Gilding
Lily

By Tatiana Boncompagni

GILDING LILY

Gilding Lily

Tatiana Boncompagni

AVON

An Imprint of HarperCollins*Publishers*

GILDING LILY. Copyright © 2008 by Tatiana Boncompagni.

FIRST EDITION

Designed by Elizabeth M. Glover

Library of Congress Cataloging-in-Publication Data
Boncompagni, Tatiana.
 Gilding Lily/ Tatiana Boncompagni —1st ed.
 p. cm.
 ISBN: 978-0-06-145101-0
 1. Women journalists—Fiction. 2. Social classes — Fiction. 3. Upper class families — Fiction. 4. Socialites — New York (State) — New York — Fiction. 5. Motherhood — Fiction. 6. Marital conflict —Fiction. 7. Seperated people — Fiction. 8. Self-esteem — Fiction. 9. New York (N.Y.) — Fiction. I. Title.
 PS3602. 06564G55 2008
 813'.6 — dc22 2008003284

08 09 10 11 12 OV/RRD 10 9 8 7 6 5 4 3 2 1

For my parents

To gild refined gold,
to paint the lily,
to throw perfume on the violet . . .
is wasteful and ridiculous excess.

—WILLIAM SHAKESPEARE, *King John*

Chapter 1

One and a half years earlier . . .

Sweeping up the main staircase of the Ludwig Collection, the Upper East Side cultural landmark and ultimate beneficiary of that evening's Spring Showers–themed fund-raiser, Lily Grace managed to ruin what would have been a perfectly splendid entrance by stomping on the hem of her silk gown and falling down in the middle of the stairs. The dress, a sea green riot in airy chiffon, had been shipped directly off a Milan runway and delivered via messenger to her apartment that day, and in her haste to get to the party, she hadn't noticed the gown's perilously long hem.

Lily looked around, noting thankfully that her face plant had gone unobserved by the party guests and paparazzi milling about at the top of the stairs, and with her right hand gathered the excess material of the dress. She'd have to hold it up all night if she didn't want to take another tumble in front of tout le monde New York—which, of course, she most assuredly did not.

Proceeding more carefully this time up the white marble staircase, she made it into the Ludwig's second-floor ballroom without further incident, surveying the room, which had been elaborately decorated to reflect the evening's theme. Swaths of blue silk blanketed twenty-five round tables, each set with white candles, floral arrangements, and dinner service for ten; while a hundred potted trees draped with ropes of Austrian crystals, white *Dendrobium* orchids and fairy lights formed a natural border around the dining area. The room smelled expensively of narcissus, fresh cut grass, and French perfume.

As Lily maneuvered through the room toward Robert's table, she returned waves from a perma-tanned socialite who had recently posed in a bikini for the cover of *Hamptons* magazine (showing off a brand-new breast enlargement) and the daughter of a Caribbean rum exporter who was known as much for her tireless social climbing as she was for her not one but two gentleman walkers, who were themselves attached at the hip (and, apparently, to the idea that ascots were remotely fashionable). Next to them stood a contingent of South American bombshells, their tagalong hair stylists and makeup artists hovering nearby, and a clique of gossiping, half-drunk fashion publicists, all thin, all dressed in trendy sequined minidresses and platform heels.

Even though Lily had been on the gala scene for less than a year, she had already deduced what these evenings were all about. They weren't about charity (if she polled the room, probably only half the guests were aware of the cause their thousand-dollar-a-plate tickets were benefiting) and they weren't about romance (the men, at least those of the hetero variety, were entirely inconsequential) but about status, the preserving of it and the getting of it. The latter being the more interesting of the two. It was remarkable to Lily how being seen or, even better, photographed with the right people, in the right dress could transform a young woman from slender wallflower to hothouse diva within a fortnight.

Lily was well past fashionably late—the waiters were already clearing the striped bass and fennel gratin entrées from the tables—but Robert had told her over the phone not to worry. "Finish your work and then come as quick as you can," he'd said over the din of the cocktail hour. "But try to be here by dessert. I took a sneak peak at the menu and they're serving your favorite."

Profiteroles. She spotted another tuxedoed waiter threading through the room with a tray of the ice-cream-stuffed pastries, making her stomach gurgle with hunger. The last thing she'd eaten all day was a ham and cheese croissant from the Au Bon Pain in her office building. Then a Silicon Valley law firm declared bankruptcy, and all hell broke loose on the newsroom floor. By the time she'd filed her story and gotten out of the bureau, she'd had just enough time to wash her face, slap on some makeup, and slip into her dress before hijacking a taxi on Park Avenue and zooming uptown for the party.

She heard the machinations of a camera lens focusing and turned to see a slim, white-haired photographer holding his camera aloft. "A photo?" he asked, and Lily obliged with a quick nod, gently angling her left hip away from the camera while sucking in her stomach and holding her right arm slightly away from her side. Getting snapped with fat-looking upper arms was a monstrous no-no in this crowd.

It had taken her a while to master what she jokingly referred to as her "PPP: Perfect Party Pose"—the pictures from when she had first started dating Robert (and hadn't learned the benefits of snapping oneself with a Polaroid camera before stepping out for an evening) could be called unflattering at best—but she was a quick study, and by the time he proposed, she looked as if she'd been doing it for a lifetime, or at least a few years longer than the short six months of their courtship. Her pose was studied, but at least her smile was genuine, or so Lily reasoned. Many of the girls had taken to pouting like supermodels every time a camera lens trained on their pretty faces.

The news of Robert's proposal had risen more than a few eyebrows around town. Not only was he handsome, charming, and well educated, but he also had a pedigree few could match for snob appeal. His great-grandfather, himself an heir to a New York banking fortune, was an avid gardener, and while puttering around at his family's summer cottage, one of the storied seaside escapes on Newport's Bellevue Drive, he had invented Blue Water, a plant fertilizer. Robert's grandfather and father further expanded what was then a small family side business by opening a chain of successful garden supply stores across the country, and Robert, who had never trimmed a hedge or mulched a weed in his life, was raised in the opulent shadow of the money tree his forebears had planted years ago, as the once-humble Blue Water Garden Supply chain eclipsed even the old bank in profitability. When he chose Lily, a relative unknown from an upper-middle-class neighborhood of Nashville as his bride, everyone took notice.

Even *Vogue* couldn't help but celebrate Lily's photogenic features and advantageous engagement by dedicating its highly coveted "Girl of the Moment" page to her. Almost overnight the magazine spread bumped her up from being just another attractive girl about town—albeit one sporting a five-carat cushion-cut diamond on her left hand—to the rarefied world of the New York socialite. She was granted unimpeded access to all the free designer clothes and accessories she could ever want to borrow (or keep, as was more and more frequently the case), as well as a spot on the junior committees of three of the city's most heavily attended fund-raisers. As Lily quickly discovered, being engaged to a Bartholomew had its privileges. Boy did it ever.

Robert spotted her first from across the ballroom. As he rose from their table, she met his brilliant blue eyes through the glittering tree branches and felt her heart quicken in anticipation of being in his arms again. She still couldn't believe that he was hers, or that her future would hold as many glamorous, champagne-filled fetes as she could bear attending. For a professor's daughter from the wrong side of the Mason-Dixon Line, it all seemed too good to be true.

They met on the dance floor, which was quickly filling with a swarm of bodies, loosened by an evening's worth of wine and cocktails, and as the band played the first few chords of "Come Fly with Me," Robert extended his hand. "Dance with me?" he asked.

Together they waltzed easily across the floor, and Lily once again thought back to her fourth grade square dancing lessons, the only formal dance training she'd ever received. If she'd been a debutante, she would have had at least a few cotillion classes under her belt, but since she'd only *lived* in Belle Meade (belonging to its exclusive country club was an altogether different thing), she hadn't had reason to learn how to execute anything more complicated than a box step. Hers was a standard American upbringing—long on education and short on luxuries—which was why Lily had been so swept away by the glamorous trappings of Robert's life. It was like winning the lottery *and* getting to go home to Leonardo DiCaprio every night. That is, if Leo wasn't only interested in models who barely spoke English, which he was, so Lily decided that her life was better than any Hollywood fairy tale anyway.

Robert twirled her out for a spin and then back in again, and she scrambled to lift the hem of her gown. *Unless you want tomorrow's Page Six headline to read "Hari-Kari by Hem," do not fall.* She kissed her fiancé on the mouth and rested her head on his shoulder. "I love you so much," she sighed. "But I'm dreaming of dessert. And a glass of champagne."

"Okay, we'll head back, but first you have to do something for me."

"But I'm scared they're going to clear the profiter—"

"Put your hand in my pocket."

"Which one?"

"Pants, left side," he instructed, pulling her a bit closer.

"I'm not going to do that here," she smirked. She began to pull away, shaking a finger at him. "You're naughty."

He held her fast. "Trust me when I say it's worth your while."

Giggling, Lily slid her hand into his pocket and felt the cool, hard touch of metal and gemstone. Pulling the long flash of diamonds from its hiding place, she gulped, "But Robert, this is far too precious."

"Nonsense," he laughed, fastening the necklace, a platinum vine set with a dozen one-carat diamonds, around her bare neck. "It was my great-grandmother's," he said. "I was going to give it to you on the night before our wedding, but I couldn't wait."

So absorbed by each other's twinkling eyes were Robert and Lily that they ceased to notice the photographers surrounding them, their camera flashes just another part of the magical setting, adding brilliance to the strands of gemstones all about.

It wouldn't be long before Lily learned the high price of extravagant decoration.

Chapter 2

It was during the first long shower Lily had taken in weeks that she dared take stock of the situation below her collarbone. Ever since she had given birth five months earlier, she hadn't had much time to think of her appearance, and that, it turns out, was a merciful thing. As the hot water cascaded down over her shoulders she inspected the wreckage that was her body. Her breasts, once the shape of navel oranges, had grown to resemble eggplants, and her stomach, saggy and still rounded, was punctured by a wrinkly, lopsided belly button. Farther down she surveyed her bikini line, or rather the lack thereof, and her overgrown paint-chipped toes.

Emerging from the shower dripping water on the marble floor of her bathroom, she thought absentmindedly that her chestnut brown shoulder-length hair could use some highlights. But with Robert now unemployed and their household budget all of a sudden running on fumes, a trip to the hair salon was regretfully out of the question. Wrapping a plush saffron-colored towel around her torso, Lily shuffled over to the vanity table in her bedroom.

"Oh mercy," she sighed as she sat down on the dressing table's silk-covered stool and peered at her still unfamiliar reflection. Her hazel eyes were rimmed with dark circles—the result of months of sleep deprivation—and a few new horizontal lines had etched their way across her forehead. Her cheeks looked like they were storing up nuts for the winter, and—what's this?—was that a gray hair? For the first time ever, Lily felt old. Okay, maybe not *old* old, but definitely not young. *Leonardo DiCaprio wouldn't give me a second glance*, she brooded.

She had never been the kind of girl who required a lot of assurances about her appearance, not like her mother, a fading beauty who compensated for her expanding waistline and multiplying crow's feet with bigger hats and ever bolder makeup.

Is it only downhill from here?

After marrying Robert, everything had spiraled out of control so quickly. She'd become pregnant while on their honeymoon, effectively preempting the year of romance they'd both anticipated spending with one another. She became flabby and cellulite-laden practically as soon as those two pink lines winked up at her from the test kit. Her face blew up. She got pimples. When she hit the five-month mark, her editor told her that she looked like a different person, and although he obviously didn't say it to hurt her feelings, neither did he mean it as a compliment.

And then, because a baby required more space and a different floor plan than Robert's hipster chic loft in SoHo could provide, they moved. Together they found an uptown two bedroom in a prewar building tucked between Park and Lexington Avenues. Lots of crown molding, a fireplace in the living room, granite countertops in the kitchen. What wasn't there to love? To celebrate the purchase, Robert's parents, Edward and Josephine, offered them a vacation at Bluebell Manor, the family's house in Palm Beach.

When they returned, Lily and Robert were surprised to find their apartment fully furnished, courtesy of Josephine. An enormous flower arrangement on the table in the foyer held a card bearing Josephine's swirly, nearly illegible handwriting: "Surprise ducklings, I've feathered your nest! Enjoy!"

Lily had walked silently through the apartment, which post-redecoration bore a heavy resemblance to Josephine's own duplex, from the cushy sofas upholstered in lustrous eggshell damasks to the heavy brushed silk curtains. There were crystal chandeliers, marble-topped side tables, vast Persian rugs, and enormous antique gilt mirrors, smoky with age. It was more than nice, but not at all what Lily had envisioned for their starter home.

She found Robert in the living room fiddling with the remote to their new flat screen television. "How could she do this without asking us? Did you know about this?"

"No, I had no idea. I'm just as stunned as you are."

She crossed her arms on top of her enormous belly. "I don't want to sound ungrateful or anything, but aren't I supposed to decorate our apartment? Isn't that the point of getting a place of our own, that it's *ours*? I mean, how did she even get in?"

"I gave her a spare set of keys in case of an emergency," Robert admitted. "I had no idea she'd do something like this."

"I think we should ask her to take everything back. We'll say thank you so much, Josephine, but we can't possibly accept such an extravagant gift."

"But she'll be crushed. She probably spent so much time, not to mention money, planning this. I'm sure she thinks she's done us an enormous favor."

Lily was starting to lose her patience. "Look around, Robert. Most of this stuff is directly out of her apartment. Look, look at this dining room table," she dragged him by the hand over to the antique Sheraton table now stationed in their crimson-and-white-striped dining room. "It's hers! This used to be in your old dining room. She probably wanted to redecorate and decided to dump all of her old stuff on us."

"It's not like this *stuff* is trash," Robert said, picking up a pair of silver candlesticks from a carved wood hutch. "These are beautiful. And we did need a bigger dining room table." Registering the shock on her face, he softened his tone. "Now we can finally have dinner parties. C'mon, Lil, dinner parties! Haven't you been talking about having some of our friends over?"

"Okay, yes, it'll be nice to be able to entertain properly, but that's not the point. The point is that this is *our* apartment, and now, every time I come in here"—Lily was shocked into momentary silence as she spied an oil portrait of Josephine, Robert, and Robert's younger sister, Colette, on the wall—"I'll feel like I'm at her place. It's a transgression of our privacy and independence. If we don't show her that there are lines she can't cross, then what's to stop her the next time?"

Robert said nothing.

"You've got to admit she's stepped over the line. We *have* to call her and ask her to take at least some of it back. We can be very polite about it."

Without replying, Robert wandered out of the dining room and down the hall, passing the nursery, which had been decorated in a red and black Scottie dog theme. In their bedroom, he flopped onto his mother and father's old canopied bed and waited for Lily to catch up to him.

"Did you see the nursery? The crib is *black*! Who buys a black crib?" She felt her pregnancy hormones, a tsunami of uncontrollable emotion, flooding her body. She wasn't in the habit of yelling—her mother had always said it was a sign of poor breeding—but there were some times when even the best of intentions couldn't keep her from breaking into tantrum mode. She began to cry loudly.

"Honey, please don't get so upset. It's not good for the baby," Robert said as he propped himself up on a pair of throw pillows. Looking around the room, he seemed to notice the frilly, flowery decor for the first time. "Man, that wallpaper is awful. It's like an old lady's bedroom in here." Picking up a ruffle-trimmed pillow in the same floral silk that was lining the walls, he pretended to retch on the bed.

"I'm not laughing," Lily said, but she'd stopped sobbing and the corner of her mouth had curled up, hinting at a smile. If there was one thing she loved about Robert—besides his fantastic ass and finely tuned moral compass—it was his ability to break her out of a bad mood. Even at moments like these, when she was snorting mad, he could reel her away from the precipice of despair with a well-timed joke. He'd make a fool of himself just to get her to crack a smile.

Swinging his long legs over the side of the bed frame, Robert gently grabbed hold of her elbows. "Let's not make this into a bigger deal than it is. Let's just tell her we love it, and then as the years go by, we can replace the things we don't like, starting with this wallpaper. He massaged the tops of her arms and her shoulders. "That way, no one's feelings get hurt. Okay?"

"Okay, I guess it's not that big a deal," she conceded. As much as she resented Josephine for overstepping their boundaries, she didn't want to fight with Robert.

Lily pulled away and walked across the room toward an antique vanity. As a little girl she'd always wanted a dressing table, and this one, with its bull's-eye mirror and marquetry details, was the prettiest she'd ever seen. It was, in fact, even nicer than the ones in the Horchow Collection catalogs her mother used to drool over on a biweekly basis. "But I think it's a mistake not to tell her that she can't do stuff like this without checking with us first. And it's not that I don't appreciate her generosity. I do. But I would have preferred to have some control over the situation. It's kind of a symbolic thing, feathering your first nest as a couple. You know?"

Robert rolled off the bed and kneeled down in front of her, grasping her hands in his. "Look, I know she's pushy, but she means well," he said. "Just let me handle her? I'll make sure she knows where we draw the line."

"Promise?"

He nodded solemnly and rose from the floor to sit next to her on the bed. They both sat there looking around the room, taking it all in fully, until Robert suddenly broke the silence. "I think it's time for . . . an adventure hug!" He lunged at Lily, who ran to the other side of the bed in an effort to avoid her husband's grasp and the eventual air toss and body slam onto a soft surface—the bed, a couch—that he often initiated after tense moments such as these.

This was one of their things. While other couples called each other improbable pet names or squeezed each other's back pimples in private, Robert and Lily engaged in amateur aerial acrobatics.

Robert grabbed her from behind, wrapping his hands around her hips as if he was about to launch her in the air.

"No! I'm pregnant. No adventure hugs until I have the baby. It's not safe."

"Okay, all right," he said, releasing her momentarily. "But only because I love you."

Now, almost a year later, Lily still felt out of place in every room in their home except their bedroom. It was the only room they'd been able to redo before Robert quit his job and she'd given birth, and they'd had a lot of fun tackling the project together over one three-day weekend last spring. While Robert ripped down the wallpaper and painted the bedroom milky white, Lily, banished from the apartment because of the paint fumes, shopped for new bed linens, lampshades, and curtains along Madison Avenue. By Monday the room had been entirely exorcized of its floral bedding, the plaid silk balloon shades and coordinating lampshades, crystal wall sconces, and bird prints in gilded frames. Awash in fresh, cooling white and devoid of the excessive swags and frippery, the room finally felt like the perfect blank slate, just what their marriage needed.

Of course, not every problem could be whitewashed over the course of a weekend.

Chapter 3

Rising from the vanity, Lily walked across the room and into her closet, where she carefully fingered her old clothes, the size two pencil skirts, clingy sweaters, and shrunken jackets. Would she ever fit in them again? Losing the forty-five pounds that still clung to her once-thin frame seemed like an impossible task. "I'll think about it tomorrow," she'd tell herself, and then tomorrow would come and she'd get as far as putting on her sports bra before she was gasping for air. These days it seemed everything made her feel short of breath: dragging the Exersaucer from the living room to the kitchen; retrieving a Pyrex dish from the back of a kitchen cabinet; even lugging a moderately light sack of groceries a few blocks. *Maybe I have asthma,* she wondered. *Can pregnancy give you asthma—in addition to stretch marks, varicose veins, copious amounts of cellulite, random new allergies, and impaired short-term memory?*

Finding a pair of velour track suit bottoms and one of her husband's old cashmere sweaters on a shelf, she pulled the lightweight V-neck over her head and breathed in his scent, the citrus and spice of Hermès Eau d'Orange Verte deodorant. Just knowing Robert would be home soon from his luncheon with Josephine made her feel marginally better. Today they were going to take the baby out for a late afternoon stroll down to the grocery store and fruit cart on Lexington.

Some women went bargain hunting at designer sample sales—

she, the fruit cart. For a dollar, the cart man, a friendly Pakistani gentleman, once sold her eight not-quite-overripe bananas that she used to make a dozen banana oat muffins and a banana loaf; just the other day she'd bagged two half pints of blueberries for a couple of dollars each.

This, of course, was a big change from how they used to shop for food. Sure the workweeks had been filled with benefit dinners and cocktail parties—or takeout in front of the television when they were mercifully homebound for the night—but weekends were reserved for cooking excessively elaborate meals with pristine (and pricey) ingredients. When Lily and Robert first moved uptown, they'd spent their weekends on a quest to find the best of everything in their neighborhood. For gelato and little green heads of Boston lettuce, they went to Citarella on Third Avenue. Pastries and raisin loaves came from Le Pain Quotidien, a Belgian café on Lexington. The fishmonger on First Avenue supplied them with wildly expensive Copper River salmon (when in season) and three-pound lobsters flown in fresh from Nova Scotia. Then they'd go home, look up recipes on the Food Network website, and pass the rest of the weekend making beef Wellington and chocolate mousse or a gratin of spring vegetables and fish en papillote. Sometimes Lily missed their old routine, watching the butcher tie up tenderloins in neat, presentlike bundles, or inhaling the pungent aroma of the cheese shop where they used to buy hunks of imported Parmesan and creamy rounds of St. Andre, but most of the time she was able to regard cutting the fat from their grocery bills as an interesting challenge.

After all, she hadn't grown up rich. Not poor, but certainly not rich. When she and her brother were young, their parents went out to dinner only on special occasions—birthdays and anniversaries and when Lily's father made tenure at Vanderbilt—and they, the kids, only got to tag along when the birthday was one of theirs. And even then it was generally to someplace like Bennigan's or Kobé Steakhouse. When it came to what they ate at home, charred (i.e., carcinogenic) chicken breasts (of the nonorganic variety) on their grill (the old-fashioned charcoal kind) were a staple. As were baked potatoes and spaghetti with whatever tomato sauce was on sale that week. It could be said that if anyone inside the 10021 zip code was predisposed to bargain shopping, it was Lily.

Hearing the front door click open, then a pair of footsteps coming down the hallway, Lily breathed a sigh of relief. Robert was finally home.

"Are you in here, honey?" he called out as he walked into the bedroom. "Did you still want to go to the store?"

"I'm just finishing getting dressed." Pulling a cotton sock on one foot, she hopped out of the closet, tripping then stumbling forward. She hit the carpet just as Robert entered the room.

"Are you okay?" he asked, helping her up. Robert was dressed in his navy suit, and, Lily noted, was looking particularly handsome, his skin still glowing with the remnants of a summer tan, his dark hair just a shade overgrown and curling attractively at the ends. *Shit, why didn't I at least put on a little blush and lip gloss?* As he leaned in for a kiss she covertly swept her tongue over her teeth, trying to remember if she had brushed them that day. *Nope.*

"*Mmm,* I missed you," he said, squeezing her waist. Lily reflexively sucked in her stomach, wishing she could also suck in the two handfuls of fat that rolled over the waistband of her sweats.

"Me, too," she said, trying not to let on that she'd been counting the hours and then minutes until Robert would be home. When he made a big deal about missing her it was sweet, but Lily didn't believe that the reverse was true: if she, the one who had been home all day with the baby, hair uncombed, teeth unbrushed, leaped on him like a Labrador every time he walked through the door, it would come off as massively pathetic. And she didn't want her husband pitying her on top of everything else. "I'll wake up Will, and then we can get going," she said.

"No, let me get him." Robert threw his tie and jacket on the bed. "You finish getting ready."

As he roused their baby up from his nap, Lily heated up a bottle of milk that she had pumped earlier in the day. In the beginning, nursing hadn't come easily to her. The lactation consultant at the hospital had proclaimed her nipples entirely inept (the bitch!) and had instructed Lily to purchase weird plastic shields that pulled her nipples into a position that made it even easier for Will to suck them into what immediately became cracked and bloody ruins. But she had been determined not to give it up, and two months— or rather, eight mother-effing weeks— later it just stopped hurting. *Poof,* and the pain was finally gone. No more wanting to swear like a drunken soldier every time Will latched on. No more biting her lower lip so hard it bled. That chapter, thankfully, was behind her.

After the pain disappeared, Lily could enjoy nursing. She relished the closeness she felt with Will as he sucked greedily and gratefully at her breast, his big monkey eyes oozing appreciation, the milky burps and gurgles that would come afterward. He relied on her for his survival and nourishment, and that alone inspired her to throw herself into motherhood with the same enthusiasm she'd once reserved for getting a front-page byline.

In fact, earlier that afternoon, she'd nursed Will to sleep, but instead of immediately transferring him to his crib for his nap, she laid him on her own bed and studied him, her face so close enough to his that she could count his long eyelashes and hear his every exhale. His skin was perfect, glowing, like it was lit from within, and softer than the finest silk. His eyebrows, wispy little rainbows, arched comically as he dreamed of something. She stifled a laugh, not wanting to wake him, and lightly kissed the rolls of fat above his knees and the dimples at his elbows. She wanted to remember him like this forever—so sweet, so pure, a warm bundle of love and magic that she had made.

Lily loved her child fiercely, almost obsessively. She felt at times like she could devour him with her love, it was so endless and unfettered. Nothing had ever felt as instinctual as caring for him:

forgoing sleep, destroying her figure, losing her career, anything and everything for this tiny seventeen-pound despot. She had lost count of the twilight hours she had passed holding him, walking around their apartment as he squirmed in her arms, trying to get back to sleep. But no matter; that was what mothers do. In fact, as Lily had taken to saying whenever anyone pointed out what a devoted mother she was, "Doing for Will is like doing for myself. I know we're not the same person, but loving him feels almost selfish in its own way."

As she lay there with her baby, she thought only of how lucky she was; all her other problems seemed to vanish when she was with him. It was only after a quarter of an hour, remembering that she needed to clean the kitchen and take a shower before Robert came home, that she forced herself to take him to his crib and get on with her chores.

"He had a dirty diaper," Robert announced as he entered the kitchen with Will cradled into the crook of his arm. The baby, still sleepy, dug his fists into his eyes and yawned.

Lily kissed the top of Will's head. "No diaper rash?" she asked as she handed Robert the bottle of warmed milk.

"Nope, but I swiped on some of that cream anyway," he said, his chest puffing out a few inches.

Alert the media, she thought. It seemed that Robert felt entitled to a father-of-the-year award every time he changed a soiled diaper, which was *maybe* three times a week. He clearly had no idea that they could probably fertilize a football field with what their son produced in a month. Still, at least Robert helped sometimes. It wasn't his fault if he came from the kind of home in which diaper duty was left to the hired help.

In the hallway, Robert nestled Will into the basket of his Bugaboo stroller as Lily retrieved a blanket from the nursery. Outside, the early September air was already hinting at the cooler temperatures to come, and she didn't want Will, who was still warm and slightly damp from his nap, to catch a cold.

On the elevator ride downstairs, she and Robert talked about buying apples for the pie Lily wanted to bake. Her mother, Margaret, had been a whiz at heating the par-baked Sara Lee desserts that she picked up at the neighborhood Kroger's, but that had been as close as her family had come to "from scratch." Lily was bent on being different; her children wouldn't have any of the trans-fat-laden bakery on which she had been raised. If she started practicing making pies and other goodies now, then by the time Will was old enough to eat them, she'd have them down pat.

"So, how was your luncheon?" Lily asked as they strolled down Third Avenue to the Food Emporium.

"Really interesting. I was seated next to this guy who runs a six-billion-dollar real estate company. He said they might be looking to hire another lawyer for their in-house legal team."

"That's great, honey."

A little more than halfway through her pregnancy, not long after Robert had convinced Lily to give up her job at the *Journal*, he confided in her that he wasn't happy at Caruthers & Caruthers, the white-shoe law firm where he toiled as a senior associate, and wanted to quit. "The hours are too long. I hate the partners in my practice area, and I'm never going to make a lot of money as a lawyer anyway," he had grumbled. Lily had asked him if he would consider switching to another firm and even offered to use her connections to set him up with interviews with other managing partners around town, but mentally he had already left the partner track behind.

The work wasn't fulfilling, he said. He felt like a cog; the real players were the guys that hired his firm—the guys he sat next to during long boardroom negotiations—and he longed to join their ranks. "I want to think strategically, to call the shots that move markets, like my grandfather did. But as a lawyer, I'm just the guy that makes sure all the i's are dotted and t's are crossed. There's no room for creativity, for big-picture thinking. Besides, financially it'll be better for us in the long run. And in the meantime, as long as we take our spending down a notch or two, we'll be fine."

At the time, Lily had been supportive of his decision, but as the months wore on she increasingly began to wonder if she'd made a mistake encouraging him to follow his heart. Without either of their salaries—she'd quit her job in the third trimester of her pregnancy—they'd had to rely entirely on the income from his trust fund, which although sizable, provided them with only enough money to cover their hefty monthly mortgage and the maintenance fees on their apartment. In the five short months since Will was born, they had amassed tens of thousands of dollars in debts. As far as Lily was concerned, the sooner her husband started working again, the better. She was desperate to pay down their debt and replenish their savings. It wouldn't be long before Will would be starting nursery school, and most of the schools in their neighborhood had annual tuitions of twelve to fourteen thousand dollars. After that it would only get worse: twenty-five thousand dollars for kindergarten, thirty thousand dollars annually for private school, and who knew how much college would cost by the time their son was ready to enroll. And that was just for one child. What if they wanted to have more?

"So, are you going to call him for an interview?" Lily asked, furtively crossing her fingers. Robert had come home from more than a few of these networking lunches and dinners with job leads that he never followed up on. She'd asked once what the point of going to these functions was unless he made use of the contacts he made, and in response he'd mumbled something about not wanting to rush into anything.

"I don't know," he hemmed. "On the one hand, it's in finance, which I *think* is the direction I want to go in, but on the other hand I'd still be just a lawyer. If he were offering me a job on the business side, I'd be really interested but—"

"Well," Lily interrupted. She was getting tired of her husband's indecisiveness. He had so many opportunities, thanks in large measure to his last name and his parents' extensive network of friends, and he wasn't taking advantage of any of them. At the start of his unemployment, she'd admired his courage—it wasn't easy embarking on a career change—but now she caught herself wondering if he had quit because he was lazy and tired of working. What's worse, the more agitated and worried she became about their financial situation, the more relaxed Robert seemed to become about his job search. "You could always call him back to get a face-to-face, and then at the meeting you could make your case for why he should hire you in a different capacity," Lily suggested.

"Yeah," Robert nodded noncommittally as they entered the grocery store. He picked up a green plastic basket. "We're not getting too much, are we?" he asked.

"No, just a few things—bread, milk, eggs, some lettuce, and the apples—"

"The thing is that I'm also thinking that I should try and do something with my dad's company. You know I've always been interested in expanding Blue Water's Internet presence," Robert said as Lily packed a head of romaine into a plastic bag.

"You've never mentioned this before, at least not to me," she said, trying to conceal her annoyance. Robert had a way of forgetting what he did and didn't tell her, but this was ridiculous. *Okay if you forget to tell me we're out of toilet paper, not okay if you forget to tell me you're thinking about making our future even more dependent on us staying in your family's good graces.*

"Really? I thought I had. Well, anyway, I've only had a preliminary conversation with Mom and Dad about it. Dad says he'll have to set up some meetings with the board to gauge their interest and then we'd go from there."

"Well, I'd still call that real estate guy back," Lily said, swapping the gallon of organic milk in their basket for the regular kind.

Chapter 4

A couple of weeks later, while eating a breakfast of buttered toast and tea, Lily was idly thumbing through her mail when she saw it—the final clue that her demotion from It girl to has-been was complete—an engraved invitation to the Ludwig Collection's annual fund-raising gala, *without her name on it.*

This final degradation should not have come as a surprise to Lily—no one had contacted her from the museum in the last few months, and she'd already been dumped by all the other benefit committees she belonged to—and yet it did. And whereas getting kicked off the other charities (Save Bucharest, the Ecology First Fund, et al.) hadn't stung her too deeply, this one had. The difference was that Lily didn't feel a personal connection to the other charities (she'd never been to Bucharest, for example), but as an art enthusiast she truly believed in the Ludwig's programs and its role in preserving and celebrating nineteenth-century art and culture.

Rationally, Lily knew that since she could neither buy a table for twelve thousand dollars nor fit into the samples provided by the designer sponsoring the event, she wasn't of much use to the Ludwig, but it still hurt to be pushed out of the inner sanctum so quickly. Frowning, she crushed the heavy cream-colored card in her hand.

"What's wrong, honey?" Robert put down the knife he was using to spread marmalade on his toast, licked his fingers, and removed the crumpled invitation from her fist. "Did you want to go to this?" he asked, smoothing it out on the table.

"No, I know we can't afford it. I'm just disappointed that I'm not on the committee this year. Of all the charities I was involved with, this one really meant something to me." She got up to throw the invitation into the trash and picked up Will, who had started crying in his bouncy seat. Sitting back down at the table, she lifted her T-shirt and let Will root around for a few moments before she gently guided his gaping, birdlike mouth to her right nipple. He began to suck hungrily, his eyes closed, grunting softly with every gulp. She smoothed his crinkled brow with her thumb and finger combed the soft Mohawk of hair on his head.

"It won't be long till we can afford to go to these things again," Robert said, squeezing his wife's free hand in reassurance. "In the meantime, I know Mom is going to a spina bifida event tonight at the Pierre. She asked me to come in place of Dad, who apparently couldn't be bothered to put on his tuxedo, and if you want I could ask her to buy an extra seat for you. You might not be at our table, but at least you'd have a chance to get all dressed up."

Dressed up in what? Lily knew she couldn't fit into any of her old evening gowns yet. "Oh, that's sweet, honey, but it's too short notice."

"Colette is coming down from Dartmouth for it," he added.

Because Lily got along famously with Robert's sister, who was in her senior year at the liberal arts college, she briefly considered changing her mind. She would have loved catching up with Colette. She was cool, beautiful, and smart as a whip. And, best of all, she loved Lily. They always had fun together, but Lily still couldn't be induced to join them. "The babysitter can't come at the drop of a hat," she said, even though Jacinta, their Puerto Rican housekeeper, had said just the other day that she would be happy to sit for the baby.

"You deserve it *mamita,* the way you take care of that baby. You the best mother I ever seen, but go out already! Take that sexy husband of yours dancing. I'll take care of *tu hijo,*" is in fact exactly what she said.

The truth was that Lily didn't want to deal with seeing Josephine, who had become an increasingly large presence in their lives in the last few months. Because Robert was trying to find a job, he was obliged to spend more time out of the house meeting his parents' friends and contacts. But to Lily, this networking seemed to coincide a little too neatly with Josephine's social itinerary. Much too often Lily found herself alone all day with the baby while Robert played a game of tennis or had lunch with one of his old college buddies, only to spend all night alone with Will as Robert squired his mother to yet another dinner party.

It's not that she didn't want to be at home with Will, padding around in her yellow flannel housecoat and slippers as he wormed around in his little cotton onesies, cooing and burping, his big, expressive eyes following her around the room as she tidied this and that. Their schedule rotated around naps, baths, and feedings, and the hours and days had a way of blurring into each other in this happy, cozy fashion. But with Robert hardly ever there to partake in the domestic bliss, she began to feel more and more neglected and underappreciated.

In fact, Robert's increasingly frequent absences were enough to cause Lily to wonder if he was having an affair. Once, after he'd been out to dinner with his mother three nights in a row, Lily actually made a joke about him having a mistress. She hadn't wanted Robert to think that she was truly worried about him sleeping around (she was supposed to trust him completely, right?), but she did want him to know (just in case he was thinking about having an affair) that she was keeping an eye out for any signs of infidelity. It was a tricky line to toe, and making a joke of it seemed like the best approach.

"So how was she tonight?" she had asked as Robert climbed into bed. The clock read 11:55 p.m., and Lily was still wide awake, pretending to read her novel.

"Mom? She's fine," he mumbled. He was already half asleep on his pillow. *Two seconds, and he's already half asleep.*

"No, I meant your girlfriend."

Without opening his eyes, Robert groaned and snaked his arm around her waist. "You're all the woman I'll ever need," he smirked, puckering his lips for a kiss, which Lily grudgingly leaned over to give.

Although the brief conversation left Lily feeling reasonably assured that her husband wasn't having an affair, she still wished that he would stay home and keep her company more often. Surely he didn't need to play tennis at his hyperexclusive, all-male club *quite* so often, and couldn't he say no to his mother every now and then?

She'd asked that question, too, this time while she was preparing lunch. They were having sandwiches—turkey cold cuts, Swiss cheese, a few leaves of lettuce, and a little mayonnaise on rye bread—and he paused between bites of a pre-sandwich pickle to say, "I wouldn't want to hurt her feelings."

She'd briefly considered smacking Robert in the face with his pickle, a bumpy penis-shaped half sour from the grocery store's deli section, but instead she let him finish it before calmly asking, "What about *my* feelings, Robert? Aren't you concerned about hurting *me*?"

Robert leaned back in his chair and exhaled sharply. "I care about them, too, of course I do. But you don't want to see Mom when she feels slighted. She goes on the warpath. You think she's tough on you now? Just wait till she thinks you've stolen me away from her. Believe me, I'm doing you a big favor by keeping her happy."

Lily wanted to tell Robert that if his idea of protecting her involved escorting his mother to a party every third night, she'd rather go without it. What was the worst thing that could happen if he dared to decline an invitation? Sometimes women like Josephine, women who were used to getting their own way all the time, only needed to be challenged once or twice before they crumbled like week-old macaroons. It was time for Robert to put her first. "So, what about tomorrow night?" Lily ventured. "Shall we rent a movie and stay in?"

"There's a cocktail party at DVF's [DVF being shorthand for Diane von Furstenberg] that I've promised Mother I'd go to," he said flatly.

"Of course there is," Lily muttered, turning toward the sink.

And that's when Robert blew up. "Look, I don't think you get how difficult it is for me. Of course I'd rather be at home sitting on the couch watching movies with you and Will. But if I did that, I'd never get a job. Do you know how hard it is walking around with the Bartholomew legacy hanging over my head? My grandfather and father built a five-billion-dollar company. They practically built the home-gardening industry, and what have I done?"

"But Robert, life is one step at a time," Lily said, adding softly, "Listen, I know you're doing a lot of networking and meeting people, but have you looked at any of those online job search engines or talked to a headhunter? Are you even sending out your résumé?"

He rose from the table, his sandwich untouched, and headed toward the door. "You don't get a good job by sending your résumé out blindly to people. In this town, you get a job by having the right connections."

"Which you do."

He glared at her. "Thanks for pointing that out."

His shoulders slumped, and Lily felt like she was once again a teenager, back at one of her high school track meets. She was a born athlete who happened to be particularly gifted at middle-distance running, a sport that required good lungs, strong legs, and a willingness to work hard, rain or shine. Lily had possessed all these attributes and quickly became the fastest female half-miler on her team. She placed first or near the top at most competitions, winning accolades from her classmates and family (particularly from her father, since her mother would have preferred that Lily excel at something more genteel, something more along the lines of ballet, for example). Running, in addition to her superior academic standing, made Lily stand out among her peers. Not popular enough to be elected to homecoming court or the student council, she nevertheless became accustomed to being recognized as a winner. Her identity, for better or worse, became inextricably linked to holding a position at "the top."

Her brother, Matthew, on the other hand, was happy to live in the realm of mediocrity. A solid C student, he also ran the 800, but not with the same skill or speed for his age and gender as Lily did. Often, as Matthew rounded his last turn, she'd squeeze her eyes shut and will all her energy into his body. She wanted him to know, if only once, what it felt like to be the best. He never won a race, however, and curiously to Lily at the time, he never seemed to mind.

Now, as an adult, she knew that the world was divided into two camps: those who were overachievers, driven to succeed, like her, and those who wanted to fill their lives with fun and friends, the work-to-live club, of which her brother was a card-carrying member. It was only after many philosophical debates—both internal and with others—that Lily was able to accept that there was nothing wrong with the way her brother wanted to live. But it wasn't for her. She wanted to *do things* with her time on earth; she wanted to *be someone*. For all Lily's previous derision of the social girls she had befriended during her short tenure on the A-list, she was also obsessed with status. After all, being on the A-list meant being the best.

"So I'm a failure," Robert said, bitter and vulnerable all at once.

"You know I didn't mean it that way," she soothed. She could tell from his tone that despite what he had said, he hadn't given up. He still wanted to *be someone,* too. She knew that she would have had trouble respecting him if that wasn't the case; however, neither did she want to be married to one of those megalomaniac investment bankers she occasionally saw striding down Park Avenue, barking into their BlackBerrys about the new palapa roof on their house in Mustique or the scratch in the paint on their Aston Martin. That kind of man she could never relate to either. Still, it was important to Lily that Robert was ambitious, that he shared her same values and believed in perseverance, productivity, and self-determination. "Besides, how can you be a failure? You're still young," she said.

"I'm thirty-five. By my age my grandfather had already opened six stores in the Midwest; by thirty-five my father had increased company profits by two hundred percent," he said, his pupils dilating with anxiety. "The time for me to start making a name for myself is now. I want to give you and Will everything this world has to offer—everything my father gave us—and to do that I need to find the *right* job. And the only way I'm going to do that is if I'm out there meeting the *right* people."

Now how could she have possibly argued with that?

Robert closed the lid on the marmalade jar. "Couldn't you call someone else to babysit? Do you want me to check around and see if any of our friends can do it?"

"No baby, that's okay. It's not worth the effort. There'll be other parties," Lily said, switching Will over to her other breast, which had become hard, dripping little droplets of milk in anticipation of the feeding. She watched as his little pink lips clamped down on her nipple and wondered, once again, whether she could love her child any more than she already did. With Robert out of the house most of the time, the baby had become her one true joy, a constant companion and a never-ending source of happiness.

"I'll ask Mom tonight what other events are coming up. You're long overdue for a night out without the baby. I worry about you,

you know, spending so much time holed up in this place." Robert stuffed the remaining piece of toast in his mouth.

"It's not so bad," she said, and shrugged.

"No, I mean it." He got up from the table and put his empty plate in the sink. "You should get out more."

"The thing is I don't really feel comfortable with how I look. Those other women are so catty, if they see me like this they'll just make fun of how much weight I've gained," she admitted lamely, looking down at her udderlike breasts. She felt like a cow, not a woman and certainly not a socialite. "I'm so embarrassed."

Robert leaned back against the kitchen counter and looked at her adoringly. "But you're hot. And I mean *hot*. Smokin'. A total MILF."

"But look at these breasts."

"Yeah, baby!" he said, Austin Powers–style. He gave her the thumbs-up sign, his face split into a silly grin, his eyes squinting into tiny slits. "I wish you could see yourself the way I do. You've never looked more lovely in your whole life. You're ravishing. Succulent."

"Please," she tutted, rolling her eyes. "That's more than enough." She knew he wanted to make her feel better, but if anything his compliments made her feel like an even bigger loser.

They were quite a pair, she thought. *He's unemployed and I'm a big fat has-been at thirty years old. What happened to our glamorous, productive lives?* Of course they were blessed to have a healthy, sweet child like Will—there were so many people who wanted to have babies and couldn't or had children with crippling disabilities—and she felt guilty for even harboring these thoughts, but she couldn't deny that she missed some of the trappings of her former life.

It felt like just yesterday that their worlds were full of possibility. Their careers were moving forward at full throttle, their lives full of privilege and romance. For her own part, Lily had felt worthy of Robert's love, fulfilled from a professional standpoint, and to top it all off she had been having fun. The dresses, the dinners, the dancing—she nearly swooned remembering it all. *Was it too much to ask to have that all back?*

"Why don't you take a walk in the park today?" Robert suggested.

"Really?"

"Sure. Get some fresh air. I'll look after Will."

"I guess I could use some time to think."

Chapter 5

Later that day, when Lily returned home from her walk, she discovered not Robert standing in the middle of their living room, but his mother, Josephine. As far as mothers-in-law go, she was a doozy. Always impeccably turned out in the latest designer offerings, from this season's de rigueur de la Renta to more avant-garde selections, like the nip-waist tartan-and-lace McQueen jacket she happened to be wearing that day, Josephine was a study in aesthetic perfection. Her makeup was always flawlessly applied, and her hair always professionally blown into a glossy black bob. She was thin, of course, and owned a jewelry collection—an endless parade of thick gold cuffs (Verdura), multistrand pearl necklaces (Mikimoto), diamond-encrusted watches (Chanel, Chopard, Charriol)—that would have made even Jennifer Lopez green with envy.

But then there was her demeanor, which could be charitably described as frosty. With one glance from her ice blue eyes, Josephine could, and often did, reduce her housekeeper to tears. She was intimidating and haughty, unapologetically judgmental and sharp—but only to those she could afford to be. Josephine was not stupid. To her peers she was charming and witty, if slightly caustic and cool. It was for the service workers—the shop girls and manicurists, the drivers and waiters—for whom she saved her most cutting commentaries. Unfortunately for Lily, Josephine had decided long ago to file her, too, under the category of underling.

"Hello, darling," Josephine said as she took in Lily's wind-blown hair and muddy (non-leather, non-Hermès) sneakers. "Did you have a pleasant walk?"

"Yes, thank you. I did." Lily scanned the room for Robert or any trace of him. *Please tell me you didn't leave the baby alone with her.* "I'm sorry; I wasn't expecting you. If I'd known you were coming over today—"

"You'd have worn your *other* jeans," Josephine smirked.

Lily's mouth fell open. She'd gotten used to her mother-in-law's snide remarks, but rarely was she so openly venal. Backhanded compliments were more Josephine's speed.

"I'm only teasing, darling." She laughed throatily (evilly, Lily thought) and rose from the couch, sweeping her arms open as a hawk might the moment before it descended upon its prey. A pair of three-carat emerald cut diamond earrings glinted through her shiny bob. "It's been what, three weeks since I saw you last?"

Lily stepped forward and submitted herself to Josephine's double air-kiss. "Probably about that."

"And you still haven't lost any more of the baby weight?"

"I really haven't started working out. Or dieting."

"No time like the present, no?" Josephine had a habit of chasing a sentence with the word *no,* a distinctly francophone tick that she had no real reason—aside from wanting to sound more worldly and sophisticated—for having adopted.

"Yes, well. I'm nursing, so it's not really a good idea to start starving myself. I would be depriving the baby of needed nutrients."

"And I thought nursing was supposed to *help* you lose weight. How curious that"—*there's that evil smirk again*—"that isn't the case for you."

Lily took a deep breath and reminded herself to keep her cool. *She's only trying to goad me into being rude back to her.* "Anyway, do you know where my husband happens to be at this moment?" she finally asked.

"Robbie?"

As if I might be married to some other guy? "Is he home?"

"In the nursery changing poor little Will's diaper. We were waiting for you so we could go out."

The fact that Josephine and Robert had plans that afternoon came as a total, horrible surprise to Lily, but not wanting to let Josephine see that she'd managed to ruffle her feathers, she excused herself and walked calmly into the nursery, where Robert was indeed changing the baby's diaper.

"Hi, sweet pumpkin," she cooed from the doorway at Will, who had his gorgeous little sausage legs lifted in the air. The baby turned his head in recognition of her voice and squealed joyously.

"Hey, honey," Robert said. "Did you have a nice walk?"

"*Umm*, it was great," she said, closing the door to the nursery. She joined him at the changing table, where she lowered her voice to a whisper (in case Josephine was eavesdropping on the other side of the door). "Do you mind telling me why in the hell your mother is here?"

"*Whoa* there, girl. Why so angry?"

"*Sshh*," she shushed, pointing to the door.

"What?" he laughed. "Mom's not listening."

Lily rolled her eyes and threw her hands up in the air. "Okay, I give up."

"I'm sorry, Lil. She called and was a block away. She said she has a big surprise for me—for us." He finished diapering the baby and propped him on his hip.

"Robert, your mother was completely horrible to me just now. Can't you talk to her? Tell her that as the mother of her only grandchild I deserve—no, I've earned—her respect."

"Why don't we *both* talk to her? Over lunch. She made reservations at Orsay."

"I'm not going."

"Lil, it's the perfect opportunity to get everything on the table. Let's hash it out, once and for all. I'll be there to back you up if she gets too nasty."

"Not today. I'm not dressed. And after what she just said to me I don't think I'd be able to express myself without resorting to some form of physical violence before our tartars arrive. I'm way too pissed off right now."

Robert sighed. "Okay then. We don't have to do it today, but let the record show that I was ready to have it out with her for you. And even if you don't want to go I *do* have to have lunch with her today. I'm already contractually bound," he said, and shrugged.

"*Uh*, fine, whatever." She knew she had a losing battle on her hands once Robert started throwing out the legal jargon. "But don't be gone for longer than two hours, okay?" She held out her hands for Will, who fell on her shoulder eagerly.

"Agreed." He smiled and gave her one of his ridiculous monster kisses, slurping a trail of saliva down the right side of Lily's face. "See you in a couple of hours."

Three hours later Lily was in the living room nursing Will, her index finger gripped tightly by his small, perfect hand, when Robert skipped—literally skipped—into the living room.

"There's something I want to show you and Will," he panted. "It's outside."

"Okay, just give me a sec," Lily said, wondering what sort of surprise Josephine had given Robert over lunch to put him in such a fantastic mood. Did she have news about a job for him with Blue Water? Or had she cut him a big check to erase their debts? What? She snapped her nursing bra back up and bundled Will in a blanket. "Where are we going?"

"You'll see." He led Lily downstairs and down the block to the parking garage where they kept their Toyota 4Runner. "Close your eyes," he said as he handed the attendant a set of keys. "Are they closed?"

"But Robert, I'm holding the baby," she reminded him. She stumbled forward, laughing nervously. Will, who could sense his parents' excitement, giggled and gripped Lily's neck with his doughy little fingers. Lily kissed the tip of his crinkled-up nose, and he swatted back at her face playfully.

"Where are we going?" she asked Robert, her heart racing with excitement as they waited for the attendant to bring them their car.

"Just close them."

Lily obeyed, and when she was given permission to open them again, she saw before her a very red, very shiny, very tiny car instead of their SUV. It was a Porsche.

After a long silence, she stammered, "There isn't even room for a baby seat!"

"Well, it's not for the baby, is it?" Robert said, flipping a dark brown lock of hair off his forehead.

"Honey, aren't we having," Lily dipped her voice so none of the garage attendants could overhear, "money problems? I can't even imagine what the payments on this are." She paused, adjusting Will on her hip. "Did you get a job and forget to tell me?"

"No, but you know, we have the monthly income from my trust and the bank's willing to lend us some money. We'll be okay for a while."

"And then what? We'll live in a Carerra?"

"No," he scoffed.

"Well then what? Tell me, because the last time we talked you said, and I quote, 'no incidentals.' This car seems like one hell of an incidental to me."

"Jesus, calm down," he said, and then in a low voice so only Lily could hear, added, "I didn't buy the car."

"Are you leasing it?" she asked, her overgrown eyebrows knitting together with confusion.

"Mom bought it for me."

"But if she wanted to help us, why didn't she give us money to pay off our credit card debt. Or, or pay down our mortgage. We didn't even need a new car."

"She thought we did."

"But this car, it's just so frivolous. And now we have to pay for an extra parking space."

"No we don't."

"She's paying for that, too?"

"No, we traded in the 4Runner."

"What?" Lily shrieked. Now they had no way to get the baby to the hospital in an emergency. How could Robert have made such an enormous, irresponsible decision without consulting her? Even her own mother, Mrs. "I'm-Constantly-out-of-the-Loop," had had some say in her father's decision to purchase the dean of admission's three-year-old Cadillac a few years ago.

"C'mon Lil, she thought the car'd cheer me up. And it did, until now." Robert unlocked the door and slid into the Porsche's unscarred tan leather interior. Pushing a pair of oversized aviator sunglasses up the bridge of his nose with his middle finger, he asked, "Why can't you just be happy for me?"

"I am, but I can't help but question the practicality of getting a new car when we're thousands of dollars in debt and barely holding onto our apartment. How would you feel if my mother took me out on a hundred-thousand-dollar shopping spree just because I needed cheering up, which, by the way, I do." Robert slammed the door and started the engine, and Lily knocked on the window. "I'm not finished," she said through the glass.

He grudgingly rolled down the window. "What else is it?"

"You said we were a team. Team players don't sneak around behind each other's backs and trade in their sensible cars for tiny Porsches."

In a tone far angrier than Lily had ever heard from her husband before, he replied, "If you want to be a team player, why don't *you* get a job."

I think I will, she thought as Robert pulled out of his five-hundred-dollar-a-month parking spot, leaving his wife and child in the wake of the shiny new car's exhaust.

Chapter 6

It was all so humiliating. Her husband spent more time with his mother than with her. She had racks of designer clothes she couldn't wear because she was too fat. And now, to top it all off, she needed to get a job.

The morning following the argument in the parking garage, Lily screwed up the nerve to call Victor, her old editor at the *World Business Journal*. When she left her job about a year ago, he had mumbled something about the door always being open for her, so she was hopeful that he might let her freelance a few pieces here and there. At least that would give her some extra spending money (maybe she would even get that long-overdue haircut) and something else besides diaper changes and nipple ointment to talk about with Robert.

"Victor Paltz," answered the gruff voice after two rings. Lily imagined him hunched over his computer terminal, pack of Doral cigarettes in his shirt's front pocket, a cup of Dunkin' Donuts coffee steaming next to the monitor.

"Victor, hi! It's Lil."

"So how's life as Park Avenue's prettiest princess treating you?" he coughed into the phone.

"Oh, great," she answered reflexively, although nothing could be further from the truth. "But I miss you guys."

"You miss us? Don't you have six maids, three nannies, and a butler to keep you company? What about the decorator? Can't you talk to her?" he teased.

Lily feigned amusement, "Oh, stop. We have a maid who comes once a week and that's it."

"So wadda ya want with a bunch of blue-collar saps like us?" Victor asked.

"Don't you want to see the baby? I thought I'd bring him down this week, but I wanted to call and find out when the best time would be. Don't want to catch you on deadline or anything."

Slurping his coffee, Victor flipped through his page-a-day organizer. "How's Friday at four? Should have everything closed by then," he finally suggested.

"Great, see you then."

After Lily hung up the receiver, she realized that if she was going to convince Victor to let her freelance for him, she needed to have a list of ideas for new stories ready by Friday. She'd also have to look a little more pulled together. Even though Victor was a reverse snob—he actually discriminated against those displaying refined manners or any amount of personal wealth—he expected her to look a certain way, and she didn't want to disappoint him.

That afternoon, Lily left Will with Jacinta, who claimed to have extensive child-minding experience, and went out to have her eyebrows threaded. Heading down Madison, she entered a Midtown office building occupied mostly by architects and art galleries, and rode the elevator up to one of the city's best-kept secrets, a postage-stamp-sized spa, crowded with Indian furniture and redolent of sandalwood incense. All the beauty editors went there because it only cost twenty dollars to have their brows threaded into arched perfection, a bargain compared to the eighty-dollar brow wax their magazines routinely recommended.

As she sat on the carved wood settee awaiting her turn in the threading chair, Lily tried to put her finger on exactly what had bothered her so much about Robert's new car. First, there was the fact that it came from Josephine, who was always looking for a new way to hook her claws into Robert. And second, it was a Porsche. She'd said her peace about that. But third, and this is what bothered her the most, it didn't seem right that Robert was driving around in a ninety-seven-thousand-dollar red sports car (she looked up the sticker price on the Internet) while she was debating whether organic milk was worth the extra expense. Of course, she couldn't have expected him to turn down a free car—what man in his right mind would do that?—but, damn it, it wasn't fair.

When Lily first found out that Robert came from a very wealthy family, she promised herself that she'd never become dependent on him for money. If he wanted to give her nice things at Christmastime or on her birthday, who was she to say no, but she wouldn't become one of those ladies who spent their days charging up a storm at Barneys, Bergdorf's, and Bliss. First off, she hadn't grown up that way. Maybe if she had, she'd feel different, but to Lily pampering and shopping was a treat, not a lifestyle. And second, although she enjoyed doing both immensely, she imagined a life spent doing nothing but getting papaya facials and shopping for designer shoes would be like eating chocolate chip cookies every day of the year; eventually she'd probably tire of them.

Her mother, who hadn't worked a day in her life, could never see the virtues of financial independence. Working mothers were a mystery to her: feminism meant having the power to write checks on her husband's bank account. "Why spend your own money when you can spend your husband's?" she'd quip to the department store sales girls as they rang up yet another Christian Dior lipstick or pair of Charles Jourdan heels. The girls would chuckle knowingly and Lily would blush with embarrassment. It's not that she would have preferred a soy-milk-drinking, braless feminist for a mother, but did her mother have to be quite so ridiculously old-fashioned?

Now, years later, it occurred to Lily that while maybe there was nothing wrong with the women of her mother's generation (and those before) enjoying the fruits of their husbands' labor, she ought to be more independent, more *liberated*, than to rely on her own husband to fix all her problems, financial and otherwise. It was up to Lily and Lily alone to get her life—her career, marriage, and social standing—back on track.

And then there was Will's future to consider. It was a sobering realization, but she couldn't rely on Robert to get another job, not at the rate things were going. Although she didn't want to believe he could be happy living life as a layabout, she couldn't rule out the possibility. What if he spent the rest of his life living off his trust, tooling around in his Porsche and at his mother's beck and call every day? If that became the case, she might have to leave him. But even if she did decide to stay and stick it out, she'd have to become a breadwinner again. Children cost money, especially in New York but even in places like Nashville. Lily had to restart her career, if only to ensure that she'd be able to get a full-time job and take care of Will on her own, if it came to that.

"Yep," she sighed while admiring a pair of tall Chloe boots— lustrous tan leather, chic golden grommets climbing up the side— on one of the spa's other patrons. "It's time to go back to work."

Or as her mother might say before slicking on yet another coat of lipstick, "The pity party's over, girl."

Chapter 7

On Friday afternoon Lily took the subway down to Wall Street, where the *World Business Journal*'s headquarters occupied seven floors of a skyscraper. She walked six extra blocks to get to the subway's handicap accessible entrance so she wouldn't have to remove Will from his stroller, but when she finally got into the slow-moving, urine-soaked lift, she wished she hadn't bothered, and she promised herself to ask a stranger to help her carry the stroller down to the train's platform on her way back.

After receiving her visitor's pass at the building's reception desk, she rode the (fast-moving, urine-free) elevator up to the fifty-third floor and slipped in through the glass security doors behind a trio of markets reporters. Veering left along a bank of cubicles, she reveled in the familiar smell of coffee and microwave popcorn and the soft sound of buzzing and bleeping from the hundreds of computer monitors, copiers, and fax machines that filled the office floor. Lily walked deeper into the maze of desks, glancing between each divide. Each cubicle was like a miniature world: In the carefully constructed collages of photos and artwork, postcards and invitations one could read into the occupant's daily lives, their friends and family, hobbies, and aspirations.

By the time Lily arrived in front of Victor's desk, reassuringly still cluttered with old papers and files, half-filled coffee cups and crumpled, empty cigarette packs, it was thirty minutes after four and he was gone.

"Smoke break, he'll be back in a second," said a familiar voice from the desk behind Victor's. Helen, one of the other legal-affairs reporters and Lily's closest friend at the *Journal*, propped her elbows on the shoulder-height divide. "How are you?" she squealed before running around the entrance of her cubicle to envelop Lily in her signature scent, a blend of grapefruit and bergamot essential oils. She leaned over the baby carriage and peered inside. "So this is Will! Isn't he adorable! I can see a lot of him in you, especially around the eyes."

Lily undid the buckles of Will's stroller and picked him up. "Do you want to hold him?" she asked, offering the baby to Helen.

"Oh no, I'm not very good with kids," Helen said, stepping backward. She pulled the pen out of the haphazard bun she had forced her marigold curls into and retwisted her hair into a tidier chignon.

"I can't believe how little everything has changed. You look great," Lily grinned, not knowing what else to say. It had been months since she and Helen had spoken, and it had been her fault for not returning any of Helen's calls or taking her up on any of her invitations to have lunch or meet for a drink.

"Thanks, so do you."

"Oh no, I'm so fat, but bless you for not pointing that out. I'm sure Victor will."

"I'm sure Victor will what?" barked her old editor as he came striding down the hallway. "Lily! My favorite Park Avenue Princess," he coughed, enrobing Lily and Will in a Doral-scented embrace.

"She's not a princess," Helen said defensively, rolling her eyes behind Victor's back.

"Oh, that's right, she only has three maids and two gardeners," he continued joking. "So this must be the little prince, huh?" he asked, passing his liver-spotted hand over Will's little head.

Victor and Helen cooed over the baby and asked all the usual questions. How was labor? Painful. Does he sleep through the night yet? On occasion, but not consistently. Are you still nursing? Yes. Can he crawl? No. Then Lily said to Victor, "There was actually something I wanted to talk with you about," and Helen had the good grace to retreat to her cubicle to call back a source.

"Have a seat," Victor said, pushing a stack of *Newsweek*s off of the chair next to his desk. They fell in a heap on the floor.

"Thanks," Lily said, resisting the urge to restack the magazines. She sat down and stuffed a pacifier in Will's mouth. He was getting fussy, knocking his little head into her chest, which she imagined was his way of saying, "Feed me now, woman." Lily felt her milk ducts fill expectantly and estimated that she had about ten minutes before her breast pads were soaked through. Clearing her throat, she launched into her pitch. "The thing is, Victor, I have a lot more free time than I thought I would . . . and, *umm,* I'd like to start writing again for you. As a freelancer."

"Really?" Victor said, the deep grooves in his forehead furrowing with confusion. "But it's not like you need to work?"

"Oh no, I don't *need* to work but I want to. I've come up with a list of story ideas," she said, fishing out of the diaper bag the ideas she had typed up earlier that morning.

"Lily, I wish I could help," he said, taking the paper from her trembling hand. "But we've had some big budget cuts since you left. There's a hiring freeze, and we aren't accepting very many freelanced pieces right now. I have a couple of stringers, but they really need the work to get by, not like you," he said, smiling.

"But need is such a relative term," Lily argued. She could use the money more than Victor could imagine, but she was too proud to go into the depressing details of her financial crisis. That and Victor was probably right that the other stringers needed it more than she did.

Forgetting the pair of reading glasses hanging around his neck as well as the pair perched on top of his computer monitor, Victor held her list of ideas out at arm's length and quickly read through them. When he was done, he regarded her sadly and said, "These are good. It's too bad you left us."

"Coming here today has reminded me," she began to say before the lump in her throat cut her off prematurely. To her surprise, she felt a large wet tear rolling down her cheek.

"Oh, c'mon, don't cry," Victor said, handing her a scratchy, company-issued tissue.

Dabbing her eyes, she tried composing herself, but the tears continued to flow.

"C'mon," he repeated. "Life can't be that bad in the manor." He handed her another couple of tissues.

Lily blew her nose and cleared her throat. "I'm sorry. I don't know what's gotten into me today."

"I'm sure it's not easy making such a big transition."

"It's just that seeing you and Helen and the offices has brought back all sorts of memories. I miss feeling like I was a part of something big and important, you know?"

"I have a feeling you're romancing what you used to do here," Victor chuckled. "Being a mother is big and important, too."

"I know. I mean, that's what I thought, too. That's what I told myself when I quit. But what if being a good mother means helping provide for my child?"

He looked at her quizzically. "Then you go back to work," he shrugged.

"I know plenty of mothers do that, but I just can't imagine spending every day away from Will. I mean, *he's* my life now. Once he's in kindergarten it'll be a different story, but for now I know I don't want a full-time job. Of course, I know plenty of women don't have a choice in the matter. They go back because they have to. So I'm lucky in that regard."

"Yes, you are."

"It's true. Believe me, I know. But what about later, when Will's in school and I feel useless? Or what if things change, financially speaking, and I really *do* need to work? No one's gonna hire me then, not when I've been out of the game for so long. I thought freelancing would be an option in the meantime, but—"

"Just because I can't give you any assignments doesn't mean you can't do it," he said firmly.

"Yes," Lily whispered, getting up from her chair. She was afraid she was going to start crying again and distracted herself by restacking the magazines that had dropped to the floor.

"Chin up," Victor said, rising from his seat. "You're smart, you've always had great instincts and you can write all the other reporters on this floor under the table. You'll find something soon, and it'll be better than anything I can offer you here."

Lily hugged her old editor good-bye and waved to Helen, who was still on the phone conducting her interview. She walked past a series of cubicles, nodding at a few of the familiar faces around the office, and went into the ladies' bathroom near the elevators. After sitting down on the toilet, she unbuttoned her shirt and unhooked her nursing bra with one hand while cradling Will into position with the other. As he sucked hungrily from her breast, his contented gulps coming fast and loud, she placed a finger in his chubby, fisted hand and told herself that Victor was right, that being a mother was more fulfilling than writing about corporate malfeasance and patent infringements. Getting pregnant with Will might have been an "accident," but now that he was in her life and she knew what it was like to feel his round bottom sagging into the palm of her hand or to smell his burps, sweet like butter cream frosting, now that she knew all this, she wouldn't trade him for anything. And yet, she—as the cliché goes—wanted to have it all: family, career, and killer Chloe boots, to boot.

As Lily switched Will over to her other breast, she heard the door to the bathroom open and saw Helen's navy ballet flats appear under the stall door.

"Lil?" she asked. "You in there?"

"*Umm,* I'm just nursing Will," she said awkwardly through the stall door. "I'll be done in a second." .

"Do you want to go down for a cup of coffee with me when you're done?"

"That'd be great." Lily buttoned her shirt back up. Squeezing her breasts to judge how empty they felt, she guessed that Will had taken in enough milk to tide him over until they got home.

Once outside of the bathroom, Lily, Will, and Helen headed down to the Au Bon Pain on the building's first level and ordered two blended iced mochas, the preferred afternoon pick-me-up for all female *Journal* staffers. "Hold the whipped cream on mine," Lily told the woman behind the register, handing her a ten-dollar bill for both coffees. "It's on me," she said to Helen.

"Thanks," Helen said, and winked.

"It's the least I could do, after being MIA for so long. I'm so sorry for not e-mailing you back. I thought about calling at least once a week, but then . . . I don't know, I guess I never got around to it."

"Don't worry about it. I know it's tough with a baby. I can't fathom what it would be like to have one of my own to take care of."

"It is a big change, especially in the beginning when you're barely sleeping and can't remember the last time you went anywhere more exciting than the Food Emporium. But I've started getting the hang of it, and I'm glad I came here to see you and Victor."

They sat down at a small iron table outdoors. "Yeah, I couldn't help but overhear your conversation with Vic," Helen began.

"I was hoping he'd give me some assignments. I could really use the work."

Helen uncapped the domed lid from her coffee and spooned a mound of whipped cream into her mouth. "I think he thinks you're so rich you couldn't possibly *want* to work," she said after swallowing the cream.

Lily took a deep breath and took off her sunglasses. "Helen, if I tell you something, do you promise to keep it a secret?"

"Of course, you can trust me," Helen said, putting her beverage on the wobbly table. She grabbed Lily's hand and squeezed it reassuringly.

"Robert and I are having some money problems. He left Caruthers & Caruthers. His trust fund is helping us, obviously, but we're stacking up a lot of debt, and I just feel like I should be doing something to help out. The other day Robert sort of suggested it, too," Lily said. Helen didn't need to know that he had basically spat the words "get a job" at her from the front seat of his brand-new sports car.

"Well, I know an editor at the *New York Sentinel*, Rebecca Burrows. They poached her away from our Endeavors section, and now she's working for the *Sentinel*'s Thursday Trends. I know she's looking to build her stable of freelancers."

"I think I vaguely remember Rebecca. Is she the really petite one with short brown hair? Likes to wear chenille cardigans with hand-carved wood buttons?"

"Yeah, that's her. Don't be fooled by her fuzzy exterior, though. She's tough," Helen said, pulling a notepad and pen out of an eggplant hobo bag. "Here's her e-mail and phone number. Tell her I suggested you get in touch." After scribbling down the address and numbers, she handed the slip to Lily.

"But Helen, Thursday Trends is notoriously hard to get into. Every freelancer in New York City wants to get their byline in there," she said, staring down at the paper. "Why would they let me write for it? I haven't done any lifestyle writing before."

"Rebecca won't hold that against you. In fact, she'd probably think it's a plus that you have a serious background."

"But what am I going to pitch her? I know legal business, Helen. That's what I've spent the last six years of my life covering."

"You must have come across a few great story ideas while rubbing shoulders with the beautiful and the damned, right? Not everyone has the kind of access to these people that you do."

Sipping her coffee, Lily thought back to when she first started accompanying Robert to charity benefits and parties. She had been constantly stunned by the excess and ostentation of his high society life and had never before thought of her comfortable existence prior to then as meager, as she had then, all of a sudden. The $7,000 annual gym memberships, weekly $600 haircuts, thousand-square-foot couture closets, these were things she had never even known existed. But having been holed up at home for the better part of the last year, Lily felt out of touch with everything chic and marvelous in the world.

Helen let go of Lily's hand and mixed the rest of the whipped cream into her drink. "Leverage your social connections, and you've got a brand-new career on your hands. I'll send Rebecca an e-mail telling her to expect to hear from you in the next couple of days."

Chapter 8

When Lily returned home, arms aching from lugging the stroller up and down the subway entrances, she found Robert in the kitchen opening a large bag of potato chips. Unlike Lily, he had the metabolism of a young colt and could eat anything he wanted: three-inch steaks marbled with fat; slabs of foie gras; entire boxes of chocolate; and bowls of full-fat ice cream.

"Hi, honey," he said, wiping his greasy hands on the tea towel hanging on the door to their Viking range. He took Will from Lily's tired arms and sat down at the kitchen table. "What did you do today with Mommy?" he asked the baby. Lily had noticed Robert was doing that more and more—asking her questions through the baby, as though their six-month-old son was some multilingual translator at the United Nations and not the drooling little milk fiend he really was.

"We went to see my old editor at the *Journal*," she answered in place of Will. "You remember Victor?"

"Oh yeah, I do. Why'd you go there?" he said.

There was a hint of suspicion in his voice, and she liked it. "I wanted to see if he'd let me freelance for him, but apparently they've had some budget cuts," Lily said, and frowned. She reached for the potato chips and then, remembering her diet, pulled a Ziploc bag filled with peeled carrots and washed celery sticks from the fridge.

"Aren't there other publications you can write for?"

"Helen offered to put me in touch with a contact of hers at the *New York Sentinel*."

"That's great, honey. You should definitely take her up on that."

"I plan to," she said, deadpan.

"So, what's for dinner? I'm starved," he said, grinning through a mouthful of chips.

Tired as she was, Lily whipped together a meal of oven-baked pork tenderloin and rice and steamed broccoli doused in extra virgin olive oil in under an hour. While she and Robert ate, she nursed Will. Then as Robert loaded the dishwasher, she gave Will a bath, nursed the baby again, and tried to put him down for the night. Of course on the very night Lily most needed him to fall asleep quickly, he refused to go down without a fight. She shushed, she cradled, she massaged—nothing worked. She rocked, she paced, and she sang, and still he was wide awake. It wasn't until 2:00 a.m., during the third consecutive feeding of the night, that Will finally succumbed to his fatigue and shuttered his long-lashed eyes for the duration.

After changing into an oversized cotton T-shirt, Lily fell into bed, half dead and reeling with exhaustion. Just as she was about to doze off, she felt Robert's hand snake around her waist and his pelvis scoot underneath her bottom. He was hard and growing harder by the second. *Maybe if I ignore it, it will go away.* She squeezed her eyes shut and lay as still as possible.

"Lil?" Robert whispered, maneuvering his hand under her T-shirt and onto her breast, the one the baby had been gnawing on practically all night.

Please, for the love of God, get your hand off my boob, she yelped inwardly. Squirreling out of Robert's grasp, she pretended to grumble sleepily, "Baby, it's the middle of the night."

"Mmm," he groaned, pretending not to hear her and moving his hands to her waist, then inside her cotton underwear. He began stroking her clitoris, trying to make her wet enough so he could slide himself inside her without resorting to the same sad tube of KY Jelly they'd been using since Lily's doctor had given her the all clear for sex. She'd gone to bed with Robert that same night and the experience had been more painful than the time she'd lost her virginity. When she consulted the Internet the following morning, she'd learned that her "vaginal dryness issues" were just another annoying side effect of childbirth and nursing. But even armed with this new knowledge, all the fumbling for lubricants and condom unwrapping made the sex feel onerous and inorganic, and so they'd stopped having it.

And now, after five very long, very sexless months, Robert had chosen a night when Lily was beyond tired and in no mood to be touched to make his move. But the way Lily looked at it she had two choices. She could either tell him how irritating his timing was and risk an argument or two, or she could just let him do what he wanted to do and chances are it would be over in ten minutes. After a few seconds of consideration, she settled on option two, but with a caveat. "Just don't go anywhere near my nipples," she told him, and this time he must have been listening because his hands didn't get anywhere near her breasts again.

Sure enough, eight minutes later Robert came and rolled off of her onto his back. "I love you, honey," he sighed, brushing a lock of her hair off her face.

"I love you, too," she whispered, pleased that she'd satisfied him and that their five-month sex drought was over. But as she dozed off to sleep, Lily wondered if she'd ever want sex the way she once had. Would it ever feel fun again, or would it always be like this, something mildly pleasurable but perfunctorily performed.

She shut her eyes and wondered, *Would it ever be as exciting as it was when we first met?*

Chapter 9

The first time Lily laid eyes on Robert was at a painful social at the New York offices of his law firm, the Chicago-born, now world-wide, partnership of Caruthers & Caruthers. The office's white-bearded managing partner insisted on introducing Lily to a few associates, apparently so they could profess to her how much they enjoyed working 120-hour workweeks for partners who barely took the time to learn their first names, and Robert was one of the associates who had been suckered into the PR mission. He was clearly unhappy about his poor luck, or the press intrusion in general, because when he initially greeted Lily over an uninspired platter of green grapes, orange cheese cubes, and red pepper sticks, it was with an unwarranted degree of disdain and distrust.

"So you're the reporter from the *Journal*," he said, sneering a little, and Lily noticed his teeth were big and square, almost shaped like Chiclets, but not so alarmingly white.

"That's right. You're Robert, the third year? What department are you in again?" she asked, her tongue feeling suddenly heavy and dry in her mouth as she met his vibrant blue eyes, the color of the Aegean Sea. It was there, in his eyes, that she got her first glimpse of the urban fairy tale—the apartment, the kids, the midafternoon weekend sex with the shades drawn, the air conditioner on, and the door locked—and discovered that she wanted it.

"M and A."

"Oh, good for you," Lily said, sipping her Chardonnay. Robert snorted, his broad shoulders heaving with laughter. He wiped a tear from his left eye.

"What's so funny?" she demanded.

"Nothing, I'm sorry. It's just something one of my mom's friends would say."

"Oh?"

"And you're probably like five years younger than I am."

"So?"

"It just struck me as a funny thing to say, that's all." Lily saw his eyes flick to a spot to the left of her head and she turned around in time to catch another male associate making an ass-grabbing gesture in her direction. He had red hair, a thick neck, and a nose that suggested he liked his gin and tonics with very little tonic. She glared at him, but instead of backing down, the associate upped the ante. Making his index and pointer fingers into the shape of a vee, he thrust his wet pink tongue licentiously between them.

"You're disgusting," she hissed at him.

"What a prick," Robert said, gently steering Lily into the hall, away from the guy who had mimed the obscenities. In the hallway, with the door to the conference room closed, he peered at her, trying to assess how angry and violated she felt. He put his hands on her shoulders. "You're shaking," he said.

"I think I should go." She wanted to tell him that she felt uncomfortable, like she was the only woman in a frat house at four o'clock in the morning, but she was too disturbed to speak. She needed to get out of there.

"No, don't go. Shit. Forget you saw that. That guy's a total asshole. He's in the real estate group," Robert said, as if that explained everything. "Why don't I give you a tour of the office? The conference rooms on thirty-four are *stun-ning*, let me tell you," he said.

"Okay." She laughed and allowed Robert to lead her up a stairwell to another floor.

His tour started in the kitchen with a thousand-dollar espresso machine, which he said none of the lawyers knew how to use, then progressed to a pretty standard-looking conference room, followed by a wood-paneled library where the firm had installed a security camera because so many associates were "getting it on in there," and finally Robert's office, a tiny windowless room painted in an uninspiring shade of pale gray. There was a wooden bookcase along one wall and a trio of framed diplomas from St. Paul's, Dartmouth College, and Harvard Law School hanging above his desk. He held out his chair for her, a swiveling seat upholstered in a darker shade of gray. "Go ahead, take a seat, feel the power."

"*Ooh,* I can feel it," Lily said as she lowered herself slowly (and, she hoped,seductively) into his chair. She noted happily that there wasn't a picture of a girlfriend on his desk and picked up the phone. "Get me the Goldman file," she barked into the receiver. He took it from her, his fingers brushing hers for a thrilling second, and put it back in its cradle.

"Now that's not a plaything, Miss Grace." He was leaning over her, one hand on the desk, and she could smell the beer on his breath. Her heart thudded violently in her chest, blocking out all the other noises—the whirr of the computer, the ticking of the clock on the wall, the sound of someone making copies down the hall.

"Are you flirting with me?" she asked boldly, willing him to kiss her with every cell and synapse in her body. If there was ever a time Lily wished she had the power of mind control, this was it.

But it was as if she'd shot him with a stun gun. Robert jerked back, looked at his watch, a sporty-looking Rolex, and announced that he had to be somewhere "like five minutes ago."

Lily rose from his chair and walked out of the office, looking both ways down the hall. *What the hell just happened?*

"Can you find your way out?" he stammered, avoiding any eye contact. He shuffled a perfectly neat stack of papers on his desk.

"I'm sure I can figure it out," she said, more than a little caustically. "Thanks for the tour."

Lily had been crushed by the rejection—she'd never felt such chemistry with anyone before—and spent a few weeks sulking, listening to Fiona Apple and burning aromatherapy candles until her best friend from college, Elizabeth Krueger, who had moved to New York with Lily after their senior year, convinced her to come to a party. "You can't stay in a funk forever," Liz had moaned, instructing Lily to change into her tightest black pants, tallest heels, and best push-up bra. Minutes later, she returned to Lily's room with an off-the-shoulder white silk peasant top. "Put this on," she said, flinging the garment across the room.

Lily went to the party, a midsummer, margarita-themed evening at Doubles, the plush red-velvet-draped, members-only club in the basement of the Sherry-Netherland. Naturally, Robert was there, and he wasn't alone. *He has a girlfriend*, Lily realized, squinting to see if his date, a tall gorgeous blonde with long thoroughbred thigh muscles and monster diamonds twinkling from her earlobes, had anything approximating an engagement ring on her left hand. She didn't. All is not lost, Lily told herself, but then Robert spent the whole night ignoring her, his eyes trained only on the bottom of his margarita glass and his flaxen-haired thoroughbred.

The following morning, Liz, despite her tequila-induced hangover, made a very noble effort to convince Lily that Robert "You-didn't-mention-he-was-a-Bartholomew" was the world's biggest snob, a selfish, chauvinistic rich boy who only dated girls whose last names appeared on the Social Register. "Count yourself lucky you never got involved," she counseled.

But Lily didn't think she was the least bit fortunate. Robert was a catch—good looking and from a good family—and that wasn't even why she was attracted to him. It was a feeling she had when they first met, a gut instinct that told her she could trust him, that she could tell him anything and he wouldn't judge her. She actually ached for him, in her bones, her eyelids, the soft tissue of her heart, everywhere.

No one was more surprised by these feelings than Lily. Before meeting Robert, she'd never cried over a man, never lost her appetite, never spent hours dissecting what exactly he meant by "Let's keep things casual" or some other such thing that men typically say when they aren't in love but are digging the sex. In high school, she was more likely to mourn a B+ than she was a bad breakup, and once Lily went so far as to ask her mother whether she might be a lesbian, since she didn't live and breathe for boys the way her girlfriends did. Her mother's response—an exasperated sigh followed by, "Of course you're not a lesbian. Don't be ridiculous"—did little to put Lily's mind at rest, and for a long time she just assumed that if she was not homosexual, she was at least asexual. In fact, it was only when she met Robert that she was truly sure of her sexual orientation. He awakened in her a desire that she hadn't known existed, and for that reason alone she already loved him. They barely knew each other, but she was sure that they were meant to be together. This was it, the love she had been waiting for.

So a couple of months after the party at Doubles, when Robert called Lily at the bureau to ask her out on a date, she made no pretense toward anger, no attempt to play hard to get.

Six months later, they were engaged.

Chapter 10

The day after her meetings with Victor and Helen, Lily cleared the unused diapers, baby bibs, Balmex cream, and box of wipes off of the living room coffee table and plugged in her laptop so she could write an e-mail to Rebecca Burrows at the *Sentinel*. She sent in a short bio, a couple of clips, and a list of three ideas. One was about a new twelve-hundred-dollar facial on offer at a new spa (she'd received a card in the mail announcing the treatment); another was about a psychic she knew a lot of the socialites consulted on a regular basis; and the third was about how expensive the engraved invitations to charity benefits were becoming (the ones for last year's Save Bucharest Ball cost fifty dollars each).

At around 9:30 a.m., she took Will out on another long walk. He loved the fresh air and all the sounds and sights, and she loved watching him take it all in. Everything, cars honking or a bicycle whooshing by, was new and fresh in his eyes. Once in the park, they stopped by the reflecting pond and watched the ducks paddling along, the other mothers and babies streaming past on their way to one of the playgrounds. She strolled a little longer, stopping at a park bench to nurse. Afterward she let Will practice crawling for a while on the grass, where she took some pictures of him with her phone—he looked so cute in his fleece hat with the round teddy bear ears poking out from the top—and sent them to Robert's BlackBerry. After waiting for close to a quarter hour for him to call or text her back, she gave up and loaded Will back up in the stroller, forging ahead with her exercise.

As she walked, she plotted. If she was going to become the family breadwinner, she had to refashion herself into a society and fashion scribe. Helen was right; she had the right pedigree and access to give her a leg up on the competition. The first step was getting back onto the party circuit so she could start sleuthing for story ideas. And if she was going to do that, she needed to blend in with the natives. In other words, she had to get back into shape. Rounding the reservoir, she thought forward to December. Robert's parents had invited them to spend the week after Christmas at their villa in St. Barths. It would be a perfect opportunity for Lily to "get out there," as Robert frequently referred to it, but New Year's was too far away. She needed to start hobnobbing as soon as possible. The only question was how. She couldn't afford to buy benefit tickets and wouldn't dream of asking Robert for the money after she'd made such a fuss about the ridiculousness of his car. She also wouldn't be able to get press passes for an event until she was a bona fide *Sentinel* freelancer.

Upon returning home, she plopped Will into his bouncy seat in the living room, clicking on the seat's vibrating mechanism as she answered her cell phone, which was buzzing on her hip.

"Hey sugar, where are you?" her mother asked.

"Hey, Mom," she sighed, disappointed it wasn't Rebecca Burrows calling from the *Sentinel*.

"Where are you? I was trying to reach you at the apartment."

"I'm home. Just got back. We went out for a walk."

"You and Will?" she asked, not waiting for a response. "Oh, that's good. Listen sugar, your father and I both think that you and Rob should move here. The economy is growing," she said vaguely.

"Mom, it's sweet that you and Dad want us nearby, but that's not really an option. We like New York."

"Just think about it. Mary Kate Hawthorne's daughter just had a baby, and Mary Kate takes care of the little girl every Friday and her daughter, you know Campbell, she goes off with her friends to the country club, has her nails done, has lunch with the girls, goes shopping. I could help you like that. Give you a break every once in a while."

"Mom, I appreciate the offer—I really do—but it's not going to happen. How's Dad?" Lily asked, hoping to change the subject. She sat down at the coffee table and turned on the computer so she could check her e-mail.

"He's fine." Margaret sighed. "Working a lot. Teaching a new course at the college this term. He's so busy, I had to mow the lawn last week, had to push the blessed mower around myself. I think one of the neighbors saw me."

"What's so bad about being seen mowing the lawn?" Lily teased, picturing her mother mowing the lawn, sweating underneath one of her wide-brimmed straw hats, black sunglasses slipping down her perspiring nose.

"It's not ladylike," Mrs. Grace said testily. "Yard work is a man's job."

Lily sighed. There was no point in arguing what passed for women's work with her mother. "All right, Mom, give my love to Matthew if you talk to him. I better go before Will wakes up."

"You do that, child, but I'm telling you, you and Rob could be real happy here in Nashville. Just think how much fun it'll be to go to Green Hills Mall together, just like when you were a little girl and wanted to buy up the entire Hello Kitty store," she sniffed.

Checking her e-mail, Lily saw there were five new messages from BabyCenter.com, one from Nikki (Subject line: 18INCHES—HASTOHURT), and one from Rebecca Burrows. She clicked on that one.

To: lily.bart2005@hotmail.com
From: rburrows@nysentinel.com
Hi Lily: I think we're going to pass on these ideas for now;
not quite enough drama, but thanks for thinking of us.
All best,
Rebecca

Feeling heavy with disappointment, Lily turned off her computer and tried to give herself a pep talk. She tiptoed over to where Will was slumbering in his vibrating bouncy seat. "The good news is that she's open to receiving ideas from me. The bad news is that I sent her my best ideas and she shot down all of them," she said to him. Will rubbed his nose in his sleep. "But don't worry. Your mommy's not gonna give up that easily."

Picking up the baby and the bouncer as one unit, she walked down the hall toward her bedroom and the master bath. Rummaging through the cabinet under the sink, Lily looked for a bottle of bubble bath she knew she had in there somewhere. Instead of drowning herself in tears, it would do her more good to luxuriate in a few thousand gardenia-scented bubbles while she flipped through the pages of the celebrity gossip magazine she picked up from the news agent's at the corner.

"I was sure it was in here somewhere," she mumbled, sticking her head into the dust-covered cubby. Tucked behind the pipes, past the lineup of baby powder, unopened boxes of toothpaste and Q-tips, Lily found a treasure trove of beauty products. There were serums, creams, masks, oils, and a litany of other potions she had been given in goody bags.

Then her eye caught on a box of hair dye.

After shutting off the tap, she studied the pamphlet inside the box. *Seems easy enough*, she thought as she skipped to the kitchen to retrieve some aluminum foil, and a couple of tea towels. Once back in the bathroom, she lit a candle to approximate a spalike atmosphere, and after carefully mixing up the dye, which promised to give her caramel-colored highlights, she divided her hair into five sections. Using a fine tooth comb she weaved a small amount of hair away from the rest, inserting a piece of foil under the strands, and slathered on the dye. "This isn't so hard," she chirped over to Will, whose lips were curling mischievously in his sleep.

Half an hour later, Lily was just finishing weaving highlights into the back of her hair when Will woke up. She had forgotten to strap him down into his bouncy chair, and as he reached up to grab hold of the arch that suspended a mirror and a few play toys over his body, he missed the mark and fell forward, smacking his forehead on the bathroom floor with an audible *thwack*.

Lily watched the fall in frozen horror. Her baby lay facedown on the floor, tensed and silent. She lunged to pick him up and hugged him tightly to her chest. "Oh, pumpkin, Mommy's sorry," she soothed before pulling him away, unhooking the strong little fingers grasping her shoulders, to make sure his forehead wasn't bleeding. Will's mouth was in a wide-open grimace, tears streaming down his red face, and he was shaking. After what seemed like an eternity but was probably only a few seconds, he finally broke into a loud wail. Lily hugged him back into her breastbone, relieved to hear his cries, and stroked his back. She started to sing his favorite song, "The Wheels on the Bus" while pacing around the apartment.

"All better now, pumpkin?" she asked, wiping away the tears on his cheeks with her hand. He reached his hand up to Lily's hair line and gurgled. "What's so funny?" she asked as Will's fingers pulled at a piece of aluminum foil.

"My hair!" she yelled, sprinting down the corridor back toward the bathroom, the baby clinging on for dear life. Detouring into to the nursery, she sat Will in his crib and slapped the On button of the toy aquarium attached to the crib rails.

Lily pawed at the foils in her hair and after hurdling into the tub, turned on the shower only to be blasted in the face with ice-cold water. She yelped and jumped aside, catching herself from falling out of the tub and onto her face, and adjusted the water temperature. She dipped her head under the showerhead (one of those steering-wheel-sized ones that are supposed to approximate the feeling of being in a rainstorm) and let the dye rinse out of her hair, keeping her eyes and mouth tightly shut. If the damage is too bad I can always go get it fixed, she reminded herself. Lily stepped out of the tub and, bracing herself with a deep breath, looked in the mirror.

Even with it wet she could see that her hair was a disaster. There were thick streaks of blonde running down the sides of her face, and the ones on the side she started with were a much lighter shade. The back of her head remained resolutely brown. It was like she was in fifth grade again, but this time she couldn't blame her mother. She had no choice. She had to call Ernesto for an emergency appointment.

"Le Hair Atelier, hello, *Est-ce que je peux vous aidez?*" answered the salon's receptionist in a nasal Long Island accent.

"Hi, yes. This is Lily Bartholomew. Hi. I'm having a bit of an emergency and I need to come in to see Ernesto right away."

"What kind of emergency are we talking about?"

"Hair color?"

"Did you try coloring yourself?"

"Yes."

"Ernesto doesn't do botch jobs," the receptionist said curtly, and hung up.

"What the hell?" Lily yelled into the phone. She wasn't going to take no for an answer. She had been going to Ernesto, or Nesto, as he asked a select few to call him, for two years, four times a year, at $500 a pop (a fortune!), plus tips ($10 for the assistant who washed her hair, $10 to the assistant who mixed the dye, $15 to the assistant who did the blow out, and $100 to Nesto). She had sent him dozens of referrals. He owed her. She was going in.

In her panic Lily called the housekeeper. "Hi, Jacinta, are you busy this afternoon?" she asked.

"No, *mamita*, what's going on? Is my baby okay?" Jacinta asked. She'd taken to calling Will her baby, and Lily didn't mind. She loved that Jacinta loved her son almost as much as she did.

"Will's fine. The problem is me, or rather, my hair," Lily admitted.

"*Uh-oh.*"

"That's putting it mildly."

"Okay mama, you sit tight. I'll be there in twenty minutes."

"Thank you, thank you, thank you!"

Lily ran into Will's nursery to rescue the baby, who had grown bored with watching the bubbles and plastic fish swim around in their faux aquarium, and slipped him in the Exersaucer she had dragged into the master bedroom earlier. She changed into dark jeans, a beige silk camisole fringed in black lace, and a gray cashmere cardigan and squeezed her feet and calves into knee-high stiletto boots. She tied a black-and-white Pucci print scarf around her head and chose a pair of purple resin sunglasses from the drawer of her bedside table. The effect was either very chic, in a Liz Hurley-while-still-fat-and-hiding-from-the-paparazzi sort of way, or very awful, in a crazy-woman-on-a-Topamax-and-Zanax-drug-cocktail sort of way.

Before she could decide which one of the two it was, the doorman buzzed to announce Jacinta's arrival, and Lily grabbed her diaper bag, then thought better of it and switched her essentials over to a small black patent leather clutch with a sleek silver closure. She knew Nesto's assistant would show her the door if she looked anything less than fantastic.

On the cab ride over to the salon, Lily racked her brain trying to think up a plausible reason for her hair's current state of duress that wouldn't be an act of social hari-kari. If she told Nesto the truth—that she had tried highlighting her own hair to save money—he would jump to the conclusion that Lily had fallen on unspeakably hard times. He would feign sympathy, and then the moment Lily left the salon, or possibly even before, depending on who was coming into the salon that day, he would pass the news on to every socialite who sat their size zero bottoms in his chair until he got hold of an even juicier piece of gossip.

Things aren't *that* bad, thought Lily, cursing herself for trying to dye her own hair. "What was I thinking?" she sighed.

Chapter 11

Panting slightly, Lily finally reached the Madison Avenue townhouse in which Le Hair Atelier occupied the second and third floors. She caught her breath and then walked up the first flight of stairs, opening the heavy gilt door to the salon, which was decorated to look like a royal French boudoir. The walls were covered in cream and mauve flocked wallpaper, there were gilt mirrors lining the walls, white orchids potted in authentic Sevres cache pots, and antique Louis XIV chairs and settees upholstered in a beige silk moiré from Scalamandré. Nesto may have been born in a favela on the outskirts of São Paulo, but his years spent working in the best salons in Paris had trained his eye. He had more refined taste than most Park Avenue wives. If Nesto wasn't coloring hair, he could have commanded a pretty penny as an interior designer.

A pale blonde bearing a not-so-slight resemblance to an Afghan dog greeted Lily from behind a mirror-topped mahogany table. "*Bonjour*, do you have an appointment?"

"No, *umm*, but Nesto's expecting me," Lily lied.

"Are you sure?" the girl asked, slouching back in her chair.

"Yes." *Best to be short.* The trick to lying is to say less, not more.

The girl sighed, visibly perturbed, and looked down the bridge of her long nose at the appointment book on the desk. "I'll have to check with him, you understand. May I take your name?"

"Tell him it's Lily," she said coolly. No last name. That would have been a dead giveaway that she wasn't on more intimate terms with Ernesto.

"Just a second." The girl disappeared around the corner. Lily took a seat on one of the couches and took off her purple sunglasses. There was a landscape painting hanging above the desk that she hadn't noticed the last time she was there. A Pissarro. Not bad.

"Lily, is that you?" Her head froze for a millisecond before turning of its own accord toward the high-pitched voice.

"Snow!"

"How *are* you, dear? We've all been wondering why we never see you anymore. Its like, 'Where's Lily? Have you seen Lily? Where is she?'" Snow rattled on in her trademark mile-a-minute exuberance. She took off her fur-lined black trench and sat down on a Louis XIV chair opposite Lily. "So where've you been, darling?"

"I've been around." Lily shrugged. "Enjoying being a mommy and all. You know how it is."

"Oh yes, aren't kids the cutest little buggers? My Lexi is already talking. She's terribly advanced."

"Oh, how wonderful."

"In fact, she said *chic* the other day. Isn't that divine? The nanny brought her in to watch me while the makeup artist was putting on the finishing touches—Valentino lent me this fabulous red dress for the Met Ball, which was, oh my God, the funnest, everyone was there, of course. I sat next to Kate Bosworth!—and then Lexi goes in this tiny baby voice *chiiic*." Snow squealed and clapped her hands.

"Oh, how adorable."

"She is. You should come over with yours for a playdate."

"We'd love to. How old is Lexi now?"

"She's eleven, no wait, almost twelve months. Hah! I lose

track," Snow giggled, shaking her honey blond tresses. "That reminds me, we're celebrating her first birthday next Tuesday. Can you come? We're not doing anything too crazy, because I absolutely do not have time to organize a major event like Di Meddling's Boobah screening party at SoHo House. Can you believe she hired Nadine Johnson to do the PR? So of course Andre Balazs showed up. And Page Six ran an item." Snow rolled her eyes and began rifling through her python Fendi Spy bag. "Anyway, we're just doing something cozy at home, champers and mini-cheeseburgers from DB Bistro—you know, the ones with foie gras and truffles in the center—and Fauchon's doing the birthday cake with cape gooseberries and those little fruit-shaped pieces of marzipan."

"Oh, how sweet. You'll get such great pictures," Lily said, picturing the scene.

"I know! Patrick is coming—but just 'cuz he's a close personal friend. Not because we hired him," she said, referring to the ne plus ultra of socialite photographers, Patrick McMullan. Snow handed Lily a large pale pink envelope.

"I meant the baby. Digging her sweet little hands into the cake? I love those photos with frosting smeared all over their faces."

"Are you kidding? Lexi's allergic to nuts. There's no way she's coming near that cake. So, what are you here for?"

"I'm here to see Nesto," Lily replied as she inspected the invitation. Engraved on heavy card stock in rose-colored ink were the words, "It's my 1st birthday" followed by the time of the party, RSVP phone line, and dress code (festive/disco chic, *whatever that means*). A separate, equally thick card listed where Lexi was registered for gifts: FAO Schwarz, Bonpoint, Jacadi, and Saks Fifth Avenue. Both cards were rimmed with glimmering disco balls and pink bubble shapes.

"I'm here to see Nesto, too!" Snow replied, running a hand through her hair. "Is he running behind or something?" she added nervously.

"Possibly." Lily shrugged again. Hopefully the receptionist wouldn't say anything to allude to her impromptu appearance. She could kiss that birthday party invitation good-bye if Snow found out she jumped in front of her to see Nesto.

Snow Foster was by no means the most attractive woman in New York. For starters, she had a pinched-in nose, most likely the result of a circa 1989 rhinoplasty, but the bigger problem was her eyes. Buggy is how most people described them, and next to the preternaturally small nose, they looked even more unattractive. But to Snow's credit, she did an admirable job making sure everything else was faultless. Her teeth were white and straight, her body, Lottie Berk lithe, and her hair, well, it was well known in certain circles that, thanks to Nesto, she had the best honey blonde highlights on the eastern seaboard.

The receptionist ducked her head around the corner and motioned for Lily to follow her.

"I guess I'm up next, see you in there?"

As Lily stepped inside Nesto's private room, a cornered-off space that boasted an enormous floor-to-ceiling window and a massive crystal chandelier, she took in the Louis XIV couch and mirrored coffee table covered in various bibelots. There were half a dozen Limoges boxes and a trio of porcelain ashtrays from Hermès all filled to the brim with cigarette butts. On a corner table stood a bottle of Tattinger champagne chilling inside a silver wine bucket, and before saying a word, Nesto, who was wearing plaid pants, a matching vest, skin-tight black T-shirt, and his trademark long black hair in a braid, poured Lily a full glass of the bubbly.

"From what I hear, you need *diis*," he purred as a greeting.

"Thanks," Lily said unsurely, taking a sip. The alcohol tickled the roof of her mouth pleasantly.

"I won't, how do you say, *bullsheet* you. There have been some *rooomors* going around. 'You fat, you getting a *deevorce.*' Why you haven't come in to see Nesto? You worry me."

"I didn't want to bother you. Remember, I couldn't do the

highlights during the pregnancy? And then I guess I lost track of time."

Without invitation or warning, Nesto stripped off Lily's scarf. "My God, Lily, who *deed* this?" he recoiled in horror.

Lily gulped.

"What happened?"

"Nesto, it was an accident. Can you fix it?"

"Of course I can *feex* it," he spat. "But I refuse to touch one hair until you tell me who *deed diis* to you?"

"I did this to myself," Lily stammered. She had come up with a lie in the cab but her mind had gone blank.

"No!"

"I don't know what I was thinking, honestly, and then Will fell and I had to comfort him and by the time I rinsed it out it was too late," she sobbed, downing the rest of her champagne.

"Don't worry. We can *feex*. But don't ever do again. Ever. *Promeese* Nesto."

Lily nodded and held her breath as he studied her in silence. After a few minutes, he finally spoke. "You have *de* same thing Brooke *Sheeilds* have? *De* depression?"

"You mean postpartum depression?" she asked, confused.

Nesto nodded, looking sadly into her eyes, and she opened her mouth to explain that her hair was just an accident and not the result of a hormonal imbalance, but then it occurred to her that Brooke Shields had made postpartum depression not only acceptable but très à la mode. She could blame her social absences, her weight gain, hell, even her hair, on a serious bout of the Baby Blues. "Yes," she nodded, matching Nesto's puppy dog expression. "It's been difficult for me."

Actually, it's not exactly a lie.

"Poor Lily. I know, so tough. But *ees* over now. Nesto take good care of you." He handed her an exquisitely embroidered white linen handkerchief.

Lily dabbed the corners of her dry eyes.

"Promeese Nesto one more thing. You lose thees weight," he said, cocking an eyebrow at Lily.

"I promise," Lily sniffed, and held her glass out for more champagne.

He paused, appraising Lily's face again. "I think we go berry blond."

"Very blond?"

"No, BEAR-YE blond."

"Like, extremely blond?"

"No, like *de* fruit, a little red. Think Nicole as in Kidman, not that mousy Ritchie girl," and with that he walked out of the room. Lily could hear him barking orders in Portuguese to his staff. An olive-skinned man in tight black leather pants and hair almost as long as Nesto's came into the room bearing a silver tray with three plastic bowls full of lavender-colored hair dye.

"Okay, we go fast. I do color now, then you go with Sandra for deep conditioning treatment," he said, winking. "On *de* house."

Once her color was done, Sandra led Lily across the main floor of the salon, which was by now packed with the post-lunch ladies-who-lunch crowd. Most of the women, dressed in Chanel tweed and flashing door-knocker-sized diamond rings, were getting blowouts and eying each other aggressively in the mirror. Sandra sat Lily down at the bank of mauve leather chairs and sinks and told her she'd be back in twenty minutes to check on the color. After the twenty minutes had elapsed, she returned, rinsed out the dye, shampooed and conditioned Lily's hair and then installed her under a heat lamp to help the conditioning treatment sink in. Then it was back to the sink, where the conditioner was rinsed out, and on to Sandra's work station, where Lily's newly (berry) blond locks were blown dry.

As she was exiting the salon, Lily bumped back into Snow, who looked much like she had when she entered the salon, her fluffy shag perhaps just a shade brighter than before. She walked straight up to Lily and clutched her arm dramatically, causing all the older women to crane their necks in hopes of catching a whiff of scandalous conversation.

"So we'll see you next Tuesday?" Snow said in a stage whisper.

"For the birthday party? Yes, of course."

"Great! Don't forget to bring your nanny. We'll have a separate room for them and the kids. Big kiss," she said, blowing Lily one.

Chapter 12

Lily arrived forty-five minutes late to Lexi Foster's first birthday party. She'd vastly misjudged the amount of time it would take to get ready, and then worked up such a sweat worming Will's little body into his green Gymboree turtleneck onesie and denim overalls that she had to change out of her ecru tunic into an equally big-tummy-friendly navy chiffon blouse. Sucking in her stomach, she attempted to fasten the top two buttons of her cream slacks, but it was no use. "Damn it," she said, glancing at the clock. There was no time for another outfit change. She left the blouse untucked and raced down the hall to find Jacinta to tell her she was finally ready to go.

"Okay, so let's go over this one more time. If the other caregivers ask you—"

"I'm Will's nanny. Not a babysitter, a nanny."

"Right, and if anyone starts asking you more questions, you just tell them that you don't understand English."

"Okay, *mamita*," Jacinta laughed. "But what if they speak Spanish?" She cocked her head to one shoulder and waited for Lily's reply, a know-it-all grin spread across her plump face.

"Oh, I hadn't thought about that," she said, and frowned. "I hate to ask you to lie, but we can't afford a full-time nanny and apparently all the other moms have them and—"

"S'okay," Jacinta interrupted her. "I don't mind. I can play it so by the time we leave, all those nannies gonna wanna come work for you." She winked and smiled broadly.

"Oh, God bless you," Lily said, bending over at the waist to hug Jacinta. "You're the absolute best."

The three of them went downstairs, Will strapped inside his Bugaboo stroller, and headed toward the subway. Since Josephine had orchestrated the trading in of their more sensible SUV for the Porsche, there would have been no point in asking Robert for a lift, even if he hadn't been at the club playing squash that afternoon.

A doorman in a hunter green cap and jacket let Lily, Jacinta, and Will into Snow's building, a prewar on Fifth Avenue overlooking Central Park. Lily announced herself to a second doorman, who checked off her name on his clipboard and pointed toward an elevator, where yet another attendant in green was standing, waiting to take them up to the ninth floor. A maid outfitted in a gray dress and white apron answered the door to Snow's apartment and escorted Lily, Will, and Jacinta into the living room, where roughly twenty-five runway-ready ladies had gathered.

The room, double height with coffered ceilings, was decorated in old American art and antiques and boasted two dark-brown studded leather couches, a collection of old architectural prints, and a leather-topped partners desk. A pair of massive landscape paintings, which Lily recognized as coming from the Hudson River school, hung above the grand piano, and on the other end, two floor-to-ceiling bookcases, their shelves lined with hardbacks and silver-framed photos, sandwiched a well-lit Monet. In the center of the room stood two tables: one small round table draped in pink linen and topped with a three-tiered cake and a stack of pink-ringed Kate Spade china plates; and another larger table, this one draped in a white eyelet tablecloth and covered with elaborately wrapped presents. Bundles of pink helium-filled balloons formed a large arc across both tables, and ten crystal vases, all packed with three dozen pink roses, had been scattered throughout the room.

Lily breathed in the flowers' heady scent and walked toward Snow, who was perched on the arm of one of the enormous couches. "Darling, you made it!" Snow embraced her as warmly as a collection of muscle and bone could.

"I'm so sorry we're late," Lily apologized, handing Snow a large blue and white bag containing Lexi's birthday gift, a smocked dress she'd found on deep discount at Jacadi.

"Oh, no worries, darling. This must be Will." She grabbed the baby's foot and shook it gently. "He's *gorge*. Don't you think, girls?" Snow asked, turning to the five other women sitting on the couch. The women, who were deep in conversation, turned their heads in unison to look at Lily and Will.

The first woman Lily recognized was Verushka Kravis, a Czech-born former fit model for Ralph Lauren who had married a wealthy paunch-bellied magazine publisher. Next to her sat two other women Lily had met only once or twice before, Umberta Verragrande, the flamboyant Peruvian daughter of Bianca Lawson (the fourth—and last—wife of J. Denver Lawson, the famous movie studio chief) who had herself married a successful investment banker in a shotgun (but nonetheless well-publicized) wedding last spring, and Kate de Santos, a headband wearing lightly freckled redhead who had grown up in Greenwich, Connecticut. Kate was married to an Argentine businessman who was said to spend more time playing polo and courting young models on South Beach than he spent either in his office or at home with his wife and twin baby girls.

Across from the coffee table, seated on an identical sofa, were Sloan Hoffman, a Dallas-born beauty with impossibly high (i.e., Restylane-enhanced) cheekbones and a well-cultivated reputation as the junior set's most outgoing hostess, and Jemima Blayton, a British import who, after quitting her job as a highly paid art consultant (her husband had been a client and, incidentally, someone else's husband at the time), spent her days making fashion statements on both sides of the pond. Perched above the other girls on the sofa's arm was Diana Meddling, a former publicity firm event planner who had married the son of a wealthy and socially connected Palm Beach heiress, thereby guaranteeing her spot among the "top girls."

Diana was part of a group of girls that Lily had once heard called the Brown Mafia, so named for the Rhode Island university they had all attended together. Diana—or Di, as her friends called her—and a half dozen other of the city's brightest young social stars were rumored to have monthly meetings deciding everything from who was going to be blackballed from various clubs around town (the Junior League, Doubles, SoHo House, Gramercy Park Hotel's Rooftop Terrace, etc.) to who would win the best costume award at the annual Central Park Conservancy Halloween charity benefit (the competition was vicious).

"He looks just like Robert," Diana said cheerlessly, her thin lips drawn into a straight, hard line.

"He has my eyes," Lily insisted.

"Oh, you can't tell about them this early on," Jemima scoffed. "Besides, yours aren't exactly about to launch a thousand ships, are they?"

The women laughed, and Lily blushed deeply. A few drops of perspiration dripped into the deep cavern of her cleavage.

Jemima sucked in her cheeks and tilted her head to one side. "I'm just teasing, darling," she said, staring at Lily with such loathing that Lily, who was still holding Will on her hip, began to tremble slightly, causing Will to clutch her more tightly, digging his tiny fingernails farther into her neck. Lily gave Will's left leg a reassuring squeeze and nuzzled him on the cheek. He immediately relaxed his vise grip, and Lily, who had plastered a smile on her face for the baby's sake, asked Jemima with as much brightness as she could muster where all the other children were.

"Upstairs in the nursery. It's up the stairs on your left. Can't miss it," Jemima said, and turned back to the group, which had already fallen back into their conversation.

"Oh, okay, thanks." Lily walked to the doorway, where Jacinta was standing, and handed her the baby. "Upstairs, on your left." She jutted her chin toward the wide wooden staircase.

"You okay?" Jacinta asked.

Lily nodded, and, pretending not to be at all bothered by the humiliation she had endured just seconds before, she shook her head and chuckled, "these women" as if they were a pack of incorrigible, ill-behaved children, which they most assuredly were not. These women were bloodthirsty sharks, as territorial and vicious as any coast-dwelling Great White, and Lily knew that if she were ever to gain acceptance among them—something she needed to do if she had any prayer of recovering her previous It-girl status—she couldn't let them get under her skin. She'd be dead in the water the second they sensed they had managed to intimidate her. That was how bullies worked: one drop of blood and they'll devour you alive.

Lily kissed Will's furry head one last time and, steeling herself for more abuse, returned to the inlaid wooden coffee table, off of which she selected a mini berry tart from a three-tiered silver cake stand. Not having had anything to eat all day (she was down two and a half pounds since last Thursday), the sudden stress of social interaction had made her feel faint. She popped the pastry in her mouth and picked up a delicate porcelain teacup and saucer from the silver tray on the table.

"Here, let me pour you a cup," said an oval-faced Asian woman. "I'm Allison Lewinberg Chung, by the way," she said, setting the flowery Bernardaud teapot gently back down on the tray after she had filled Lily's cup and hers to the rim. "I saw your son from across the room. Looks about the same age as mine. He's very cute."

Lily swallowed her tart, half-chewed, and wiped the crumbs off her mouth, careful not to smudge her lipstick. "Thanks. I hope I'll get to meet yours later."

...n you believe they call this a birthday party?" whispered
...son as she led Lily to a vacant corner of the room so the two
of them could speak freely. "Do you know that it costs a thousand
bucks to get someone from Patrick McMullan's team to come to
your party? I mean, do you think Lexi actually cares whether she
makes New York Social Diary dot-com?"

Lily stifled a chuckle. "But Snow told me that Patrick is a friend
of hers."

"Please," Allison rolled her eyes. "He's friends with all of us.
But that doesn't mean his assistant won't be sending Snow a bill
tomorrow."

Lily took a sip of her too-hot tea, scalding the roof of her mouth.
She coughed, biting back the pain, and asked, "Are we going to
play with the babies at some point?"

"Are you kidding? Can you imagine Umberta getting on the
floor in that Missoni?"

"It *is* knitwear."

"There's only one reason Umberta Verragrande's knees touch
the floor, and it doesn't have anything to do with her baby. You
heard about her and that photographer in the bathroom of the
Gramercy Park Hotel's Private Roof Club, right? Why hire a publicist when you can just suck paparazzi dick instead?"

Lily snorted. "I think that is hands down the most disgusting
thing I've heard all year."

"No crap, hands down," Allison said, then winked.

"You're horrible."

"No, just really fucking pissed off. I don't know how much more
of this bunch I can take. I'm on the Five Boroughs Student Aid
Ball committee with Morgan de Rambouillet," Allison nodded over
to the couch, where a beyond-skinny woman—whose only flaw
was the Angelina Jolie–like vein vertically traversing her oversized
forehead—had sparked a flurry of hugs and kisses upon arrival
just moments earlier and appeared to be holding court. "Last week
I had to bring Justin with me to one of our meetings and he got

hungry, so I nursed him. No big whoop. I was being modest; I had a little blanket over my shoulder so it's not like my boob was completely hangin' out there in the breeze. But Morgan flipped out and in the middle of the meeting, in front of everyone, told me to go to the bathroom if I had to nurse. The irony is that if *Vogue* suddenly declared nursing chic, you can bet she'd be the first one whipping out her nonexistent tits every meeting." Allison lowered her voice to barely above a whisper. "Morg already has osteoporosis because she's been a rexi for so long."

"But if she's truly anorexic, why haven't any of her friends staged an intervention?" Lily whispered back.

"Oh, but we did try, years ago."

"And what happened?"

"She told us we were all—and I quote—jealous, hideously fat bitches, and started wearing armfuls of those evil-eye bracelets, as if she has to protect herself from all the evil thoughts we're lancing her way. As if we don't have anything better to do than sit around wishing we were as bone-thin and bitchy as she is. She's fucking paranoid delusional if you ask me. But anyway, back to what I was saying before, at the Five Boroughs meeting I kept my mouth shut and went to the bathroom to finish nursing Justin, and then yesterday Morg called me at home and said the group had decided that babies were 'too distracting' and I shouldn't bring him anymore. Can you believe that? She even asked me if I planned on nursing for a whole year, as if that's any of her business."

"Well are you? I mean—planning on nursing for that long?" Lily asked.

"Of course. It's totally bonding. Plus *hel-lo*? Does anybody read the newspapers? Breast milk is the best form of nourishment for a growing baby."

"That's why I stuck with it through the engorgement and cracked nipples, but it's a lie that it doesn't ruin your breasts. I feel like crying every time I see them in the mirror; they're so saggy. Do you think they'll ever go back to where they were before?"

"No. Why do you think God invented the boob lift?"

Lily laughed. "Robert would never go for that. He hates plastic surgery."

"The trick is asking for one *before* you get pregnant. That's what Verushka did. She wanted to hire a surrogate to have the baby for her, but her husband said he didn't want a stranger carrying their baby, so she compromised and told him that she'd do it if he transferred the money for a boob job and a tummy tuck into her bank account as soon as they found out they were pregnant."

"So what does a good boob job cost these days anyway?"

"Ballpark? Thirty to forty thousand."

Hearing the enormous sum, Lily sputtered. "Gosh that's a lot of money. But it wouldn't be enough to convince me to have a child if I really didn't want to have one in the first place. Deep down Verushka must have wanted a baby, right?"

"I think deep down she was thinking about her future financial security."

"Prenup?"

"You have to pinky swear that you aren't going to repeat this, but I heard that Verushka's prenup stipulates that she has to have two children in the first five years of marriage or her husband has grounds for divorce. She'd get zilch. These baby clauses are all the rage, apparently. Thank God I didn't have one. Not that I would need one as an incentive to have children, but still, it's degrading."

Lily and Allison continued talking until Umberta beckoned Allison over to the couch. "Guess we better join the others," she said, disappointed that their tête-à-tête was coming to an end. "But I definitely want to get your number. We should have coffee sometime."

"I'd love that," Lily beamed. She'd been cut off from the outside world for so long, she'd forgotten how wonderful and thrilling it was to form a connection, however tenuous and superficial, with another woman.

Sitting down on the couch next to Verushka, Lily reached over to grab an asparagus stick wrapped in prosciutto and a bacon-wrapped prune. As she chewed, she listened to the women discussing—predictably—nursery school admissions.

"It's all about the letters of recommendation and knowing someone on the board, even if they deny that it isn't," Kate de Santos said knowingly.

"If that's the case, my husband plays squash with two of the board members from the Ninety-second Street Y, so I think we can safely say that Daniella is getting in there," Morgan said, turning to address Lily. "Speaking of squash, I hear Rob's playing a lot these days."

Lily nearly choked on her asparagus tip. Was the queen bee of social New York actually talking to her? Swallowing hard on a stringy piece of prosciutto and wondering why she even bothered to eat at these parties, Lily managed to squeak out, "He can't seem to get enough of it. It's his new passion."

"Christian says he's getting tough to beat," Morgan said, running a bony hand through her nipple-length, chocolate brown locks. "Tell me, how does Rob manage to get in so much practice?"

"*Um,* well I guess he just makes the time."

"Oh yes, that's right. I forgot. He's left Caruthers, right?"

"He's making a transition to hedge funds," Lily said, trying without success to make eye contact with Allison or even Snow, who was staring at a plate of miniature cupcakes with pink frosting as if any moment they were going to get up and dance the Nutcracker ballet for her.

"Oh God. Well isn't that what everyone's trying to do these days," Morgan quipped.

"I wouldn't know, really," Lily stammered. "I think Robert feels like he's ready for a more challenging opportunity. His legal background makes him uniquely qualified to—"

"You can save the résumé rundown for someone else," Morgan said.

"Someone who cares," Lily overheard Diana saying to Jemima behind a cupped hand.

Morgan continued, "Anyway, I'm more interested in hearing about what you've been up to. Anything interesting?"

Well, let's see. I did just have a baby. "Taking care of the baby takes up most of my time."

"Isn't that what the nanny's there for?" Sloan asked, crinkling her nose—and her forehead if it hadn't already been Botoxed to hell and back—in confusion.

And I was worried about Jacinta giving up the jig. Lily racked her brain in search of a plausible recovery. "Well, I'm very hands-on."

"Hands on the Ho Hos, from the looks of it," Diana whispered to Jemima, who, attempting to stifle her laughter, snorted into her teacup.

Just then a dark-haired boy with cherry-colored lips, vampire-pale skin, and a Grecian nose swaggered into the room. "Hello, ladies," he said, and twenty-five hands dug into purses and pockets in search of their lip plumpers and powder compacts. Lily wondered if the boy was an up-and-coming model or actor and that's why all the women were primping so ostentatiously, but when he pulled a large black camera from his messenger bag, she realized that he was the photographer Snow had mentioned (several times) would be coming. "Patrick sends his regards," said the model-photographer—Chaz was his name, Lily later learned—as he started crouching and clicking away, capturing the pretty pink party decorations and well-dressed guests from all angles.

"If someone has a party and no photographer is there to capture it, does the party really happen?" Lily murmured to Verushka, who looked at her blankly before getting up and joining Umberta and Morgan for a picture next to the cake from Fauchon. Umberta plucked a cape gooseberry off the fondant frosting and held it over her mouth, her head tilted back and eyes half closed. It was a sensual tableau, not at all appropriate for a child's birthday party.

Chaz took a couple of shots, and then Umberta let the exotic fruit fall into her mouth. She held the round golden fruit between her teeth, snapping off the stem as she winked at Chaz.

"Thanks for coming, darling," Snow hollered to Chaz. "I'll just go call the nannies and we can get this show on the road."

Abandoned by her host, Lily felt awkward and self-conscious sitting on the far end of the sofa, and just as she was considering leaving the other mothers to go check on Will and Jacinta, a long train of children and nannies entered the room.

"Time to cut the cake!" Snow honked from the front of the line. She cued the maid to dim the overhead lights, close the curtains, and open the double doors to the living room. A disco ball descended from the ceiling and began to spin out shards of multicolored light as a bubble machine filled the room with baseball-sized bubbles. A man in a tuxedo and five women dressed in pink leather sixties-style shifts entered the room.

"Is that Belinda Carlisle?" someone whispered.

"Oh my God. It's the friggin' Go-Go's," her friend whispered back. "How totally gauche. Just goes to show that money can't buy everything."

"Apparently not."

The Go-Gos began singing "The Birthday Song" to Lexi, who was sucking on her thumb and staring at the disco ball, totally oblivious to her pop-icon serenaders. When the song ended, Snow took her daughter, who was dressed in a Bonpoint pink cashmere cardigan, pink taffeta party dress, and the most gorgeous pink suede baby booties Lily had ever seen, and posed with her behind the cake before blowing out the lone candle herself.

As soon as the lights came back on and the disco ball was retracted up toward the ceiling, Morgan glanced down at the diamond-encrusted bezel of her watch and shrieked, "Look at the time." As she retrieved her chinchilla vest from one of the sofas, she announced, "I must go. Maison Gerard is delivering the Ruhlmann cabinet today."

The ladies watched her stride out of the room toward the front door and then, as if Morgan's departure had called an end to the party, they too began announcing their good-byes. Lily wondered if Morgan had forgotten about her baby and nanny, who was lining up for a wedge of cake, and turned to alert Snow. "I think she's left without Daniella," she whispered discreetly to her.

"Morgan never travels with her. The baby and nanny have their own car," Snow said, before depositing a tiny forkful of the marzipan filling into her mouth. "*Mmm,* that was good. I only allow myself one treat per party and only at the end. You should try doing that. Really keeps the calorie count in check," she said.

"Thanks for the advice," Lily said, deciding to forgo her own slice of cake entirely. She turned to find Jacinta struggling to keep her own piece from falling off her plate and onto the floor while at the same time holding a squirming and obviously cranky Will. "Here, I'll hold him so you can eat," Lily said, taking the baby. "I'm just going to go get his diaper bag, and then we can go back home. It's way past Will's nap time."

Up the flight of stairs and down a long hallway, Lily discovered Lexi's nursery, which was decorated with a rocking chair upholstered in soft pink silk shantung, a giant pink crystal chandelier, a round white crib with its own gauzy canopy, and two enormous white armoires hand painted with little bunches of rosebuds. Above a white marble fireplace hung an original Mary Cassatt *Mother and Child* painting. Lily found her black nylon diaper bag next to the rocking chair and was about to leave when Allison walked in and retrieved a lone pacifier lying on the floor. She stuck it in her mouth, gave it a quick suck, and placed it back into Justin's mouth.

"Hey, not sure if you and Will are free, but I'm trying to start a playgroup for the mommies and babies. Wanna come? It's next Thursday afternoon at four. I'm booking some manicurists."

"Oh, what a treat," Lily replied.

"Not for us, silly, for the nannies."

"What?"

"I figure they deserve a little pampering, and in the meantime we'll be in the nursery with the babies. For once," Allison rolled her eyes.

"The other moms are going to freak out."

"That's the point. So can I count on you?"

"Wouldn't miss it," Lily promised.

Chapter 13

The afternoon after Lexi's birthday party, Lily recharged her laptop and pulled up her old list of contacts, cross-referencing for family law attorneys. If what Allison said about baby quotas being all the rage in prenuptial agreements was true, she might have a perfect Thursday Trends article on her hands. She was confident Rebecca would love the idea, but first she needed to make sure she would be able to come through with some sources. If she pitched a story that she wouldn't be able to deliver on, she'd lose all her credibility, and then Rebecca would never want to work with her.

After jotting down a few names and numbers of lawyers, she started calling. The first lawyer was out to lunch, the next had left the firm to start her own practice, and the third promised to call Lily back as soon as he was out of a client meeting. Waiting for the phone to ring, she thought about how difficult it was going to be to convince the women with baby quotas hanging over their heads to talk about their prenups.

Lily knew from firsthand experience what a touchy subject these agreements could be: Robert had presented her with one just a day before her wedding, and it succeeded in turning what should have been the best weekend of her life into one of the most stressful.

It had rained heavily the week before they got married. So

heavily, in fact, that the workers at Nashville's Brentwood Country Club weren't sure they'd be able to put up the tent in which the wedding dinner was to take place. On Wednesday night the club's event planner proclaimed that if it stopped raining by Friday afternoon, the grounds would have a chance to dry overnight and they could get the tent up in time for the six o'clock reception. But if the rains continued, they would have no choice but to serve dinner in the poolside grill house.

On Thursday, the local meteorologist, whose yellow-cake hair and blue-plaid suits hadn't changed since he started on the five o'clock news twenty years ago, predicted continued thunderstorms through Saturday, prompting Lily and her mother to begin redrawing the seating arrangements while Lily's father took Robert and his parents to a rib joint near the university. When her father came home, a mere hour and a half later, the first out of his mouth was, "That mother-in-law of yours sure is a piece of work," and then proceeded to fill Lily and her mother in on all the gory details from lunch.

"First, we had to change tables twice because one booth was under the air-conditioning vent and the other was too close to the kitchen. Then, when we were finally seated, Josephine starts asking why we didn't have the wedding at the Belle Meade Country Club."

"Oh no," Margaret gasped, slapping her forehead with her hand.

"Oh yes, so of course I had to tell her that we're not members there. And then Josephine says that she wished you,"—he pointed at Lily—"had said something about that because apparently she could have gotten us in," her father snorted.

"Oh Lord," her mother gasped again.

"Then she says something like, 'I'm sure Lily would have preferred to have her wedding some place chicer,' and Edward goes ballistic. He slams down his menu and tells her, basically, to shut her big face, and then Josephine just gets up from the table, walks outside, and we don't see her again. Edward thinks she called a cab and went back to the hotel. He insisted that we stay and have lunch, and then he wouldn't let me pick up the tab."

Lily should have known there would be some fallout for her from the catastrophic lunch because a day later, amid the continued chaos of the wedding preparations, Robert reluctantly surprised her with what in some circles would be referred to as an "ironclad prenup." The agreement was sixty-five pages long, required multiple signatures in front of a notary, and stipulated exactly how much money Lily was entitled to (very little) in case of various scenarios. Robert gave her the hefty document right after he came over for a quick breakfast of coffee and blueberry muffins. They were in her bedroom, kissing and talking excitedly like couples tend to do in the days preceding their wedding, when he suddenly handed it to her. Lily's reaction could have best been described as livid.

"Robert, if you knew your family was going to make me sign one of these, don't you think the respectful, upstanding, correct thing to do would have been to show me it at least a few months in advance?" she demanded. "I don't even have time to get a lawyer to look over it for me."

"The reason I didn't talk to you about it was because they didn't show me the damn thing until today. I'm as opposed to it as you are, but my parents are forcing me to do this. They told me that if I don't get you to sign it and I go ahead with the wedding, they'll disinherit me."

"Your father wouldn't say that," she said, although she knew what Robert's father did or didn't say was immaterial. Up until that point Lily had only spent a dozen evenings with the Bartholomews, but she could already tell who wore the pants in their family. Edward was a charming, affable man—he frequently told Lily how much he liked her—however, when it came to controlling his wife's behavior, he left a lot to be desired. Robert said it was because his father abhorred all kinds of confrontation—he once delegated the firing of Blue Water's CFO to their chief legal counsel—and only dared to reprimand people when he felt that it was absolutely necessary.

"Maybe, but Dad's not going to live as long as my mom, and when he dies, she gets all the money."

"Edward might outlive Josephine," she said, horrified by her own words. "I can't believe we're even having this discussion. It's so morbid. We're supposed to be talking about our vows and practicing our first dance, not arguing about which of your parents is going to die first."

Robert ran a hand through his thick dark brown hair. "You just have to trust me. I'm doing this for us. To secure *our* future."

"Actually, Robert, this prenup seems to be mainly concerned with securing *your* future," she snapped.

"Try to understand my position. You love me, not my money, right?"

"How dare you say that," she whispered angrily. If her mother, Margaret, overheard them talking like this, she'd be scandalized. "Is that what your mother thinks? That I'm after your money? That I'm a gold digger?"

"Please don't make this into something it's not. No one gets married these days without one. Ask any of your married friends in New York. I want to marry you. I love you. So please just make this easy on me and sign the fucking thing." Robert hurled the agreement on her bed and left the room.

Lily picked up the prenup with resignation. She couldn't tell her parents about it. They might tell her to call off the wedding or end up resenting Robert, and she couldn't bear the thought of that. Robert was everything she'd ever dreamed of in a husband. He was gorgeous, well-educated, and it didn't hurt that he had a last name that could open doors for their future children. But above all this, he grounded her. She'd always been prone to sinking into her own misery whenever anything went wrong—it was one of the curses of being an overachiever—and he had an uncanny ability to lift her out of her gloomiest moods to make her laugh, or at least help her regard her situation with a little less self-pity. He made her feel safe, from the world and from herself, and she couldn't imagine going back to a time when he wasn't a part of her life.

Lily opened the door of her bedroom and found Robert sitting next to it, head in hands, body curved into a ball. When he looked up, she could see that he'd been crying. "Call the notary," she said, kneeling next to him and hugging his head sideways into her chest.

Twenty minutes after making her first batch of calls (and one snack run to the kitchen later), the phone finally rang. It was Dean Gold, an attorney at a Los Angeles–based law firm who specialized in marital law. Lily quickly told him about the story she was researching and who she was writing for, leaving out the fact that the *Sentinel* hadn't actually commissioned the piece yet. If he knew she didn't have the assignment yet, he'd never spend an hour talking to her in favor of racking up another six hundred dollars in billables.

"So, I guess my question is are you seeing more baby quotas and if so what do they look like?" she summarized, her fingers hovering above the keyboard, ready to begin note taking.

There was a long pause, never a good sign, before Dean finally stammered, "You know what, I don't think this is the kind of story I want to participate in. But please feel free to contact me in the future." *Click.*

Lily slumped down in her chair. If she couldn't even get a media-savvy lawyer to talk to her, how on earth was she going to find any women willing to go on the record? Feeling frustrated, Lily walked into the kitchen and poured herself a glass of iced tea. It occurred to her that the same lawyers who were eager to get their name in the *World Business Journal* might not be so interested in getting into Thursday Trends. Returning to her computer, Lily did a quick search on the Internet and looked up names of other attorneys who'd been in divorce stories in the *Sentinel* and *New York* magazine. Then she found their numbers through Martindale-Hubbell's online attorney registry and began dialing.

On her first call she was patched straight through to Gene Samuels. "I'm so glad you called," he said. "I think your idea's right on the money. I'm seeing more and more of these baby-quota clauses, as you call them," Gene said, and chuckled. "I even have a client for you to interview for your piece."

"Oh yeah? Can you tell me her name?"

"Sure can—its Sloan Hoffman."

"I think I might know her," Lily said, trying not to sound too overeager.

Chapter 14

"Do you think we'll be out later than ten?" Lily asked Robert over breakfast on Friday morning. Robert's mother had called at 8:05 a.m. to ask her son out to dinner, and Lily had insisted, for once, that she come along. Josephine was easily prodded into divulging gossip about her friends, and Lily hoped that she might stumble across another story idea while listening to her mother-in-law vilify her unwitting confidants.

"Huh?" Robert asked, tipping down the corner of the *Financial Times* section he was reading.

"I should let Jacinta know, just in case," Lily explained as Rob's eyes flitted back to the Markets page he was reading. She picked up the salmon-colored paper's discarded Weekend section and turned to the fashion pages. "Well, should I? Call Jacinta?"

"Sure, why not? We could take our time and walk home from the restaurant. It's supposed to be a beautiful night," he said from behind his paper.

"Oh, that's a great idea." A moonlit walk with Robert would be wonderful, especially since they hadn't spent much time with each other in the last few weeks. Robert, in addition to accompanying Josephine to at least two cocktail parties or dinners per week, had started passing more and more time at his exclusive all-male tennis club. Apparently he was meeting a lot of people, potential employers he said, on the squash courts and in the steam rooms. He'd even lined up some interviews, which Lily considered a step in the right direction. "I should bring a jacket in case it gets cool," Lily thought out loud.

"Just don't forget to thank my parents for dinner."

"Robert," Lily huffed, "I made that mistake once. And by the way, why don't you ever thank them for the meal?"

"Because I'm their son. I don't have to."

"But I do."

He put the paper down and took Lily's hand from across the table. "Yes," he sighed. "Can you please pass the sugar?"

"All righty then, glad we cleared that up." Lily fought the urge to pelt a handful of raw sugar cubes at her husband's smug-looking face. She slid the bowl of sugar across the table and picked up Will, who was inch-worming his round behind across the tile floor, and carried him into the nursery. Popping the nipple of his bottle into his mouth, she watched as he sucked greedily on his formula, his eyelids slowly shuttering closed. Stopping breast-feeding had been harder than Lily thought it would be. Not only had her breasts swollen into miniature boulders, but she missed feeling so acutely needed by her son. Anyone could mix him a bottle of formula.

After putting Will down for his morning nap, Lily sat down at her computer and typed out a one-page pitch letter for her baby-clause story that summarized her idea and the anecdotes she had found so far. "Please, please, please love my idea," Lily whispered at the screen as she sent the e-mail on its way to Rebecca Burrows at the *Sentinel*. She got up to refresh her cup of coffee.

On the way back from the kitchen, the phone rang. "Hello, is this Lily Bartholomew?" asked the gravelly voice on the other line.

"Yes, this is she."

"Rebecca Burrows."

"Oh, hi, I just e-mailed you."

"That's why I'm calling. Love the pitch and so does Ford," she said, mentioning the chief editor of the Trends section, Ford Davies. He was a legend among the New York glitterati. Catch his eye with your writing and you could write for any publication (aside from maybe *Vanity Fair*) in the country.

"Oh, really? That's great. Thank you," Lily said, almost breathless with excitement.

"When can you get the piece to me by?"

"*Umm*," Lily hummed. She'd imagined that Rebecca would take a couple of days, if not more, to get back to her. She wasn't prepared to suggest a deadline.

"How about a week and a half from today?" Rebecca asked.

How am I going to come up with fifteen hundred words of scintillating prose in ten days, she panicked.

"Lily?" Rebecca prompted. "Is two weeks enough time?"

"*Umm*, yes. It should be."

"Good, I'll expect your copy before noon. We pay two dollars a word. Call me if you have any questions," she instructed before hanging up.

As she placed the receiver back onto the base of the phone, Lily exhaled loudly. She couldn't believe she was on her way to becoming a Thursday Trends writer. Now all she had to do was finish reporting and writing the best article of her career—in less than two weeks. It wouldn't be easy, but she'd pull an all-nighter to finish it if she had to. For Will's sake, she had to start pulling down a paycheck. This article could be the key to restarting her career.

Later that day, in the early evening after Lily had put Will down for his second nap of the day, she went through what in another era would have been called a full toilette. After showering, she blew her hair dry and rolled it up in Velcro rollers, applied a layer of foundation and swept the apples of her cheeks with an apricot-colored blush. She lined her eyes in dark brown and gray, glossed her lips, and spritzed on a gardenia-scented perfume before slipping into an old leaf-printed Diane von Furstenberg wrap dress and a pair of peep-toed platforms.

Just as she was buckling the straps on her heels, Lily heard Will cry out and rushed into his room. She found him up on his hands and knees, running his index finger along a large yellow-brown smudge on the crib's bottom sheet.

"Shit, shit, shit!" Will had pooped with such force that it had ricocheted out of his diaper, all the way up his back to his neck. It was now seeping through the back of his cream cashmere jumper from Bonpoint, a shower gift from a friend of Josephine's, a friend that Josephine had forced Lily to invite and then spent the entire shower gossiping with in a corner. Lily started panicking, "What am I going to put you in now?" she yelled at Will, who kicked a poop-splattered leg toward her face in response. Lily set the baby back down in the crib and quickly stripped off his jumper, which she threw down on the soiled sheet.

Charging into the bathroom, she laid a towel down on the floor, put Will's wriggling body on top of it and started filling the plastic baby tub with sudsy water. She then stripped off her dress (thankfully poop-free) and set Will in his tub, scrubbing away at his bottom, back, and hair (there was shit in it, too). Will, who hated baths, cried the whole time, grabbing at Lily's face and arms with his wet hands. Once Lily was satisfied that he was clean, she pulled him out of the tub and carried him to the linen closet, where she retrieved a clean towel in which to wrap Will's slippery wet body.

Dashing back to the nursery—Jacinta was due to arrive any minute—Lily dug through Will's clothes to find him another outfit. After settling on a Ralph Lauren knit sweater and corduroy overalls, she changed Will and looked at her watch. She had five minutes to take the rollers out of her hair and get dressed again. Running down the corridor, she almost slipped on a puddle outside Will's bathroom and skidded into the living room, where she planned on handing Will off to Robert.

He was sitting on the round silk-covered ottoman near the fireplace and was holding a glass of scotch on the rocks. He stared at her, momentarily speechless.

"Please take the baby," Lily blurted out, holding the baby out toward him.

"Well, hello Lily," said a deep voice from behind her back. Lily spun around to see her father-in-law standing at the entrance to the living room. In his hand was a hand-etched crystal highball glass. Beside Edward stood Josephine.

"Didn't Robbie tell you that we were going to drop by before dinner to see the baby?" asked Josephine.

"Oh my God! I'm so sorry," Lily yelped, turning back around to Robert. She forced the baby into his lap, spilling Robert's drink.

"Jesus, Lily," he gasped, wiping the pale amber liquid off his khaki trousers. He set his drink down and then, peering at her face, asked, "Is that shit on your cheek?"

She sprinted back out of the living room, past Josephine and Edward, who were standing under the living room archway, and headed straight for the bathroom to assess the damage.

Which was bad. Her white lace bra and panties had been drenched by Will's wet body and were now completely translucent. Her rollers were still in. There was indeed some of Will's poop on her cheek, and her painstakingly applied smoky eyeliner had dribbled down her cheeks. In her sexy heels, barely there underwear, rollers, and dirty face, she looked like a crazy whore. No, make that a crazy whore who allows her clients to defecate on her. Lily felt the sting of embarrassment and shame rise up from her belly and into her throat. Josephine would never let her live this down.

Just then the doorbell rang, announcing Jacinta's arrival, and she could hear Robert calling out to her from down the hall: "The reservations are for eight. We need to leave now, babe."

The restaurant, located on a busy street in the East Sixties, was as painfully hip as Lily guessed it would be. The sleek glass bar on the first floor was crowded with plump-lipped models and their dates, banker types in French-cuffed shirts. Following Josephine and the maître d' up the stairs to the formal dining room, Lily noted with relief that the lighting in the dining room was as dim as it was downstairs in the bar. She had only had a minute to get dressed, pull the rollers out of her hair, and wipe the feces and mascara from her cheeks, and compared to Josephine, who was dressed in a floral-printed Emanuel Ungaro skirt suit, she felt unkempt and inferior.

Throughout the dinner Lily stayed quiet and listened to Josephine prattle on about her friends, their new houses and plastic surgeries, drug problems and paramours, but Lily didn't hear anything that sounded like fodder for a Trends article. She focused on her plates of tuna carpaccio and grilled scallops in sunchoke sauce (it had been a long while since she'd had such delicious food, and she was savoring every morsel), and when the dessert tray arrived at the table, Josephine turned to address Lily for the first time that evening.

"Darling, how are you preparing yourself for St. Barths?" she asked.

"*Umm,* how do you mean, exactly? I'm very excited about it."

"Yes, well, you should be, dear," she smiled wryly. "It's so much fun, isn't it, Robbie?" she asked, turning toward her son.

"Yes, of course, Mom," Robert answered. "I know Lily's going to love it."

"We'll be going to a lot of parties, of course."

"Fun," Lily replied, smile plastered on her face. She turned and mouthed the words, "Where is she going with this?" to Robert, who shrugged, apparently just as clueless as she was, in reply.

"It's important that you are *bien habille,*" Josephine said slowly. "Do you know what I mean?"

"I studied French in high school, Josephine, so yes, I understand your meaning." Lily tugged the neckline of her dress closed and sat up a bit straighter in her chair. She hated, more than anything else, when Josephine acted condescendingly toward her.

"*Mais oui, tres bien.* Of course I don't expect you to know how to dress for these soirees. I'm assuming you've never been on a yacht before."

"Actually, I have. My second summer here I had a share in the Hamptons and—"

"The beach, darling. Say the beach, not the Hamptons," Josephine clucked.

"What's wrong with saying the Hamptons?" Edward protested, throwing his napkin down.

"C'mon, Mom," Robert seconded. "Let. It. Go."

"Oh, so I suppose she's *not* interested in coming to the cruise collection trunk shows with me next week?" she asked Robert and Edward.

"Why don't you ask her directly, Josie. She *is* sitting right here," Edward said.

"I'd love to go," Lily said, hoping to dissipate the tension building at the table. As much as she hated the idea of going anywhere with Josephine, this was just the sort of event she should be attending as a Trends writer.

"Mother, Lily has plenty of clothes," Robert interjected.

"Oh, Robbie, don't be such a spoilsport," warned Josephine as a waiter pulled up to the table with a dessert trolley, it's little bell ringing merrily and calling an end to the trunk show conversation.

Robert pointed at an espresso cup full of tiramisu on the dessert tray, and Lily, feeling giddy with excitement and in celebratory mood, indicated to the waiter that she wanted one of the cheesecake lollipops from the tray.

But just as the dessert was set before her and Lily's fork was brought to bear, Josephine grabbed Lily's wrist lightly and looked her straight in the eyes. "The empire waist is out this season," she whispered before letting go of her arm. "Just something to keep in mind, darling."

Lily set her fork down.

"Good girl," smiled Josephine, tucking a piece of smooth raven hair behind her ear.

After dinner, Lily remembered to thank her host.

Chapter 15

"You should have eaten that cheesecake," Allison yelled, slapping a spatula full of icing on the top of a miniature poppy-seed cake. "What a bitch!"

"I know, but I just feel so intimidated around her." Lily had come over to Allison's townhouse on a tree-lined block in Turtle Bay an hour early so she could help set up for the mommy-and-me group meeting. So far her only contribution had been relieving Allison of one very large, very foul-tasting mug of green tea in her enormous kitchen.

And what a kitchen it was. Everything from the Viking range to the glass-front cabinetry was polished to gleaming perfection. There was a massive Sub-Zero, a warming drawer, and a row of silver tins that held a bevy of exotic spices, sugars, and salts. A set of stainless steel All-Clad pans hung above the white marble-topped island where Lily was seated, mindlessly tracing the marble slab's blue veins as she watched Allison put the finishing touches on her baked goods.

"Listen to me. Mothers-in-law can not be given an inch of wiggle room. Today she bars you from eating dessert, tomorrow she's telling you where to send Will to preschool."

"Please," Lily scoffed. "Not even Josephine would try that."

"You say that today, but talk to me in two years."

"You sound like you're speaking from experience."

"My mother-in-law is a five-foot-two manipluatrix. I watch her like a hawk," Allison said, jabbing her index and middle fingers forward in front of her eyes.

"Josephine's crafty all right, but she *is* taking me shopping."

"Because she doesn't want to be embarrassed by you!" Allison screeched.

"I don't care! I don't want to be embarrassed by myself either. Besides, she's Robert's mother. Shouldn't I at least be making a good faith effort to get along with her? I'm thinking that the more time we spend together, the more she'll get to know me and like me."

"No good deed goes unpunished," Allison warned before pointing at a pastry bag on the kitchen island countertop. "Hey, can you pass me that?"

As Lily handed it to her, she said, "Anyway, I need to find some more inspiration for my writing."

"I didn't know that you're a writer."

"I am, well, I was," she paused, feeling suddenly nervous about telling Allison that she was writing for the *Sentinel*. What if Allison didn't want to be friends with a lifestyle-section writer? "Remember that thing you told me about Verushka having to have a baby because it's in her prenup?" she asked.

"Yeah?"

"I'm writing about that, or rather, baby quotas in general, for Thursday Trends." Lily held her breath, bracing herself for Allison's reaction.

"I can't *wait* to read the article."

"You're not mad?"

"Why would I be mad?"

Lily opened her mouth to explain that she had technically violated Allison's trust by using something she had told her in confidence to get a story assignment, but just then the doorbell rang. While Allison went downstairs to let in the first guests, Lily took a plate of freshly baked cranberry scones into the living room, depositing them on a table already crammed with letter-shaped cookies, individual-sized Bundt cakes dribbled with lemon icing, and double-chocolate-macadamia-nut brownies. Then Lily ran upstairs to summon Jacinta and Will and Justin and his nanny, Lusita.

The nursery, an open space that took up the entire fourth floor, had been painted Creamsicle orange and decorated with a David Netto natural wood crib and matching changing table. Twin built-in bookcases, broken by a picture window, were filled with stacks of books and toys, and lined up against one wall were five child-sized vintage tin fire trucks, one of which was being commandeered by an antique Steiff teddy bear.

Lily picked up Will, who was slithering along the white shag pile rug blanketing the floor, and swung him onto her hip. As she walked back toward the stairs, she sung over her shoulder, "Jacinta, Lusita, time for your pedicures."

Downstairs, three of the mothers were standing in the living room looking thoroughly confused. "Di, *you* take Dixon Jr. upstairs to the nursery," explained Allison as she took the carrot-topped little boy in head-to-toe Burberry plaid from his nanny's arms and handed him to his mother. "The nannies will be down here getting the spa treatments."

"We won't be gone long, Beverly," Diana said to her nanny, a large Jamaican woman who was trying unsuccessfully to get comfortable on a black leather-and-steel Mies van der Rohe Barcelona chair. Pulling Dixon Jr.'s hands away from her black pearl necklace, Diana turned to the other two ladies. "Can you believe this?" she asked, her nostrils flaring with indignation. "Allison and her fucking communist notions." She stomped upstairs with her child.

Lily listened as two women whom she recalled were publicists whispered to one another. "I say we get out of here while we still can," the shorter one said, pulling out her BlackBerry. "I've got a zillion e-mails to respond to. That Choo dinner isn't going to organize itself. Maybe let's offer free bags—let's tell the girls they can have whichever one they want—in addition to free shoes this year? And free hair and makeup for the day of the event. And let's definitely try to snag a *Vogue* editor. See if Alexandra Kotur doesn't have anything else on her agenda that day. Everyone wants face time with her. Hell, let's send an invite to Paula Froelich from Page Six. All the girls want to get cozy with her now, too. Oh, and we've *got* to start sending out invites for that weekend getaway to Morocco. The client expects us to nail down at least five socials plus someone Hollywood—I'm thinking Anne Hathaway, she loves this stuff—and I need to make sure we're going to get coverage on Style dot-com and *Fashion Week Daily*. I mean, at the bare minimum, we can get that, right? Shit, there's so much to do. I don't have time to sit around singing effing nursery rhymes today."

"I think you mean, *recite* effing nursery rhymes."

"*Kristen*," she warned in a don't-mess-with-me tone.

"But Amy, we can't just up and leave. Allison agreed to host the benefit party at the Ferragamo store next Thursday, remember? We have to stay."

"Thirty minutes, Kristen, that's all," Amy compromised while trying to pry her baby's fingers from around his nanny's neck. The little boy, Jeffrey, was dressed like a mini rap-mogul in Timberland boots, low-slung jeans, a black T-shirt, and a silver puffer jacket with a fur-trimmed hood. Jeffrey's nanny made the sign of the cross as she watched his mother climb up the stairs on her five-inch Brian Atwood platforms, her son bucking and kicking all the way.

One by one the rest of the mothers arrived and trudged with their children upstairs, where a professional storybook reader was reading selected rhymes from *The Real Mother Goose*. Once everyone was settled in a circle around the rug, the reader led them through "The Itsy Bitsy Spider" and then began "The Hungry Caterpillar." Lily, who had zoned out somewhere between the reciting and storytelling, was thinking about her upcoming afternoon with Rob's mother when she felt her ears prickle. Out of the corner of her eye, she saw Di nudge Morgan and glance in Lily's direction. Instinctively Lily looked down at her clothes, a blush-colored V-neck sweater and heather gray slacks, to check for crumbs, milk stains, or exposed underwear. All clear. She nonchalantly took Will into Justin's frog-themed bathroom en suite and checked in the bathroom mirror for stray nose hairs and migrating eyeliner, but she didn't see any. Feeling uneasy and self-conscious, Lily rejoined the group. *Something is definitely up.*

Thirty-five minutes later the class finally ended, and the women (except Amy and Kristen, who had left midway through the parachute game) collectively groaned with relief, apparently exhausted by playing with their infants. For a bunch of Pilates and yoga enthusiasts, they tired awfully easily. Lily watched the women hobble toward the staircase.

"Shall we go see how the nannies are doing?" Sloan asked Umberta, who was once again clad in a clingy dress, this one designed by Gucci and made of an emerald knit jersey that matched her heavily applied eye makeup. *Green eye shadow and fake eyelashes before 5:00 p.m— nice.*

"If mine thinks I'm paying for this hour, she has another think coming," Umberta replied as she headed downstairs.

"I'm just praying that mine hasn't painted her toes lavender," cracked Jemima. "She has horrendous taste. Remind me to tell you about the time I sent her to Bendel's to pick up a gift for my acupuncturist. What a disaster!"

Back downstairs Lily was bent down behind the kitchen island, picking up the pile of linen napkins she had accidentally brushed to the floor, when she overheard Morgan and Di whispering to each other on the other side of the butcher block.

"Why the fuck did Allison invite her to join our group?" Diana asked.

"I know, it's bad enough she was at Snow's the other day," Morgan replied. "Randoms like her just bring the whole level of the group down."

"Well, she's not exactly a random. She *is* married to Robert Bartholomew," Di pointed out.

"But for how long? He'll tire of having a fat hausfrau for a wife soon enough. He could have done *soo* much better."

"Sans doute, darling," Diana cackled. "I still can't believe she was a Girl of the Moment."

"Yeah, talk about a literal *moment*," Morgan cackled.

"She's totally trying to worm her way into our group. I mean, I get that she wants to be our friend—"

"Obviously."

"But can't she see that she doesn't belong?" Diana asked as she and Morgan wandered back out of the kitchen.

When Lily was suitably sure that the two women had left the kitchen, she rose from her crouched position below the lip of the butcher block and scanned the living room in search of Jacinta, who was at that moment wiggling ten sparkly pink nails in front of Will's face. She practically ran across the room and grabbed one of Jacinta's hands for inspection.

"It's Dee-your," her babysitter said.

"And it's lovely."

Managing to conceal her impending breakdown, Lily told Jacinta that she didn't need her to come back to the apartment with her, as was the original plan, and scuttled downstairs with Will. In record time she clicked him into his stroller and was outside starting her trek back uptown when Allison came barreling after her.

"You're leaving?" she asked.

Lily turned her back and started walking quickly up the block. "Yes, see you next time," she yelled, trying to sound like she wasn't about to burst into tears.

"Wait, Lil!" Allison shouted as she caught up to her, her Giuseppe Zanotti heels clicking along the pavement. "Can you believe Amy stormed off like that? She must have passed Jeffrey back and forth with his nanny like ten times," Allison was bent over double, cracking up. She lifted her head and saw that Lily's eyes were welling with tears, her lips pulled into an unnatural smile. "It's okay, you can laugh now. They're gone."

Lily bit down hard on her lower lip. "I think it's depressing—not funny—that these kids feel closer to their nannies than their mothers. That's what I think."

"What's wrong? Did something happen in there?" Allison asked.

"Morg and Di are what happened," Lily said, suddenly feeling more angry than sad.

"What did those two mother-fucking bitches do now?"

"They called me a fat hausfrau. And they said that my marriage wouldn't last," Lily said furiously, looking down at her sweet baby, totally oblivious to the drama.

Allison pursed her lips in a way that told Lily everything she needed to know: that this wasn't the first time the girls had said disparaging things about her. "Let's go back inside," she suggested, shivering in the autumn chill.

"No, I want to go home. I'll be fine. I just need some time to get over it," Lily said.

"Okay, I'll let you go, but try not to take what they said personally."

"But how can I not?" Lily gasped. "Morgan said Robert could have done so much better!"

"Sweetie, I know it's hard, but you're the new girl, at least as far as Di and Morg are concerned. We all had to go through this bullshit at one point. You didn't think joining the chicest mommy-and-me group in the city would be easy, did you?" Allison said, and then turned to walk back toward her townhouse.

Chapter 16

It took Lily a few days to recover from overhearing Diana and Morgan's cruel comments, but when she did she felt even more driven to become a regular contributor to Thursday Trends. Not only did she want to reclaim some financial independence from Robert, she yearned to show Diana, Morgan, Josephine, and anyone else who doubted her station in their world that she wasn't *a random*, a person of no consequence who could be snubbed and skewered without the slightest censure or reproof. She mattered, God damn it! And if writing about New York's urban gentry and their Veblenesque consumption was what it would take to earn their respect, then she'd do it. After all, others had climbed up the ladder in far less honorable ways.

Not long ago, there was a woman who mounted, so to speak, her way to the top. She landed a big ticket marriage to a well connected hotelier before anyone had the chance to figure out that she had once been a high-class call girl—in Fort Lauderdale of all places. She had curly blond hair then, as opposed to the burnished auburn hue she dyed it before she wedded her catch, but eventually her tawdry past caught up to her in the form of a widely circulated X-rated JPEG. Of course by then she was already "in," having used buckets of her husband's money to win herself a few key friendships.

And then there was the case of a young woman who managed to turn the fashion-society-media world on its ear. Pretty, stylish, and sprightly enough to catch the eye of an influential editor, she quickly found herself on all the right guest lists. It was only later discovered that she had been a kept woman, the girlfriend of a rich drug dealer, at the same time that she had made her ascent on the scene. These two examples were just the tip of the iceberg—Lily could think of several others that had filtered down to her through gossip or that she had read about as blind items on Page Six—and while the particulars of each story were slightly different, they both provided further evidence that the old society truism was still, well, true: Once you're at the top, people have a way of forgetting how you got there.

But for Lily, there was more at stake than just her place in society. There was her marriage to consider. It seemed to her that ever since she had fallen from her pedestal, tipped over, and shattered into a million little pieces at the feet of women like Morgan and Diana, Robert had gradually ceased loving her as he once did. There was a time when she thought their love for one another was legendary and if not that, at least enduring. But the first year of their marriage had pulverized even that illusion, and she was unsure that their relationship could survive the crushing arguments and hurtful silences that had so quickly and unexpectedly accumulated in their wake. Robert was once so proud of her that she could see it in his eyes, and Lily wanted, more than social stature or journalistic recognition, or anything really, for him to look at her that way again, to find her between the spangled branches of their lives to mouth the words, "I love you."

At precisely three o'clock on Tuesday afternoon, Lily climbed into the town car Josephine had hired for the afternoon. If she was at all late, she'd end up on the receiving end of Josephine's speech about punctuality, and that was the last thing she wanted to deal with now. When Lily got into the car, however, she saw that Josephine wasn't even inside to mark her arrival time.

"Change of plans," the driver grumpily informed her, and they drove to Josephine's apartment building to wait for her to finish getting ready. Motor running, they waited there for twenty minutes before Lily's mobile rang. On the line was Josephine's assistant, Greyson.

"Mrs. Bartholomew . . . behind . . . feel free . . . champagne . . . the car." Greyson spoke so quietly and in such a low voice that Lily could barely make out what she was saying.

"Okay, we'll wait here," Lily said, and clicked her phone closed.

"Wha'd she say," the driver grunted over his shoulder. He had a heavy Brooklyn accent and a thick salt-and-pepper mustache that further muffled his already garbled words.

"*Umm,* just that we should stay here for a while. She'll be down shortly."

After twenty more minutes of waiting, Lily began looking around the back of the car for the champagne Greyson had mentioned. Tapping open the lacquered walnut console on the side of the car, she found a bottle of 1989 Veuve Cliquot La Grande Dame chilling on ice. Lily twisted off the metal wrapping, popped off the cork, and slowly filled a crystal flute with the pale yellow, effervescing liquid while she mentally justified the early drink. After enduring the most grueling edit of her life—three editors had laid their hands on the piece and each had demanded she make major changes—she deserved to enjoy herself today. Toasting an imaginary companion, she took her first sip. "*Mmm,*" she raved.

"That good, huh?" the driver asked cheerlessly.

"I'll tell you what, it makes waiting around in a car not such a bad way to spend an afternoon," she said, and then, deciding it would be rude not to make a little small talk, she asked the driver, "Have you been driving for Mrs. Bartholomew long?"

"Just today."

"Oh, so this isn't your first stop today?"

"Are you kiddin'? She hasn't stopped since nine a.m. I took her and her son—your husband, right?—to breakfast and then they went shopping. Hermès, Armani, Gucci. Trunk was loaded with bags by the time we dropped him off at the tennis club," he said.

"But that can't be right." Just as she started to explain that Josephine's only son, her husband, Robert, happened to be a hundred miles north of the city hunting pheasant and quail that morning, the door to the limo opened, and Josephine's heavily shellacked head popped through the doorway.

"What can't be right?" she asked, settling into the car's plush banquet. She was wearing a celadon tweed suit with a fox collar and cuffs. No pantyhose, despite the chill, and crocodile pumps. "Oh, I see you are having a glass of champagne," Josephine noted with surprise.

"Yes, it's delicious. Thank you. May I pour you a glass?" Lily offered.

Josephine ignored her and started rattling off directions to the driver. When she was done she turned her frosty gaze back to Lily. "I must admit, I'm a bit shocked you took it upon yourself to open *my* champagne, Lily. *C'est tres mal éléve*," she seethed.

"But, your assistant—"

"An apology would be sufficient, Lily."

Lily could feel her cheeks burning. She hadn't been spoken to like that since she was a child. "I'm sorry," she said, adding indignantly, "but Greyson told me to help myself to it."

Josephine tutted angrily and retrieved a pair of gold-rimmed reading glasses from her croc Hermès Birkin. "I need to review my notes," she announced, putting on her glasses and opening a Smythson of Bond Street blue leather notebook.

As the car pulled in front of the Ortensia de la Reina boutique, Josephine closed her book and returned her attention to Lily. "Before we go in, I have something to say to you."

Uh-oh. Here it comes. Lily downed the rest of her champagne and placed the flute back in the side console.

"I know you have had the privilege of *borrowing* beautiful

dresses in the past, but it is a completely different thing to be a *customer*. You are not expected to—how should I put this?—*drool* over everything. The sales girls are trying to please you, not the other way around. *Tu comprends?*"

"Yes, I understand *completely*. Thank you so much for your guidance," Lily said, wondering why she ever thought going shopping with Josephine would be a good idea.

"You are welcome, *cherie*," Josephine said. "You are at a great disadvantage, you know, having grown up in such a different sort of environment, but I will do what I can to help you assimilate."

"Josephine, it's not like I grew up in the slums."

While Robert and his father never made Lily feel bad about her middle-class upbringing, Josephine seemed to actively seek out opportunities to point it out, as though it was something that Lily should be ashamed of, which she resolutely was not, as hard as Josephine tried to make her feel otherwise. Lily was proud of her father. Maybe he didn't make a lot of money as a professor, but he was principled and intelligent, as well as highly regarded in his field and beloved by his students and fellow faculty members. Her mother, well, she tried not to spend too much money at the Chanel makeup counter. And she always meant well. That was a heck of a lot more than Josephine could say for herself.

"Of course you didn't, dear." She patted Lily's knee lightly and offered up one of her patented smirks. "But if you had grown up here—or any place with a certain degree of sophistication, really—you would have known not to wear black to a boutique. Someone might mistake you for a salesgirl."

Once inside the boutique, Lily and Josephine were escorted to a private room in the back of the store's second floor. Near the entrance of the room a large cut-crystal vase had been filled with white orchids and roses and set on a mirrored table. Josephine blew past it, and the two champagne flutes that the nervous-looking salesgirl was holding out for them, and glided across the beige carpeting to the other side of the room. She sat down in a chair in front of a black lacquer desk and started thumbing through the designer's look book.

"Hello? Is anyone going to help me?" Josephine complained loudly, shooting the salesgirl the look of death from across the room.

"Y-Yes, coming right away, Mrs. Bartholomew," stuttered the girl as she replaced the tray of champagne on the entrance table and sprinted across the room to attend to Josephine. Lily followed her, also forgoing the champagne—she was already feeling tipsy from the glass she drank in the back of the car—and sat in the chair next to Josephine's. The salesgirl, who was indeed dressed in a tailored onyx worsted-wool dress quite similar to the one Lily was wearing, handed Lily her own book.

"Just earmark the looks you like, and then once you've made your decisions I can show you the samples or we can go ahead and start filling out the order form," she said. "My name is Bella and—"

"We don't need to know your name," Josephine snapped, her eyes never leaving the look book. She licked the tip of her pointer finger and flipped a page.

Lily offered Bella a sympathetic, I-feel-for-you eye roll. "I'm sorry," she mouthed. Bella nodded discretely and retreated back to the front of the room while Josephine continued to study the book.

The clothes were marvelous. There were hip-hugging white sailor pants and super-thin, slightly see-through cashmere sweaters in nautical prints. Red cotton skinny trousers with white mother-of-pearl buttons running up the side of one leg and a sleeveless silk tie-front blouse in a cream and navy anchor print caught Josephine's eye. She ordered them, plus two pairs of platform ostrich espadrilles and an off-the-shoulder teal blouse and pencil skirt made from linen muslin and satin. "I'll wear it with my hair slicked back and my pink sapphire and diamond hoops. So easy!" Josephine clapped.

Yeah, if by easy you mean pairing twenty thousand dollars' worth of jewelry with the best of this year's cruise collection.

"And for you, Madame?" asked the salesgirl.

There were no prices on any of the pages, so Lily wasn't sure what, if anything, was in her budget, or if she even had a budget. She and Robert hadn't spoken about their monetary situation since the day he had come home with the Porsche, but she guessed it would be okay for her to spend a few hundred dollars on something new. Pointing at a well-tailored white cotton blouse with oversized gold buttons, she asked the salesgirl if it came in any other colors.

"Just white."

"Okay, I'll take it in white then."

"Just the one?"

"Yes, that will be sufficient."

"Excellent. What about the matching skirt?" It was an A-line navy skirt with a dozen white anchors embroidered along the hem. It looked expensive.

"I'm not sure," Lily responded, biting her lip. "It's not really my style."

"Very good." The salesgirl nodded politely, not a trace of disappointment on her face (Lily already liked her immensely), and started noting the style number of the blouse when Josephine tutted loudly, "Of course it's your style. It's gorgeous. She'll take that as well."

The girl looked back at Lily, waiting for her direction.

"Did you not hear me?" Josephine snapped her fingers inches away from the girl's face. "Hello? Are you deaf?"

The girl recoiled, momentarily stunned by Josephine's finger snapping.

"*Umm*, okay, I'll take it," Lily gulped, hoping to save the salesgirl from further abuse and thinking that she could always call the store the next day and cancel the skirt. But then it also occurred to her that Josephine might be secretly planning on treating her to the clothes. After all, she had taken Robert shopping that morning and she knew full well that they were buried in an avalanche of credit card debt.

Only problem was, Josephine had no intention of buying Lily's clothes. After she'd finished making her final selections, Josephine ordered the salesgirl to tally up their bills and then another woman (also clad in black) came in to retrieve Lily's credit card information (Josephine's was on file at the store). Handing over her AmEx to yet another saleswoman (dressed in a black trouser suit, of course), Lily was informed that thirteen hundred dollars would be charged on her account and that the items would be sent via messenger to her apartment as soon as they arrived in the store.

Next stop Henri Bendel. The trunk show, which was actually for three young, CFDA-approved up-and-coming designers, took place in a roped-off area on the department store's top floor. As soon as Lily walked into the space she saw Morgan and Diana posing for a photograph, their Birkin bags (not croc) crooked casually into their elbow joints.

"Thank you, ladies," said the white-haired photographer who had been clicking photos of the women. He turned to see if anyone else of importance had arrived, and as he looked Lily up and down, she thought she saw the gleam of recognition in his eyes before he noticed Josephine standing next to her. "Josie, a photo?" he asked, lifting his camera. Josephine turned her slim frame away from him, then rolled back her front shoulder, twisting slightly from the hip. As soon as she was in position the photographer started snapping away. "Beautiful as always," he said, and winked.

So that's how it is done. Lily was in awe of her mother-in-law's ability to strike a pose without so much as an inkling of self-consciousness. Even at the height of her pre-baby popularity, Lily hadn't been able to match Josephine's serenity in front of the cameras. She'd always felt a bit awkward posing. Should she smile, and if so, should she show her teeth or not? A half smile, or did that look too unnatural? Then there was the question of what to do with her arms and hands: resting on the hips, or hanging at her sides?

Josephine turned to look for Lily, who had been hanging out in the foreground sipping a glass of sauvignon blanc, and grabbed her arm lightly as they walked toward the chairs that had been set up for the fashion show. "You'll be in the second row," she said, pointing at a seat directly behind Josephine's with Greyson's name taped on it.

"Perfect," Lily said, and sat down in the chair. *Finally a moment to relax!* As she was studying the list of looks that were going to be coming down the runway, she felt a tap on her shoulder and looked up to see five feet seven inches of glossy, toned, and tailored perfection. It was Morgan, of course.

"Lily? I knew it was you! Di said it couldn't be you because you weren't on the guest list. But here you are nonetheless." She flicked a brown ringlet behind a shoulder blade jutting through the fabric of her Rachel Roy trench coat.

How can an anorexic have such lustrous hair, Lily wondered as she painted a smile across her face. "Hello, Morgan. So nice to see you," she lied.

"It *is* Lily over here!" Morgan called across the room to Diana, who was talking to a short round man whom Lily recognized as one of the show's three featured designers.

"You know, I told Morgan here that it couldn't be you, since I helped put together the guest list and I know for a fact that you aren't on it."

Thanks, I got that the first time.

"I didn't figure you for a crasher," Di said teasingly as she sauntered over.

"I'm here with Josephine."

"Oh, yes, Robert's mother. Such a lovely lady." Di took a sip of wine. "Are you filling in for her assistant Greyson?"

"Yes, but I'm not her assistant."

Morgan and Di exchanged glances. "Darling we know that, obviously," Di snickered. "Greyson has the most fabulous legs."

And I don't. Have great legs, that is.

"And taste. Greyson has an incredible eye," added Morgan for good measure.

Which I must also not possess. Lily nodded blithely and repeated what was fast becoming her new mantra: *No blood in the water.*

"So if you aren't filling in for Greyson, are you here as a spectator?" inquired Morgan.

As in someone who sits on the sidelines. Not a player.

"I'm here to shop," Lily said before she could stop herself.

Di regarded her dubiously. "Okay, then. Happy shopping!"

"Thanks, you too."

Lily groaned inwardly. Why did she have to say that? This meant that she was going to have to buy a few things just to show Diana and Morgan that she had money to burn. And that she had a sense of style. *So much for sitting back and enjoying the show.*

A hip-hop song started playing over the loudspeakers, cueing everyone to rush to their chairs. As Lily settled back into her second-tier seat, Josephine turned around, tapping her on the knee with her pen. "I didn't know you were friends with Morgan and Diana," she said, making eye contact with Lily for the first time since they left the car. "Such lovely girls." Josephine turned back around to face the show.

Great, so being friends with Diana and Morgan wins me her approval? Forget raising healthy kids or being a loyal wife—Di, Morgan, and me as best buds, that's what she wants to see.

A pin-thin teenager, even more skeletal than Morgan, appeared in front of the white canvas curtain at the base of the runway. She was wearing a crotch-high miniskirt and a crystal-encrusted triangle bikini top, and the front row clapped gleefully in appreciation. Then, everyone started scribbling in their folders. Lily, not wanting to stick out as the only non-note-taker in the crowd, wrote in her folder, "Maybe if I weighed 100 pounds." Five more girls in mere strips of clothing stomped down the runway. There was more note taking, some *oohs* and *ahhs,* and then the music changed.

Skeleton girl appeared again, this time wearing a long cotton cardigan cinched with a wide black patent leather belt. This was more like it. Lily drew stars next to the look numbers corresponding with a white linen shirtdress worn with a pink patent leather belt and an electric blue silk bomber jacket with a seashell-print lining. If she was going to buy something, it might as well be something she loved.

As soon as the show ended the women jumped up on their platform pumps and rushed toward the racks of clothes from the show. Lily saw one forty-something woman in a leopard-print dress lunge toward an azure Grecian-style column only to be beaten to the punch by a twenty-something girl with waist-length blond extensions. Lily scanned the racks of clothes and saw Josephine fingering her beloved blue bomber. "I love this one," Lily commented, running her hand over the soft fabric.

"*Hmm,* perhaps you are learning from me?" she said, and turned to the salesgirl who was hovering next to her. "I'll take this one in a size two."

"Darn," Lily cursed under her breath. She scanned the racks for something else that she not only liked but that would also impress Morgan and Di and eventually settled on a mint green pique sundress with an empire waist (which was actually still in fashion, despite Josephine's assertion to the contrary) and the pink patent leather belt she had seen on the runway. Not only were her selections beautiful and well priced compared to Ortensia de La Reina's offerings, but the salesgirls fawned all over her, right in front of Di and Morgan. It was a thousand dollars well spent.

Back in the car Josephine poured two glasses of the champagne and handed one to Lily. "To fabulous clothes and ideal friends," she toasted.

At the next stop Lily watched as Josephine, now glowing with retail-induced euphoria, ordered a pair of slim cut seersucker pants, a shrunken navy blazer, a taffeta pouf skirt in sapphire, and an ecru lace blouse with crystal buttons. Lily bought a gray A-line skirt, which she planned to pair with a white cotton tank and her new pink belt. Back in the car, Josephine poured them more champagne. And it was a good thing, too—otherwise Lily might have been sober enough to realize that she had spent almost three thousand dollars (her entire first paycheck from the *Sentinel*) in less than four hours.

Chapter 17

On Saturday morning, still in good spirits from her (overall) successful shopping trip with Josephine, Lily decided to prepare Nutella-filled crepes, Robert's favorite, for breakfast. After feeding Will his morning bottle, she brewed a strong pot of coffee and whipped together a bowl of crepe batter. While the batter settled she gave Will a bath and dressed him in a rugby shirt and jeans. She was frying up a pan of apple-wood smoked bacon when Robert finally stumbled in, dressed just in his boxer shorts, his eyes still heavy with sleep.

"*Oooh*, what's all this?" he said, yawning audibly and picking up Will in his muscular arms.

"Hi, honey," she said, furtively admiring her husband's toned physique. All those squash games at the club were doing him good.

"Look what Mommy made for us," Robert cooed at Will, who in reply stuck his left hand in his father's mouth. "*Umm, umm, umm,* I'm going to eat your hand!" Robert smacked, pretending to gnaw on the tips of Will's fingers as Lily, who had just finished juicing a dozen oranges, handed him a glass of the orange liquid. "Let me just go take a quick shower." He lowered Will back into his Exersaucer and retreated back toward the bedroom, juice in hand.

Ten minutes later Robert returned to the kitchen and sat down at the table, which was laid with a plate of crepes and another of bacon, plus a small carafe of coffee, and asked Lily what she wanted to do that day.

"No squash games, no bridge luncheons?" she questioned, teasingly.

"Nope, I'm all yours," he said between mouthfuls.

"Well, I was hoping we could go to the park. I'd like to get some pictures of you and Will with the fall foliage in the background." She set the egg-white omelet she had prepared for herself earlier on the table and sat down.

"Yeah, that could be fun," Robert said. "By the way, Mom called me yesterday. She wanted to talk about you."

"Oh?" Lily's mind flashed back to her mother-in-law's various reprimands on the day of their shopping spree, starting with the incident with the champagne. Girding herself for yet another Bartholomew sermon, she pushed her ice-cold omelet away and asked, "So what did she have to say?"

"She said that she had a wonderful time with you."

"Really? She didn't mention anything else?"

"Not really. She said that she helped you pick out some nice things."

"She did?" Lily was both shocked and relieved that Josephine hadn't told Robert about how she had been mistaken for a salesgirl at the trunk show or how the photographer hadn't even bothered taking her photo.

"Didn't she?" Robert asked, confused.

"I guess," Lily shrugged. "I'm just surprised she admitted that she had a nice time."

"Well I think it's great you two had a chance to bond."

"Yeah, there's nothing like spending a boatload of cash together to bond two women."

"*You* didn't spend a lot, did you?"

She gulped, feeling suddenly embarrassed by the sum of her expenditures. "About three thousand," she finally said.

"Lily, I thought you understood our situation," Robert said grimly.

"I do, but your mom was pressuring me to buy a lot of things."

"Lily, I know you. You're not so easy to push around."

"I figured that if she was encouraging me to spend money then—"

"Then what?" he said, the tension rising in his voice.

"Well, to be honest, at first I thought she might be planning to buy the clothes for me, which in retrospect I realize was completely stupid. And then I ran into Diana Meddling and Morgan de Rambouillet at the trunk show, and they asked me if I was planning on buying anything—it was like they were implying that I was there as your mother's assistant—and then I *had* to buy something just to show them. I really didn't spend that much compared to the other women."

"You have to return those clothes."

"But it's not fair that I don't even have jeans that fit while you're tooling around in a brand-new sports car," she said, frustration tingeing her voice with whininess. "Your mother's driver told me that Josephine took you shopping when, by the way, you told me you were going to be hunting with your friend from Tuxedo Park!"

"The hunt got canceled and Mother asked me to come run a few errands with her that morning," he explained curtly. "Is that okay with you?"

"The driver said you went to Hermès and Armani."

"We did. Mom bought me some new suits and ties." He pushed back from the table, wiped his mouth with a paper napkin, and rose from the table. "Thank you for breakfast," he said.

"So you get new clothes, but I have to go on looking like a bag lady?" Lily knew she was heading down a dangerous path, but there were some things that shouldn't be left unsaid, and this was one of them. Just because she hadn't grown up with a lot—there had been no fancy trips, country estates, or lavish sweet sixteen parties in her childhood—that didn't mean that she should be the only one making sacrifices. It wasn't fair that Robert continued to live the high life while she was literally monitoring her use of paper towels and comparison shopping for Windex. They should both have to make sacrifices in the bad times. Wasn't that what marriage was all about?

"What happened to for richer, for poorer?" she asked Robert, her voice full of accusation and hurt.

"Don't be so dramatic." He turned his back to her and dumped his dirty plates in the sink. Without turning around, he added, "Look, now's not the time to start throwing our money around. I need those suits and ties *for my interviews*."

"I'm not saying you don't," she protested, hurt and shamed by his words.

Robert turned around slowly and crossed his arms in front of his chest. He looked as angry and frustrated as she felt, but then his expression softened. "If I land one of these jobs you can pick any store in the city, and I'll take you there and treat you to whatever you want. But until then, we can't afford any shopping sprees. You have two choices. Either you can return those clothes or you can find a way to pay for them yourself. My AmEx is maxed out as it is." Breezing past her into the hall, he walked off in the direction of his office.

"Are we still going to the park?" Lily called after him.

"Yeah, sure, whatever," he said before disappearing into his study.

Lily picked Will up from off the floor and kissed the top of his head. "Forget everything you just saw. Mommy and Daddy love each other very much," she reassured him before setting him back down. Lily had always sworn to herself that she would never fight in the presence of her children, and even though she knew that Will was too young to understand what was going on, she didn't want to fall into the habit of bickering in front of him. From time to time her parents had argued in front of her and her brother, and the tension between them had always made her feel nervous and scared.

As Lily got to work scraping crepe batter off the countertops and grease from the backsplash, she turned her argument with Robert over in her head. Perhaps she'd been wrong to insinuate that because Josephine had taken Robert shopping, he should understand why she wanted some new things for herself. And perhaps it was irresponsible of her to spend all that money. But still, couldn't he see things from her point of view for a second? Couldn't he be more sympathetic? On top of all this, it troubled her that Robert was taking less and less interest in spending time with Will. When Will was just born, he had helped with changing diapers and rocking him back to sleep in the middle of the night. But now Lily had to bug him just to whip up a bottle of formula. Where was her supportive, loving husband? And would she have him back once he found a job?

After cleaning the kitchen and loading the dishwasher, Lily set Will down for a nap and went into the dining room, where she turned on her computer and surfed the Internet in search for new ideas for the *Sentinel*. Her article on baby quotas was running on Thursday, and Rebecca was so pleased with how it had turned out that she had called Lily at home to ask her to whip up a new batch of ideas.

After a while of fruitless portal-hopping Lily became bored and wandered into Robert's office, a wood-paneled room with built-in bookshelves. Josephine had decorated it with a leather couch, two antique library-step end tables, and velvet drapes. On the wall above his desk she had hung an abstract painting that depicted a man holding a woman, but if you looked long enough at the shapes, you could also make out a third woman, positioned directly behind the first. It gave Lily the creeps, and she shuddered lightly as she entered the room to find Robert staring blankly at what looked like his résumé on the computer screen. Poor thing, she thought guiltily, remembering what he had said about having such a massive legacy to live up to. His father hadn't been able to convince the board to let Robert open a new Internet initiative at Blue Water, and he was now fully, but somewhat begrudgingly, focused on finding employment with a hedge fund.

"Honey, let's not fight about money." Lily bolted over to his desk before he could shoo her away. She was tempted to tell him that she'd be able to pay for her new clothes once she received her check from the *Sentinel*. But as good as it would feel to throw that in his face, she couldn't bring herself to do it, so instead she said vaguely, "I have a way to pay for the clothes. I'll be able to pay you back in a few weeks."

Robert closed the document he was working on and looked up at her. "It's not a big deal," he sighed. "But what I don't get is that you have a closet full of clothes that you don't use, and then you go off and buy new stuff we can't afford. You know we're in debt."

Lily perched herself on his desk. "The thing is that I still don't fit into most of the clothes in my closet. I'm still too big," she said.

"Then why don't you get rid of them. They're just taking up space."

His words hit her like a bucket of ice water in the face. She'd opened herself up to him—talked about her *fatness* for God's sake—and he'd responded without reassurance or affection, but cool indifference. *He's a heartless jerk,* she thought. He hadn't even tried to understand how vulnerable and insecure she felt. There was no point in her trying to explain herself. Lily sighed and looked up at the ceiling.

"I really need to get some work done today. Can we do the park thing tomorrow maybe?" Robert asked.

"I have a lot of stuff I can do today, anyway," she said. She closed the door on her way out.

Lily walked back to the dining room and sat down again behind her computer. She discovered little of inspiration and eventually found herself on eBay creating an online seller account. Then she headed for her closet to cull the-impossibly-tiny and the-not-particularly-beautiful from her wardrobe.

As she was picking through her dresses and skirts, Robert walked into the closet to tell her that he was going to the club. "I should be back by dinnertime," he announced, crouching down to the floor of the closet where she had piled some of the pieces she planned to sell. "You don't fit in this one?" he asked, fingering a red silk dress with capped sleeves and a low neckline.

Lily nodded. "It's not really my style anyway."

"Oh," he frowned, "that's a shame."

Lily glared at him. "Not really," she said, pulling the dress out of his hands.

Robert sauntered out of the closet to pack his leather gym bag, and she waited until she heard his footsteps leave the bedroom before she emerged from the closet with another pile of clothes. "Too busy to go to the park, but not too busy for a game of squash," she muttered under her breath.

As if on cue, Robert walked back into the bedroom and drew Lily into his arms. "Let's have a date tonight," he said, squeezing one of her butt cheeks a little too hard.

"Are you sure you won't be too tired from squash?" she asked, her right eyebrow arched challengingly. She pulled away from him and threw the clothes in her arms onto the growing heap on the bed.

"Not a chance," Robert said and lifted her hair to kiss the back of her neck. "See you later."

After she was sure Robert had left, Lily transferred the pile of clothes on her bed to the living room couch. One by one, she laid each piece on their Oriental rug and photographed it with her digital camera, taking close-ups of the tiny details she thought were noteworthy—a lace trim here, a toggle closure there—and was about to start loading the photos onto her computer when the phone rang.

"Why haven't you called me?" It was Liz.

"Mom?" Lily teased.

"Very funny. I left you two messages last week and no response. What gives?"

"It's been a crazy few weeks. I've actually been to the hairdresser's *and* to two parties. And I'm trying to get my writing career back on track."

"So now do you regret quitting your job?"

"Just say it."

"Say what?" There was a pause. "You mean I told you so? Because I'd never say that."

"But that's exactly what you think."

Back when Lily was debating whether or not she should quit the *Journal*, Liz had advised her against it. She'd seen Lily work her way through college and then up to reporter status. "You are the smartest girl I know. It's not right for you to just chuck it all in to have babies," she'd said. But Lily's mind had been made up, and she'd told Liz that until she was also married and pregnant she couldn't possibly understand. It was a condescending thing to say, and before Lily knew it they were fighting, absurdly, about girl power and the legacy of the Spice Girls. A lot of hurtful, cutting things were said—Liz had parried Lily's "You're just jealous that I'm happily married and you're not" with "At least I'm not a pathetic little *housewife*"— and although they made up a few weeks later, their relationship had never fully recovered from the argument. By the time Will was born, they were speaking to one another only once or twice a month, and their e-mails had become equally stilted and infrequent.

Perhaps Liz had been right, but at the time quitting seemed like the right thing to do. At the time, Lily had rationalized that since she and Robert didn't need the money her bimonthly paycheck provided, continuing work would be selfish, in service of nothing but her ego. She remembered believing that there was more nobility in the sacrifice of her career for the well-being of her children than there was in slogging away at a nine to five in search of professional recognition and shopping money.

"Sometimes I wonder if I made the right decision," Lily said in order to break the silence and hopefully bury the hatchet for good. "But you know what they say about hindsight being twenty-twenty. All I can do is focus on what I'm doing now. And since I've started writing again, I've started feeling like my old self again."

"That's wonderful," Liz said in the same voice one might use on a small child trying to put together his first puzzle.

"Anyway, enough about me," Lily sighed. "Tell me about the fabulous things you're doing these days. Dating anyone special?"

"I wish. I think you snagged the last decent guy in New York. But at least things are going a bit better for me on the work front. I was offered a job with Henri Fontaine, the French jeweler, in VIP relations. I get to outfit all the stars before big awards shows."

"Does this mean you're moving to Los Angeles?"

"No, but the job requires a lot of travel. I'll spend Oscar season in L.A., but then I'll be in Cannes for the film festival, London for the BAFTA's, Miami for New Year's, New York for the CFDA's and the Met Ball, blah, blah, blah."

"Sounds anything but blah to me. What an incredible job! Congrats," Lily said. She couldn't think of anyone better suited to a life spent tripping across the globe with celebrities, but she also had to be honest with herself—the thought of Liz living out such a glamorous existence made her envious. Still, she was happy for her and proceeded to barrage her with a million different questions about how she got the job and how they selected the celebrities they were going to try to outfit for an event.

"We also do socialites," Liz said, leadingly.

"Tell me you don't mean me."

"I do."

"I don't know if you've noticed, but the last time I graced the social pages was about two years ago. Do you know what I'm doing right now? I'm selling clothes on eBay. That's how desperate the situation is. I think it's safe to say you will *never* be loaning me any of your goodies."

"Never say never," Liz teased. "There's a pair of pearl and diamond earrings that I think would look perfect on you."

Chapter 18

On the Thursday morning her article was slated to appear in the paper, Lily woke to find Robert already showered and dressed in a business suit.

"Hey, honey, I have an interview today, but I should be home in time for dinner," he said, shaking her bare shoulder gently.

Lily blinked her eyes in the morning sun. "Good luck, sweetie," she yawned and went back to sleep only to be woken by Will's cries from inside his crib ten minutes later. She pulled on her jeans, rescued the baby with a bottle of milk, plopped him in his stroller, and went downstairs to the news agent kiosk on Lexington. She paid for a copy of the *Sentinel* and the new *Cookie* magazine and returned home, too nervous to look at her article on the street.

In the kitchen, as she waited for the coffee to brew, Lily opened up the paper to the Thursday Trends section. At the top of the page there was a huge picture of Sloan Hoffman and her two twin girls looking cozy and beautiful on a pink-and-green striped couch, a plate of lemon squares glistening on a silver tray on the coffee table. Below the picture read the headline:

AND YOU THINK YOUR PRENUP'S AWFUL
Baby Quotas In the Age of Mommy Mania

Lily couldn't believe it. She had that week's lead article. All of the New York social world was going to be talking about it, and how perfect that today's playgroup was scheduled at Morgan's place in SoHo. The timing couldn't have been better. *Fat hausfrau, my ass.*

Morgan's apartment, an enormous and much photographed (*Town & Country, Harper's Bazaar,* and *Architectural Digest* had all run spreads) triplex loft, belonged to her husband, the famously handsome and debonair French count Christian de Rambouillet, who worked for the very successful hedge fund of which Morgan's father, Thomas Howard III, happened to be a founding partner. From the looks of the de Rambouillet's spread, it was a successful fund indeed. The apartment boasted a two-story living room–dining room decorated in Art Deco pieces, including the new Ruhlmann rosewood cabinet Morgan had mentioned at Lexi Foster's birthday party and a Jules Leleu dining table, matching bergère chairs, and a carved wood settee with ivory inlays. The jutting, asymmetrical angles, glass edges, and white-on-white decor made it the least baby-friendly room Lily had ever seen.

Morgan, who was dressed in a winter white Balenciaga pantsuit, greeted Lily, Will, and Jacinta in the foyer. "Welcome," she said in a tone that conveyed quite the opposite. She flashed two rows of brilliant white veneers in a rather poor approximation of a smile. "Allison mentioned that she had invited you."

"She did, yes. Is that alright? I haven't put you out, have I?"

"No, not in the slightest. The more the merrier."

Ha!

"I just didn't realize you were friends with anyone here. Besides Allison, I mean. "

Lily stood there, placid and confident, refusing to be flummoxed by the inhospitable greeting.

No blood in the water.

"Oh, well. Here we are," Lily said.

Morgan sighed wearily and turned to Jacinta. "Babies and nannies in the nursery. Take the steps at the end of the hall, through that door," she instructed. "*Do not* go into the great room. It is *prohibido*. Got it? That room is off-limits."

"So where are the mommies?" Lily asked.

"On the roof terrace," Morgan said as she stalked up the stairs on her stiltlike legs.

After giving Will a quick kiss on the cheek, Lily followed Morgan up two flights of stairs to the apartment's rooftop terrace, a fifteen-hundred-square-foot wonderland of potted topiaries, expertly trimmed evergreens, and boxwood hedges. (*Wow!* was all Lily could say.) There was even a sunken Koi pond with a mosaic tile border. Morgan had thrown down a trio of kilim rugs and sandwiched a low Moroccan coffee table between two benches, one upholstered in vibrant orange velvet and the other in faded aqua silk shantung. The three overhead space heaters were working efficiently enough that the women didn't need to keep on their fur coats, but they did anyway.

Umberta was standing next to a mother-of-pearl inlaid bar wearing a cropped grayish white fur coat over a peach-colored tulip skirt. Lily walked up to the bar and asked for a Kir Royal from the bartender, who was dressed in just a turban and a pair of balloon pants. As she watched him pour Perrier-Jouët over a splash of crème de cassis, she said casually to Umberta, "Love your fox."

"J. Mendel does do the best furs," she said, brushing her long blond bangs off her forehead. "But you must get Gilles to do you a one-off, otherwise before you know it you'll be flipping through *In Style* and *boom,* there's a picture of Mariah Carey in your coat." She stuck out her tongue. "Gross!"

"Oh no, heaven forbid," Lily deadpanned.

"So, I saw you at the Henri Bendel trunk show the other day. I was across the aisle. In the front row."

Whereas I was in the second row.

"Wasn't the show divine? I wanted to buy everything, and I guess I nearly did. Of course, since I'm friends with the designers, I get to buy at wholesale. Nobody pays full price these days."

Except for me, it would appear.

"But anyway, didn't you love everything? I'm so psyched for the holidays now."

"To be honest some of the pieces I found a bit juvenile. It's like they're designing for teenagers."

"It's true that Alec designs for a slim silhouette. Not for you I guess," she smirked, eyeing Lily's waist. "Personally I admire women who really own their hips, but I could never pull off the curvy look. Besides, I have such a fast metabolism, I can't seem to keep any weight on," she added, lighting a cigarette before asking the buff bartender, "Could I have an ashtray please?" She smiled flirtatiously, two smoke coils blowing from her tiny nostrils.

"Lily, get your ass over here," she heard Allison calling to her from across the rooftop.

"I better go, sounds urgent," Lily said to Umberta, turning on her heel and skipping over to Allison, who was waving wildly from her perch on a tufted ottoman in patchwork brocades. "Perfect timing," Lily whispered when she plopped down next to Allison.

"Anytime. Can you believe Morgan splashed out like this? I don't think Kublai Khan had it so good," she chortled.

"Have you checked out the guy over there with the tray?"

"Duh? Who hasn't? I'm practically creaming over here."

"Allison!"

"What? Like you don't want him to lay you down on this rug and—"

"Okay, that's enough," Lily cut her short. "Has anyone ever told you that you have a dirty mouth?"

"My husband, about three times a week."

"Three times? I don't believe you."

"Believe it." Allison bit the insides of her mouth to keep from grinning.

"Okay, Miss Sexpert, if you're such great shakes in the sack, tell me why my husband hasn't come on to me more than once in the last four months."

"Maybe because you're waiting for him to make the first move. Why don't you try initiating once in a while? And I should take you shopping to my favorite lingerie shop, Maya. What are your thoughts on crotchless panties?"

Lily snorted uncontrollably, the champagne filling her nose. "Can't say that I have any," she said, holding her nostrils through the burn.

"Maybe it's time you do," Allison said, twisting her mouth to one side and raising her eyebrows.

"Changing the subject, did you happen to see my piece in the *Sentinel* today?"

"Of course I did. Who didn't?"

"You don't think I threw Sloan under the bus do you?"

"Sloan's a big girl. She knew what she was doing when she agreed to that interview," Allison said knowingly. "I wouldn't worry, but she's coming today, so I'm sure she'll let you know exactly what she thinks. In the meantime, more bubbly? Your glass is looking a little low to me."

"Actually, before we do any more toasting, I really need to pee. Where's the ladies' room?"

"Down one flight to your left. Make sure you take a peek into the nursery down the hall. You're in for the shock of your life," Allison warned.

Lily raised her eyebrows questioningly.

"You'll see."

After Lily used the lemon verbena scented powder room on the third floor, she took a short detour toward the nursery, and when she walked through the double doors, she nearly dislocated her jaw. The room was decorated entirely in black and white and reminded Lily of the room at the Blakes Hotel she and Robert had stayed in while on short vacation in London. Was it possible that

Morgan had commissioned the world-famous Anoushka Hempel to decorate her nursery? Next to one of the black-lacquer-painted walls stood a white crib outfitted in white linens with black monograms, and on the opposite wall were two matching chests of drawers painted in white and accented with black handles and trim. The floor, finished in a glossy black-and-white-checkerboard pattern, and the windows, draped in white-and-black-striped curtains, made the room ideal for a photo shoot, but questionable in its appropriateness for a baby. Where were the toys and books, the stuffed animals and diapers?

However, the pièce de résistance of the room's decor—what Allison must have been referring to when she said Lily would be in for a massive surprise—was the four-by-four wall-mounted black-and-white photograph depicting Morgan and her newborn daughter. She looked so perfect in the photograph; there wasn't a smudge of eye makeup, a drop of perspiration, or even a renegade curl marring her beaming appearance. *Leave it to Morgan to make even childbirth look soigné.*

How different Lily's experience had been. She'd gone into labor during brunch at the Four Seasons hotel in Midtown. Robert's parents were in town, and Robert had wanted to tell his parents in person that he had quit the firm. That morning, they'd argued about whether or not Lily also had to go.

"Can't you just tell them I wasn't feeling up to it?" she'd asked from underneath the duvet cover.

"I need your support," he insisted.

She complied with a sigh, rolling her big belly out of bed, her feet thumping heavily on the floor.

"That's my girl," he'd said, and smiled, his eyes crinkling sadly in the morning light.

At brunch, the waiter had just filled Lily's glass with freshly squeezed orange juice when she felt a rippling of pain in her lower pelvis, like a cramp. She excused herself to the bathroom, where she sat down on the toilet and waited for the feeling to pass. Once the pain had subsided she went back to the table, and midway between the entrance to the restaurant and their circular table in the center of the main room, she felt a gush of liquid streaming down her leg onto the restaurant's beige marble floor. She stumbled the last ten paces to the table, careful not to slip on her own fluids.

"Robert," she said to her husband's back as she neared the table, now blanketed in plates of eggs Benedict, bagels, smoked salmon, and her waffle, swimming in butter and maple syrup. "I think I just peed on myself," she whispered to him.

As he turned around, she took in the hard line of his mouth, the color drained from his face, and realized that he must have broken the news about his job when she was in the bathroom. "What? Are you sure?" he asked, studying her pants.

"I had a cramp and then—"

"Are you sure your *water* didn't just break? I think your water just broke," he stammered.

"It has?" Lily looked over at Josephine and Edward. "I can't believe it's finally time!"

Josephine snorted loudly. "Well, speaking of timing, I think yours could use some work. We were just in the middle of a very important *family* conversation," she snapped, reaching for her quilted Chanel handbag. "I guess we'll see you at the hospital," she said to Robert.

"Mother, wait." Robert snatched the bag's gold chain before Josephine could reach it.

"Don't make a scene, Robert," she seethed, rolling her eyes. "Your wife's doing a good enough job for the both of you."

Edward shook his head in disgust. "Lily, are you all right?" he asked kindly, helping her into a chair. "Maybe we should get you home."

Lily felt another searing cramp ripple through her belly and pelvis and watched, paralyzed, as Robert chased his mother out of the restaurant: "Good idea," Lily exhaled after the last of the pain had left her body. Taking Edward's arm she walked slowly out of the restaurant.

As they neared the marble expanse in the hotel's front foyer, she overheard Josephine's shrill whisper echoing off of the walls of the cavernous space. "Who goes into labor at the Four Seasons? Answer me that."

"Mom, be nice. It's not like she planned this."

"On purpose, by accident, it doesn't matter," Josephine threw her hands up in the air, her set of gold bangles clanking loudly. "Why she didn't want to schedule her C-section at Lenox Hill like everyone else's daughter I'll never know. You know it's really selfish of her to put the baby through the stress of labor just so she can give birth like one of those hillbillies in their RVs."

"It's not like she's having the baby at home. We're going to the hospital," Robert interjected.

Wagging her finger in her son's face, Josephine continued her rampage. "I warned you that she would be totally out of place in our world, but oh no, you had to marry her."

"And I don't regret it—not for one second."

"Bravo, dear! So go home and be happy with your little hillbilly."

Oh no she didn't.

"The answer is no, you can not have an advance from your trust fund. End of story."

Lily watched as Josephine pivoted on her Louboutins and clicked her way out the door and onto Fifty-seventh Street's double-wide pale gray sidewalk. Frowning, Robert turned around to see his father and wife standing less than ten feet behind him. "Oh, baby," he croaked, his eyes brimming with apology. "She really doesn't—"

"Just take me home," Lily pleaded.

"Get her home, son," Edward said, beckoning Robert back across the foyer before turning toward Lily. "Not that you have any reason to, but please try to forgive my wife's behavior. I think

she's finding it a bit difficult to think of herself as a grandmother."
He kissed her on the cheek and embraced her lightly. "I, on the
other hand, am thrilled to be a grandfather. You make sure Robert
calls me the second that baby arrives, okay?"

"Yes, of course, Edward," she nodded.

"We'll call you," Robert seconded before leading Lily outside
and into a taxi.

For the next seven hours, Lily labored in the relative comfort
of their apartment. Robert rubbed her back and encouraged her
to *hee-hee-hoo* through her contractions until the pain became
too much for her to bear without the help of medication. At ten
o'clock Robert retrieved her already packed overnight bag from the
bedroom and they headed for the hospital, where she was swiftly
admitted into the maternity ward, hooked up to a fetal heart-rate
monitoring belt, and administered an epidural. The spinal block
instantly numbed the pain of her contractions and allowed both
of them to finally get some rest.

The following afternoon, after twenty-four hours of active labor
and forty-five minutes of pushing, the obstetrician handed Lily
her purple-pink, eight-pound bundle of joy. As she held her son
for the first time, noticing his tiny toes, the soft hairs blanketing
the tops of his earlobes, the way his chest rose and fell with every
breath of air, she wept from exhaustion, relief, and, yes, happiness. "You've done it, sweetheart," Robert said, stroking her sweat-
soaked forehead. "You've made a perfect baby."

It was a sweet moment, but soigné it was not.

By the time Lily returned to the party on Morgan's terrace, the
women had gathered around the Moroccan table and Sloan Hoffman, the apparent woman of the hour.

"There she is," Sloan said as soon as she eyed Lily approach-
ing the table. Lily's stomach tensed in anticipation of what Sloan
would say next. "I was just telling the girls that thanks to your
faaabulous article, I've sold an entertaining guide, and the Food

Network wants to test me for a thirty-minute show based on the book."

"Really? That all happened just today?" Lily asked.

"Yes ma'am. The *Today* show called, too, but Amy says we should definitely give *Oprah* the exclusive."

Lily looked to Amy, who nodded in agreement. "We've set up a conference call with Oprah's people tomorrow. We'll plan it so the show premiers the week before her book launch."

"And I'm going to personally make sure you're invited to the cocktail party," Sloan said to Lily.

"But not the dinner party," Di murmured to Morgan within Lily's earshot.

Lily, having once been an in-demand Girl of the Moment, knew that there was a clear line of demarcation between those who made the dinner cut and those who were relegated to the cocktail parties that fell before or after the dinner. Lily hadn't yet made the dinner list; she was still on the B-list, if that.

Lily shook off Di's comment. "But is you husband okay with the piece?"

"You don't know?" Morgan guffawed.

"We were going to split up anyway," Sloan said, and shrugged. "At least now I'll have the public's sympathy on my side. Did I mention Page Six called, too? They're calling us the divorce of the year," she added excitedly.

Out of the corner of her eye Lily noticed Kate de Santos downing her glass of champagne in one gulp.

The women spent the rest of the afternoon talking about where they were spending the holidays and what "little trinkets" they were putting on their lists for Santa. By the end of the afternoon, the ten of them had quaffed the better part of a case of champagne. Kate, who had gotten particularly tipsy that afternoon, nearly fell down the steps leading back down to the apartment. When she lost her balance, she grabbed the side rail, flinging her gift bag into the air. The gift inside, a heart-shaped paperweight from Baccarat, was propelled into the Chagall lithograph on the opposite wall and succeeded in shattering the glass frame.

Lily rushed down the stairs to make sure Kate was okay while all the other moms gaped from the top of the stairs. But as she helped Kate to the front door, Lily couldn't help feeling a bit relieved that someone else was going to be the subject of the following week's gossip and ridicule. As Lily would soon find out, Kate's marriage was rumored to be doomed, and the Baccarat mishap would only fuel more speculation of an impending divorce.

Chapter 19

New York in December is a magical place. The department store windows come alive with groovy interpretations of storybook tales; office building foyers are strung with twinkling lights and decorated with menorahs and Christmas trees; and hundreds of private apartments across the city are transformed into bijoux-box boutiques, selling everything from French-milled soaps to Portuguese baby clothes.

On the Tuesday following Morgan's Moroccan-themed mommy-and-me, Lily was pleasantly surprised to receive a phone call from Verushka Kravis, who was throwing a "Holiday Shopping Night" at her ultramodern Columbus Circle penthouse.

"You'll have fun," Verushka promised.

"Sounds great! When is it?"

"Tonight."

Tonight? "I'll have to see if Rob's free."

Silence: They both knew Lily was a last-minute addition to the guest list.

"Thank you so much for inviting us. What—" Lily was going to ask which charity the event was benefiting when Verushka cut her off. "Look darling, I have to go. It's the caterers on the other line."

Click.

That night, having assumed that the evening had been organized to benefit a certain (if yet unveiled) cause, Lily was shocked to discover that the proceeds of the event were destined not for charity, but for the Cayman Island bank accounts of the evening's socialite purveyors.

However, the first thing Lily noticed when she and Robert walked into Verushka's apartment was not the debatable hypocrisy of the city's best-known philanthropists trying to make a buck for themselves, but the eighteen-foot Douglas fir that had been erected in the living room. Decorated in yards of opalescent platinum French ribbon and white fairy lights, the evergreen's branches were draped in mounds of costume jewelry instead of ornaments, and a diamante necklace, in lieu of the traditional angel or star, sparkled from the apex of the tree.

"That's quite a tree," Robert said, wrapping his arm around Lily's waist. "But where's the mistletoe?"

"Forget the mistletoe," she whispered, and he kissed her lightly on the lips.

"I'm going to find the bar, can I get you anything?"

"Champagne if they have it, otherwise a glass of wine?" she said, watching as her husband disappeared around a white marble column in search of their drinks.

Turning her attention back to the magnificent tree, she fingered a faux ruby and diamond chandelier earring hanging off the end of one branch. It was finer than any of the costume pieces she had folded away in her jewelry roll.

Verushka, who was dressed in a curve-hugging dress and Roger Vivier ostrich-feather pumps, walked up beside Lily. "Isn't it marvelous?" she remarked, nodding her shiny black head of hair at the tree.

"Did you do this?"

"Oh God no, Jerry hires someone every year to come up with a new idea. This one is my favorite so far."

"It would be mine, too. My only question is who gets to keep the jewelry?" Lily giggled.

"Me, of course. But that's not even the best part. Jerry's planting a real piece, my Christmas present, in there somewhere on Christmas morning. I have to look for it!" she hooted.

"How fun!" Lily exclaimed, feeling a small twinge of envy for Verushka's spoiled lifestyle. But then she spotted Robert crossing back through the living room with a glass of champagne for her, and her heart flooded with feelings of guilt. She loved him whether or not he showered her with designer clothes and golf-ball-sized cocktail rings. Their love was real, not built on the tawdry quid pro quos of a trophy wife existence.

"Robert, darling, so good to see you," Verushka said to Robert in a tone far nicer than she had ever used addressing Lily. "There are some magnificent little pieces on Umberta's table. I'm sure Lily would *love* to find one of those bangles under the tree," she purred, pointing over at a table of jewelry.

"I'm sure you're right," Robert chuckled gamely.

After a few minutes of small talk, Verushka said she had to check on the hors d'oeuvres, but before leaving she leaned in and murmured in Lily's ear, "If you want to tell your editors at the *Sentinel* about this event, let me know. I think it would be a *fa-bu-lous* story for you."

"*Hmm.* Well, that is an interesting idea," Lily said, realizing that she and Robert had only been invited because Verushka wanted to be featured in Thursday Trends. Perhaps she, like Sloan Hoffman, had an entertaining book up her sleeve.

Cocking his head toward a group of men organized near one of the floor-to-ceiling windows, Robert announced that he was going over to join them. "You don't mind, do you?" he asked.

"No honey. You go ahead."

Walking around the room, Lily surveyed the wares on display. Thanks to her eBay sales and her first freelancing check from the *Sentinel*, Lily had been able to pay Robert back for the things she'd bought with Josephine and still had enough left over to buy Christmas presents for her family and Robert's. Her plan was to start collecting gifts tonight.

On one table there were rows of white-gold filigree earrings and multistrand necklaces, while another held a collection of alligator and python clutches. A pyramid of boxed perfumes and scented candles and soaps had been built on another table, and the last held a collection of pint-sized cashmere rompers, smocked dresses, Peter Pan–collared shirts and wool toggle coats.

It was—Lily thought wryly as she walked over to Snow's aromatic table—the New York socialite's version of a lemonade stand. Except instead of lemonade these women were hawking $3,000 jeweled hoops, $200 toddler sweaters, and $100 bath salts. As much as she hated to give Verushka any press, Lily had to admit that she was right: this could be a good story for her. She'd pitch the piece to Rebecca tomorrow.

"Divine packaging," Lily smiled as she fingered a $75 set of minicandles.

"This one is a great hostess gift," Snow said, handing her a $50 box of hand-milled soaps.

Handing her two twenties and a ten from her handbag, Lily said, "Yeah, it is. Perfect for my mother-in-law."

Snow, who had caught the tint of sourness in Lily's voice, whispered conspiratorially, "I've got one, too," and snuck the minicandle set into Lily's white shopping tote. "This one's on the house. Maybe it'll warm old Josie up a bit," she said, and winked.

"I know this is going to sound a little creepy, but if you were a man, I'd be tempted to leave Robert for you."

"You are creepy, but I like you anyway," Snow said, laughing.

Next Lily waltzed over to Umberta's table, where she picked up a lovely cameo pendant chiseled from the pale pink underbelly of a conch shell and nestled in a ring of tiny seed pearls. "This is gorgeous," Lily gushed.

"All the top girls are wearing them," Umberta said. "The best ones are made to order, of course."

"Made to order. Like couture cameos?"

"See this one?" she asked, pulling a cameo pendant from her cleavage. "Our master craftsman will do one in your likeness. But you have to go to Venice so he can see you in person. And not everyone can have one. Only the top girls," she reiterated.

Yes, yes, not me. I'm not a top girl. I got it already, thankyouverymuch.

"So you might like this one instead," Umberta said, showing her another pendant, this one set in white gold and studded with pale blue sapphires. "It's the next best thing to having an original."

Lily was inspecting the cameo and its whopping $10K price tag (*imagine what the couture version costs*) when she heard Robert laughing loudly across the room. She turned around to see what the source of hilarity was.

He was standing with Morgan's sister, the renowned party girl Cecilia Howard—CeCe to those who knew her—and Morgan and her husband, Christian. They were all laughing at something, and Christian's arm was wrapped jovially around Robert's shoulders. *Man, they look chummy*, Lily thought as she handed back the pendant and asked for a card from Umberta. Shuffling across the room, she stepped into the trio's intimate semicircle and Robert introduced her to the famous French count and Bungalow 8 fixture.

"Christian de Rambouillet," Morgan's husband said while executing a short bow to Lily. His high cheekbones, cleft chin, and thick black hair made him look more like a star soccer player than a successful and infinitely pedigreed financier. *Aren't French counts supposed to be half-wit inbreeds with receding hairlines and bad teeth?* Christian took Lily's hand and lifted it inches from his rosy lips. "It turns out we are all going to be in St. Barths at the same time," he said, raising a dark eyebrow.

"Oh yes, that's right." Lily blushed.

"You'll have to visit us on our yacht," he added.

He's so nice! "Sounds great. I—"

"And you guys are definitely coming over for a round of tennis," Robert added, cutting Lily off.

"Robert, you know I am *terrible* at tennis," Morgan giggled, and tossed yet another handful of hair over her shoulder. "I'll just watch on the sidelines."

"Then you can keep score," Lily said amiably.

"Oh, I'm very good at that," Morgan said, glaring at Lily.

"I love tennis," CeCe said, out of step with the conversation.

All that cocaine must have done some real damage. Lily guessed that CeCe, who purportedly worked for her father's hedge fund, didn't actually spend that much time in the office. She was far too thin, tan, and relaxed and didn't have any trace of the dark under-eye circles that all of the female lawyers Lily used to interview for the *Journal* sported with unerring regularity.

"Well, I guess I better finish making the Grand Tour," Lily said, cocking her head in the direction of the tables. "It was nice meeting you," she said to Christian and CeCe.

"Likewise," Christian said, bowing again, a curly smile playing upon his lips.

Man, he's trouble, Lily thought as she clicked back toward the mounting shopping frenzy and twinkling tree.

Chapter 20

Lily was in high spirits the weeks before Christmas. Rebecca had loved her idea on socialite shopping nights and commissioned a fifteen-hundred word piece on the topic, and Lily managed to turn the article around much more quickly than the last, thanks in large measure to the cooperation of Verushka and the other women involved in the retail event. The day that the article appeared, she found herself once again worried about getting angry feedback from her sources, namely Verushka and her ilk. The tone of the piece wasn't exactly mean, but she did include some rather cutting comments from a curmudgeonly society columnist and a highly respected social historian. She'd find out soon enough—everyone in the playgroup had decided to skip their next meeting in favor of the annual Santa Comes to Town event at Doubles, which was slated for the following Tuesday.

In the meantime, Lily needed to come up with another idea for Rebecca, and for inspiration she decided to go out shopping with Will. Despite the interminable crowds and unhelpful sales staff, Lily happened to enjoy shopping for Christmas presents. First on her list was Robert, and for him she planned to go to Loro Piano, the überexpensive Italian clothes shop that specialized in cashmere socks, scarves, and slippers, leather gloves and jackets, and understatedly chic separates for men and women. When she got there, at around 4:00 p.m. on a Friday, the store was crowded beyond capacity. After selecting a quilted vest, she beat her way to the back to the till to pay for her purchase.

"So book me a seaweed wrap and manicure and pedicure for tomorrow afternoon at five," the man waiting in line in front of her was saying when she joined the queue. Lily knew she'd heard the voice—light Spanish accent, full of machismo—before, but she couldn't quite place him. He slid his BlackBerry back into his jacket pocket for less than a minute and then pulled out another phone, this one thin and sleek with gold-rimmed buttons, and dialed a new number.

"*Mi amour,* we're still on for Per Se tomorrow night, no?" he asked. "I'll swing by and pick you up at seven thirty." Lily could hear a high-pitched woman's voice squawking through the minuscule phone's speaker. "No, because I'll be coming directly from the Tennis Club. . . . No, because I'm getting a, *um,* sports massage there at five. . . . *Mi cara,* I must go. See you tomorrow." *Click.*

As the man paid for the leather jacket in his arms, Lily processed the information she had gleaned from his phone calls. The Tennis Club was the men-only Fifth Avenue bastion of the Manhattan gentry to which Robert belonged. *So what the hell were they doing offering seaweed wraps and manicures?* Robert had never mentioned anything about there being a spa at his club, but come to think of it, his fingernails and toenails always seemed buffed and trimmed, and once she could have sworn he was wearing a clear coat of gloss on them. I'll be damned, she thought. The Tennis Club has a secret spa in it. Lily couldn't think of a more perfect story for Thursday Trends.

Of course, there was one pitfall: Robert was likely to catch some heat from her article once it was published. His friends would probably give him a hard time, and the club leadership might even come down on him and put him on probation for a while, but if she didn't tell him about what she was working on, then at least he would be able to deny knowing anything about it before it was published. How could the club's board members punish him for something he knew nothing about? It would be difficult, but she'd have to keep her article a secret from Robert until the piece came out. Once it did, they could deal with the fallout together. Surely, if Robert knew what the situation was, he would want her to go after the story.

Feeling chipper and excited, Lily headed to Hermès to buy Josephine a scarf. She had decided to give her the soaps and candles she'd gotten from Snow at Verushka's party as a hostess gift once they were in St. Barths, but Lily still needed to find something appropriate (and generous) for her mother-in-law for Christmas. An Hermès scarf would fit the bill and, considering all the time she would be spending with Josephine over the holidays, it seemed like a good investment of Lily's hard-earned cash.

Next she headed west to Bergdorf Goodman, where she picked up a heather green cashmere turtleneck she had found on deep discount (there was a tiny hole near the hem on the back of the sweater) for her mother, a Ralph Lauren button-down shirt for her father, and a gray wool scarf with a paisley-printed silk lining on one side for her brother. Matthew, who was married with two children and working in Nashville for a midsized advertising firm, didn't expect a gift from her this year, but she wanted him to know she was thinking of him. For Robert's only sibling, his younger sister, Colette, Lily had ordered a canvas duffle bag monogrammed with her initials from J. Crew, but Lily also decided last minute to pick up a set of Lancôme lip glosses for her and a set of makeup brushes for Matthew's wife, Beth, on the basement beauty level.

Then she ran across the street to FAO Schwarz and stocked up on Thomas the Tank Engine paraphernalia for Matthew's twin three-year-old sons. For Will she bought a wooden train with removable stacking blocks. Her last stop of the day was Fauchon, the French chocolatier on Park Avenue, where she bought a box of truffles for Robert's father. After that it was time to go home and start wrapping everyone's gifts.

At the apartment, she dashed off a quick e-mail to Rebecca about the Tennis Club idea and then wrote out cards for each of the gifts she had purchased.

On her mother's card she wrote,

Hope you don't mind the little hole in the back. It was on sale. It's a medium. You haven't gained any more weight have you?? It's okay if you have. Grandmas are supposed to be chubby . . .

All my love, Lily

On her father's card she wrote,

Can't wait to spend some quality time with you very soon. Biggest kiss!!!

All my love, Lily

Then the phone rang, interrupting her gift wrapping. It was Rebecca, who wanted to know how Lily planned to scout out the piece.

"I could sneak into the club undercover, as a spa technician or a caterer?" she suggested.

"But you'd need to find some on-the-record sources as well."

"That's a problem. They've kicked out long-standing members for lesser offenses."

"Well, what about one of those guys who's been kicked out? Or someone who didn't get in?"

"Three of my husband's friends from his old firm were black-balled from the club when they applied for membership," she said, realizing that they might talk to her on the record if they were harboring a big enough grudge.

"Call them. And if you do sneak into the Tennis Club and get caught, we're disavowing all knowledge of you."

"I understand the terms of the assignment," Lily laughed, and hung up.

Rushing to finish wrapping the Christmas presents before Will woke up, she scrawled out the rest of the cards and divided the gifts into two separate bags—one for her family and one for Robert's.

The following day Jacinta arrived at the apartment to take care of Will while Lily got a jump on her Tennis Club espionage. The week before Christmas was sure to be a busy time there, and Lily wanted to make use of some of the inevitable craziness. The night before she had devised a plan to infiltrate the club as a spa technician. But to do that, she needed to look the part. Most of the facialists and masseuses she'd encountered at other spas around the city were from Eastern Europe or Russia, but if she posed as one of them, she'd be easily caught out. After much consideration she finally decided that she had the best chance of winging it as a Latina.

Pulling on an oversized T-shirt, a pair of still-too-tight jeans, and old tennis shoes, she doused herself in perfume, slicked on some bright pink lipstick, gelled her hair back into a tight bun, and stuck a pair of large gold hoops in her ears.

"Ta-da!" she said, stepping into the living room to show Jacinta her disguise.

"Not bad, *mamita,* but something's missing," Jacinta said, tapping a finger on her upper lip. She went to the front hall closet and retrieved her beloved blue and gray Yankees jacket. "You wanna look Puerto Rican? You gotta wear this," she said, tossing Lily the jacket.

"Thanks," Lily said, squeezing her babysitter in an embrace. "Wish me luck."

"You mean *buena suerta,*" Jacinta winked. "You gonna knock 'em dead, *mamita.*"

In a mirror in the lobby of her building, Lily appraised her appearance. As long as she didn't run into Robert or any of his friends, she'd have no trouble passing as a spa worker.

She was right. The Tennis Club's doorman, dressed in a navy overcoat, cap, and white gloves, helped her push her way through the revolving door, which was so heavy it nearly negated the need for a no-women policy—it alone would have been enough to keep them out. Once inside, she walked across the hunter green lobby toward the brass reception sign, her sneakers squeaking on the plush carpeting.

"*Hola,*" she said. "*Busco el espa?*"

"Hablas inglés?" asked the man behind the old walnut desk.

She shook her head. "*Yo soy una assistente en el spa,*" she announced, thankful for Jacinta's last-minute vocabulary primer.

"*Hmmm.* The spa didn't," he mumbled, frowning down at a large plastic binder. He wasn't expecting anyone, and she saw him reaching toward the phone.

"I do seaweed wrap," she blurted out in English, trying her best to sound like Jacinta. "*Soy nueva,*" she shrugged impishly.

Pointing to the plastic name tag clipped to his navy suit, he warned, "Make sure they issue you one of these."

Lily nodded and entered one of the velvet-lined elevators, avoiding making eye contact with the attendant as he pressed an unmarked button. They were whisked upward to the unknown floor, where the door opened onto a large wood-paneled suite. Lily stepped forward, taking in the big picture windows overlooking Fifth Avenue, a six-foot-high granite fireplace, and two large green velvet sofas. The air, scented lightly with rosewood and the smell of burning embers, lent the room the feel of a majestic Norman château, and she half expected to find a snifter of calvados in the mirror-backed open bar.

Tiptoeing toward one of the wingback chairs next to the fireplace, she spotted a pile of service menus. With one of those, she'd have the hard evidence needed to prove the spa existed, and her heart quickened in anticipation of landing such a prize. But just as Lily was about to slip into the pocket of her puffy jacket one of the cream-colored engraved booklets, a stocky blond-haired woman dressed in clinical whites yelled at her in a thick Eastern European accent, "Doze menus are not for de staff. We have dem printed out on compuder paper if you wand to become familiar wid de suite of services we offer."

Lily regretfully dropped the booklet. She'd have to pick it up later when no one was watching.

"Come wid me," the blond woman said, stepping out of the doorway to reveal a long corridor. "I'll get you into a uniform and den you can help Alisa wid her five o'clock seaweed wrap."

"*Si, bueno*," Lily nodded, following the woman down the hall to a room lined with shelves crowded with piles of freshly washed linens and giant plastic tubs of body lotions, oils, and other spa staples.

The woman regarded her so sternly that for a moment Lily thought she was caught out. She motioned for Lily to turn around in a circle.

Once Lily had, she said, "You'll do. Some of de patrons like a larger backside."

What the . . . ?

She handed Lily a white button-down uniform and a pair of terry-cloth slippers. "Tomorrow I expect you to wear de shoes de agency send to you, but today you can wear deese."

"*Gracias.*"

"Elisa is waiding for you in room five," the woman said frostily before leaving Lily in the locker room.

Peeling off her clothes with lightning speed, Lily changed into the uniform (a surprisingly snug fit) and searched the room for useful evidence. In less than thirty seconds she had pocketed one of the engraved menus, a washcloth embroidered with "The Spa at the Tennis Club, New York," a small sandalwood-scented soap stamped with the club's emblem, and the biggest score of all: a copy of that week's appointment bookings. She had the name, membership number, and service requested for each of the spa's patrons. *Bingo.*

Then she hightailed it into room five, where another blonde, this one as sinewy as the other was sturdy, was prepping the room for a client. The top buttons of her uniform had popped open, revealing the top of a red lace bra.

"You're late," Elisa said, and then exited the room on a pair of white platform heels.

Oh my God, are those stripper shoes? Lily was beginning to realize that the spa had more than one reason for wanting to remain a secret.

When she returned, she was followed by a tall man in a plush terry cloth robe who Lily instantly recognized as the man in the cash-register line at Loro Piano. As Lily stood gaping at him from the corner of the room, he undid the belt of his robe, dropped it to the floor and climbed onto the tin-foil-and-cellophane-covered table.

"So Mr. de Santos, we do the seaweed wrap for you today, yes?" Elisa asked.

Mr. de Santos? Not Alejandro de Santos, Kate's husband? Lily couldn't believe that she was staring down at the hairy thighs and uncircumcised, sluglike penis of her friend's husband. *Oh, shit.* How was she supposed to keep her composure now? And how would she ever face Kate again?

Trying to avert her eyes as much as possible, Lily helped Elisa rub a citrus-scented exfoliating cream all over Alejandro's legs and arms—luckily Elisa was intent on commandeering the more sensitive torso areas. When he finally flipped over onto his stomach, Lily felt a rush of relief, but only a few minutes later she was once again confronted with his nakedness as she and Elisa showered the exfoliant's granules off of his hairy body. It was a disgusting job, but Lily hadn't realized how gross it was until he got an erection during the final body massage and Elisa mouthed the words

"Out, now" to Lily, effectively dismissing her from the room.

As soon as Lily closed the door behind her, she bolted for the changing room and gathered her belongings in one of the spa's canvas bags. Then she found the stairs and ran down them and out the back entrance as fast as she could. It was only when she was a few blocks away from the club that she allowed herself to slow down.

"*Dios mio*," she wheezed, her lungs burning from the fast sprint. "This is going to be my best story yet."

Chapter 21

Exactly one week later Lily found herself on the same stretch of New York sidewalk, this time looking nothing like the Latina spa worker who had slipped between the Tennis Club's gilded doors. The *Sentinel* had run her story on its secret spa that morning, and within hours CNN, NPR, and Gawker had all picked up on the piece, elevating her fluffy exposé to national news. She'd also gotten a call from a reporter from Page Six, which was planning on writing an item about her tomorrow.

Who's not a top girl now, Umberta?

To celebrate the occasion, she had booked a last-minute appointment for a blow-out at Ernesto's salon, and as a result was looking glossy-maned and chic in her Chloe boots and a sharply tailored princess coat when she arrived in the ruby-drenched lobby of the Doubles Club.

"Over here," called one of the photographers on duty. It was the Grecian-nosed boy who'd been sent from Patrick McMullan's stable to photograph Lexi Foster's birthday party.

"It's Chaz, right?" Lily asked, hoisting a velvet-romper-clad Will on her hip.

"Oh, that's great. Just like that," he said, snapping a half a dozen photos. "Gorgeous!"

Lily had to admit, it felt great being in the spotlight again. At the birthday party Chaz hadn't even bothered taking a photo of her. Now he knew her name.

After grabbing a pair of felt reindeer ears and a stuffed dog toy for Will, Lily meandered through the bar and descended farther into the club, where she spotted Robert and Josephine at one of the round tables near the dance floor. She had been hoping that Josephine would be late so she'd have a chance to talk to Robert about the article, which she had decided not to warn him about so he would be able to tell the club's board members that he had nothing to do with the piece if they questioned him. In other words, she wanted him to have plausible deniability.

"Hi, honey," she said, passing the baby to his father. Will wrapped his plump arms around Robert's neck and squealed joyfully, head-butting him in the neck. "Have you all been here long?" Lily asked.

She caught Josephine rolling her eyes.

"Not really," Robert said, not making eye contact. "Should we go take a photo with Santa, since the line's not that bad?" he asked his mother.

Lily unbuttoned her coat and laid it down along with her purse on the seat next to Robert's. It was clear that he was angry at her—probably someone had said something to him about the article—but that didn't excuse his rudeness. And there was no way she was going to let him take their Christmas photo without her. But by the time she caught up with Robert and Josephine at the picture platform, they were already arranged on the bench next to Santa.

"Wait for me," Lily told the photographer and stepped behind the bench.

"Oh dear, do you mind if we take a few of just us?" Josephine asked.

Lily glared at Robert, willing him to stand up for her, but his only reply was a slightly apologetic smirk. As she watched her mother-in-law smile warmly for the photographer's lens, Lily was tempted to grab her child from Josephine's bony chicken-skinny arms and wedge her bottom onto the bench next to the benevolent Santa, but then she realized that doing so would only make her seem childish and petty. *Let her have the damn picture if that's what she wants.*

"I think we got next year's Christmas card," Josephine trilled merrily as she got up from the bench.

Lily took her spot on the bench and the bemused photographer took another set of photos. When Lily, Robert, and Will returned to the table, Josephine announced her intention to use the powder room and minced her way across the tiny square of a dance floor toward the restrooms.

"I can't believe you let her kick me out of my own child's Christmas photo," Lily hissed across the table at Robert. She handed Will a crumbly butter cookie.

"Don't get started with me today. I'm hardly in the mood." He glared at her for a few seconds and then added, "Your article in the paper this morning?"

"Yes?"

"Why on earth didn't you tell me about it? I showed up at the club this morning looking like an ass. Everyone knew about it except me."

"I know, but it will be fine. I purposefully left you in the dark so you could deny knowing anything."

"The president called me into his office. The board voted unanimously to expel me. They even put my father on probation."

"Are you serious?"

Robert stared at her, annoyed.

"But they can't do that. You didn't know anything about the article. It wasn't your fault. Didn't you tell them that?"

"And look like the kind of husband who has zero knowledge of what his wife is up to? Lily, for *fucking* sake, how could you have thought this wasn't going to get me in trouble?"

"I don't know. I just didn't."

"Didn't think? That's obvious," he scoffed. "I'm sure this was a big story for you, but I can't believe you didn't think about the consequences. Those guys that you quoted, they're totally fucked. Not only is the Tennis Club blackballing them for life, but their applications at the Racquet Club and the River Club have been pulled."

"Does that mean that you won't be able to join those other clubs either?"

"I don't know," he said, and sighed. "Mom says she knows the president of the River Club pretty well. She's gonna make a big donation, but it's no guarantee."

"So it's Mamma and her money to the rescue once again, huh? Thank goodness you have one more reason to keep kissing her ass."

"Don't you dare talk about her like that," he spat back at her, throwing down his napkin.

"Oh, and she can say whatever she likes about me? Need I remind you that she once called me a *hillbilly*?"

"You know what? This time it isn't about her. It's about you and what you've done to fuck things up. The last thing you should be doing is dragging my mother into this, when she's the one who's going to have to clean up the mess you made. If anything, you should be showing a little gratitude right about now." Robert shut his mouth as if he was afraid to say anything else and leaned back in his chair. After a long silent pause he said, "You never admit it when you're wrong, do you?"

"I said I was sorry," she said.

Robert got up from the table and handed Will back to her. "I'm going to say hello to Tom Howard," he announced crisply. She watched him cross the room toward his mother and Morgan's gray haired, pinstripe-clad father.

A few days earlier Robert had mentioned that Mr. Howard, a founding partner of International Investment Partners of Greenwich, commonly known as IIPG, was considering recommending him for a job. Although Lily didn't relish the idea of having her family's financial well-being attached to anything Morgan had influence over, she was anxious for Robert to rejoin the working world. Maybe then he'd stop spending almost every night with his mother and start spending more time where he belonged, at home with her and the baby.

Stranded alone with Will at her table, Lily accepted a glass of wine from the waiter and took off the reindeer-ear headband she had donned earlier. Robert was never going to forgive her for getting him kicked out of his beloved club, she brooded. He was so angry, even angrier than he was that day in the parking lot when she failed to share his exuberance for the new Porsche. Once again, Josephine had played the situation perfectly and had made herself out to be the hero, while Lily came off as the selfish wife. How had she let this happen to her, again?

She began to gather her things—Lily couldn't take the festive atmosphere much longer—but just as she had slipped on her coat she spotted Verushka making a beeline toward her from across the dance floor. She looked mad.

"Why haven't you returned any of my calls?" Verushka huffed, crossing her bangle-covered arms, the gold spheres jangling noisily.

"You've been calling me?"

"Three times since this morning! Mind if I sit down?"

"Please," Lily said, pulling out a chair for her. "Christmas cookie?" she asked, offering her a small red plastic plate.

Verushka shook her head and grasped Lily's hands.

Here it comes.

"Darling, I have the best news."

"You do?"

"Jerry read your story about our shopping night and your *fab-u-lous* piece this morning. Don't tell anyone but those anti-Semites at the Tennis Club rejected his application. Anyway, he thinks you're an *amaaazing* writer. He's asked one of his staff at *Townhouse* to write a feature about you," she said. *Townhouse*, the society magazine that appeared magically in the lobbies of New York's better East Side buildings, was considered a must-read in certain circles. Every month it featured a different It girl or power couple inside its pages. "He wants you on the cover."

"But Verushka—"

"Consider it my little thank-you." She winked and then got up from the table. "Peppy Brown is going to call you to set up the shoot, and then one of the editors will call you to set up the interview."

It was great news that Verushka's husband wanted to put her on the cover of *Townhouse*, but considering how angry Robert was at her, she wasn't sure how he was going to respond to the news. Feeling even more overwhelmed than before, Lily got up from the table. She found Robert in the bar talking with an older woman Lily hadn't met before, and although she could tell Robert didn't want her to come anywhere near them, she had to let him know that she was leaving.

"I'm so sorry to interrupt," she said to the woman, whose face was preternaturally smooth for her age; she had cheeks as plump as a Dutch milkmaid's. "I have an awful headache, Robert. Can I give you the ticket for the stroller or do you want me to take Will home?"

"You can take Will," he said quickly, refusing to make eye contact.

Lily managed to get the baby in his stroller and into the elevator without any major waterworks from either Will or her. But as she turned the stroller off of Fifth in the direction of Madison Avenue, she felt her eyes begin to prickle. She'd messed up big time, and the only person she had to blame was herself. Robert was right, she hadn't thought about the consequences of her doing that piece. *Would this be the straw that broke the camel's back? Could he really leave me over this?* Rifling through her bag for a packet of tissues, she heard a pair of footsteps clomp up behind her and a hand on her shoulder.

"Wait a second." The cold winter air blew Robert's suit jacket open and his silk tie over his shoulder.

"What are you doing out here without your coat? You're going to catch a cold," Lily said, her nose red and stuffy. She wiped away a tear.

Grabbing her at the elbows he pulled her into him and held her gaze. "I just want you to know that I love you. I think that what you did was stupid and reckless but I still love you. Just promise me you'll keep me informed about what you're working on. If it's something that's going to affect our lives, I should know about it."

"Oh, Robert, I promise. Never again. You have my word," she said, the relief flooding her voice with tremors. "I never meant to get you kicked out. I never imagined that would happen."

"I know you didn't, which is why you should have told me. The article you wrote has caused a huge scandal. You have no idea."

"But where's their sense of humor?"

"Lily, these people don't have one."

"Then why would you want to belong there anyway?"

"*Uhh,* I don't know, maybe because the most powerful men in the city dine there on a regular basis or possibly because my great-grandfather was a charter member?" he said sarcastically. "Lily, I thought you understood that I don't go to the club because I'm a nut for racquet sports. To tell you the truth, if I never played another game of squash I couldn't care less."

"So then why are you so mad about getting kicked out?"

"Because the guys that I was playing with are incredibly well connected. Any one of them could have helped me land a good job or at least an introductory interview."

"Robert, I'm so sorry. I honestly didn't think it would come to this."

He shook his head and sighed. "I know you didn't."

"You're still mad."

"I'll get over it," he said softly, shivering in the cold wind. "Wait here while I get my coat. Okay?"

Lily watched as her husband dashed back inside the Sherry-Netherland to get his coat, turning her attention to the windows of Crate & Barrel as he disappeared around the corner. Peering inside the shop's windows at the tinsel wreaths and tables set for Christmas dinner, she felt flush with holiday spirit.

Robert really did love her.

And she was going to be on the cover of *Townhouse*.

Chapter 22

The following Monday, Lily got a call from Peppy Brown, the middle-aged sittings editor of *Townhouse* magazine. Lily had heard rumors that Peppy was a ridiculous snob—she'd once axed a layout when she found out the subject lived in a rental apartment—and spoke with an affected British accent meant to cover up her Alabama drawl and blue-collar roots.

As expected, Peppy took no time letting Lily know who was in charge: "We'll be there on Wednesday at noon," she said. Make sure your apartment is spotless and that the caterers include some vegetarian options. Serena Bass does a nice roasted-fennel salad that the crew likes very much."

Gulping at the thought of having to shell out for an expensive catered lunch, Lily stammered, "And how many members of the crew are there?"

"Eight, give or take a few."

"This won't be too short notice to get Serena Bass to do the catering?"

"Just tell whomever you speak with that it's for us. They'll make the exception," Peppy said, and then, after doling out a few more directions, bade Lily a very curt good-bye.

Dashing into the bathroom where Robert was preparing to shave, Lily finally told him about the *Townhouse* article. Over the weekend things between them had thawed considerably, and she felt confident that he would be equally excited about her cover shoot.

Except, he wasn't. "Aren't you supposed to be a member of the press?" he asked pointedly.

"Yes, and?"

"I'm just wondering if you want to present yourself as a socialite when you've basically spent the past couple months making fun of them in your articles."

"My articles don't make fun of socialites."

Robert picked up his razor and began to run it down his upper lip. "Could'a fooled me," he said, a little caustically.

"You know, I thought you would be happy for me." Lily sat down on the lid of the toilet.

"Hey, I'm just looking out for your interests. Don't get mad at me if something you *want* to do isn't something you *should* do."

"But I've already said yes."

"You can always tell them that you've changed your mind."

"But I don't want to. I want to do this."

He paused, his razor halfway between his ear and his chin, and shot her a look in the mirror.

"And I think it's something I *should* do," she said, mocking his admonishing tone. "I don't see how upping my profile a little could harm my career. If anything, it makes me look more like an insider."

"Okay then, Lily. Whatever you want." Robert washed his razor under the sink, toweled off the rest of the shaving cream, and walked out of the bathroom.

Lily followed him into their bedroom, and after watching him put on a new suit and tie (probably one of the Armani ones he had picked up with Josephine), she asked him what he was doing that day that required him to be so well dressed.

"I'm having lunch with Tom Howard, Morgan's father. I think

he's going to offer me that position at IIPG soon," he said, striding out of the bedroom.

Lily stood rooted in her spot. *Did Robert just say that he was close to getting hired by Morgan's father?* On the one hand, she was thrilled that Robert was finally close to landing a job, but on the other hand, *did the job have to be with IIPG?* The fund was practically a family business. Besides Mr. Howard, Morgan's husband, Christian, and her sister, CeCe Howard, worked there. If Robert started working for IIPG, Lily would have to take every snooty look and abrasive comment Morgan dished her way with a smile. Still, it was better than the alternative of them having to give up their apartment because they couldn't make the mortgage. And if working for the fund made Robert happy, well then, she had no choice but to support him in any way she could. That was her job as his wife, right?

After rousing Will from his crib, she changed his diaper and bundled him into a snowsuit. She was tempted to skip her morning workout, but there were less than two weeks left before she was due to bare her thighs on a beach in St. Barths, and at this point she couldn't afford to miss a morning sweat session. Even though she'd been pleased to note in the mirror that morning that her stomach had lost most of its Doughboy flabbiness and her upper arms were finally showing some tone, she also realized that what passed for fit in most corners of the globe wasn't going to turn any heads on the beaches of St. Barths. Of course, Lily knew the best that she could hope for at this point was a body that wouldn't incite any incidents of mass vomiting.

Halfway through her power walk, Lily's mother called her on her cell phone. After filling Margaret in on the news of her *Sentinel* article and the upcoming photo shoot, her mother asked, "Is *Townhouse* like *Vogue?*"

"No, it's more like *Town & Country,* but it's just in New York and they give it away for free," she said.

Dead air.

"A lot of important people read it, though."

"Oh, I'm sure," her mother responded, adopting the same voice Lily had once heard her use at Kroger's when one of the grocery store workers tried to sell her a packet of frozen soy burgers.

"Anyway, I'm really excited about it," Lily explained.

"Is Robert excited about it, too?"

"Oh yes. He thinks it's great," Lily lied. Their conversation that morning had made it clear that he was less than thrilled about it.

"Well, I was just calling to tell you that we received the Christmas presents you sent."

"You did? No peeking, okay?"

"I remember how much work you used to put into the presents you made for your father and me," she laughed. "You'd spend weeks collecting wildflowers in the woods behind our house, and then you'd dry them in between the pages of your books. You'd make these gorgeous little collages, and once you glued the flowers on to a picture frame you made in art class. I still have that somewhere."

"You're so good about holding on to things."

"It's a little easier when you have an attic and basement instead of a few measly closets' worth of storage space. What y'all pay for that apartment I'll never understand," her mother sighed. "Anyway, congratulations on getting the cover of—what's that magazine called again?—*Penthouse*?"

"Mom, *Penthouse* is a porn magazine. The magazine I'm going to be in is called *Townhouse*."

"Oh, Lordy, ain't that confusing?" Margaret remarked before wishing Lily a good day.

Allowing her mind to wander to the upcoming photo shoot, Lily continued her walk through the snow-covered park. Beneath the icicle laden branches, she envisioned a portrait of herself curled up on the living room's damask sofa, the high sheen of her life on languid display.

Chapter 23

It was at half past noon on Wednesday afternoon when Peppy Brown, dressed in head-to-toe peach tweed Chanel, arrived at Lily's door with a coterie of *Townhouse* interns, a hairstylist, makeup artist, and wardrobe consultant.

Lucas, the Australian-born hairstylist in black leather pants, was the first to lay hands on Lily. Rolling a small black case over the doorjamb to her bedroom he announced in his Down Under twang that they had a lot of work to do. He sat Lily down on a chair in the middle of the bathroom, and while the others hovered over their roasted fennel salads and grilled polenta squares, he snipped three inches off of the bottom of her hair and touched up her roots with some blond highlights. Although she was happy with the cut, the styling reminded her a bit of Josephine's bob. That Peppy Brown approved of the transformation was of little consolation.

Still, had Lily been predisposed to throwing public tantrums, there was no time for fretting. Two hours had passed since Lucas began his coiffing, and Lily still needed to be made up and dressed. Not wasting any more time, Fatima, a gorgeous, generously built black makeup artist, marched into the bathroom and smeared a blob of foundation over her face. After dusting her cheeks with an opalescent apricot blush, she applied lipstick, multiple coats of mascara, and three shades of eye shadow. Then, as the photographer scouted the house for locations, the stylist and Peppy showed Lily her wardrobe options, eventually talking her into a nearly neon shift and helping her pile on about two hundred thousand dollars' worth of gold necklaces and cuff bracelets on loan from Verdura. ("Can I keep it?" she couldn't help but snort.)

The photographer took a couple rolls of Lily giving Will a bath and of them playing on the braided black and cream rug in the nursery. Midway through the third roll, Robert appeared bearing an armful of flowers for Lily and his apologies for not being there from the start of the shoot. "I was stuck in an interview and there was no way I could make an early exit," he explained in the bedroom while she was changing into a lamé cocktail dress.

"It's okay," she said. "I've been having so much fun I barely noticed you weren't here."

He kissed the tip of her nose. "You look gorgeous, by the way."

The photographer set up the next shot in the dining room, where Lily wrapped a floral apron around her waist and pretended to feed Will a dinner of mashed carrots. Then she changed once again into a long black gown from Monique Lhuillier. Another three rolls of Lily on the couch, on the Persian rug, and by the fireplace and the photo shoot was over. By 10:00 p.m. everyone except for Lucas had packed up and left.

As Robert put an overtired Will to bed, Lily helped Lucas finish packing up his case. "I hope you like your hair," he said. "I know it's a big change, but a woman like you needs to present herself in a certain way."

"What do you mean?"

"Polish is everything."

"What am I, a brass knocker?" she joked.

"I'm serious, babe. In this town, it's not enough to be beautiful and down to earth. Nature is for the parks, not the ballroom."

Lily smiled at Lucas. She could tell he was trying to level with her, hairdresser to socialite or whatever she was these days.

Out in the hall, as they waited together for the elevator, Lucas said, "Call me when you have something big and important to attend." He handed her his card.

"Will do."

"Because you really shouldn't be trying to style your hair by yourself," he added.

As the elevator door closed, Lily swallowed the lump in her throat.

Chapter 24

Josephine had decided on a Czarist Russia theme for this year's Christmas party. The tree, a fourteen-foot Scotch pine, was bedecked in gold-trimmed red velvet ribbon, grapefruit-sized glass spheres, and gilded ornaments that were meant to look like Fabergé eggs. A brown mink throw was draped across the two eighteenth-century sofas and the usual bibelots on display, a collection of heirloom Limoges boxes and a rainbow of Lalique crystal fishes had been replaced with Russian icons and a nativity scene. On the marquetry coffee table a silver tray held a half dozen crystal champagne flutes and shot glasses, an open bottle of Dom Pérignon and another of Grey Goose vodka in a cylinder of ice. Next to it, a kilo tin of Beluga caviar was nestled on a bed of shaved ice, and three small silver bowls held chopped egg white, onion, crème fraîche, and lemon. There were warm blinis and toast points stacked on a porcelain plate rimmed in purple enamel and a half a dozen tiny spoons made out of mother-of-pearl piled on a monogrammed linen napkin.

Josephine's live-in maid took Lily's and Robert's coats and murmured in broken English that Josephine and Edward would be joining them soon. In the living room, they found Robert's sister, Colette, curled up on the sofa drinking a glass of champagne and chatting into her mobile. She said good-bye, or rather, "ex-oh-ex-oh" to her friend and jumped up to give Lily a hug, nearly spilling champagne on the baby's head.

"Oops, silly me," she said, catching a small amount of the liquid before it dribbled off her chin and onto her dress, a barely-there dash of ecru chiffon. Colette obviously wasn't on her first glass.

"Can I hold this scrumptious little guy?" she pleaded, holding her arms out for Will.

Lily handed the baby over slowly. "Please be careful."

"Oh, don't worry. I've been around tons of babies," Colette soothed, holding Will high above her head.

Brushing past his sister on the way to the tree, Robert barked, "Hey, don't drop him," and distributed the gifts they had brought under the tree while Lily kept an eye on Colette and Will.

"Donnes moi le bebé," Josephine said throatily as she entered the living room, her arms outstretched just as Colette's had been moments before. Josephine, who was dressed in a midnight blue cocktail suit and a coordinating diamond and sapphire parure, peeled a giggling Will from Colette's arms and started chanting a French lullaby in the baby's ear. Edward, trailing not far behind his wife, sat down next to Robert on the couch and heaped a generous tablespoon of caviar onto a blin.

"Hello, Mr. Bartholomew," Lily said, smiling graciously and taking a seat next to her father-in-law. "Merry Christmas."

"Indeed." He smiled as he poured her a glass of the Dom Pérignon.

Everyone drank and nibbled on the caviar as Josephine related the five-star details from her and Edward's recent travels through Spain and Switzerland, Japan and New Zealand.

Pouncing on a lull in the Josephine-dominated conversation, Lily announced, "I was photographed for the cover of *Townhouse*."

"That insipid little magazine?" Josephine sneered.

"Weren't you on the cover of it once?" Edward said. Lily caught a glimpse of glee on the old man's face.

Josephine snorted indelicately. "Years ago, dear. They had different standards then."

Lily shot a look across the room at Robert, who cleared his throat and readied the room for his own announcement. "I have some exciting news," he said.

"*Qu'est-ce que c'est, cherie?*" Josephine asked, flashing a diamond-flanked sapphire as she smoothed down the side of her chignon.

"I got a job at IIPG. I'm going to be selling their new fund." He raised his glass. "A toast. To you, Mom and Dad, for your unwavering support of Lily and me." Robert stood up and walked toward his mother.

That's what he calls unwavering support? Doesn't he remember what happened at the Four Seasons when my water broke?

"Bravo, Robert!" Josephine clapped, rising from her high-backed chair to press a rouged cheek against both sides of her son's face.

Lily, who was upset that Robert hadn't shared the news of his job offer with her in private before announcing it to his whole family, looked over to where Will was sitting on Colette's lap sucking on a madeleine. Catching Lily's attention, Colette jerked her head in the direction of her bedroom. "You. Go. First," she mouthed.

A few minutes later, Colette stumbled into her bedroom and found Lily lying facedown on her canopied bed. She shook Lily's calf roughly and said, "I suggest we stay in here for the remainder of the evening, because," and then, in an imperious voice meant to sound like Jospehine's, sang, "tonight, we celebrate for Robert."

"Did she just say that?" Lily lifted her head off the bedspread.

"*Mais oui.* My darling, we are so proud of you," she said, handing over Will and opening a window. "Where are my cigarettes?" she muttered, searching through her desk drawers.

"Hey, little guy," Lily said to her son. She sat him down on the floor and helped him practice standing.

Colette lit a cigarette with an etched gold lighter and took a long drag. "Don't worry, I'm blowing all the smoke out the window," she said after registering Lily's disapproving stare. "Doesn't it piss you off how much Robert kisses up to her?"

"Sure it does, but what am I supposed to do? Wave my hands and say, 'Hey, Robert, remember me? Your wife? The woman who gave birth to your child after twenty-four hours of hard labor? The woman who makes your dinner from scratch every night? The woman who—" Lily stopped herself short.

"What?" Colette demanded, blowing smoke out of her nose.

"No, I can't say it. It's too vulgar," she said, blushing.

"You're no fun," Colette teased, poking her with the toe of her Gucci stiletto.

"Besides, it's been a while since I've done *that*," Lily joked.

"Well maybe if you did *that* more often, he'd have toasted you tonight!" Colette giggled, snuffing out her cigarette on the windowsill.

They heard a rap on the door. "Girls, I know you're in there," said Edward. Colette jumped up and let him inside. "Can't say I blame you for wanting to hide out in here, but it's present opening time and—"

"Okay, Dad, we're coming," Colette said, and she and Lily followed Edward back into the living room.

"Colette, how many times do I have to tell you that it's considered rude to just up and leave a party," Josephine scowled as she walked over to the tree. She retrieved a small oblong box and handed it to Robert. "This is from your father and me."

Robert ripped the paper off and tore off the top of the box, flinging it aside. Inside was a leather watch roll, which he quickly prized open. "It's the Franck Muller I wanted!" he exclaimed, getting up to air-kiss his mother yet again. "How did you know this was the one I wanted?" he asked, sliding the six-figure watch onto his wrist.

Lily caught Colette's eye and stuck her finger in her mouth.

"Is something caught in your throat?" Josephine asked Lily primly.

"*Mmm*, yes, I think I have a bit of blin . . ." Lily coughed, then took a large sip of champagne. Robert gave her a quizzical look, and Lily clutched her throat daintily.

The present opening continued. Josephine received a red coral necklace with a diamond and gold clasp, plus a new fur coat, from Edward, who received a humidor and a few boxes of Cuban cigars from Josephine. Besides his watch, Robert got a leather desk set from Scully & Scully, the Loro Piano vest from Lily, and a pair of Lacoste white tennis shirts from his sister. Colette received from her parents a diamond cross necklace from Tiffany's and a quilted Chanel purse from her parents.

Then Josephine opened another gift with the same wrapping paper Lily had used to wrap her mother's present. "To Mom," Josephine announced, reading the name on the envelope. "Guess that's me?" She sliced open the card with a red-lacquered nail and read the note that was meant for Lily's mother. Pursing her lips, she tore open the package and pulled out the cashmere sweater.

"Oh hell," Lily croaked, trying to figure out how Josephine ended up with her mother's sweater and what exactly she had written on the card. Something about being a fat grandmother and the hole in the sweater, she remembered. Panicking, she looked over to Robert, who was admiring his watch, and then to the tree. Where were the other gifts? Out of the corner of her eye she saw Edward lifting up a pair of socks and a package of golf balls, and met her father-in-law's watery blue stare.

"I look forward to spending more time with you, too," he said uneasily.

Lily nodded sheepishly. She'd managed to insult her mother-in-law and hit on her father-in-law in one go and on Christmas Eve, no less. *Bravo me.*

Not wishing to draw any more attention to herself, Lily quietly opened the first present that Colette—who had ended up with her brother's scarf—had brought over to her. It was an antique pedal car for Will. She opened five more gifts from Josephine for her son:

two outfits from Papo D'Anjou; a set of imported baby bubble bath and lotion in cut crystal bottles (*because crystal is so safe to have around babies*); a Steiff bear; and a MacBook Pro computer.

"It's never too early to start familiarizing them with technology, dear," Josephine said when Lily opened up the laptop.

"But Mom, you don't even have an e-mail account," Colette snorted.

"Feel free to use that one yourself until Will's ready for it," Edward added.

"Maybe I will," Lily said, smiling at Edward. "I have to admit that this one is even nicer than the one I've been using."

At the bottom of the heap of Will's presents, Lily finally found a gift for herself, a heavy gift bag with a couple of scrunched up pieces of tissue barely concealing its contents. Beneath the paper she found a package of engraved stationery from Mrs. John L. Strong plus a book on manners from etiquette guru Emily Post. The note taped to the cover of the book read,

SO IMPORTANT TO KNOW HOW TO
WRITE A GOOD THANK-YOU NOTE.

XX, JOSEPHINE

Lily thanked Robert's mother, who gave her the same smile she did after she scolded Lily for drinking her champagne in the town car, and then opened a package from Colette containing two designer T-shirts and a studded-leather belt. Her last gift was a Chanel handbag that was identical to the one Josephine had given her daughter. "Thank you," Lily said again to Josephine, this time with some real enthusiasm. The purse was classic and chic, not to mention very expensive.

"Don't thank me, my dear. That's from your husband."

Lily checked the card that was attached to the present and it indeed read, "To Lily. Love, Robert." It was clearly written by a woman, probably the shop girl at Chanel or Greyson, Josephine's assistant. "Oh, then thank *you*," she said, turning to look at Robert, a saccharine smile plastered across her face.

(*The bastard didn't even buy my Christmas gift himself.*)

"You're welcome, sweetie," he smiled from across the room, clueless to Lily's inner fury. Lily poured herself another glass of bubbly and sank a soupçon farther into the fur-covered couch.

Chapter 25

The first thing Lily did on Christmas morning was take two Tylenols for her massive champagne-and-vodka-induced hangover. Then, after the medication had a chance to work its magic and she no longer felt like she was drowning in her own toxicity, she called her parents. They had just finished opening gifts (unlike the Bartholomews, they opened presents on Christmas Day rather than Christmas Eve) and were thrilled with the ones Lily had sent. She quickly decided that there was no point in explaining the mix-up. Then, when there was no further reason to postpone it, she broke the news about Robert's new job.

"I suppose this means you won't be moving back home any time soon," her mother sniffled.

"That was never going to happen."

"And why on earth not?" her mother asked.

Again Lily was in the position of not wanting to hurt her mother's feelings. She couldn't tell her what she really thought, that Nashville, as much as it had to offer, was ultimately a small, sweet town compared to New York City, or that the prospect of living just miles from her parents, as much as she loved them, was hardly appealing. She wasn't sure she belonged in New York, but she was certain that she didn't want to go back to Nashville. To do so would be like going full circle, and she wasn't ready to close that gap, at least not yet. "This is where we live. Our friends are here," Lily finally sighed.

"But you could get used to living here," her mother pressed. "It's great for young families. For what you pay for that apartment, you could have a nice home with a big lawn. The private schools are great; we have nice restaurants, parks, shopping. Your brother and his wife have a wonderful quality of life. They're very happy."

"I'm sure they are, but there's no point even discussing it now that Robert has found a job in New York. If we move anywhere, it'll be to Greenwich." Mentioning Greenwich was a big mistake. Lily spent the rest of the call telling her mother everything she knew about the land of hedge funds and lower taxes.

Later on that afternoon she and Robert started packing for St. Barths. Dusting off their old suitcases, which hadn't been used in over a year, she folded her clothes in leaves of tissue paper, wedging in the crevices of her bag a collection of shoes, belts, scarves, costume jewelry, and toiletries. But even with all the extra accessories, Will's bag ended up weighing more than hers did. Between his shoes and clothes, the stacks of diapers and beach essentials, Lily could barely close the suitcase. Seeing Lily struggle with the bag's zipper, Robert quipped, "You know, they have babies in St. Barths, too."

"Oh, really?" Lily said sarcastically as she piled in the extra toys and baby sunblock in multiple SPFs. It was a ridiculous amount of stuff for a weeklong beach vacation, but she didn't want to get stuck buying thirty-dollar packs of diapers. Apparently everything cost almost three times as much on the island.

The following morning, Lily, Robert, and Will took a cab to JFK and met Josephine, Edward, and Collette near the check-in counters. They were already snapping at each other—Josephine was upset that Edward had refused to charter a plane to take them directly to St. Barths— and by the time they boarded the plane Lily felt grateful that she, Robert, and Will were sandwiched together in the economy cabin while the rest of the family bickered over warm nuts in First Class. "Thank God we're at the back of the bus," Robert winked as they found their seats on the airplane.

Lily dozed with Will asleep in her arms for most of the flight from New York to St. Martin. But once they got to the Caribbean Island's airport and had to claim their luggage and recheck it with the airline that ran the hourly shuttles between St. Martin and St. Barths, chaos erupted all over again. The baggage claim area was clogged with sweaty tourists, all equally anxious to move on to their final destinations, and a group of island women, dressed in vibrantly colored muumuus and heaps of gold jewelry, were moving slowly throughout the crowd, hawking their woven handbags and other Caribbean kitsch to the novice travelers. A light breeze filtered through the open windows that did little to reduce the stifling heat and humidity.

Just as Lily was contemplating sitting down on the dirty linoleum floor, their bags appeared—all fifteen of them. Robert flagged down a porter to help them with the luggage, but there were just too many pieces and everyone, with the exception of Josephine, who claimed that carrying her overstuffed Hermès Birkin was as much strain as her back could take, ended up having to cart at least one suitcase. Lily lifted Will's duffel bag and slung its strap over her shoulder. Then she grabbed her suitcase with her left hand and Will and his diaper bag with her right. Stumbling on her way to the check-in counter, she almost fell and would have squashed the baby and fallen on her face if not for the quick reflexes of an airline worker. In the rush to get to the next plane, none of the Bartholomews seemed to notice her near tumble.

The next plane was a small, probably decades-old twin-engine aircraft with ripped vinyl-covered seating and a funky odor. The flight lasted less than twenty minutes, but it was so bumpy and hot that it felt like an hour. Will, who Lily had never seen produce one drop of perspiration, sweated so much he soaked through his clothes, and when the plane landed, nose-diving onto a narrow strip between the beach and a green mountain cliff, she nearly vomited from fear.

Once on the ground, Lily began to feel much better. As Robert and Edward signed for their rental cars and left to install the baby seat in the back of one, Lily and Will joined Colette and Josephine for an espresso at the open-air cafeteria at the airport. The coffee was strong and hot—as good as any Parisian café's—and there was a cool breeze coming off the ocean. Gazing out at a pair of windsurfers traversing the sparkling blue ocean, Lily sighed contentedly. "I love it here already," she said.

"*Ahh*, to be on vacation is good, *n'est-ce pas?*" Josephine sighed, taking a sip of her coffee.

"When *aren't* you on vacation," Colette snorted. Lily hid a smirk behind her espresso cup.

Josephine gasped and quickly rose from her chair. "I'm going to find your father," she said tersely, throwing a handful of euros on the table.

Robert found Lily and Colette nursing their second cups of coffee in the café. "Let's go," he said, clapping his hands. He hoisted Will up on his shoulders and picked up his diaper bag. "*Chop, chop.*"

They all piled into the rented open-topped Jeep and drove along the long chain of beach clubs, outdoor cafés, and chic little clothing boutiques that formed the waterfront. At a glass-front bakery Robert stopped the car and bought a selection of sandwich baguettes, a bottle of rosé, and a box of chocolates. Back on the road they passed a group of teenagers making the daily pilgrimage to the beach and a family of four eating ice-cream cones. Then Robert turned the car onto a side street leading them up into the mountains and past a series of private gated villas. Eventually they reached the Bartholomews' villa, which overlooked St. Jean, a sandy cove dotted with small, exclusive beach resorts.

The one-story stucco house was painted white and surrounded by banana trees, hibiscus, frangipani, and bougainvillea. The honeyed scent of the exotic flowers wafted through the front door into the living room, decorated minimally yet comfortably with cushy white canvas sofas and chairs and a wet bar already stocked with drinks and snacks. Each of the three bedrooms featured a king-sized bed draped in white mosquito net, a bathroom en suite, and a private patio. Situated at the back of the villa was an expansive deck outfitted with lounge chairs, a teakwood table, and three massive sun umbrellas, as well as a bean-shaped swimming pool with one infinity edge. Robert had warned Lily not to expect anything too luxurious, but if this was "a bit rustic," she'd shudder to think how the Bartholomews would describe her grandparents' old cabin in the Smoky Mountains.

Lily unpacked her suitcase, assembled Will's travel crib, and after feeding the baby a bottle of formula and a handful of Cheerios, put him down for his nap. Kicking off her sneakers, she flopped down on the mattress next to Robert, who had fallen onto the bed immediately upon arrival.

"Honey, the baby's asleep." She traced a large circle on his back.

"*Mmmh?*" he groaned, turning over on his side to face Lily.

"Do you want to, *umm*, make love?" she asked, wishing she was the sort of woman who could initiate sex or talk dirty without feeling silly and self-conscious.

"Okay," he said, unbuttoning his shirt.

Lily unbuttoned her blouse and shimmied out of her jeans. It had been months since she and Robert had made love. Part of the problem was that they both ended up going to bed at different times. Either Lily was up late writing or Robert was out networking, and they weren't the kind of couple that would have spontaneous middle-of-the-night sex sessions, at least not anymore. Lily once tried to wake Robert up with a blow job after reading an article entitled "Rev Up Your Sex Life Tonight." But just as she was about to open the front flap of his boxer shorts, he flipped over, kneeing her in the nose and throwing her off balance. She ended up half naked on the bedroom floor, nursing a banged-up nose and a bruised tailbone.

Climbing under the white duvet, Robert pulled her toward him so she could feel his erect penis pressing into her. He ran his palms along her ass and snaked his fingers inside her Cosabella thong. He stripped them down to her knees with one hand, while the other unhooked her bra. She felt his mouth on her nipple, sucking and biting it gently as he fingered her rhythmically. Then, to Lily's surprise because he hadn't done this in ages, his head went lower. With his fingers he spread her open and with only the tip of his tongue he began to trace small circles on her clit, slowly increasing the pressure until she was highly aroused.

"How does that feel?" he whispered.

"Like heaven," Lily whispered back, and before she knew it she was moaning and shuddering. Sayonara vaginal-dryness issues. She hadn't been this wet in ages. Robert finished stripping off her panties and flipped her onto her stomach, pushing himself between her legs, the roughness of his movements jarring her, making her gasp with pleasure. She had to bite her lip to keep from crying out. He rolled her onto her back, holding her hips in the air so her legs extended just past her head, and pounded into her. She pushed back with each thrust, trying unsuccessfully to remember the last time sex had felt *this* incredible. Finally Robert came, pulling out right before he ejaculated. He pumped his penis, shooting a milky pool of come into her belly button and between her breasts.

"That was great," he said, kissing Lily on the lips and collarbone and handing her a wad of tissues. She watched him bounce off the bed and walk into the bathroom, his legs as sinewy as the first time she'd seen them in their postcoital, naked glory. As he washed himself off in the sink, she cleaned off the mess on her belly and searched the sheets for her damp underwear, then smoothed the duvet into a wrinkleless plane of Pratesi linen. (Josephine had once left a note indicating that it was Lily's responsibility—not the staff's—to remake the bed if she and Robert chose to "rumple the bed sheets" midday.)

After changing into her lemon yellow bathing suit and a thigh-skimming white cotton tunic, she snaked her head around the crack in the bathroom door. "I'm going out by the pool."

Robert was on the toilet and smiled up at her. "Okay, honey, see you out there."

Stepping out on to the pool deck, Lily sighed contentedly. The hot afternoon sun beamed down on her face. In the distance she could see white-capped waves crashing against a rock at the outer edge of the cove. She laid a towel on one of the chaise longues and pulled off her tunic.

"Hey there," Colette said, plopping down in the chair next to Lily's.

Her triangle-topped string bikini made Lily feel matronly in her bathing suit. "God I hate you," she said, squinting at Colette in the sunlight. "You have not one ounce of body fat."

"I'm sure you didn't either when you were my age," Colette replied, popping a potato chip in her mouth.

"If you're trying to be nice, try harder," laughed Lily, snatching a chip from between Colette's fingers and lying down on her chair.

"Maybe you're the one who should be trying harder," Colette taunted, stealing the chip back.

"She's right, dear," clucked Josephine as she clicked by on a pair of Christian Dior mules. She was wearing a wide-brimmed straw hat and a black bikini. Lily gulped at the sight of Josephine's stomach, which was just as taut as her daughter's.

Is that a six-pack?

Colette rolled her eyes at her mother.

"I've lost thirty pounds," Lily declared before she could stop herself.

"Good for you. You can tell," smiled Josephine. "I don't know how you girls do it—gaining and losing all that weight. Must be awful on the body, no?"

"Well I can tell you it hasn't been easy, and next time . . ."

"In my day we didn't gain so much. You never heard of girls putting on fifty, sixty pounds," tsked Josephine. "I put on seventeen pounds when I was carrying Robert and nineteen with Colette. You really don't need to put on more than that; the rest is just fat," she said, leaning back in her chair and crossing one long leg over another.

"Well, I'm sure you're right. I certainly wouldn't advise anyone to do what I did. But I didn't set out at the beginning of my pregnancy to get fat. It just happened."

"Oh, please. That's ridiculous. No one gets fat for no reason. You ate too much. It's quite simple. I think this is why we have an obesity epidemic in the United States. People sit in their cars stuffing their faces with hamburgers and milk shakes and then say, 'Oh no, how did I get to be so fat?' There's a word for that kind of behavior: gluttony."

Lily opened her mouth to say something in her defense, but what could she possibly argue? It was true that she had eaten too much while pregnant, and it was also true—this she now realized with foreboding clarity—that she was not like Josephine and Colette: she had not been born with their superior genetics, their sylphlike bodies and easy grace. For her, these things did not come naturally. Imagining their little poolside tableaux as a sophisticated, adult version of the old Sesame Street vignette, the one in which an unseen chorus implores the audience to pick the thing that "is not like the others," Lily knew it was she that did not belong. Despite all her efforts, this could never change.

Standing up from her chaise, the sun suddenly too hot on her shoulders, she plunged headfirst into the pool. Remaining underwater as long as she could, Lily allowed her form to rise to the surface only when her lungs burned and her brain fried with panic.

"There's my girl," Robert said as soon as her ears cleared the water. "I thought I was going to have to jump in there and save you."

Oh, but you still do.

She swam to the edge of the pool where he sat crouched and grinning and let him help her out of the water.

Chapter 26

According to the sheet that had been slipped underneath Robert and Lily's door while they had been taking their afternoon "nap," everyone was expected to be ready to leave for dinner that evening at exactly 8:30 p.m. The dinner reservations were not until 9:15 p.m., but the restaurant, located in the Hotel Carl Gustaf, was on the other side of the island. Lily had read in one of the guide books that St. Barths was only eight miles long and much less wide, so she couldn't understand why they had to set out forty-five minutes in advance for what must be a five- to ten-minute journey. But the reason was abundantly clear when they hit gridlock in front of the Tom Beach Hotel in the village of St. Jean. Still, she didn't mind being stuck in the traffic; it gave her a chance to study what the other women were wearing as well as scan the windows of the clothes shops, which at 9:00 p.m. were doing a surprisingly brisk business. In one window she spotted a mushroom brown tunic with turquoise embroidery around the plunging neckline. A rope-and-leather belt hung loosely around the mannequin's hips, giving the dress some shape.

"Look," she pointed out of the Jeep's window. "Can we go there tomorrow?"

"Sure," Robert said, patting Lily on the knee. "You see something you like?"

"*Uh-huh,*" she replied. Her attention had moved on to a woman in a white bandeau top that was so tight you could make out not only the size of her nipples, but the shade of her areolas as well.

Despite their early departure, they arrived five minutes late for dinner, which was unacceptable according to the maître d' of the restaurant, a short man with thin lips and large ears. He began making a fuss, but Josephine breathed something in French in one of his mammoth hairy ears, and he promptly led them all to a circular table overlooking the outdoor pool and harbor. Dozens of yachts and mega yachts were moored there, and the lights that had been strung on the masts and hulls of the boats twinkled up into the sky.

Lily took a seat in one of the table's rattan chairs and surveyed the packed dining room. Every table was draped in perfect white cotton cloths, set with heavy porcelain plates and silverware and commandeered by impeccably dressed patrons, their gold watches and diamond earrings twinkling in the candlelight. Lily detected someone playing the piano near the old dark-wood bar, but the restaurant remained so blissfully hushed that even the chiming of wineglasses three tables over, or the gentle splashing of the water on the edge of the pool, could be heard.

A waiter handed Lily a leather-bound menu, and she began to scan the hand-calligraphed list of appetizers. Everything was in French. She knew enough of the language to muddle through a weekend in Paris, but not enough to decipher the restaurant's haute cuisine offerings.

"Excuse me, I'd like a menu in English, *s'il vous plait*," Lily asked the maître d' politely.

"We do not have any available, Madame," he responded curtly and circled around the table to where Edward was inspecting the wine list. "Would you like to speak with the sommelier, Monsieur?" he asked.

Edward nodded, and the sommelier promptly appeared. "Could you tell me about this one?" he asked, pointing his finger at the list.

As the sommelier summarized the distinct attributes of the wine, a white Burgundy from the Loire district of France, Robert leaned over and whispered to Lily, "You can figure it out, right?"

"There are a few tricky words, but I guess I can work around them," she said, although the truth was that nothing made sense and she was going to have to make her selection by playing eeny-meeny-miny-moe.

The sommelier returned with the wine and poured an ounce of it into a glass, swirling it around the bowl and handing it to Edward for approval.

"Delicious," Edward pronounced, and the sommelier handed the bottle to a waiter who went around the table pouring everyone a glass.

Once he was done pouring, the waiter took Josephine's and Colette's orders before turning to Lily. "*Et pour vous, Madame?*" he asked, cocking his head to the side. "*Vous avez choisi?*" he repeated slowly, mockingly.

"I'll have the *asperges blancs* to start, but I'm debating between the *andouillettes* and the *Rillons* for the *plat principal*," she stalled, choosing the two least expensive choices for her main course. "*Lequel des deux vous preferez?*"

"*Ah, ça c'est facile, pour moi, j'adore les andouillettes*," he said in his rapid fire argot. "It is a specialty of *la maison*."

Snapping shut her menu, Lily smiled up at the waiter. "Sounds wonderful. I'll have that, then." She took a sip of the wine and turned her attention back to the marvelous view of the marina.

The white asparagus, which had arrived at the table drenched in a thick white sauce that had already congealed around the edges of the plate, turned out to be a poor choice. As Lily tried to rescue the tender stalks from underneath the blanket of béchamel, she listened to Josephine's animated retelling of an unfortunate incident involving a newly separated couple who were in St. Barths on the same yacht, but each with different partners. The yacht, *Shore Bliss*, was currently occupied by its joint owners, Jack and Sandra

Forthright, plus their two lovers (he had taken up with the owner of a chain of trendy clothing boutiques and she with a handsome Upper East Side dermatologist who was about to launch his own skincare line) and their two twenty-something daughters.

The Forthrights were in the midst of a very nasty, very public divorce (Page Six wrote about them at least once a month) and neither would agree to give up what had become their annual family trip to St. Barths. At the last minute their lawyers drew up a deal for the couple to share the yacht, splitting the staff down the middle and designating which bedrooms each would occupy. The agreement, a reportedly forty-page document, stipulated when Mr. and Mrs. Forthright could take their meals on board and how many guests they were each allowed to have as well as when each was allowed to use the screening room, game room, sun deck, and the various toys—which Lily came to learn meant speedboats, Jet Skis and the like—on the vessel. Apparently the detailed agreement hadn't been able to prevent whatever argument erupted yesterday, because Mrs. Forthright had been seen screaming hysterically and throwing armfuls of men's clothing off the side of the deck. Obviously, it was all anyone on the tiny island could talk about.

Lily's first course was whisked away and replaced by another dish, which turned out to be a coupling of sausages garnished with a peppery watercress salad. Slicing off the tail end of one of the sausages, she deposited the hot, fatty piece of meat in her mouth.

Josephine eyed Lily's plate over the cluster of votive candles in the center of the table and inquired, "Do you like your andouillettes?"

"They're delicious, thank you. And how is yours?" Josephine's Dover sole, which Lily had noted cost over a hundred euros, came on a silver charger and was garnished with a cheesecloth-wrapped lemon half and a pat of butter that had been molded into the shape of a rose and dusted with gold.

"The sole here is incredible. It's really the only thing to order. Though I must say that I'm impressed you chose the tripe," Josephine smirked, lifting her wineglass by the stem. "I didn't know you had such an adventurous palate."

Lily had been tested enough times by Josephine—and now the Killer Socialites—to know when to play it cool. Lily tipped her wineglass back at Josephine and smiled gamely. "I have eaten andouillettes since I was a little girl."

"Oh dear," she chuckled, a malevolent spark in her eye. "I don't think chitlins really count. Andouillettes are a very refined food, nothing like what you're accustomed to eating with your cheese grits and corn bread. Though darling, *I* found the menu at your wedding charming. No matter what everyone else said."

Robert gave his mother a warning look. "Well, as long as *you* enjoyed yourself, Mother, that's the most important thing," he said sarcastically.

"Ha!" Edward laughed, gurgling his wine at the back of his mouth. "Good one, son."

Robert grabbed Lily's knee under the table and squeezed. Later that night, they had sex again.

Chapter 27

The following morning, after drinking fresh-pressed orange juice and espressos at a coffee shop in the town of St. Jean, Lily and Robert took Will to the beach, where they rented a pair of umbrella-shaded chairs on the stretch of white sand in front of La Plage, a lively restaurant that was famous for blaring dance music and serving stiff drinks from 11:00 a.m. onward. After undressing Will and slathering him in SPF 50+ sunblock, Robert carried him down to the edge of the turquoise water. As Lily watched her husband dip Will's foot into the tide and then quickly lift him back up again, her son's pale little body convulsing with laughter, she felt a wave of relief wash over her. Robert was finally taking an active interest in their son. For months he had picked up the baby only when asked and rarely took the initiative to change his diaper or make him a bottle; now he barely wanted to put him down.

One plastic cup of rosé and two hours in the sun later, Lily was desperate to escape the *thud-thud-thud* of the club music the restaurant's disc jockey was playing for the bronzed and beautiful pre-lunch crowd. Passing a table of women in matching Missoni bikinis, Lily went into the bathroom to change back into her shorts and T-shirt and then returned to take Will off Robert's hands. "I'm going to go explore," she said, hoisting the baby on to her hip. "If you need to find me, I'll be in one of the shops we passed last night."

"Aren't you forgetting something?" he asked, squinting into the sun.

She patted the front of her shorts. "I have my credit card."

"I meant a smooch for your ever-loving husband," he said, readying his lips for a kiss.

She leaned over and granted him one. "How could I have forgotten!" She laughed and headed back onto the main road, where the boutique in which she had spotted the mushroom-colored tunic dress was located. As she walked into the shop a woman with leathery brown skin, pin-thin legs, and a pile of dyed-blond hair arranged in a nestlike bundle on the top of her head asked if she could be of any help. When Lily said "*Non, merci,*" the woman retreated to the stool behind the cash register and lit a cigarette. "I'm here if you change your mind," she said in her French-accented English and picked a piece of tobacco from between her yellow teeth.

After a few minutes of browsing, Lily found the dress she liked and took it into the dressing room in the back of the store. She closed the plywood door and put Will down on the floor so she could strip down to her underwear. But as she was about to slip the dress on over her head, Will pushed open the door and began to speed crawl into the middle of the shop. Lily covered her breasts with one arm and dashed out after him, scooping Will up with her other arm just as a trio of men sitting in the leather chairs in the middle of the store turned to ogle her. *Was that Christian?* She lifted her son to cover her bare chest and spun around. Standing in front of her was none other than Morgan.

"What on earth are you doing?" she exclaimed, the vein on her forehead popping out a bit farther than usual.

"Just doing a little shopping," Lily squawked while backing up in the direction of the dressing rooms. "Let me get some clothes on and I'll be right out."

Lily managed to block Will from crawling out again while she changed back into her own clothes. Then he pooped (*fantastic timing!*), and she had to change his diaper. So by the time she and the baby exited the dressing room (both fully dressed), Morgan was posing in front of the three-way mirror in the same dress Lily had in her hands, plus the leather hip belt and coordinating shoes.

"So, I heard you guys are coming to my parents' New Year's party?" Morgan said.

Curious, I only detect a moderate level of hate and distrust today.

She looked over her skeletal shoulder to inspect the rear view of the tunic ensemble in the mirror. "Christian, what do you think of this one?" she called over to her husband.

"Beautiful," he said without glancing up from his BlackBerry. Morgan disappeared back into the dressing room and Christian walked over to Lily. Bowing slightly he took her hand up to his mouth, this time letting his lips graze the top of her fingers.

"And how is our fair Lily today?"

"A little less fair, I suppose. The sun out there is brutal. Look," she said, showing him the pale patch of skin under her watch, the Tank Francaise Robert had given her for her birthday more than two years ago.

Christian took her wrist, his thumb grazing its underside in such a way that caused the little hairs on the back of Lily's neck to stand up. "Are there any other tan lines you'd like to show me?" he asked.

"Didn't you just see all of them?" she asked, blushing all over again as she took her wrist away. *Is he out of his mind? His wife is a world-renowned beauty and high-society poster child, not to mention standing within earshot, and my husband is about to become his business partner.*

"There's actually something I wanted to talk to you about."

"Oh, really?"

"I've been handling the art investments for IIPG for the last five years. We've built up an impressive collection of important works.

Why not do a story on it? *Architectural Digest, Elle Decor,* and *Town & Country* want to come shoot our offices—we've built a Rothko gallery that rivals the one at the Phillips in Washington—but I'd much prefer having some exposure in the *Sentinel.* Would you consider pitching the story to your editors?"

Morgan reemerged from the dressing room wearing a pale pink minidress and floral silk espadrilles. Lily and Christian watched as she jutted out an impossibly bony hipbone. "Do you think it's too long?" she asked, hitching up the hem a couple centimeters.

"Perhaps," Christian said noncommittally and turned his attention back to Lily.

"But I'm hardly an art expert. Wouldn't you want—"

"That's not what Robert said. When we showed him around the gallery, he mentioned you have a degree in art history."

"I majored in international law. The art history was a minor," Lily corrected.

"Major, minor, what's the difference? You love art, have some passion for it, am I right?"

"Yes," she conceded. The story would be right for Thursday Trends, and art collections in offices would be an interesting topic for her to tackle. But she'd have to write the piece with attitude, poke a little fun at the pretentiousness of having a gallery worth a hundred million dollars, or whatever the value of the art was, inside a hedge fund's offices, and she definitely didn't want to get Robert into any trouble with his new bosses. Plus, it wouldn't be entirely ethical for her to do the piece. "Christian, I'd love to do it, but now that Robert is working at IIPG it would be considered unethical for me to write about the fund, even if I was just writing about your office decor. There are strict rules against that sort of thing."

"You don't have to tell anyone he's working with us, do you?"

"No, but I could get into a lot of trouble if they found out."

"Don't you think the most worthy pursuits in life are just a tad risky?"

Lily blushed, a scarlet hue spreading from her neck up to her forehead.

"Christian," Morgan called as she emerged from the dressing room with a pile of clothes under her arm. "I need your advice. Get over here now please!"

Christian rolled his eyes and leaned in a few inches closer to Lily's face. "It looks like I'm being summoned."

"It's okay, I should pay for this and get back to Robert," she said, holding up the mushroom tunic.

"There's one more thing I think you should consider before you make your decision," he said, whispering in her ear, making the little hairs on her neck stand up one more time. "Robert's new at the fund and he'll learn in time that we're all expected to bring our own special set of advantages to the table. For some of us it's our social connections that are our most valuable commodities. I see an enormous potential in your husband, but I have to tell you, not everyone does. I'm sure if you were able to bring the firm some positive publicity, the skeptics might change their minds, and we could make his position a permanent one."

"I didn't realize . . . ," Lily stammered. She took a deep breath and started over. "I didn't realize that I could be of help that way." *Was Robert only working at IIPG on a trial basis? If so, why didn't he tell me? Surely I have a right to know that kind of thing.*

She walked over to the till and handed the dress to the woman, who hadn't budged from her perch on the stool. "Two hundred euro," the woman said, and Lily reluctantly handed her a credit card. That much money for a scrap of cotton was too much, she thought guiltily as the charge went through and a machine crunched out a tiny, barely legible receipt for her to sign.

Just outside the shop, she spotted Christian smoking a cigarette. "See you on New Year's!" she chirped nervously.

He waved her over. "What I've confided in you has made you anxious, yes?" He blew a puff of smoke away from her face.

"Yes," she said quietly.

"I shouldn't have told you." He shook his head and a dark lock fell attractively over one of his eyes. "That was a mistake."

"No, it's fine, really."

"When the time is right, I'll tell Robert what he needs to know. It shouldn't come from you. And don't worry; I'll look out for him in the meantime."

"Thank you." She sighed, relieved that she wouldn't be the one who had to tell Robert that he didn't have the full support of the fund's leadership. As his wife, it wasn't really her place, was it? And if she told him now when his confidence was still so shaky, would he relapse into his depression or resent her for bearing the bad news?

As she walked away, Christian called out to her, "Think about the article. You can give me your answer on New Year's."

Four nights later on New Year's Eve, Lily found herself scrunched next to Colette in the backseat of their rented Jeep. Her nose was just inches away from Josephine's perfumed neck, and the syrupy scent was making Lily feel nauseous. She longed to dip her head between her legs, but there wasn't enough room, since Josephine had scooted her seat back as far back as possible in order to accommodate the tulle skirt of her Oscar de la Renta gown. "You have enough room back there?" Josephine had asked as she pinned Lily's calves against the car's backseat.

The traffic was worse than ever, but luckily the Howards' villa wasn't too far from the Bartholomews', and the journey took a little less than half an hour. It was another story once they reached the gated driveway, where a uniformed guard with a clipboard was checking names and waving through the cars. The people in the car in front of them apparently weren't on the list, because after ten minutes of waiting for them to move forward Edward had to back up the Jeep to let the other car pull out of the driveway. "Party crashers are such a nuisance," Josephine tutted.

Once inside the villa, Lily, Robert, Edward, and Colette made a beeline for the drinks table, leaving Josephine to her circle of

Restylane-plumped, laser-resurfaced friends. *"Yuck!"* Colette shivered as they walked away from the group. "Shoot me if I ever look like that."

Robert took two glasses of champagne from a white-jacketed bartender and handed one to his sister and the other to Lily. "Let's check this place out," he said, offering his arms to the women. Together the three of them walked the perimeter of the party and admired the view from the lodga, but then they lost Robert to a circle of men he said were IIPG investors, and soon thereafter Colette splintered off to smoke a cigarette outside.

Entering the bathroom Lily bumped into the infamous Mrs. Forthright, who was in the process of freshening her makeup. "For once, I don't care what everyone's saying. It felt good to—" she stopped talking as Lily walked in.

"I'm sorry," Lily apologized, blushing. "I'll leave."

"It's all right, honey," Mrs. Forthright said, snapping her compact shut and slipping it into a golden egg-shaped clutch. "Come on in. I'm assuming that since you're at this party you already know my whole life story."

"Not the whole story, just how you like to do your husband's laundry."

"Ex-husband," she corrected, "and you're funny." She offered her hand, which was tanned, strong, and noticeably unadorned. "Call me Sandy."

"Lily Bartholomew."

"*Mmm-hmmm,* a Bartholomew, huh?" She squinted her eyes knowingly at Lily. "You know I was about your age when, as my childhood minister used to say, I lost the path. I fell in love with a rich boy who gave me everything a girl could ever want. Big diamonds, big houses, big cars, the works," she said, ticking off each item on her fingers. "Everyone thought I had the best life, but you know what? I was miserable with a capital *M*. I'd let myself get sucked into this competitive, shallow world where all anyone cared about was where their kids went to school, what building their apartment was in, and what fund-raisers they were chairing that year. Anyway, after thirty years of marriage my husband, out of the blue, serves me with divorce papers. When I ask him why, he says it's because I've become a bitter old bitch."

"Just out of the blue? That's awful," Lily said.

Mrs. Forthright leaned back on the bathroom counter and tucked a wayward piece of blond hair behind her ear. "So I tell him, 'Of course I'm bitter. I never eat, never say what I *really* mean, never put one foot wrong.' I have this theory about women as they age. They either get fat or they get mean. It's either one or the other, and I've decided as of today, I'm gonna get fat. Screw it," she laughed.

"Good for you!" Lily clapped.

"You look like a nice girl," Mrs. Forthright said. "So I'm gonna give you the best piece of advice I've got. Don't buy into the same crap I did. You'll save yourself a lot of grief. "

"That's one of those things that falls into the category of easier said than done," Lily said.

"And yet." Mrs. Forthright raised an eyebrow and smiled. She lifted up the hem of her dress, a classy column made from pistachio-colored silk, and pushed open the bathroom door. "Enjoy the party, honey."

Back in the living room, underneath an enormous chandelier, its arms spread like crystal tentacles over the sunken living room, Lily scanned the party, sifting through the guests and waiters for Christian's face. She had been struggling with whether or not she should agree to pitch his art collection story to her editors. It was doubtlessly unethical for her to write the piece, so she would have to pass the story idea on to another reporter at the paper. However this also made her nervous because she'd have no control over the direction of the article *and* she would still be the one blamed in case it was a total catastrophe. Her only other option, as she saw it, was to wait a few weeks and then lie to Christian and tell him she had pitched the idea to her editors and that they had rejected it. How would he ever know the difference? And if she never had any intention to work on the piece, then she'd also never have to tell Rob about it. He'd surely spot the ethics problem immediately and be suspicious as to why she was even considering doing it.

She eventually found Christian standing alone near the edge of the pool. He was smoking a cigarette and looking oddly morose given the context of the evening's festivities. Reflexively she smoothed down the silk of her dress's skirt as she walked toward him.

He greeted her with an air kiss and as she leaned in, she could feel his hand, warm and soft, on a patch of bare skin at the small of her back. "Happy New Year," he said.

"And to you. What a great party!"

"Don't the Howards throw the most marvelous parties?"

Lily was startled by the acid edge in his voice, and they both gazed at the candles floating in the pool until she finally said, "I just wanted to tell you that I've decided to go ahead and pitch the art collection story to my editors."

"Superb news." He turned to face her and grasped both of her hands in his. "How about I arrange a tour of the gallery for you?"

"Okay." Lily smiled uneasily and took her hands away.

Christian took another drag from his cigarette. "There's your husband," he said, nodding across the room to where Tom Howard, wearing the self-satisfied look of an obscenely successful man, was standing next to Robert, who was bent over double, laughing. For a moment Lily felt embarrassed by her husband's obviousness, but then the moment passed as quickly as it had arrived, and she chided herself for being so disloyal.

"I should go join him. Happy New Year, again." She crossed back over the pool deck in search of Robert, who had been swallowed up by a crowd of partygoers.

Much, much later, after the clock had struck midnight and many of the evening's guests had already gone home to their villas and yachts, Robert led Lily to the lodga and kissed her. He held her long enough that she could smell the slightly sour scent of his perspiration and hear the galloping pace of his heart.

"I love you," he slurred. "I know being married to me hasn't cracked up to be everything you might've thought it would be. I know I've been an ass. But I promise, only clear skies from here on out. Things are going to get easier."

Lily wanted to believe that the worst was behind them, but in the twilight fog—she could just make out the white-capped waves crashing on the rocks below—she feared that it wasn't. Not yet.

Chapter 28

Back in New York, Lily spent the first week after the New Year unpacking suitcases and opening mail. Now that she was, according to Gawker.com, the *New York Sentinel*'s hottest new writer, every publicity firm in town wanted her at their events, each offering to send over a hired car and a designer outfit for the night in question. The following Thursday night Lily had no less than seven parties to choose from, including a shoe collection launch at the Hollywould shop in Nolita, the opening of a new furrier on the Upper East Side, a book signing at Saks Fifth Avenue, an opening night reception for a new exhibition at the Gagosian Gallery, and, finally, a private dinner (*yes, a dinner!*) celebrating the engagement of a blond girl with a questionable past and the son of a successful restaurant franchiser, neither of whom Lily had ever had occasion to meet. New York was funny that way. It mattered not who you knew, but who knew you—or, even better, who wanted to know you.

Lily tucked all the invitations into a file folder she had bought just for that purpose. Without organization, she was bound to show up on the wrong night or at the wrong place or (heaven forbid) dressed in the wrong way, and her new social butterfly lifestyle (and status) left no room for such errors. As a veteran of the scene, she instinctively knew which parties were going to attract the best crowd, serve the best drinks, offer the best goody bags, and—most importantly—garner the most press coverage, and considering all these things, she decided to kick off her Thursday night with the book signing at Saks Fifth Avenue.

The party, in honor of a *Vanity Fair* contributor who'd written a well-reviewed memoir about her disillusionment with fashion journalism, was being hosted by the daughters of an aging rocker and was close to capacity by the time Lily arrived alongside a crush of publicity firm interns. After a few minutes wandering around the gathering, she spotted Allison holding a pink-colored cocktail and sucking on a wedge of ruby-red grapefruit. Next to her stood a twenty-something girl with wide, almost startled-looking eyes, thin chestnut brown hair, and overglossed lips that peeled back to reveal a set of glassy gray teeth. The girl looked vaguely familiar, and Lily remembered seeing her in a few of the back issues of *Townhouse* that Peppy Brown had brought over for her to look through.

"Hey, babe, thought you'd never make it," Allison said, turning her back against the girl.

"I'm sorry. Jacinta kept me talking again," Lily said as she leaned in for an air kiss.

The girl stepped around Allison's body block and Lily noticed that her face and neck had been clumsily dusted in bronzing powder, probably in an attempt to hide her terrible skin. "Emily Leiberwaller, so nice to meet you," she said, offering an orange-tinted hand.

"I'm going back for a refill," Allison said to Lily before walking off in the opposite direction of the bar.

Emily let out a high-pitched laugh. "Have you read the book yet?" she inquired nervously.

"Not yet, no. But I'm looking forward to reading it. Have you read it?" Lily was asking, when Di came up behind her and dragged her by the arm to the other side of the room.

"Do you know who you were just talking to?" Di demanded as

she pulled Lily behind a six-foot-high poster of the book's cover.

"What's the big deal?" she shrugged. *What is it that everyone has against Emily,* she wondered. *So what if she's a little weird and brash? So are half the people here.*

"That," Di said, "is Emily Leiberwaller, a total social piranha. Nobody likes her. The only reason she's invited to these things is because her publicist bullies everyone into sending her an invitation."

"The poor girl."

"Don't fall for her little nice girl crap. She's a shameless party crasher. She begged me to invite her to Umberta's baby shower and even though she hardly knows Umba she showed up sans invite and made a huge scene. I had to have the security guard ask her to leave."

"But why would Emily want to go to Umberta's baby shower if she doesn't even know her?"

Di's eyes narrowed. "You should write a story about her."

"Oh, I couldn't. It would be too mean. And I don't do mean."

"You won't be saying that in a couple of weeks when she starts calling you ten times a day."

"But she doesn't even have my number."

"Yeah, but her publicist does," Di said just as they were interrupted by a photographer.

"Hey, Di and Lily, a photo?" asked Chaz.

"Give me a sec." Di swung Lily over to her other side and pointed to the side of her face still facing the camera. "This is my good side," she whispered. "We can't pose together unless I can be on this side."

Lily, who had not yet ascertained her "better side," nodded sheepishly.

"I look like a fucking drag queen from the other side," Di explained in a whisper.

Lily laughed, and then the flash popped in both their faces.

It wasn't until the following Monday, during lunch with Rebecca and Helen, that Lily saw the picture that the *New York Post* ran of her and Di talking at the book party.

"Aren't *Journal* reporters supposed to be above reading the gossip rags?" Lily asked as she spotted the broadsheet on their table at Fred's, the airy eatery on the ninth floor of Bergdorf Goodman.

"Not when it features a certain former *Journal* reporter turned, and I quote, 'sexy socialite scribe,'" Helen snickered.

"Did they really say that?" Lily asked, grabbing for the paper. Rebecca snatched it away and began reading the caption out loud:

"Perennially chic **Diana Meddling** and sexy socialite scribe **Lily Bartholomew** share a laugh at the Saks Fifth Avenue party for *Diamond Dust and All that Glitters*."

The waiter arrived at the table with their menus and a basket of bread. "Congrats on all the articles, by the way," Helen said before dipping a piece of ciabatta into the olive oil dish. "Victor has your piece on the Tennis Club's secret spa tacked up next to his monitor. Says he's starting a shrine."

Rebecca picked a hunk of focaccia out of the bread basket. "Speaking of articles, do you have any new ideas for me? Ford thinks you have terrific instincts, and he's impressed with the access you've gotten on past articles."

"Wow, he really said that?" Lily gasped, incredulous.

"Don't look so shocked. You're doing really well," Rebecca laughed. "But you're only as good as your last piece, so . . ."

Lily searched her mental database for something interesting and slightly edgy, and came up empty-handed. "I've got nothing," she shrugged.

"Nothing? Really?" Helen asked. "There's got to be a new nighttime hot spot or fitness craze you can write about?"

Lily shrugged. "None that I know of."

"How about a new It girl?" Rebecca asked.

"Besides you," Helen smirked.

"There's always someone new on the scene. How about I e-mail you later today, once I've had some time to think?"

Rebecca nodded and motioned to the waiter that they were ready to give their order.

Before their food arrived, they talked about Lily's struggle to juggle motherhood and her writing, Helen's latest disappointment in the dating arena, and the cooking class Rebecca had recently decided to enroll in. Jabbing a fork into a pesto-covered pillow of pasta, Rebecca asked, "So, Lily, go to any good parties lately?"

"They all have a way of melting into one another. Been to one, been to them all. But I must admit, I'm having fun. There's this fast-paced energy that's so intoxicating—if you're not already drunk on all the free champagne, that is. And you meet a lot of interesting characters." Lily chewed a piece of chicken. "At that book party, for example." She gestured toward the copy of the *Post* tucked in Helen's bag. "I met this girl. The word is that she hired a publicist to help her get into A-list events. A lot of girls do this, but only once they've already climbed their way to a certain stratum. Then it's the publicist's job to take you to the next level. Get you in the papers, a nice spread on your closet in *Domino* or the cover of *Quest,* for example. There's one socialite, Umberta Verragrande—"

"*Ooh,* I've heard of her," said Helen.

"She hired Paul Wilmot after she'd been asked to join the Guggenheim Museum's Artist's Ball committee. Then, voilà, there's a spread on her in *Harper's Bazaar,* and she's blogging for *New York* magazine. Coincidence? I think not. But the thing is that Emily—that's her name, Emily Leiberwaller—she isn't following these rules. She's completely jumped the gun. She hasn't paid her dues, and there's a rumor that she, through her publicist, pays the photographers under the table so they'll take her picture.

She *wants* to be an It girl, but she's not. All the real socialites despise her."

"So let me get this straight," Helen said, rolling a creamy fork of pasta. "This girl isn't promoting anything other than herself? It's not like she's got a business, like a clothing line or a shop or something?"

"She just wants to get photographed rubbing shoulders with the glitterati."

"That's the most pathetic, ridiculous thing I've ever heard," Helen said. She blew a ringlet of marigold curls out of her eye and frowned. "It's so sad."

"And perfect," Rebecca said, she popped another ravioli in her mouth.

"Perfect for what?" Lily asked.

"For your next story," Rebecca said.

"No way," Lily protested. "It's too mean."

Rebecca ignored her. "If you think about it, it's not too different from what people used to do to gain social entrée in this town."

"And what was that?" Helen asked.

"During the Golden Age, people with a lot of money but no social status would throw dinner parties for people who were socially connected but had fallen on hard times. The nouveau riche basically preyed upon the impoverished members of the old guard and used them to open doors for them. And come to think of it, all the big-time robber barons had publicists to help get the word out about their philanthropic endeavors. Although they weren't called publicists back then. What's the girl's name again? Do you know her backstory?"

"It's Emily Leiberwaller and I don't, not yet," Lily said.

"But you will?" she asked.

"No, I won't," Lily said. "I don't want to skewer this girl, okay?"

"Lily, you can do this story without skewering her. We'll be sure to say that this is common practice these days. We can point out well-regarded socialites who have used them, so there's no stigma.

This is your next story, Lily. I'm assigning it, and I want to see copy in a week," Rebecca said.

"But Rebecca—"

"This is a great story, you know it is."

"Helen?" Lily asked. "What would you do?"

"It's a tough call, Lil. I guess one argument for doing it would be that if you don't do it, someone else will. And maybe they won't be so nice about it."

"That is true," Lily acknowledged.

"So it's settled. You're doing it," Rebecca said. "Remember, copy's due in one week."

Chapter 29

Walking home from lunch at Fred's, the cold January wind whipping her in the face, Lily received a call on her cell phone. There were no pleasantries, no hello or may I speak to, before a determined voice demanded, "Are you going to Elrod's birthday thing tonight?"

Lily recognized the high-pitched voice immediately; it was the woman of the hour.

"Is this Emily Leiberwaller? Why are you calling me?" Di had predicted she would call, but Lily hadn't imagined herself worthy of having her own ("wannabe") socialite stalker. And it seemed like an incredible coincidence that Lily had just been talking about Emily and less than an hour later, she was calling her. But there was no way Emily could know about her new assignment for Thursday Trends.

"Oh, we must have a bad connection. I asked if you were going to Elrod's party tonight," Emily repeated.

Elrod Hamlin, a semisuccessful designer who frequently escorted pretty blond socialites to public functions, was celebrating his birthday as he did every year, with a private, over-the-top dinner at one of the city's chicer eateries. It was an A-list-only event, a see-and-be-seen orgy of fabulousness for the well heeled and blithely hip. Just that morning Elrod had messengered Lily an outfit to wear—a 50s-style alabaster cocktail dress from his latest collection—with a note begging her to attend.

"Yes, I think so," Lily said, although she had originally planned to skip the dinner in favor of a night home with Robert and Will. It was Robert's first day at IIPG, and she had wanted to mark the occasion with a bottle of expensive red wine and beef Wellington. She'd already set out a box of frozen puff pastry to thaw and had been looking forward to spending the afternoon searing tenderloin and sautéing mushrooms in Marsala. But considering her tight deadline, she had no choice but to postpone the dinner and spend the night dressed in alabaster shantung with Emily, the so-called social piranha, by her side.

"So why don't you come over to my place tonight at seven and then we can head uptown together," Emily suggested.

Uptown? That's not right. The dinner was being hosted *downtown* at Buddakan, the ultrahip Asian fusion restaurant that was in the meatpacking district. Elrod was commandeering the long banquet hall table in the downstairs eating area. "Don't you mean downtown?" Lily asked.

"Oh yeah, that's what I meant to say. Did I say uptown? Silly me," Emily giggled lightly, but there was something in her laugh that led Lily to believe that Emily actually had no idea where Elrod's party was happening. *And if that's true, then she's trying to use me to crash his party.*

Di was right; the girl was a shameless party crasher. Lily felt a pang of sorrow for Emily. She wanted what everyone wanted, to feel like she belonged, and Lily could relate to that, certainly. But the group Emily wanted to join would never accept her, and because she was fragile and awkward, she had no chance of surviving her swim with the sharks. Lily thought that maybe by doing this story, she could help guide Emily back to shallower, safer waters. She would encourage her to get a job, find a new group of friends and a new purpose for her life. It occurred to Lily that she could help Emily *and* get the story for Rebecca. The two were not mutually exclusive. "So listen," Lily said. "I'm not sure if you'd be interested in doing this, but my editor's asked me to pick a girl about town and write a piece about her life."

"You mean like a day in the life of a socialite?"

"Sort of."

"And you want me to be the socialite?" Emily said the word *socialite* like most people might say Olympic gold medalist or Nobel Peace Prize recipient.

"That's the idea."

"Oh my God, that would be fantastic!" she shouted, and Lily had to hold the phone away from her ear.

Lily wrapped up the conversation and jotted down Emily's address on a scrap of paper in her purse. As she walked home, she decided that Rebecca was right in that Emily's quest for a place among the gifted and glamorous said a lot about modern society—its perpetual obsession with status and the new ways of achieving it. She would write the piece as a cautionary tale, a Fitzgeraldian tragedy for contemporary times, and if she did it right, it would be her best article to date, something of which she could really be proud. She'd finally have a chance to shine a light on the world of the New York socialite, to show that it could be silly and cruel, destructive in its vapidity.

Lily arrived at what turned out to be Emily's parents' apartment at 7:00 p.m. on the dot. She had tucked a notepad and pen as well as a tape recorder in the Chanel purse Robert had given her for Christmas and she pulled all of them out as Emily, already outfitted in a long-sleeved, last season Elrod wrap dress (everyone would be dressed in *next* season's dresses, making Emily's appearance ever more conspicuous) and scuffed-up silver pumps, gave her a tour of her parents' two-bedroom abode, which looked noticeably worse for wear. The carpets needed changing—there were stained, mottled brown patches here and there—and the sofa and chair cushions frowned with overuse. Emily's room could have also used an update; its lavender walls and bubble-gum pink carpeting seemed better suited to a ten-year-old girl than a woman in her late twenties. The teddy bears lining the top of the bureau and the eyelet-trimmed heart-shaped pillows stacked on the bed were hallmarks of an adolescence better left behind.

"I was just about to put on a little bronzer before you came in," Emily said, showing Lily a pot of gold-flecked powder. "You can use some if you like."

Just then Lily had a thought. She jumped up from her perch among the pillows and stuffed animals on Emily's bed. "Can I do your makeup? We're in no rush, after all. The party won't get started for another hour."

"Would you?"

Lily stood behind Emily as the two of them gazed into the mirror. "Sure, this will be fun. Let me look at you for a sec," Lily said, turning Emily to face her. She pushed back a wisp of Emily's baby fine hair and considered her skin, which was sallow, dry in patches and oily in others. A smattering of pimples dotted her forehead and chin. Her lips were dry and cracked. "You have such beautiful eyes," Lily said.

"Really?" There was that startled stare again. It was as if she hadn't been paid a compliment by anyone in a long time.

"But why do you use so much bronzer? I think you'd look really lovely with just a little blush, here." Lily pointed to the apples of her own cheeks. "Do you have some?" she asked.

"I'm not sure. I usually just use the bronzer." Emily opened the top drawer of her bureau and rifled around in a plastic basket filled with makeup. "But I know my mom has some. I could go look in her room. You can fish around in here and look while I'm gone."

"And look for some ChapStick or something. Your lips are a little dry," Lily called after her as she picked through old mascara wands, empty pots of eye shadow, handfuls of half-used lip and eye pencils. A dusty compact held a concealer in a shade too dark for Emily's complexion; there were three bottles of eye makeup remover, five tins of Altoids, and seven tubes of lip gloss. She pulled the drawer out farther to expose a medium-sized box covered in a rose print, Laura Ashley circa 1989. "Maybe in here," she wondered aloud, lifting the box top to reveal a trio of jumbo-sized prescription bottles: Klonopin, Vicodin, and Ambien. A smaller bottle of Prozac was wedged at the front of the box. Lily quickly replaced the top, closed the drawer, and sat back down on the bed to digest what she had seen. Emily was taking an antidepressant, tranquilizers, painkillers, and sleeping pills. And by the size of those bottles, it looked like she had a serious addiction to the latter three. *How on earth did she get her hands on those? What kind of doctor prescribes those kinds of pills in that amount to someone so obviously troubled?* Sitting there on Emily's bed, Lily felt more resolved than ever to rescue the girl from herself.

"Found one," Emily sang as she returned with her mother's blush, a peach and pink duo in a round silver compact.

Lily forced herself to smile brightly. "Great, now let's get to work."

Thirty minutes later they were heading downtown to Buddhakan when Lily suddenly remembered that she was supposed to be interviewing Emily for the story. "Do you mind if I start asking you a few questions for the article?" she asked, clicking the Record button of her tape recorder. For most of the remainder of the cab ride she listened to Emily identify all the important New York girls she was "best friends" with at Brearley—a school for whose tuition, Lily would later learn, her parents took out a second mortgage on their apartment to afford. Emily's list of friends included all the usual suspects, and Lily had a hunch that the women mentioned would not be happy when they found out they were going to be associated with Emily in the *New York Sentinel* of all places.

"So what is it you do now?" Lily asked, trying to move the interview forward.

"Nothing really. I had a job with McKinsey out of college, but I hated the long hours."

"And when was that?"

"Four years ago."

"And you've done nothing since? Don't you want to *do* something with your life?"

"Well, I do *do* a lot. I'm involved in a lot of charities. In fact, you should refer to me in your article as a philanthropist. Write that down," she said, tapping her index finger on Lily's pad. There was a large callus on her knuckle.

"What's this?" Lily asked, holding Emily's hand up to the light.

"Oh, it's nothing. I take boxing at my gym sometimes."

Lily knew she was lying. And suddenly something crystallized in Lily's mind: Emily was bulimic. All the clues fell into place. The callus on her index finger (from thrusting it down her throat so she could purge), the brittle hair and horrible skin, the translucent teeth and the breath mints. Emily was popping pills and vomiting. She belonged in rehab, not at Elrod Hamil's overhyped birthday dinner.

The rest of the night Emily stuck to Lily like the double-sided tape holding her dress closed. Lily pretended not to notice Di and Morgan's dirty looks and introduced everyone to Emily as though she was her close friend. In the dim light, with her new makeup on, Emily looked like she belonged. She didn't have to ask any of the photographers to take her picture, and Elrod insisted Lily bring Emily to his upcoming fashion show. When they left the dinner at fifteen minutes to midnight, Emily told Lily she'd had the most fun of her entire life.

Chapter 30

Entitled *The Modern Girl's Guide to Social Climbing*, the article about Emily had been disquietingly easy to report. After only a few phone calls, Emily's publicist broke down and admitted that she had worked with Emily on a "consulting basis" and Emily's so-called former best friends had come forth with numerous anecdotes highlighting her obsession with social rank. Still, Lily portrayed Emily sympathetically, as nothing more than a victim of a world gone haywire with its values. She didn't include anything on her addiction issues, eating disorder, or the run-down state of her parents' apartment. The article, Lily thought, was critical of society but kind to Emily.

"What can I say? I have a soft spot for underdogs," she'd told Rebecca when she turned in the piece on Wednesday.

"Even status-seeking party crashers like Emily Leiberwaller?" Rebecca teased.

"Even them. I'm just worried that Emily won't understand that I'm condemning society, not her personally. I hope she gets that. I have this feeling that she's very . . . fragile."

"I'm sure she'll be fine," Rebecca said. "But if you're worried, you can check all the quotes with her. It's not required, but it might be a good idea in this case."

"I'll do it as soon as I get off the phone with you." Lily hung up the phone and dialed Emily's number. A half hour later, Emily had signed off on all her quotes.

The piece ran the following Thursday. Lily had barely a chance to skim the piece and leave a message on Emily's cell phone before she was due, along with Jacinta and Will and all the other mothers, babies, and nannies, at Diana Meddling's co-op on Eighty-fifth Street at nine thirty in the morning. According to Di, breakfast was the new cocktail hour. "Not unless you're serving us cocktails," Allison had quipped.

Alas, there were no cocktails, but there were plenty of mimosas on offer. Di had set up in her hunting-lodge-inspired living room a buffet of breakfast goodies, including a chef-manned egg-white omelet station and croissants flown in from Laduree in Paris by her father's jet. Even Snow, one of the most attentive waist-watchers in the bunch, had succumbed to her carb craving and was feasting on a pastry when she greeted Lily under the low-hanging deer-antler chandelier.

"Have you tried?" she asked, holding up the remaining bit of croissant, her eyes half-mast with pleasure. "Totally worth it."

"I'll get one now."

"We were just talking about you—well, about your article—before you came in," Snow said, glancing back over to the cowhide-upholstered settee where Morgan, Di, and Verushka remained huddled over their espresso cups.

"Oh, really?" Lily said blithely. "Do you want a coffee? I think I need a coffee first." She nodded in the direction of the couch, and they walked over to join the women. "Hi, everyone," Lily said when she caught them eyeing her. "Verushka, did you manage to find that bauble in the tree?"

"Oh yes. See!" Verushka giggled, setting down her espresso cup. She shook a double-wide strand of diamonds on her wrist. "Sparkly, no?"

"Very," Lily said.

"Why don't you sit down?" Di asked, motioning to a stool made out of an elephant's foot.

Did she just invite me to sit down?

"Yes, please join us," seconded Morgan.

Lily took a seat and Di continued. "We loved your piece in today's paper. Thank God someone finally did something about that girl. She's such a nuisance."

"Oh, that. Yes, well Emily's not so—"

Di leaned over and squeezed Lily's hand. "It just so happens that there's a spot open on the Save Bucharest Foundation benefit committee. Some ladies who were *going* to be on the committee aren't exactly sample size anymore," she said, shifting her gaze momentarily to Kate de Santos, who had put on a good ten pounds over the holiday break.

Rumor had it that Kate's husband had installed one of his many mistresses in their apartment while Kate and the children were celebrating Christmas with her parents in Connecticut. Upon returning to the city, Kate received an anonymous tip, cluing her in on the overnight visitor, and she apparently decided then and there that her husband had finally crossed the line. She ordered all the locks on their apartment to be changed while he was in Miami "on a deal."

Morgan picked up where Di left off. "Would you be interested in cochairing it with us?" she asked.

"Oh my goodness, yes!" Lily gushed, and then added a bit more calmly, "It's such an amazing cause. Thank you. I'll do whatever I can to help."

"We know you will. The main thing is that Ortensia de la Reina is sponsoring the event, so we all have to wear something from her spring line, which happens to be horrible, so it's going to be a sacrifice for all of us," Morgan pouted.

"Really? I was in her boutique recently and bought a couple of pieces from her resort collection, which was lovely. I'm sure it's not that bad," Lily ventured.

"Trust us, its *hidi-o*," Di grimaced. "But it's part of the deal. Also every cochair, in addition to buying two tickets, is required to secure at least two items for the silent auction. For example, we know your mother-in-law is friends with Donald Trump. Maybe she could call him up and ask him to donate a lunch date?"

"Or a guest spot on his TV show?" Verushka chimed in.

"*That* would get some high bids," Morgan added enthusiastically.

"I'm not so sure about that. Josephine is really protective of her connections, and I'm not sure how well she knows—"

"Let us know as soon as he agrees," Di interrupted.

Uncrossing her Christian Louboutin leopard-print heels, Morgan whispered, "Excuse me for a while, girls. I have to go get a closer look at Kate. I think she's pushing one forty. What would you say, Di?"

"If she's not there yet, she'll be there soon," she snickered. "She's already eaten, like, three éclairs."

Chapter 31

In early February, after canceling twice on Christian's secretary, Lily finally followed through on her promise to come in for a tour of IIPG's new art gallery. On her way over, she tried calling Robert to tell him she'd be in the building—she thought it would be fun for them to look at the paintings together—but he was in an all-day conference at a midtown hotel and couldn't be reached.

Dressed in an ecru wool pencil skirt, chocolate sweater, her Jimmy Choo boots, and princess coat, she entered the glass-front office building and rode the elevator up to the hedge fund's suite on the thirty-seventh floor. Christian's secretary, a meaty, thick-ankled woman who looked as bossy as she had sounded over the phone, marched Lily to a couch in Christian's enormous corner office and then left, shutting the door behind her.

Christian came into his office a few minutes later and seemed surprised to see Lily seated on his couch. "Lily, to what do I owe the pleasure?" he grinned, kissing her lightly on both cheeks. He sat behind his desk and motioned for her to sit in a chair closer to him.

"Your secretary scheduled a tour of the art gallery for me today. I assumed your marketing coordinator was going to be the one showing me around, but then I was brought here. Didn't she tell you I was coming?" Lily asked, confused.

Christian checked the clock on the wall. "She didn't, no," he sighed. "But lucky for you my client dinner was canceled. Why don't I give you a quick tour of the gallery, give you all the materials you need to move forward with the story, and then if you have any more questions you can ask me them over dinner." He lifted a black cashmere coat with a chinchilla collar off of the coat rack.

Lily felt awkward agreeing to have dinner with Christian, but she also didn't want to be rude to the man who was helping her husband at his work. *Think of Robert,* she told herself. *If I can become better friends with Christian, he'll be even more invested in helping him.*

Christian led her through a series of hallways to the small gallery, which featured an unfocused array of impressive pieces, everything from a luminous still life by Fantin-Latour to a swirly, vibrant Chagall. As he rattled off intriguing facts about each work, Lily soaked up the serene atmosphere, allowing herself to respond emotionally to the paintings.

Once they were done with the tour, they took the elevator down to the main lobby and hopped into a company car idling by the curb. Ten minutes later they were seated at a small table in the upstairs room of Felidia, a popular Italian restaurant off Second Avenue. Christian ordered a bottle of Barolo, and as Lily took her first sips of the wine, she decided to enjoy the evening. Robert went out all the time for dinner with his colleagues and friends.

After dinner the company car was once again waiting by the curb for them. They slipped inside the backseat, and Christian leaned forward, placing a warm hand on top of Lily's left knee as he told the driver her address. When he leaned back he let his hand move farther up her leg so it was resting on her upper thigh, his thumb just inches from her crotch. He continued their conversation about a restaurant they had both been to while in St. Barths, as though he wasn't mere inches from initiating an adulterous affair, and Lily decided to ignore his hand—*he's probably just tired and a little drunk and not even aware of where his hand* is, she told herself. A few minutes later the driver pulled up to her building.

"Well, this is me," she announced, making a move toward the door.

"Wait," he squeezed her thigh. "The driver will open the door for you."

She looked down and blushed. "Oh."

He lifted her chin with his finger and looked into her eyes. "You embarrass too easily. I see the heart of an adventurous woman in there."

She lunged toward the door, driver be damned, and hopped out of the car as fast as she could. Outside she breathed in the night air, trying to clear her mind, which felt fuzzy with alcohol. "Thank you for dinner and for the tour," she said through the open window.

"It was my pleasure," he replied.

"See you soon," she waved, feeling more than a little uneasy.

When Lily opened the door to their apartment, she found Robert in the living room hunched over a takeout container of General Tso's chicken. Will was already sleeping in his crib—Robert had dismissed Jacinta an hour ago, he said—and Lily was hit with a wave of guilt as strong as the smell of the Chinese. From time to time she had heard the working mothers at the *Journal* talk about feeling guilty for missing out on so much of their children's development, and back then Lily had thought they were being disingenuous, that deep down those mothers were actually more than happy to get away from their children for most hours of the day. Now she knew better. It was, in fact, quite possible for a woman to love her child with every ounce of her being and still need something else beyond motherhood to define her.

For Lily, this was certainly the case. While it was true that she had stumbled into her new career, once she discovered that she had a talent for lifestyle writing, it became almost an obsession.

She particularly craved the writing process; the search for clarity in her prose brought her so much joy that when she wasn't working on a story she felt comparatively irritable and morose. It would seem that the key to her happiness was work, and realizing this fact was at once thrilling and unmooring. Thrilling in that she was attempting to have it all—the elusive trinity of marriage, child, and career—and unmooring in that the very idea of prioritizing other things above her family prompted angst-ridden introspection (*Am I a bad mother? Am I selfish?*). It also created a fair degree of tension between her and Robert.

It was ironic. She had jumped back into journalism in hopes of winning back her husband's affection, but the more time she spent working, the more distance there was between them. He wanted her to be happy, but he also wanted to find a home-cooked meal and a freshly scrubbed child waiting for him when he returned from the office. And therein lay the problem: a woman can only do so much with two hands and twenty-four hours that when she chooses to pursue her own dreams, often ones that require manicured nails and networking cocktails, she can't help but drop a couple of balls at home.

Robert had certainly noticed the lack of inspiration in their recent meals. One night when they were eating pasta with commercial pesto sauce and salad from a bag, he reminisced about the broiled lamb chops, roasted rosemary potatoes, and salad with homemade Maille mustard vinaigrette she used to make for their dinners. "When my schedule slows down a bit, I'll do more cooking," she'd said, but secretly she was angered by his assumption that it was up to her to prepare a gourmet meal every night. If he wasn't happy with what she was cooking, couldn't he take the initiative to make something?

They'd also started fighting about Will and the division of labor when it came to his care. Now that she was working, Lily believed that Robert should pitch in more with the diaper changes and baths and had started imposing those duties on him. As a result, he resented her for badgering him into chores he considered maternal in nature, and she him for not having a better attitude.

One night, when they were fighting over who was going to give him a bath, Lily lost her temper and blurted out, "I just don't get it. He's your son. Don't you want to bond with him?"

"I can bond with him in other ways," he said.

She hadn't even had the strength to continue the argument.

"Fine then, he'll go without a bath tonight," she snapped.

Still, despite the added guilt and marital stress, Lily told herself she was doing the right thing. *How can I be a good mother and wife if I'm not satisfied with my life? If my happiness doesn't come first, then at least it should be balanced with everyone else's, right?*

Robert put down his chopsticks and the container of chicken. "Jacinta said you went out to dinner with someone?" he asked, patting the seat next to him on the couch.

She sat down, kissed him on the mouth and began unzipping her boots. "I was at your office today, actually," she said.

Robert picked up his beer from the coffee table and took a swig. "Oh?"

"I tried calling you, but you were at that conference. Anyway, Christian told me about IIPG's art gallery while we were in St. Barths, and I thought someone else was going to give me the tour, but I guess it's his baby and he wanted to do it. Then the next thing I know we're having dinner at Felidia," she shrugged. "I'm sorry I didn't call you. I guess I figured you would be working late again tonight."

"Was it good?" Robert asked flatly.

"The tour or the food?"

"Both. Either?"

"Well, I loved seeing the art up close like that—it's quite a collection, we should take a look at it together one day—and the food was delicious. I don't think I'll need to eat again for days."

Lily lifted herself off the couch and picked up her boots. Her feet, which had been stuck in heels for most of the day, felt tender on the hardwood floor. "I'm going to change out of these clothes. See you in bed?"

"Yep," he said, his eyes not leaving the television. "See you in there."

Chapter 32

The following day Lily had a lunch scheduled with Josephine at La Goulue, the uptown see-and-be-seen crowd's favorite French bistro on Madison Avenue. She had called Josephine on her way home from Diana's breakfast meeting to ask for her help with the Save Bucharest silent auction and was hoping that the reason why Josephine had convened the lunch was to tell her that she'd managed to get Donald Trump to agree to Lily's request.

"How's the renovation in Palm Beach going?" Lily inquired as soon as Josephine sat down, only twenty minutes late, at their front-room table.

The Bartholomews were renovating the kitchen of Bluebell Manor, and as a result Josephine was, unfortunately for Lily, in an especially sour mood that day. Josephine had just gotten off the phone with one of her girlfriends, who had gushed nonstop for forty minutes about the previous night's cocktail party in an antiques shop on Worth Avenue, and was livid that she had missed the soiree. Last summer, when the kitchen renovation had been scheduled, Josephine had decided that she didn't want to be around while the workers were streaming in and out of the house and didn't think it would be a big deal to miss a few weeks of parties. But now she was furious at herself for agreeing to a February renovation and even angrier that she hadn't been able to convince

Edward to rent another house or apartment there for the season. They were stuck in New York with nothing to do and no one to see. To Josephine, the situation was too pitiful for words. Smoothing down the lapel of her Ralph Lauren riding jacket, she griped, "Fine I imagine. But it's taking so long."

"Oh, well, I suppose that's to be expected?"

"Yes, but it's such a bore to be in New York. No one and I mean absolutely no one is here right now," she grumbled. "Aren't all your little friends going down?"

"Actually only three of the mothers in Will's playgroup are gone, and the rest are here for the moment. I'm sure some of the others would go, but they're busy with charity work," Lily said.

"Ah yes, I don't know why any of you agree to put on fund-raisers this time of year. When I was your age we had January and February off. It was so much more civilized that way. The social calendar is a complete mess these days. You have girls chairing six, seven, eight benefits. It's terribly gauche, don't you think?"

"*Um,* well, I guess things have changed a bit. There's no stigma attached to wanting to help a lot of causes," Lily said.

"Things haven't changed *that* much," Josephine snorted. "The chicest girls your age chair only one or maybe two events a year. *And* they manage to stay out of Page Six. I hope now that you seem to have *somehow* found your way into that crowd, you won't be whoring the Bartholomew name all around town."

Lily was speechless. Did Josephine really just say *whoring*? First of all, it was the most indelicate thing she'd ever heard her mother-in-law say. And second, hadn't Josephine lauded Morgan and Di, girls who chair at least five galas a year and regularly appear in the *Post*'s gossip columns?

What right does she have to decide how I can and can not use my last name?

Josephine, née Josephine Johnson of St. Louis, Missouri, was no more a Bartholomew than she was. Before she met Edward, Josephine was just another pretty, upper-class coed hoping to land a rich husband before her freewheeling campus days were over.

Lily took a sip of water and tried to rise above the situation. "I've only been asked to cochair Save Bucharest, so I guess that isn't an issue." She forced a smile. "Shall we order?"

"Yes, excellent idea. Waiter!" Josephine yelled over to their server. "How long am I expected to wait here?"

He scurried over and took Josephine's order—two truffle-oil salads and roast chicken entrées for herself and Lily.

After the waiter brought out their *salades foules*, Lily decided to broach the subject of the charity's silent auction. "Have you had a chance to call Donald about Save Bucharest?" she asked, lifting a forkful of lettuce to her lips.

"About that, Lily, I made a few calls, but nobody thought he would be interested."

"So you didn't ask him directly?"

"That's not how it's done," Josephine chuckled.

"What about Barbara Walters or Jane Fonda?" Lily asked, mentioning two of Josephine's friends that they had discussed her calling.

"It's not like you are raising money for the Princess Grace Foundation," she smirked. "I mean, Save Bucharest is kind of a B-class charity. None of my friends would want to be associated with it."

"Well, actually last year *Vogue* featured it as the 'party of the season,' so I'd say it is definitely a first-class event," Lily said stridently. She had been holding out hope that Josephine was giving her such a hard time because she had done her a favor and felt somehow justified in browbeating her a little more than usual, but now it occurred to Lily that her mother-in-law was simply having fun slapping her around without having to worry about raising Edward's or Robert's ire.

"I'm just repeating what my friends said," Josephine shrugged.

"Who did you speak with exactly?"

"Why does it matter if they're not interested?"

"Maybe they'd change their minds if they knew about all the

great architectural treasures Save Bucharest is helping to restore."

"Dear girl, these are *very* private people, and I wouldn't want you embarrassing yourself by pressuring them to do something they don't want to do," she snapped. "Now on to more interesting topics. Have I told you about the mix-up with Bisazza? They sent us the wrong tiles. . . ."

Not daring to betray an ounce of her fury, Lily pretended to listen as Josephine prattled on about her kitchen renovation and the misery of having to spend February in Manhattan. Somewhere in the middle of her ranting, it dawned on Lily that she had been running herself ragged trying to win Josephine's approval when that was never even a possibility. It didn't matter that she had scaled to the top of the social ladder in less than six months; it didn't matter that she had refashioned herself into a respected society journalist; and it certainly didn't matter that other reporters were heralding her as the next Alex Kuczynski. Josephine was committed to despising Lily no matter what.

So it was there, at their tony table in the middle of La Goulue, that Lily finally had an epiphany: She didn't want to be the kind of woman her mother-in-law would (at least in theory) be supportive of. With new eyes she watched as Josephine sliced off a sliver of the roast chicken breast and deposited it between her crimson lips. While it could be said that she was a highly polished woman— she'd figured out long ago how to paint her face and dress the part—underneath all those layers of Chantecaille face powder and designer clothes lay an insecure, deeply troubled woman.

Lily motioned to the waiter for the bill.

"You're not going to leave right now?" Josephine asked, looking up from her entrée. "You just can't leave in the middle of lunch."

"Actually, Josephine, I can," Lily responded, leaning forward and looking her mother-in-law in the eyes. "For as long as I can remember you've been making me feel like I'm not good enough to be a Bartholomew. My parents didn't belong to Belle Meade Country Club. Our name isn't on the Social Registry. I didn't go to a fancy prep school," she said, ticking each strike against her on her fingers. "But today you finally crossed the line. You can't treat me like I'm dirt. I won't take it anymore."

"Who said you were dirt?" Josephine balked.

"Why can't you just give me a break? I'm not a bad person. I've never done anything mean to you, have I? So why are you making it so hard for me? All I want to do—all I've ever wanted to do—is make your son happy. Don't you want Robert to be happy?"

Josephine looked around the room, nervous that someone might be overhearing their conversation, while Lily continued, "If you want to be miserable, fine. Be miserable. Be bitter, but give Robert and me a chance to be happy."

For once the tables had been turned, and it was Josephine who was shocked into silence. Lily grabbed her purse from the back of the chair. "Don't worry. I'll get the check," she added before depositing $130, all the cash that was in her wallet, on the table. Hopefully it was enough to cover their bill and a twenty percent tip.

Slipping into her coat, she walked out of the restaurant, the little bell on the front door jangling merrily as she swung it open. Outside it was cold and drizzling, but Lily decided to walk home anyway. She wanted to feel the raindrops on her face and the sidewalk, its concrete squares glistening wet and clean, beneath her feet.

That, and she didn't have any cab fare.

Chapter 33

As a Save Bucharest cochair, Lily was scheduled for a fitting at the Ortensia de la Reina showroom at 11:00 a.m. on the Monday after her disastrous lunch with Josephine. It was the first day the dresses would be made available for the cochairs to see, and she knew enough about the other girls' hoarding habits to snag the earliest appointment. Getting stuck with some pouf-ball monstrosity would have been considered a major stroke of bad luck, especially since Lily's debut as benefit cochair marked her real reentry into high society. Every editor and style guru in town would be noting her dress selection. A good choice could secure her a spot on the party pages of *Vogue* and *W*; a bad one, her spot *off* them.

Plus, despite the current turmoil at home, she wanted to enjoy the evening as much as possible. After walking out on her lunch with Josephine, Robert had come home from work ready to harangue her for "misbehaving" around his mother, but she refused to listen to the lecture.

"I don't want to hear it," she said. "She practically called me a whore, and I told her that she couldn't treat me that way anymore. There's only so much you can expect me to swallow from her. It's not like I was really nasty back to her, although believe me, I could have been, and it would have been totally justified."

"She called you a whore?"

"Well, not technically. She said she didn't want me to start whoring out the Bartholomew name."

"She did?" he snorted up a laugh and sighed. "Well in that case I'm glad you didn't let her get away with it. But you walked out in the middle of lunch. You should have stayed, worked through your issues," he argued.

"What issues? She's a bitch."

"Lily, for God's sake."

"She was beyond rude to me!"

"You walked out on her. If that doesn't qualify as rude, I don't know what does."

Lily had heard enough. "Look, *I'm* your wife and the mother of your child," she said, jabbing her chest with her finger. "You deal with your mother if you want to, but your first loyalty should be to me. Why do you automatically assume that I'm the one at fault?"

"I don't. But I do hold you to a higher standard. Why can't you take the high road and quit being so sensitive when it comes to issues with my mother?"

They barely spoke for the rest of the weekend. Robert slept on the living room sofa on Friday night and worked all day Saturday. For breakfast on Sunday she made him crepes, but they did little to soften the edge in his voice, the few times he did talk to her. By Monday, Lily was ready to try a more direct approach and stopped him in the foyer as he was about to leave for work. "Can't we move past this?" she asked.

Robert put his hand on the doorknob. "It's important to me that you try to get along with Mom," he replied before opening the door and leaving. "For Will's sake, if not mine."

Lily felt defeated. She'd thought that Robert's unemployment was the main source of their problems, that when he did start working again, they would be able to begin a happier chapter in their marriage. Not so. The money pressures had disappeared, but all the other issues hadn't. They still argued about Josephine and how many nights Robert spent away from home, except now his excuse was work.

She felt like crying, but instead she went into Will's nursery, which she knew would be awash in buttery morning light and the sweet smell of baby. Already awake, playing with his Fisher-Price aquarium, he grinned his gummy smile, the threads of drool pooling on his pajama top as she entered the room. She carried him into the kitchen, where she fed him his bottle and watched as he walked around the perimeter of a chair, all the way holding on for support. The morning passed quickly, and by ten Jacinta was at the door, ready to take over so that Lily could leave for her big fitting at Ortensia de la Reina's showroom in the garment district.

The showroom itself was drab and devoid of any decoration aside from a few mirrored tables and flower arrangements, but the two long racks, both full of formal dresses of varying lengths and styles, stood like an explosion of color and texture in the middle of the room. The designer's publicist, a young socialite named Kyra Kemp, had already pulled two dresses in anticipation of Lily's arrival. The first of which featured a fishtail hem (never an attractive look on those with hips wider than a fourteen-year-old boy's) while the second, a floaty mustard-colored concoction, washed her out.

"Would it be all right if I looked through the racks for something that might, *um,* suit me better?" Lily asked.

"Yeah, of course," Kyra said before disappearing into a closet.

Lily picked through the rest of the gowns, settling on two other dresses, one with tiers of eggplant-colored tulle and another hot pink one with a dramatic off-the-shoulder neckline.

"Try this one, too," Kyra said, emerging from a closet holding a silver gray satin and lace strapless gown, "It's very flattering on."

"I bet," Lily agreed, fingering the lace bodice. "I'll definitely try it on."

With the publicist's help, Lily stepped into the dress made out of tulle. Kyra buttoned up the back and then brought out a small wooden box for Lily to step on so the tailor would be able to baste up the hem of the gown if need be. "I like it, but I still want to try on the others," Lily said, checking her rear view in the mirror before stepping back off the box and shimmying into the next options, the purple and pink frocks she had chosen.

Eventually Lily settled on the gray satin and lace dress that Kyra had suggested. The other dresses were just as gorgeous, but Kyra sold her on the gown's sophisticated allure. "It does fit the winter on ice theme perfectly," Lily admitted.

"Trust me, it's *the* dress," Kyra said. "You're lucky I didn't let Morgan see it. She would have snapped it up in a heartbeat."

"Morgan's been here already?" Lily asked, astonished. She had thought hers was the first appointment that morning.

"Yeah, she was originally scheduled to come in after you, but she called me last night—I was in the middle of a date at SoHo House, for fuck's sake—and demanded that I let her in early. Can you believe she had the nerve to threaten to go to another designer if we didn't give her first pick? I mean this is after we donated a hundred thousand dollars as underwriters of the Save Bucharest Ball. Most designers give half that to sponsor a major event," Kyra griped.

"Well, that's Morgan for you," she sighed. "What can you do?"

Months ago Lily might have delighted in hearing (and spreading) any gossip about Morgan de Rambouillet, the more mean-spirited and venomous, the better. But now that she knew Morgan's life was less than perfect, that her husband was a philandering malcontent of the first order, and that Morgan's greatest accomplishment was winning the admiration of insecure acolytes, Lily was able to see her in a more forgiving light. What was Morgan but an overgrown enfant terrible, the product of a cultural ethos that favored peacocks over swans?

"Live and let live, right?" she added with a shrug.

"Maybe," Kyra smiled devilishly. "Or maybe not. Now tell me. What shoes are you planning to wear?"

Chapter 34

Lily's next duty as a Save Bucharest cochair was to host (i.e., show up at) a cocktail party in Henri Fontaine's newly renovated boutique on Madison Avenue. The company, which was now owned by a major French luxury goods conglomerate, had decided to cosponsor the Save Bucharest event in an attempt to link its name with the city's young and beautiful—its current clientele of Park Avenue dowagers being an obviously dying breed. For Lily and the other cochairs this meant that in addition to donning gowns from Ortensia de la Reina, they were invited (expected) to borrow a couple pieces from the store's catalogue of overpriced bijouterie for the pre-party and ball.

Lily's friend Liz, who had started working for Henri Fontaine a few months earlier, had e-mailed Lily in mid-February to tell her that she'd been drafted to help organize the company's in-store party preceding the Save Bucharest benefit and had noticed Lily's name on the list of social chairs. Lily was thrilled to be back in touch with Liz—they hadn't seen each other over the holiday season—and e-mailed her back saying that she was looking forward to catching up. "Wait till you hear about what I said to Josephine the other day," she wrote.

They had decided to meet in front of the Madison Avenue townhouse in which Henri Fontaine occupied the first two floors. Liz would help her pick out a few baubles to borrow for the following week's events, and then they would walk down to Serafina on Sixty-first Street for lunch.

Liz was standing outside, a few paces from the front door, smoking a cigarette, when Lily arrived. After stubbing out her cigarette, Liz quickly ushered Lily into the store, where she gave her a quick tour of the showroom before leading her up a flight of stairs and into a private room decorated with a sleek ebonized wood table, three Art Nouveau armchairs, and a gilt-edged mirror.

"Because you're one of my best friends," Liz prefaced, "I'm showing you the very best piece we have to loan out." She pulled a black velvet box out of the vault in the wall and brought it back to the desk. Opening the box, she revealed a pair of dramatic South Sea pearl and diamond chandelier earrings.

"Wow!" Lily gasped.

Liz clipped the earrings carefully on Lily's ears and took a step back. "The opalescence of the pearls and the sparkling diamonds illuminate your entire face," she said, guiding Lily to the mirror.

"Jesus, it's like I have a spotlight on my face. Can I really borrow these?"

"Of course you can, but don't you dare lose one. Beyoncé is wearing them to the Oscars in a couple weeks."

Over their pizza lunch, Lily learned that Liz was happier than she'd ever been. She'd started dating an architect who sounded kind and attentive and was taking gemology and marketing classes in the evening. Liz was planning to start designing her own line of jewelry the following year. "I'm in such a good place right now," Liz said before stuffing a wedge of pizza in her mouth.

As genuinely happy as Lily was for her friend, she couldn't help but feel a little envious. From the outside, Lily knew her life looked perfect—she had an exciting career, a spot among the Manhattan glitterati, a gorgeous baby, and a blue-chip marriage—but something was missing. And that something, she realized, was a feeling of security, not in her position in society or in her job, but in her relationship with Robert. She knew he would stay with her as long as she didn't cause any (more) problems because, well, that's the kind of man he was. Maybe he wasn't the most sensitive guy in the world, but Robert, thanks in part to his legal training, had a keen sense of what was right and wrong and always wanted to be on the side of the right. That was one of the things Lily loved most about him, yet she didn't want him to stay married to her out of a sense of obligation. She wanted him to stay because he so loved her, so enjoyed the life they had built together that the idea of them not being together would scare him to tears, the way that it did her.

The following Wednesday night a bevy of photographers from Style.com, Patrick McMullan and WireImage, greeted Lily as she entered the Henri Fontaine store dressed in a form-fitting rose-colored skirt suit and the enormous pink tourmaline and diamond ring Liz had helped her select for the party. Posing alone in front of the photographers, she suddenly longed for Robert to be standing next to her. Despite their still-frosty relations, he had originally planned on attending the party with her, but had been slammed that afternoon with a new project and wasn't able to get away. It would have done them a world of good to have a few drinks together in a fun environment, and it saddened Lily that they weren't going to have the opportunity.

Waving a small thank-you to the men and women behind the lenses, Lily escaped into the "mosh" of bodies that were clogging the first level of the boutique. After snatching a glass of champagne from one of the waiter's trays, she bumped into Allison, who looked dazzling in a vintage Alaia minidress and golden gladiator heels.

"Hey Allison, have you seen Emily Leiberwaller tonight? I invited her to this party and called her a bunch of times, but she never picked up. I'm starting to get worried. Have you seen her at any parties since my article came out. Has anyone heard from her?"

"Lily, forget about Emily, you currently have bigger problems," Allison said, gripping Lily's shoulders.

"What? What are you talking about?"

"You mean you haven't seen it yet?" she asked.

"Seen what?"

"The article in *Townhouse*? You really haven't seen it yet?"

"No, I didn't even know that it was out yet," she said, taking a sip of her champagne. With everything that had been happening in the last few weeks, she had almost completely forgotten about doing the photo shoot and interview. "Am I on the cover?"

"The cover is divine—you and Will look so cute," Allison said. "You know, most people don't even read the articles so this really isn't *that* big of a deal. It's not like you got skewered in *W* or anything—"

"Wait, are you telling me I got skewered?"

Allison took a deep breath and lowered her voice almost to a whisper. "You said that you take Will with you to as many parties as you can so you don't have to pay for babysitting."

"What's so bad about that? It's the truth," Lily laughed. "My Lord, I thought you were going to tell me something terrible."

"I don't think you realize . . . What you said makes you sound," she paused, searching for the right word. "Not rich."

"You mean poor?" Lily snorted into her champagne glass. She couldn't believe Allison was getting so worked up over something so silly.

Allison grabbed her arm. "This is serious. New York is still a town that runs on money, no matter what people say. That comment doesn't make you—or Robert—look good. People are already talking about it."

"Oh my God, Robert," Lily gasped, clapping her hand over her mouth. "He's going to kill me."

"You should hire Amy to handle your publicity. She's helping Kate spin in her favor that stuff on Gawker about her being a binge eater. She could definitely help you minimize the damage of the *Townhouse* piece."

"No, I can't do that. It would be too hypocritical after what I wrote about Emily. Speaking of, have you seen her anywhere?"

"Lily, forget Emily. I think I heard she went somewhere on vacation or something."

"Oh, that's good," Lily said. Maybe Emily's family had sent her to rehab, someplace nice like Promises in Malibu, she thought.

Allison snapped her fingers in front of Lily's face. "Listen up, lady. You've got to make sure you look totally glam from now on. Tell every reporter in this room that you live in an exclusive co-op, went to St. Barths for New Year's, and have a new Porsche in the garage. And make sure they get a good look at that engagement ring on your finger. It also wouldn't hurt if you and Robert made a sizable donation to Save Bucharest Friday night."

Lily groaned. "What have I gotten myself into?"

"Don't worry. Lesser women have survived worse," Allison said, wrapping her arm around Lily's shoulder and guiding them back into the center of the party.

"Thanks for sticking by me," Lily said, wishing she had the time to confide everything in Allison, to tell her about her dinner with Christian, her blowup with Josephine, and subsequent argument with Robert.

This couldn't be happening at a worse time. Of course, there's never a good time to get bad press, is there?

"Do you want to come over for lunch tomorrow?" Allison asked.

Lily shook her head. "Tomorrow I'm so busy. Petra Nemcova is in town, and I'm trying to convince her to let us auction off a date with her for Save Bucharest. Technically she's Czech, not Romanian, but I'm hoping she'll want to help out, since we're sort of working in the region. And she likes charity balls. On top of that

I have to come up with another idea for Thursday Trends. Which reminds me, have you seen Morgan's husband anywhere?"

The sooner Lily told Christian that her editors had taken a pass on her hedge fund story, the better. Then maybe he'd stop calling her at home. Didn't he know that everyone had caller ID these days?

"Last time I saw him he was at the bar."

"Let's talk later, after the ball when things are calm again," Lily said before weaving her way through the crowd toward the bar.

She didn't see Christian, but after drinking a glass of champagne, she needed to use the bathroom. A waiter gave her directions to the one in the hallway in the back of the shop, since the one upstairs already had a long line waiting for it. "It's technically for the store staff only, but no one's using it, so I don't think they'll care," he winked at Lily.

Letting the bathroom's heavy wood door close behind her, she groped along the wall to find the switch for the light. Just as her fingers brushed over the rim of the gilded switch plate, the door reopened and she felt a man's arms wrap around her, his hands moving quickly to her breasts.

As Lily whirled around in the pitch-dark, she heard the door click closed and felt the man's hand underneath her skirt, cupping her buttocks. Within a split second she was pinned against the wall, his mouth on hers, his fingers trying to jam their way up her vagina.

"Get off of me!" she screamed as she wrenched herself out of the man's embrace.

Sliding his hand back under her skirt, he laughed, "Don't act like you don't want this."

"Christian?" she stuttered. "What the hell are you doing?"

"Isn't it obvious? I'm crazy about you. I can't get you out of my head," he said, unbuttoning her suit jacket and squeezing her left breast. He pinched her nipple.

She pushed him away. "Get your hands off of me! I love my

husband!" she blurted out, surprised by the resolve in her voice and the tears welling in her eyes. Her heart flooded with emotion, and she struggled to take a breath. After months of wondering whether she and Robert had rushed into their marriage or if they really did belong together, Lily now had her answer.

"Your husband's an idiot," Christian spat, "a limp-dick lawyer who only got his job because his mummy begged us to give him one."

"How dare you talk about him that way," Lily snarled, animal-like in her anger. She slapped Christian across the face. One of the prongs of the pink toumaline-and-diamond ring caught on his cheek, splitting the skin.

"You cut me, you whore," he said, flipping on the light. In the mirror, he touched his cheek, which was bleeding. There were already spots of blood accumulating on the pristine front of his shirt. "You pathetic little social climber. I can't believe I wanted to fuck you!" he spat at her in the reflection.

Frozen in her spot, Lily watched as Christian turned on the faucet and began cleaning his cut. Thick droplets of blood fell from his chin into the sink basin. There was blood in the water. Not a good omen, to say the least.

Not mine, not mine. Not my blood.

Lily stumbled toward the door to the bathroom, unlocking and opening it as quickly as she could. As she was buttoning her jacket in the hallway, Liz came around the corner.

"What happened?" she gasped, taking in Lily's heavily disheveled appearance.

"Liz, I have to get out of here. Is there a back exit?"

Chapter 35

When Jacinta laid eyes on Lily's mascara-streaked cheeks and red nose she jumped to the conclusion that Lily had had a fight with Robert at the party.

"Robert wasn't even at the party. Something else happened," she said as another tear rolled down her face leaving a trail of eye makeup behind.

Jacinta handed her a box of tissues and led her to the couch in the living room. "Wha'happened, mamita," she asked.

Taking a deep breath, Lily quickly divulged the whole sordid tale, starting with Christian's flirtatious comments to her in St. Barths and ending with what had happened in the bathroom in Henri Fontaine. "You can't breathe any of this to anyone. *Comprendas?*"

If word got out that Christian had attacked Lily in the bathroom, it would be a major scandal, not just for both of their families but for IIPG as well. Robert, who was a probationary hire anyway, would probably be fired immediately, and the fund would have no choice but to rally behind Christian, given his familial connections and seniority.

"Don't worry about me. Worry about how you gonna explain this to Roberto."

Lily bit her lip. "How *am* I going to explain this to Roberto? I mean, Robert."

"It won't be easy, but better you than that *conjo pendejo*," Jacinta said, standing up from the couch. She put away a few of Will's toys, gathered her things, gave Lily one last hug, and left for the evening.

By 10:00 p.m., Lily had taken a shower and was tucked up in bed, reading the *Townhouse* in which she and Will appeared on the cover. The editors had decided to use the shot of her cuddling with him in the nursery. Sitting cross-legged on the yellow toile rug she looked natural and happy, as if she routinely bathed her son while swathed in cashmere and silk, draped in gold and jewels. *It's all an illusion,* she thought as she turned out the light and pulled the covers over her head. She had allowed herself to be seduced by the glitz and glamour of high-society life and in the pursuit of it had rolled the dice on the one thing in her life that truly mattered—her marriage.

Lily realized that everything she had done in the last six months had been in service of her bruised ego. If she hadn't been so insecure, she wouldn't have cared what Morgan and Di, or even Josephine, had thought of her. Her life had been better than good enough, but she'd wanted more, a small measure of fame, a place in the spotlight, to make her feel like *she* was good enough. She resolved to come clean with Robert about the fiasco with Christian the following morning. She would tell him that she was ready to make amends with his mother and that he'd been right about the *Townhouse* article: She shouldn't have done it.

Except Robert was gone by the time Lily woke up. He'd left a note, telling her he hadn't been able to finish the project he was working on and would be in meetings all day. There was a chance he would have to fly to Chicago that night, but promised he would be back in town for the Save Bucharest gala the following evening. "Wouldn't miss your big night," he wrote. "I love you."

Lily picked up the note, which had been left on her bedside

table, on top of her copy of *Townhouse*, and wandered into the kitchen to brew a pot of coffee. The good news was that Robert had apparently forgiven her for walking out on Josephine at La Goulue. The bad news was that she wouldn't have a chance to talk to him about Christian and everything else before the gala.

Chapter 36

Lily started getting ready for the ball at about 3:00 p.m. While Jacinta watched Will, she took a jasmine-scented bath and smeared a revitalizing mask on her face. Then Lucas arrived, toting his little black rolling box full of hair products and styling tools, and demanded to see her dress and jewelry, which she had all laid out carefully on her bed along with her new silver Manolos (Kyra Kemp insisted Lily rush out and buy them) and a simple silver python clutch, a gift from Nancy Gonzalez for hosting an event thrown by her handbag company.

"Very chic," Lucas commended, nodding at the ensemble. "I'm thinking that we'll do an updated chignon. We can cut some long bangs and angle them across your face."

"Sounds perfect," Lily said, and smiled. "I'm sure whatever you do will look great."

Lucas finished washing, cutting, and styling Lily's hair by 5:30 p.m., leaving Lily an hour to apply her makeup and get dressed. She was supposed to be at Cipriani 42nd Street at 7:00 p.m. even though the party started half an hour later. The committee was expected to come early to make sure everything was set up to their exact specifications and (more importantly) to honor the request of a photographer from *Vogue* who wanted to take their pictures without the distraction of the rest of the crowd. Lily was just applying a last coat of mascara to her lashes when Robert arrived home from his trip, depositing his bags and quickly changing into his tuxedo in time to escort Lily downstairs and into one of the IIPG company cars.

"You look absolutely spectacular," he said, and whistled as they slipped into the backseat of the car.

"Thank you," she said, her voice quavering.

"Are you okay?" he asked, taking her hand. "You're shaking."

"I'm just nervous, I guess." She smiled and took a deep breath. *Later, we'll talk later.*

Because of traffic, Lily and Robert arrived ten minutes late to the benefit's cavernous venue, a former bank turned upscale party space. Everyone was buzzing around, checking the brochures for the silent auction and testing the microphones and spotlights. Others were giving interviews to a large woman with lips painted an unflattering shade of cinnamon. Off in a corner a photographer and his two assistants were setting up the lighting for the group shot. By the bar Lily spotted Di looking fashionably elegant in an empire-waist emerald taffeta dress. Next to her stood Jemima, ever the fashion star in a beaded yellow bubble, and Verushka, dressed to kill in plunging purple silk, her glorious *poitrine* on full show.

"How about a drink?" Robert asked Lily, clasping her hand tightly as he led her toward the bar.

She noticed Verushka whispering to Di and Jemima, who both turned to look at Lily before erupting into a cacophony of snorts and cackles. In a flash Lily realized that Verushka had been the mastermind behind the article about her in *Townhouse*; she must have been angry at Lily for the few biting remarks she'd included in the article about her Christmas shopping night and had taken her revenge in print.

As Robert and Lily neared the bar and the women's laughter grew louder, Lily started trembling again.

Robert squeezed her hand. "Don't be nervous, honey. You've deserved to have a night like this for a long time. I want you to enjoy every second," he whispered in her ear.

They drank a glass of champagne on the far end of the bar, away from the others, and then headed over to where the photographer was organizing everyone for the group picture. Behind a trio of gilded chairs the photographer's assistant lined Verushka, Jemima, and Morgan, who was dressed in a red silk dress with an asymmetrical neckline and cabochon ruby chandeliers that didn't quite match the wattage of Lily's earrings, then directed Lily, Di, and a doe-eyed Hollywood starlet, to be seated in front. Lily made sure she kept her back straight, her stomach pulled in, and her chin down for every flash. After the shoot was over, she went straight from her chair to the bathroom to check her hair, reapply her lip gloss, and take a few more deep breaths.

On the way back from the ladies' room she was stopped by Morgan. "Well isn't that a lovely dress," she remarked icily. "Is it from Ortensia? You know that we're obliged to wear something from her line, right?"

"It's one of the samples from her spring collection."

"That's interesting because I know I had the first appointment. and I didn't see it there."

"Oh, really? Well, maybe you just missed it. There were a lot of dresses to choose from."

"No, I would have seen that one. Silver gray is *my* signature color," she challenged.

Lily couldn't help but laugh. "Morgan, it's not like you own this color."

"Yes, *actually*, I do."

"What do you want me to do? Go home and change? Because by the time I come back I'm sure there will be four more girls wearing silver gray dresses. What are you going to do about them? Bar them from entering?" She crossed her arms over her chest and stared at her.

"I don't care what a bunch of nobodies are wearing. No one's going to be taking pictures of *them*. Everyone who matters knows silver gray is *my* color. And don't think for a second I'm going to let you plead ignorance on me," Morgan huffed portentously.

"This is ridiculous. You're acting like a spoiled brat."

"Just don't be surprised when you aren't asked to chair an event of this caliber again."

"If I were you I'd check my delusions of grandeur at the door," Lily advised coolly. "You don't run this town, and you can't tell me what to do. Now if you'll excuse me, I was on my way to say hello to Snow and Allison."

Later, during the seated dinner, Morgan glared at Lily over the ice-block centerpieces, and everyone seated at their table could feel the chill between the two women. Christian, who was seated to Lily's left, took great pains to avoid talking to her, and her other dining companion, Jemima's husband, Paul, kept looking over Lily's head to see where everyone else was seated around the room. During the main course he disappeared altogether, and Lily was left to saw at her overcooked filet mignon by herself. She tried entering an ongoing conversation between Verushka and Di's husband, Dixon, but Verushka leaned over so far Lily couldn't even see Dixon's face. *There's no doubt about it, the freeze is on.*

Lily tried to flag Robert's attention to tell him she was going home, but he had been seated next to Morgan and was so engrossed in his discussion with her that he didn't notice her signals from across the table. As the plates of passion fruit mousse hit the table, she got up from her chair and walked around to where he was sitting, wedging herself between him and Morgan.

"I'm feeling really tired all of a sudden. Can we go home, honey?" she asked.

"Really, so soon?"

"Yes, Lily, so soon?" Morgan parroted, pulling her chair away from the table. "The night has just begun. You're not going to make Robert leave all of his friends just because you're feeling tired, are you?"

"You keep out of this," Lily growled, trying to keep her voice out of others' earshot. She didn't want a scene.

"What's gotten into you?" Robert asked, his cheeks reddening.

"She's absolutely disturbed," Morgan said loudly, garnering the attention of the rest of the table.

"Now hold on a second—" Robert started to say before Di, calling out from across the table, interrupted him. "*Sans doute*, she's totally gone off the deep end."

Robert threw his napkin on the table. "If you think I'm gonna allow you two to talk about my wife that way in front of me, you're wrong. Morgan and Diana, you owe Lily an apology. Right now."

"Ha!" snorted Morgan.

"Robert, let's just go home," Lily begged.

He turned around in his seat and their eyes locked. "What's going on here?" he asked, his eyes searching hers for the answer.

"Can't she just get a taxi home?" Di chuckled to Verushka.

"Or the subway, if you wanted to save a few bucks," Verushka hiccupped in return. The rest of the women laughed uproariously. Now they had the attention of their whole table as well as everyone seated at the two tables on either side of theirs.

Composing herself, Morgan added, "Seriously, you should go home if you're feeling like you're coming down with something. Whatever it is, it might be catching."

Lily glimpsed the look of haughty indifference on Morgan's face. "I'm so sick of you," she hissed.

"Honey, *what* is going on?" Robert repeated, he reached out and squeezed her arm in an attempt to get her to focus on answering him. Lily wanted to answer him, but she couldn't speak; her mouth felt like it was stuffed with champagne corks.

"I'll tell you *what's* going on," Morgan sneered, a half smile playing about her lips. "She's embarrassed because she tried to seduce my husband and he rejected her. She threw herself at him in the bathroom of Henri Fontaine's. She probably did it because she's so jealous of me."

All eyes turned to Christian. "It's true, I'm afraid," he sighed heavily. "I'm sorry, Lily. I didn't want to embarrass you any more than you've already been. But I thought my wife had the right to know what had happened." He shook his head and turned to Verushka. "I just wanted to be nice. She said she wanted to do a story about our little art gallery at the fund."

"You're unbelievable." Lily glowered at Christian.

"Is this true?" Robert asked Lily. "Did you really make a pass at Christian?"

"No, he's the one who kissed me!" she yelped.

Morgan pointed at the scab on her husband's face. "You see his cheek? She clawed him when he refused to let her—I don't know how to say this without sounding indelicate—pleasure him."

Di reached over and patted Christian's back. "You poor thing," she cooed.

"He's lying. Ask Liz Krueger! She helped me out of the store that night. Someone find her and ask her!" Lily gasped.

"I think it's best if we leave now," Robert said, grabbing Lily by the elbow. As she turned away from the table she felt a tug on her skirt. Turning back around, she noticed that the hem of her dress had gotten caught underneath Morgan's chair. Panicking, she yanked at the skirt, ripping the fabric and leaving a long shard of silver gray material on the floor.

"Oh no," she yelped again, gathering the tattered skirt in her hands.

Robert escorted her out of the building, his mouth set in a hard line and his face red with anger and humiliation. Outside, he hailed over a cab and put her in it.

"You're not going back in there, are you?"

"No, of course not. You think I want to face those people after what just happened?"

"Then come inside," she said, scooting over to make room for him.

"I'm not going home with you, Lily. I'll spend the night at Mom's."

As he closed the door, she scooted back over and rolled down the window. "Robert, please tell me you don't believe them. It's all lies. I promise you that Christian was the one who wanted to have sex with me. *I* refused and Morgan's mad at me because I wore her color and I wouldn't go home and change," Lily cried.

"Now you're not making any sense."

"Please don't make me go home alone tonight. I need you. I love you. Tell me you love me," she begged, and when he didn't say anything, she added, "at least tell me you don't believe them."

"Honestly, I don't know what to believe," he said walking away, down the darkened street in the direction of Park Avenue, where he would hail another cab to take him to his parents' duplex.

Chapter 37

Lily woke up the following morning in a fog. As she rose from bed she thought momentarily that the previous evening had simply been an awful nightmare, but then she saw her ripped dress crumpled on the floor and knew otherwise. In the span of an hour her entire life had come crashing down around her. Morgan and Christian had made a fool of her in front of the crème de la crème of New York society and, more guttingly, her husband. After making a pot of coffee, she called Robert and left a message, asking him to call her back as soon as possible. "Please, honey, I need to speak with you," she'd said.

Walking into Will's nursery, the room glowing in the morning sunlight, she retrieved him from his crib and let him stick his chubby baby fingers in her mouth as she carried him into the kitchen for his bottle and then back into the living room.

She was changing his diaper, heavy with a night's worth of urine, when the phone rang. Hoping it was Robert, she dove for it.

"Brace yourself," Allison said ominously.

"What is it *now*?" she asked.

"Maybe I should come over and tell you in person."

"Just tell me, what's going on?" Lily asked, the dread coating her throat and constricting her airway. She struggled to take a deep breath. "How much more can go wrong?"

"Emily Leiberwaller killed herself yesterday afternoon."

Lily's mind flashed to Emily's room and the sad, glassy eyes of one of the teddy bears on her dresser. "No. No, this didn't happen. Tell me this didn't happen."

"There's an article in today's *Post* about her suicide," Allison said, pausing. "I'm going to assume you also haven't seen the item on Page Six about what happened at the benefit last night."

"Oh shit. It's about me, isn't it?"

"Your dustup with Morgan was all anyone could talk about after you left. It's not true about you hitting on Christian at the jewelry store cocktail, is it?"

Lily explained what had really happened at Henri Fontaine's and how Christian had been calling her for days. "I have the phone logs," she said. "Do you think I should send them to the *Post*?"

"No, that would only encourage them to keep on writing about the incident. And anyway, everyone knows Christian's a total dog. Last year he was briefly fucking a publicist who works for Gucci. She was, like, barely out of college. And he apparently used to brag about giving it to her up the ass in the steam room at the Tennis Club. That was humiliating enough for the poor girl, no one's gonna date her now, but there were others who suffered even worse fates. A couple of years ago there were rumors of Christian and another girl meeting every Thursday afternoon at the Carlyle. I mean, you'd think that he'd at least choose someplace a little more off the grid, ya know?"

"Who was it? Who was the girl?" Lily asked. If Christian had a reputation for sleeping around, her story wouldn't seem so implausible.

"Lara Banner."

"Who?"

"Exactly. She left town after he ended the affair. I think she moved to Los Angeles and became a buyer for Fred Segal or something. She was a Girl of the Moment once upon a time, too. Then suddenly no designers would lend her clothes, no one invited her to any of their parties. When she was invited, none of the photographers would take her picture. She couldn't get into Bungalow or Marquee, not even on a Saturday night in the summer. It was all Morgan's doing. She had her thrown off all the benefit committees and basically made her life miserable."

"That's what she threatened to do to me if I didn't go home and change my dress."

"Yeah, I meant to ask you about that. What were you thinking wearing silver gray last night? Everyone knows that's her color."

"Do you realize how ridiculous that sounds? Besides, the publicist was the one who convinced me to wear that dress, which, by the way, is now ruined."

"Kyra really fucked you over. Everyone knows that she hates Morgan because Morgan treats her like crap, and there's nothing she can do about it because her job *literally* is to get Morgan in Ortensia de la Reina's gowns for big events. So Kyra did the next best thing and used you as her unwitting pawn to get under Morgan's skin."

"You know what? None of this seems vaguely important anymore." Lily could hear a click on the line. Allison had another call coming in, probably from someone looking for an inside angle on the scoop du jour. "You should get that, and I need to go get a paper," Lily said.

"Let me know if there is anything I can do. I'm here for you anytime day or night," Allison pledged before hanging up.

As soon as Lily and Will got to the news agent's she picked up a copy of the *Post* and turned to the article about Emily's suicide. It was a short piece, buried between an article about a toddler falling down a flight of stairs in Brooklyn and a police raid on a prostitution ring in the Bronx. Emily wouldn't have been happy with the placement. She'd spent her whole life scheming to get her name in Page Six, but even in death she'd missed the mark by a few pages.

Lily read on. According to the police report, Emily had taken a mixture of sleeping pills and prescription pain relievers while her mother was at a bridge tournament on Fifty-seventh Street, exactly fifteen blocks from their apartment. When Mrs. Leiberwaller came home she discovered her daughter passed out on her bed and called the paramedics, who were unable to resuscitate her. Emily was pronounced dead on arrival at Lenox Hill Hospital. Her funeral had been scheduled for Tuesday morning. The paper listed among her survivors a younger brother, a junior at Middlebury College in Vermont, as well as her parents. Lily closed the paper and tucked it into her diaper bag.

Back at home, she rocked Will to sleep, all the while thinking about the Leiberwallers' tremendous loss. It hadn't mattered that Lily had portrayed their daughter sympathetically; the article had illuminated Emily's alienation and struggle, and that had been too much for her fragile psyche to bear. Lily closed her eyes and pictured Mrs. Leiberwaller discovering Emily's limp, fleshy body on her bed, the eyelet pillows and empty pill bottles scattered on the bubble gum pink rug.

After reluctantly transferring Will to his crib, she crept out to the hallway and pulled the *Post* from her diaper bag. Allison had said there was something about her on Page Six. Even though her public humiliation seemed of little importance in light of Emily's death, she needed to know what was in the paper if for no other reason, so she could understand what kind of fallout Robert might be dealing with at work.

Hers was the lead item.

Last night at the Save Bucharest gala scrawny socialite **Morgan de Rambouillet** publicly accused rising *New York Sentinel* society scribe **Lily Bartholomew** of trying to seduce her husband in the bathroom of the French jewelry boutique Henri Fontaine during an in-store party there on Tuesday night. Sources say Mrs. Bartholomew baited the debonair French count, **Christian de Rambouillet**, by telling him she wanted to write an article

about the recent art acquisitions of International Investment Partners of Greenwich, the hedge fund at which Mr. Rambouillet—and
incidentally Mrs. Bartholomew's own husband, Blue Water heir
Robert Bartholomew—are employed. We can only guess who
won't be chairing any more $1,000-a-plate fund-raisers in the
near future. . . .

It couldn't have been worse. She hadn't imagined that both Robert's name and the name of the hedge fund would be mentioned.
They'd also managed to include the *Sentinel* and IIPG's art collection. Dropping the paper, she dashed to her cell phone, which was
buzzing from inside her evening bag on the table in the foyer.

Before answering, she checked the number on her caller ID,
which indicated the call was coming from Josephine's apartment
on Park.

"Robert?" she asked, answering the phone. More than anything,
she wanted to hear his voice telling her that he was going to come
home and that they would work through this awful situation
together.

"No, darling," said the voice Lily wanted to hear the least.

Oh shit.

"Hello, Josephine."

"I hope you're happy now."

"If you're—" Lily began stammering.

"From the moment you pushed your way into this family,
you've done everything you can to bring dishonor on the Bartholomew name. First that awful, tawdry little story you dug up
on the Tennis Club, and now this. Coming on to Christian de
Rambouillet—a family man for God's sake—and driving that
innocent little Leiberwaller girl to kill herself? My God, Lily! I
knew you were trouble, but I had no idea you were *this* deceitful
and spiteful. If there's one good thing that comes of this, it's that
my son, *my* Robert, now knows what kind of woman you are.

"I'll never forget when he told me that you were unhappy with the way I decorated your apartment. You'd manipulated him into thinking that I had somehow invaded your privacy, or some non-sense like that, but really you just weren't happy with my hand-me-downs, were you? Robert's priceless family heirlooms weren't good enough for you, were they? You wanted me to shell out for some brand new dreck, some trendy modular couches probably. *Me* consult *you* for design advice? Ha! That's a laugh.

"At the time I thought to myself, how ungrateful and spoiled can one girl be? And then little by little, you did your very best to destroy each and every one of Robert's relationships with his friends and family. You nagged and nagged until he felt guilty spending time with me or his father or any of his oldest and dear-est friends, the people who *truly* care about him. He was so turned around by you, he didn't know which way was up or down. I'm sure you're also responsible for him to quitting his perfectly good job at Caruthers so he could make more money in finance. You're so greedy and ungrateful, a partner's salary wasn't enough for you, was it? Thank God we forced him to get that prenup. He fought so hard against it, but I bet he's thanking his lucky stars now. You know you're not going to get a dime in the divorce."

"Is that all, Josephine?"

"You have nothing to say for yourself?"

"I have no idea what an appropriate response to what you've just said is."

"That's right, because you have no manners. I bet you've never been appropriate a day in your life," Josephine snapped before clicking off the line.

Lily sat down on the couch and stared at the wall. She replayed in her mind what Josephine had said, remembering her vicious words almost verbatim. She'd known for a long time that her mother-in-law didn't like or approve of her, but she hadn't known the depth and ferocity of her hate. Now it was all in the open.

She felt angry, shocked, and guilty all at once. Angry because Josephine had been cruel and vile and had assumed the worst was true; shocked because she'd never imagined receiving a call like that in her lifetime; and guilty because it was true that she had brought dishonor on the Bartholomew name, if only by accident. If she had never tried to swim with the socialites, none of this would have ever happened. Why had she allowed herself to get sucked into their lifestyle? It was so staged anyway. There was nothing real or meaningful to it.

God damn it, why did you have to be a player? Why couldn't you have been happy standing on the sidelines like everyone else?

There was a big lump in her throat and a hole burning its way through her stomach. She wanted to talk to Robert. Why hadn't he called her back? Did he know his mother had called her and decimated her with her acid tongue?

Eventually she picked her cell phone back up and dialed Rebecca at the bureau. She had to put Josephine's call—and Robert's failure to call—out of her mind and do some damage control.

"I can explain," she said preemptively as soon as her editor picked up.

"That's good, because you'll need to do it in person. Ford wants to see you as soon as possible."

Lily called Jacinta, who was trapped in Brooklyn at a family function and couldn't come until the afternoon. Then she called Liz, who arrived within an hour, and Lily was able to get to the *Sentinel*'s headquarters in Midtown by noon. The security guard gave her a pass and told her to go up to the tenth floor, where Rebecca would be meeting her by the elevator bank. Together they walked silently into Ford's corner office, which was decorated with modular steel and white laminate office furniture. There wasn't an ounce of clutter on his desk, not one coffee-stained notebook or misplaced paper clip.

Lily sat in one of two chairs opposite his desk and waited for Ford to complete his phone call. He was younger and shorter than Lily had expected, and his dirty-blond curls, long Roman nose, and wire-rimmed glasses gave him the air of a playwright or artist.

"Okay, so let me know what the lawyers say," he said, yanking a wireless headset off of his head. He looked at Rebecca and sighed and then turned his attention to Lily. "Now tell us your side of the story," he said, pulling a pen and a pad of unlined paper from the drawer of his desk.

"Where do you want me to start, with the incident at Henri Fontaine's or before?"

"Just start from the beginning," Ford said, and she did. She told him about joining the playgroup and how Morgan called her a nobody, about Christian flirting with her in St. Barths and how he used Robert to pressure her into agreeing to pitch the art gallery story, even though that was just a ruse to get her to spend time with him. Then finally, she told him about fighting with Morgan about the color of her dress and how Morgan threatened to make sure she never chaired another ball again. When she was done telling him about everything, including how she had never intended to pitch the article on IIPG's art collection because she recognized the obvious ethics issue, Ford put his pen down and leaned back in his Aeron chair.

"Well, I believe you," he said, taking off his eyeglasses to reveal a pair of jade green eyes. "But it'll be the managing editor's call whether you can continue writing for us and what the *Sentinel*'s public face on this is going to be. I'm going to recommend that we stand one hundred percent behind you on this, as well as the Emily Leiberwaller story. *New York* magazine is doing a piece on her suicide, and if they contact you, let us know immediately. In fact, you should probably speak to one of our in-house lawyers now." Ford wrote the name and number of the lawyer on a separate sheet of paper and handed it to Lily. "Give him a call as soon as you get home."

Lily nodded solemnly and closed her eyes. "I should have never pitched that piece on Emily," she lamented.

Rebecca patted her on the knee. "Her death wasn't your fault."

"But the press is going to try and spin it that way," Ford said, pinching the bridge of his nose. He walked around to the front of the desk and leaned his weight backward on it, crossing one sneakered foot over another. "This hasn't been a good week for you, has it?"

"That's the understatement of the year!" Rebecca snorted.

"Before I go," Lily said. "I just want you to know how grateful I am to have your support, no matter what the paper decides to do. I've loved working with Rebecca these past few months."

Ford shook her hand and the thought crossed Lily's mind that she probably would have been better off marrying someone like him, a smart editor with an upper-middle-class background similar to her own. They'd live in a brownstone in Brooklyn, send their kids to public school, and read the Sunday papers in bed with their Free Trade coffee in mugs from the Conran shop. But she'd married Robert, a wealthy heir, handsome, smart, and likable. A total package, as one of her friends had crassly called him, but part of that package was some not-so-wonderful things, like the snobby, difficult mother, or his sometimes spoiled, selfish impulses. *For better or worse*, she reminded herself as she walked back toward the elevator bank with Rebecca.

"Let me know if anyone from *New York* calls," Rebecca said.

Lily nodded solemnly as she stepped into the crowded elevator. "Talk soon," she said as the doors closed and she, along with the rest of the passengers, was swooped back down to the ground floor.

Chapter 38

Lily spent the rest of the week talking on the phone with Rebecca, Ford, and the *Sentinel*'s managing editor and lawyers. While the press seemed to have lost interest in her argument with Morgan at the Save Bucharest ball, Emily Leiberwaller's suicide was threatening to become national news, with Lily at the center of the scandal surrounding her death.

On Monday, Gawker.com and fashionweekdaily.com all reported that Beth Janklow, a freelance writer who had a reputation for penning unflattering articles about the über-rich and famous, was working on a piece about Emily's suicide for *New York* magazine. Sure enough, two days later Lily received a call from the reporter.

Following the counsel of the *Sentinel*'s lawyers, she agreed to the interview. The lawyers told her that it was okay for her to show remorse, but if she admitted to any wrongdoing she'd be opening herself and the newspaper to financial liability. They encouraged her to insist that Beth include in her piece that the article had been fact-checked with Emily prior to its publication and that Emily hadn't disputed a single quote that had appeared. Factually, there were no errors. She should repeat that as many times as deemed necessary.

Beth and Lily met for coffee in a small café near Gramercy

Park in early March. Beth, a forty-something woman in a tailored dove-colored pantsuit and Hermès scarf, started the interview by asking Lily how she was able to convince Emily to do the interview. "What did you tell her the article was going to be about?" she asked, taking a sip of her black coffee as she waited for a response.

"I told her that I wanted to write a feature about a girl about town—those were the exact words I used—and asked if she'd be interested. She said yes."

"Emily told her parents that you wanted to shadow a prominent socialite and had chosen her."

"I remember she sort of rephrased what I said so it sounded like I was doing a day-in-the-life kind of piece. And I think I said that it could be something like that. I wasn't specific about it."

"You let her believe what she wanted to believe."

"I was vague because I wasn't sure exactly what I was going to write. I had an idea, but I was still toying with different angles. As a reporter, you know how it is. I mean, do you already know what the slant of the piece you're interviewing me for is even though you haven't finished your reporting?"

Beth didn't respond to Lily's question and pressed forward with hers. "The Leiberwallers feel like you purposefully misled their daughter and had planned all along to portray Emily as a pathetic loser. *Those were the exact words they used*," she said, challenging her from across the table. "They think you used Emily to advance your career."

"That's an unfair accusation," Lily replied calmly. "Every reporter uses their sources to advance their career to some degree. The real challenge is to make sure you're being ethical about *how* you use them. Ideally you'd always be able to be sensitive to your sources' needs and preferences, but sometimes that's just not possible. For example, are you considering how this article is affecting me and my personal life?"

"No."

"See."

"There's a difference. You're a journalist; you know how this works."

"It could be argued that Emily was media savvy. Her publicist gave her pointers on how to handle herself in front of reporters."

Beth let out an exasperated huff. "Let's continue with the interview. Did you mislead Emily Leiberwaller?"

"No, I did not," Lily said plainly. She looked outside through the café's window. There was a group of moms chatting as their babies slept in their strollers. One woman had a large Florida-shaped milk stain on the front of her trench coat, another a pacifier clipped to her fleece jacket. Where were these kinds of mothers when she needed them? If only she'd befriended a different, more normal, set of moms when she was feeling so lonely, she could have avoided everything that had happened. "Look, I'm very conscientious about my subjects' feelings. My articles are fair, and I fact-check all my stories myself. Emily knew exactly what was going to appear in the article." She took a deep breath. "I'm *deeply* sorry for the Leiberwallers' loss. I never wanted this to happen."

"Why did you write that story? I heard that you were trying to impress Di Meddling who apparently disliked Emily and orchestrated her being kicked out of Umberta Verragrande's baby shower. You wrote about that in your piece," she said, as if Lily needed reminding.

"It wasn't anything like that. I interviewed Diana for my article, but I wasn't trying to *impress* her. I wanted to do the story because I wanted to highlight how ridiculous it is that an educated young woman like Emily could throw her life away in pursuit of something as superficial as getting her picture taken at parties. Why do people think it's meaningful to be called a socialite? Emily would have worn that title like a crown, but believe me, it's overrated. She never got to discover that for herself, which is what I'm most sorry about."

"This is a bit unrelated, but I have to ask you about the article you were planning on writing about IIPG's art collection. Doesn't your husband work there? Wouldn't it be unethical for you to write a flattering piece about his employers?" Beth asked.

"I'm happy you're bringing this up, because there's been a lot of . . . *umm,* confusion surrounding that," Lily began. Then she told Beth everything she had told Ford and Rebecca, leaving out only how Christian had used Robert's precarious position at the fund to manipulate her into spending time with him.

When the interview was over and Beth had left the coffee shop, she called Arthur Rubenstein, the *Sentinel*'s lawyer, on her cell phone and told him what questions Beth had asked and how she'd answered them. Arthur said she'd done a good job and asked her to call him again if Beth asked for a follow-up.

Next Lily called Ford, who thanked her for keeping him updated on the developments. "It sounds like they're going to put you through the wringer for this," he said. "And since there's no way of proving that you didn't mislead Emily, the public will assume that you did. Everybody loves blaming a journalist."

They spoke for a while about Beth, her direct interviewing style and journalistic pedigree, and then Lily mustered up the courage to pose the question she'd been dreading asking. "So, has it been decided whether or not I can keep writing for you?"

"This wasn't my call," he started. "But we, as in the powers that be, think it's best if you take a little vacation from writing for us. Just for the next few months until the buzz dies down."

His response was no surprise, but hearing it made Lily feel unexpectedly relieved. "You know what? A little vacation from a lot of things sounds good."

Chapter 39

New York in March is depressing. The weather can't make its mind up; one day it's sunny and warm, the next it's gray and cold. It often snows, but unlike the storms of January and February, these hold no charm. The icy drifts turn to dirty slush the moment they hit the sidewalk, causing the city to collectively grumble, "Enough already!" while kicking the muck off its metaphorical boots. Even with a full circuit of parties to keep everyone busy, those given the opportunity to head down to Miami or farther south in search of warmth and sunshine, do.

Lily, however, stayed put. She didn't leave New York, although her parents eagerly suggested she come down to Nashville for a break, and she didn't go to any more parties. She kept as far away from the spotlight as possible, and saw only a handful of friends—Allison, Kate, Liz, and Helen—for walks in the park or milky coffees at Le Pain Quotidien near her apartment. But mainly Lily sat in her apartment, taking care of Will and waiting for Robert to call or e-mail, which he did exactly three times a week, "just to check in on Will" (*i.e., not me*). He came over to see the baby as well, always on Sunday afternoon from 2:00 to 4:00 p.m., the only time when he wasn't otherwise busy, he said.

Robert's visits could be best described as awkward. Lily and he never talked about what happened at Save Bucharest, what had appeared in the *Post,* or the phone call from Josephine that had followed. Robert avoided making eye contact and she, conversation. They skirted around any topic that could lead to an argument; this meant that his work, family, and the majority of his friends or hers were off limits. For three weeks she never veered from three subjects—their wonderful son, the miserable weather, and her credit card bills. Then, on the last Sunday in March, Robert finally suggested that they talk next time he came over. Not just talk, as in the safe chatter they'd been having for the past several weeks, but *talk* talk, as in discuss their future, a conversation full of consequence and import.

"Come for dinner. I'll make something. I'm sure you're not getting any home-cooked food these days," she offered, figuring that Robert wasn't the kind of man who would ask for a divorce over roast chicken and mashed potatoes.

"You don't have to."

"No, really. I don't mind. I want to do it," she insisted.

The following Sunday, Robert arrived on their doorstep at 7:00 p.m. on the dot. He was wearing jeans and an old cashmere pullover and bore a bottle of pinot noir. There were dark circles under his eyes and he hadn't shaved, but he smelled clean and masculine and she wanted to bury her head in his chest. Taking the bottle of wine from him, she led him into the living room, where Will was playing with a musical tool bench.

"He just loves that thing," she said, pointing at the toy. "You really hit the nail on the head with that one."

"*Bu-dump, bump,*" he said, beating his fingers on an imaginary drum set.

She smiled meekly, threw her hands in the air as if to say, *I'm trying, okay?* and cleared her throat. "So. Why don't you wait in here while I finish preparing everything? Unless you'd rather join me in the kitchen?"

"No, that's all right. I'll wait here."

After Lily set the dishes of roasted chicken, buttered green beans, and a gratin of potatoes on the table, she called Robert into the dining room. If he noticed that she had taken down the portrait of him, Josephine, and Colette or that she'd repainted the formerly red-and-white striped room a mossy shade of green, he didn't comment. After slipping Will into his high chair, he opened the wine and poured Lily a generous glass. "I don't exactly know where to begin," he said, fumbling with his napkin.

She spooned the green beans and potatoes on his plate and then hers. "Robert, I swear I didn't come on to Christian," she blurted out.

"I know that, Lily. Some of my friends from the club told me about Christian's reputation with women. The fucking prick can't take being rejected. But it's not like you didn't lead him on."

"Did you just say that *I* led him on?" she sputtered.

"I see your phone bills," he said. "He called you several times last month."

"But I didn't pick up more than a few times," she started to explain.

"Why would he be wasting his time calling here if you hadn't encouraged him?" Robert asked, interrupting her. "I saw you two together while we were in St. Barths. Don't deny that you were attracted to him."

"Maybe originally, yes. But even at that point I never considered sleeping with him."

"Then why didn't you tell me about what happened in the bathroom of that jewelry store?"

"Because I was afraid you'd get mad at me."

"That's ridiculous," he scoffed.

"You were so exasperated with me already. Remember? We weren't talking. I had gotten into that argument with your mother," she reminded him. "Besides, the only reason I started spending time with Christian was so he would help you."

"And why would I need that asshole's help?" The tips of his ears turned pink with anger.

"He said the board of directors wasn't convinced you were IIPG material. If I brought some good press to the fund, the board members might be more accepting of you. I knew I couldn't write about the fund, but I thought I could make sure you had an ally in Christian. If I could make him my friend, then he would be yours, too."

"You have so little faith in me that you just took what he said at face value. You must think I'm this big, stupid loser, huh?"

"I defended you to him."

"This is exactly why I moved out. You don't believe in me. You don't trust me. In fact, you trusted an asshole like Christian instead of me, your husband. How was that supposed to make me feel?" Robert shook his head and scratched the scruff on his jaw. "Just so you know, the board would have hated seeing an article like that in the press. It only would have drawn attention to us, which is, believe it or not, a very bad thing in the hedge fund community. Not everyone wants attention from the media. Even supposedly good press can slice both ways, but I guess *Townhouse* already taught you that lesson," he said.

His words were meant to sting, and they did. "You don't have to be mean," she said.

Robert forged on, barely registering the hurt written all over Lily's face. "That art gallery was something Tom Howard agreed to let Christian do, but most of the board was mad as hell when he approved the expenditure. If anyone doesn't have the full support of the board, it's Christian. At one time he helped the fund raise a lot of money in Europe, but now that we have a solid presence there, he's not worth the ten million a year he draws. At some point, maybe as soon as next year, they're going to let him go."

Lily suddenly remembered the way Christian had looked at Mr. Howard and Robert at the New Year's Eve party. He was full of contempt, jealousy even. It suddenly dawned on Lily that he had been afraid that Robert was going to take his place at the firm. "I've been so stupid," she whispered, resting her fork and knife crossways along her plate. Nothing like chagrin to kill the appetite. She transferred onto Will's tray a couple of her cheese-covered potato slices, which he quickly fisted into his mouth.

Robert took a sip of his wine. "Why do I feel like a broken record when I say that this all could have been avoided if you'd only come to me. If only you had talked to me about what was going on, Lily."

Lily didn't know what to say. As a reporter, she should have known to consider the source of her information, and as a wife she shouldn't have kept any secrets from her husband. Her instincts had been all wrong. *Again.*

She'd also been wrong about Emily, too. She should have never written that article and she should have admitted that to Beth, the reporter from *New York* magazine, in her interview. Being factually correct wasn't enough in this case; sometimes a little extra sensitivity *was* required. Lily had known that Emily was troubled. The eating disorder, the painkillers—those had been red flags. Why hadn't she paid attention to them? She'd justified doing the piece by painting Emily as the victim, but whose victim was she? The other women may have excluded her and Emily may have willingly submitted herself to their ridicule, but Lily had shined a light on it all, embarrassing her publicly. She decided to call Beth to tell her that she now realized that she had indeed made some questionable ethical decisions when writing the piece about Emily.

Robert ate the rest of his dinner in silence, occasionally leaning over to ruffle Will's hair and hand him a green bean.

"Are you going to lose your job?" Lily asked.

"It's possible they'll find a reason to get rid of me, but it won't be because I didn't have the support of the board, at least not initially," he said, the anger creeping back into his temporarily placid demeanor.

"Will you ever forgive me?" she asked.

He regarded the place where the portrait of him and his mother used to hang and scratched his chin. Lily knew he was wondering where she had put it, but he didn't ask. Instead he said, "You used to be so strong. When I met you, you were an independent, intelligent person. The old Lily wouldn't have gotten worked up over what a bunch of stupid girls thought of you." Robert pushed his plate away and wiped the corners of his mouth with his napkin. "You've changed."

Slamming her wineglass down on the table, Lily shouted, "That's not fair!" The red liquid sloshed onto the white tablecloth, creating a mushroom-cloud-shaped stain. She lowered her voice for the sake of Will, who sat startled in his high chair, half a green bean hanging out of his mouth. "If I've changed, it's because I thought I had to. I wanted to fit into your world. I wanted to make you believe that I belonged, that I wasn't this dead weight, a freaking albatross, bringing you down, no, *dragging* you down to my level, my—dare I say it?— middle-class level. That's how everyone made me feel. Morgan and Di said you could have done better. So did Josephine. She called me a hillbilly, for crying out loud. So what was I supposed to think when you shut me out and started spending more and more time with her instead of me? You know she called me after what happened at Save Bucharest, don't you? She said I tried to destroy your life, that it's my fault you quit your job at Caruthers. She's hated me all along. And you never defended me because you never wanted to offend her. So instead you let her walk all over me. What chance did our marriage have unless we were both unequivocally first in each other's hearts?" Lily knew she had made some colossal mistakes in the last few months, but she wanted Robert to recognize that he had also played a part in their estrangement.

"Look, Lily, I'm sorry Mom called you. I didn't find out about it until recently. Why didn't you call me to tell me what she'd done?"

"I'd called you once already that morning. I wasn't going to hound you when you so obviously wanted nothing to do with me."

"Well, Colette finally told me about it a couple weeks ago. Mom let it slip one day when she was on one of her tirades, complaining about you, and Colette defended you. Mom proudly admitted that she'd called you and told you you were ungrateful and spoiled."

"Don't forget deceitful and spiteful," Lily snorted ruefully.

"Mom said you had nothing to say for yourself."

"Oh, I did. But it wouldn't have been polite."

"After Colette told me about Mom's phone call, I left work and dragged her out of one of her insipid little luncheons at the Carlyle. I made her tell me exactly what she had said right there in the lobby of the hotel. She was mortified, of course. I caused a huge scene, but I couldn't help it. I'd never been so angry in my life. I told her she couldn't talk to you like that and that I didn't want to see her face or hear her voice again until she apologized to you—both in writing *and* in person."

"That couldn't have gone well."

"No, it didn't. I moved out. I've been sleeping at my friend Henry's for the last couple weeks. He's got a futon in his living room."

Lily picked up her wine and drained the small amount that hadn't already spilled out. She set the empty glass back down. "I can't say that I'm unhappy you're not living with Josephine anymore, but if there's one thing I've come to realize this past month, it's that she's not the source of all our problems. A lot of them, yes. But not all. Do you remember the day you brought home the Porsche?" she asked.

"Oh God, not the Porsche, again." Robert stood up to undo the clips harnessing Will into his high chair. Lifting him up, he placed Will on the hardwood floor and watched him take a few uncertain, wobbly steps away from the table.

"That day," she continued, "you told me to get a job, and I did. Then I spent six months working my ass off to make something of myself so that you would be proud of me."

"I've always been proud of you."

"What about all those months you didn't want to have sex with me? All those times you were holed up in your office, or at the club, or, yes, at a party with your mother, rather than with me and Will, the family that you created? Were you proud of me then? So proud you couldn't stand being with me?" she asked sarcastically. "I was *desperate* for your company, to know what was going on in your head, to have you know what was going on in mine, but you gave me nothing. What a few kind words, some acknowledgment of my hard work as a mother would have done for me then. What choice did I have but to try and get your attention some other way?"

Lily looked over at Will, who was holding onto the side of her chair, looking up at her expectantly with his round eyes. She hated herself for fighting with Robert in front of him. "Mama!" Will shrieked, bouncing up and down on his chubby little legs. She scooped him into her arms, inhaling the scent of his hair.

"My sweetheart," she whispered in Will's ear, stroking his soft head.

"I was depressed. I couldn't find a job. I felt like a failure." Robert threw his napkin down on the table, the plane of his brow furrowing in distress. "I'm sorry I wasn't there for you," he added after a long, heavy pause.

Lily stood up from the table and tucked in her chair. "I made some pie," she said, more like a question than a statement.

"I think I should go. It's getting late," he sighed. He held his arms out for Will. "Here, I'll take the little guy."

Robert put Will to bed while Lily cleared the table and cleaned up the kitchen. She cut a few slices of the blueberry pie and put them in a Tupperware for Robert to take with him. At the door, he kissed her good night on the cheek and thanked her for dinner.

"What's going to happen to us?" she asked. Their discussion had brought up feelings of anger for both of them, but now that they were finally talking after so many weeks of silence, she didn't want to stop. It felt good to let it out, to get to the bottom of

Robert's anger and her resentment. Stopping talking meant that they'd given up on their marriage, and she wasn't ready for that to happen, at least not yet. "When are you coming home?"

"I don't know. But I'd like to see Will every weekend, maybe have him for one night a week?"

"Is this a separation?" she asked, stunned by the realization that Robert had come to their apartment knowing full well that he was going to spend the entire summer on his friend's futon.

"Let's not call it that. I just need some time to work things out," he said, leaving Lily standing in the doorway of their apartment, holding the bag of warm pie.

The following week Allison invited Lily and Will over for a playdate. Although they'd spoken several times since Save Bucharest, Lily was looking forward to the coffee klatch and promised a batch of homemade chocolate chip cookies. When she and Will arrived—through a blustering March snow shower no less—the townhouse was filled with the aroma of vanilla and sugar. Allison's nanny, Lusita, greeted them at the bottom of the steps and led them into the living room, where she had set up a play area filled with toys and touch-and-feel books.

"I'm in the kitchen," yelled Allison as soon as Lily had settled Will on the floor with a plastic rendition of Noah's Arc. She pressed a few buttons and the toy came alive with blinking colored lights and sounds—an elephant's cry followed by a horse's whinny— sending Will into a state of hiccupping, drooling excitement.

"Can I leave him here a sec with you?" Lily asked Lusita.

"Yes, no problem." Lusita smiled warmly, shooing her into the kitchen. "He be okay with me."

Lily ducked around the corner into Allison's gleaming kitchen to find her at the marble-topped kitchen island pouring out two cups of coffee from a stainless steel carafe. "It smells heavenly in here," Lily said, reaching for a cup.

"And you look—"

"Not so good."

"Too thin." Allison slipped a warm cookie onto Lily's saucer. "Look at you. You're swimming in your clothes."

"I have no appetite. And sitting around the apartment doing nothing drives me crazy, so basically we spend the whole day wandering around the city. Will hasn't napped in his crib once in the past week, since he's always in the stroller. I'm worried the Bugaboo's going to give out on me."

"So I take it things didn't go so well with Robert last week?"

Lily poured cream in her coffee. "Let's see, where shall we begin? He's still really angry with me for believing that he didn't have the support of IIPG's board. Then there's the fact that I didn't tell him that Christian mauled me in a jewelry store bathroom," she said, ticking her offenses off on her fingers. "And last, there's the not so very small issue that he hates the person I've become. Apparently it's weak and shallow to care about what everyone's saying about you behind your back."

"Oh, Lily, I'm sure he doesn't think that."

"No, he pretty much does and you know what? He's right. I am pathetic. I mean, Di and Morgan used to make me literally shake with fear. Why on earth I ever wanted to be their friend is beyond me now. Of course, I realize this only *after* I've shot my marriage to hell. I destroyed everything because I wanted to be a socialite. A socialite! What the hell was I thinking?"

"You can't be so hard on yourself. You were going through a hard time. You lost your sense of self and forgot what mattered for a little while. It happens to a lot of new mothers."

"It didn't happen to you," Lily pointed out glumly.

"Yes it did, but my husband wasn't also going through an identity crisis, so he was there to give me the support I needed. You had to go it alone because Robert was dealing with his own issues at the same time. Both of you were down in the dumps. *Of course* your marriage was going to suffer. How could it not?"

"But even if you're right, Robert and I obviously can't communicate. How can we have a healthy marriage if we can't open up to each other? When we got married I envisioned that we'd be there for each other. I'd make him feel better when things didn't go his way and vice versa. That's how it should be."

"Get real, Lily!" Allison snorted. "Only people who aren't married have this idealized vision of what marriage should be. In practice it's messy and confusing and ugly and dirty. But you stick with it. You muddle through all the muck. Give Robert some time to lick his wounds. He'll figure it all out and come back to you."

"You don't know that for sure."

"Yes, I do," she said, swinging her shiny mane of long black hair behind her back. "He'd be a fool not to, and I know he's no fool." Allison grasped Lily's hand across the marble. "Now eat your cookie. You're not allowed to leave the kitchen until you do."

Chapter 40

In the middle of July the article by Beth Janklow ran in *New York* magazine. Its title, *Meet the Real Mean Girls*, introduced a scathing depiction of the cabal of manipulative, power-drunk socialites led by Morgan de Rambouillet and Diana Meddling. The piece focused mainly on Emily's death but also uncovered other casualties of the women's intrigues, including Lara Banner, the Hollywood stylist who had once succumbed to Christian's charms and was later run out of town by Morgan and Diana. Even more indicting, Mrs. Leiberwaller had unearthed a series of e-mails from Di to Emily following Emily's request to cochair an event benefiting the Ludwig Collection. A sidebar to the article, quoted one of the e-mails in its entirety:

> *Dear Emily, There's no way we'd let you cochair. First of all, you can't afford a $20,000 table, can you? And second, cochairs are supposed to bring people to the event. Having your name on the invitation would have the opposite effect, don't you think? xx Diana*

Lily flipped to the section about her. After her dinner with Robert she'd called Beth and come clean about Di having been the one to suggest she do the piece and how she regretted having written it. Beth had subsequently rewarded Lily's honesty and contrition with a nearly empathetic treatment:

> Weeks after our initial interview Mrs. Bartholomew called me at home to tell me that she felt wracked with guilt over Emily's suicide. With a voice full of regret she said she'd been dishonest with me during our first face-to-face meeting. We met a second time, when she broke down in tears. "People tell you, 'Oh, you're not responsible for her suicide,' and you believe them. And they are right, but to a point. I saw all the warning signs and I didn't pay attention to them. I figured that Emily would read the article and see how silly she was being for wanting to become a socialite. I thought I was helping her by writing that piece. Of course, I realize how wrong I was now. Emily was too sensitive. I should have used someone tougher—emotionally tougher, I mean—to illustrate the point I was making in that piece. One thing I've learned in the past year is that to be a socialite you have to have thick skin. Like a shark's. Or thicker."

The fallout from Beth's piece was tremendous, inspiring a series of op-eds about adult bullying in the *New York Observer* and other Manhattan-based publications. *Primetime Live* dedicated an hour to the subject. There was even a backlash against charity balls, with attendance at some of the A-list events plunging nearly 50 percent from the previous year. Many of the women's magazines temporarily reduced their coverage of society doyennes both young and old, and as a result a handful of top-tier designers stopped lending out their gowns and handing out free handbags and shoes to any girl who could snag a spot on a benefit committee.

Of course, the boycott wouldn't last long. By wintertime the article would be all but forgotten, and the parties, the girls, and the perks would have returned to their normal state of abnormal. The only difference would be that Morgan and Di, although certainly still a part of the scene, no longer reigned as the queen bees of the junior set.

Chapter 41

In August, Lily's mother came to New York for a two-week visit. The days were hot, and Lily warned her mother that the smells of decaying fish and other rotting refuse rose from the baking pavement into the air, but Margaret refused to be dissuaded. "I have a right to see my youngest grandchild. You've kept him from me long enough," she said over the phone, ending any potential dispute about her stay or its length.

But when her mother arrived, dressed in cranberry palazzo pants, a straw sun hat, and lashings of rose perfume, Lily was glad she had come. "You smell so good, Mama," Lily said, embracing her mother heartily.

They spent their days browsing through the sales racks and their evenings cooking simple dinners and lingering over glasses of cold white wine. Margaret's wonderment over the convenience of having both a grocery store and pharmacy within a few minutes' walk and her excitement at exploring the air-conditioned floors of Saks Fifth Avenue and Bergdorf Goodman reminded Lily to appreciate the city she'd started taking for granted—and wanting to flee.

The night before her scheduled departure and after a dinner of hot biscuits and butter lettuce salads, her mother set down her glass of Chardonnay and gave Lily her best it's-time-to-come-clean look. "Are you ready to talk about what's going on between you and Robert?" she asked.

Lily regarded her mother across the table. "I was wondering when you were going to ask me that."

"Okay, then," she said, raising her eyebrows. Margaret's dark pink lipstick had seeped deeper into the wrinkles around her mouth, and her lashes were so heavily coated in mascara they reached out like spider arms.

"You're so beautiful," Lily said, feeling a sudden burst of love for her mother.

"Stop stalling, girl."

"I wasn't stalling. Honestly, Mama, I've already told you everything there is to know. As far as I know, Robert's been able to keep his job at the fund and he's living at his friend's place."

"That's not what I'm asking. I want to know what you're feeling. Before that thing happened"—her mother would only refer to the Save Bucharest debacle as "that thing"—"you didn't seem terribly happy with how things were going between you two."

"People talk about how hard marriage is, but I never anticipated that our first years together would be *this* hard. What happened to the honeymoon period?"

"Oh, there's no such thing. Everyone knows the first years are the hardest, sugar. The *real* honeymoon doesn't come until much later."

"How much later?"

"I'm still waiting."

Lily laughed. "Okay, I get it. Marriage is never easy." Margaret got up to start clearing the dinner dishes. Picking up the plates on the table, she headed into the kitchen. Lily followed her with their glasses and the nearly empty bottle of wine. "But maybe Robert and I just aren't meant to be together?" she shrugged.

"There was a time when I felt the same exact way about my own marriage with your father. Matthew had started kindergarten but you were still at home with me. Your father had just been named assistant professor and was intent on keeping an open-door policy for his students. Some nights he wouldn't get home until nine or ten, those little bastards would keep him for so long. By then, of course, I was dog tired from running after you kids all day and just dying for a little adult conversation. But all he wanted to do was eat his dinner and go to bed. He couldn't see how I was falling apart inside. And that he couldn't see that made me think that I'd made a mistake marrying him," her mother said as she filled the sink with water and pulled a pair of bright yellow kitchen gloves over her hands. "Can you hand me the Palmolive?"

Lily squirted the green soap under the tap.

As Lily's mother watched the bubbles form, filling the kitchen with their synthetic scent, she said, "Your father and I fought a lot when you and Matthew were little."

"You needn't remind me."

"He was so emotionally unavailable, although back then they didn't call it that. He was a man's man," Margaret lifted her arms out of the soapy water and made quote marks on either side of her head, next to her ears. "I used to sometimes wish that he'd get into a car accident."

"You didn't!" Lily gasped.

"Of course I didn't really want him to die." She paused, hesitating. "No, not really. But I sure passed some time imagining a life without him."

"Mama!" Lily wasn't sure she wanted to hear her mother confess to wanting her father dead, even if she didn't really mean it. She knew her parents hadn't had a perfect marriage, but it had seemed happy enough.

"He would infuriate me so much. He'd refuse to deal with problems, then I'd blow up at him just to get some kind of reaction, and then he'd call me crazy. He just didn't get how lonely I was, and unlike you, I didn't have any choice but to put up with it."

"It was a different era. Mothers and wives were supposed to be mothers and wives and that's it."

"I'm not talking about getting a job. I could have become a realtor or worked in a shop if I really wanted to. What I meant was that you have a choice whether or not to stay married. Back then and in the community we lived in, getting divorced was still a big deal. I'm not saying this is a good thing, but everyone's getting a divorce these days. When you were young, it was still taboo. There was no surer way to get yourself ostracized." Margaret finished drying the last dish. "I didn't have very many girlfriends when you and Matthew were little and if I'd divorced your father, I can guarantee you I would have had none."

"Oh, Mama, how do you know that?"

"One of your friend's mothers got divorced—her husband was cheating on her with a woman in Memphis—and after that she was never invited to any dinner parties, not even potlucks," Margaret said as she picked Will up from the kitchen floor. "I think it's somebody's bedtime," she sang, nuzzling her nose into his neck. Will responded by joyfully jabbing his finger in Margaret's eye. "No, baby," she said, grabbing his fingers lightly. "That ain't no way to treat your Grandmamma."

Lily padded into the living room, now stripped of its fussy needlepoint pillows and repainted in apple blossom white. The porcelain animal figurines lining the fireplace mantel had been replaced with a series of pewter-framed family photos, the silk-covered sofas had been reupholstered in blue poplin. The room, removed of its oppressive grandeur, now felt casual, airy, and modest. It was more to Lily's taste.

Margaret rejoined Lily on one of the sofas. "So, where were we?" she asked, pulling her daughter's feet into her ample lap.

"Do you think I should divorce Robert?" she asked.

"Do you think you would be happier if you did?"

"I love him. I can't imagine life without him."

"Then there's your answer."

"But life's never that black and white. Maybe love isn't enough. Maybe I want the kind of marriage he could never give me."

"Whatever it is you decide to do, the most important thing is that you don't spend the rest of your life regretting your decision," Margaret said, patting her daughter's leg.

"Do you regret staying with Dad?" Lily asked.

Her mother cupped her hands over her eyes and took a deep breath. "No, pumpkin, but I do regret spending so much time resenting him for being able to go on living like he always had when my life had changed so much. I wasn't the beauty queen with ten boys proposing marriage anymore. I was just another housewife with two kids to carpool and a house to keep clean. Men have their midlife crises and everyone gets it, but if a woman breaks down after getting married, having children, and watching her hips spread year after year, people say, "What's she complaining about? Her husband isn't cheating on her. She doesn't have to work a nine to five. Hell, *she's* the one who's got it easy.'" Margaret shook her head, rising from the couch and chuckling ruefully. "It is what it is. I wish I'd found my peace with it earlier."

"Marriage sucks," Lily said glumly. "You're either the one screwing up or the one being screwed over."

"Or both," they said in unison.

"Welcome to adulthood, sweetheart," her mother said.

Chapter 42

At the end of August, Lily began to write again. Her articles, which focused mainly on beauty and baby-related trends, were unlikely to raise more than a couple of finely groomed eyebrows and were subsequently buried in the center pages of the Thursday Trends section. Still, the work kept her mind active and her days busy, and pretty soon she fell into a comfortable routine, working while Will napped and spending the afternoons at mommy-and-me classes or running errands. There were times when Lily was struck with loneliness or anxiety, but generally those moments were confined to the Saturday afternoons when Robert would come by to pick up Will.

It was on one such Saturday in mid-September that Robert announced his decision to rent a studio a few blocks from his office. He was fumbling with Will's overnight bag and sippy cup when he turned to her and uttered casually, "I thought I should give you my new address, in case of emergencies."

"You're moving?" she asked, completely alarmed and unsettled by the news. If Robert was moving to a new apartment, it could mean that their separation was becoming permanent. "Can you wait here while I put him down for a nap?" she asked nervously as Will, who had been busy clutching her leg and trying to climb up it, immediately let go and started scampering down the hall.

"No, no, no, no!" he yelled as he hurled his tiny body down the hall.

"This might take a while," Lily sighed. "Feel free to help yourself to a beer in the fridge." She ran to catch up with Will and swung him under her arm as she elbowed open the door to the nursery.

Twenty minutes later, Lily reemerged from the nursery to find Robert in the living room staring at a picture of all of them together on the beach in St. Barths. "Hard to believe this was taken just nine months ago," he said.

"Yeah, it is."

He placed the framed photo back with the others on the mantel, crossing his arms over his chest, the chest she still wanted to bury her face in at any given moment of any given day. *Get a grip, Lily.* "So about your new apartment . . . I'm assuming that you've rented it because you have no intention of moving back here," she said, her voice not betraying the heavy thudding of her heart.

Robert slumped on the poplin sofa. "I didn't say that. I can't stay at Henry's forever. He's a single guy; he can't have a kid hanging around his apartment every weekend."

"Robert, we can't live like this anymore. *I* can't live like this anymore. You need to tell me once and for all whether or not you want to try and make this work."

"I need more time," he said, rubbing his eyes. She noticed that Robert looked haggard and tired, the bags under his eyes shaded a translucent purple.

Lily sat down on the opposite end of the couch and pulled her feet up underneath her. If he'd hinted even once in the last three months that he still loved her, she might have felt inclined to give him more time to figure out what he wanted. But as it was, she felt like she had no choice but to let him go.

"I love you, Robert," she said. "But I need your answer now."

He nodded, refusing to meet her gaze.

"So then it's over?"

Robert's eyes were shining, full of tears.

"God damn it, say something," she said, growing impatient, her own emotions threatening to bubble over and spill forth.

"I need more time," he said again. "Just give me a few more months."

Lily felt her nostrils burning, but she resisted the urge to cry. "If saving our marriage isn't enough of a reason to forgive me, then you'll never be able to. Either you love me and you want to stay with me or you don't. How can a few months change anything at this point?"

When he didn't say anything, she threw her hands in the air and stood up. "It's over, Robert."

He picked up his jacket and left, and for a minute the world was bathed in such silence that Lily could hear the lock on the front door click closed and the sound of Robert's soles hitting the carpet in the hall, each step taking him farther away from her. She picked up one of the sofa cushions, pressed it to her face and let out a long howl, her body shaking with the force of her sobs. Within minutes her tears, the ones she'd been holding back for months, had drenched her face, the pillow, her blouse.

"My marriage is over," she said aloud, the sentence falling awkwardly from her mouth. "My marriage is over," she repeated again and again and again until the words blurred together and held no meaning whatsoever. She sat on the couch for a long time, her throat hoarse from crying, a zillion thoughts racing through her head: *Should I move back to Nashville? Should I go back to work? Will Robert get remarried? If he does, I'll kill him.* And then she thought of Will, who would have to grow up between two households, jostled back and forth from week to week, never knowing what it was like to have all of his belongings in one place, and she started to cry all over again.

A good while later—twenty minutes or maybe sixty, she wasn't sure—Lily picked herself off of the sofa and walked zombielike down the hall into her bathroom, where she splashed her face with cold water. Tiptoeing back down the hall into the nursery, she found Will sleeping peacefully in his crib, his arms splayed out above his head. He looked like an angel.

"It'll be alright, sweetie," she whispered, choking back a fresh gush of tears.

Chapter 43

In late November, Lily was invited to a fund-raiser benefiting a Bronx-based children's charity. She had been purposely leading a low-profile life since the night of the Save Bucharest ball and wasn't looking forward to facing the inevitable whispers and stares in her direction. Although Beth Janklow had given her an easy ride in her article for *New York* magazine, Ford had been right in that everyone, *especially* the rich and semifamous, loved to blame a journalist. They'd fed Lily dirt on their best friends, sent her invitations to the best parties, but after one slip she'd been kicked to the curb faster than she could say "VIPs only." It was a good thing that she no longer harbored even the slightest interest in reclaiming her spot on the A-list. Her last tour on the charity circuit had been more like a trip through a meat grinder. It had left her battered and raw, predigested and disoriented. She would never subject herself to that again. Not in a million years.

Still, she missed her friends, or rather, the women she had mistakenly considered her friends. Most of them wanted nothing to do with her. If they bumped into her, say, shopping for baby clothes at Barneys, they'd duck into the Mrs. John L. Strong stationery boutique next to the children's shop. At the swings in Central Park, they'd make a hasty departure for the sandbox. She even caught Snow dashing across Park Avenue, nearly getting clipped by a Fresh Direct truck, to avoid her. Being slighted by Snow, one of the few women Lily had previously counted as a true friend, initially hurt her feelings. But the pain quickly faded to disappointment—in Snow. Although she was fun, she was only a fair-weather friend, and Lily had had her fill of those.

Of the half a dozen women she'd befriended in the past year, only Allison and Kate had proven themselves loyal. Allison's friendship hadn't surprised Lily—Allison was a freethinker and had always seen Morgan and Diana for the bullies that they were—but Lily had been shocked by Kate's allegiance. She was also incredibly thankful for it. Like Lily, Kate was going through a divorce and had been the subject of a lot of nasty gossip, so they had plenty to talk about. Kate had taken to saying things like, "I knew I was in trouble when I started daydreaming about referring to Alejandro as my ex-husband," and they would both roll to the floor snorting with laughter. Their lives had taken a turn toward the absurd; what else could they do but find the humor in it? Over the summer, they buoyed each other's spirits and swapped self-help books, women's magazines, and legal advice. By the time fall arrived, they had formed an unbreakable bond.

In fact, it was Kate who insisted that Lily join her and Allison's table for the Children Are Love benefit. "But you must come," she had whined. "Otherwise we'll have an open seat and everything will be out of order."

After a couple of days of pestering, Lily finally agreed to be their tenth.

A few minutes after Lily succumbed to Kate's pestering, her phone rang. It was Allison. "Do you have something fabulous to wear?" she asked.

"I'm sure I can come up with something," Lily replied.

"Do you want me to call Carlos at Valentino? Samantha at Angel Sanchez? His gowns are such showstoppers. And Sam's such a doll, I'm sure she'd—"

"No, God, please don't call anyone," Lily protested. "Now can we talk about something besides who's wearing what?"

Later that evening, after putting Will to bed, Lily dove into the recesses of her closet and pulled out every black-tie appropriate gown she owned. Then, one by one, she tried them on. Most of the dresses didn't fit—Lily had gained back about ten pounds and now teetered more on the side of a six than a four—but one did. It was black, long, and devoid of any ornamentation. It was the kind of simple column that cried out for an important piece of jewelry. Her diamond and platinum necklace would have fit the bill perfectly, but it was in the lockbox that Robert kept at the bank, and she didn't feel comfortable asking him for the key. Beyond that, she questioned the appropriateness of wearing an heirloom from a family to which she no longer belonged.

Just as she was about to unhook the back of her dress the doorbell rang. She wasn't expecting anyone and for a moment wondered if Jacinta had decided to drop by to peek in on Will. Now that Lily wasn't going out as much, she sometimes did that, just so she could give him a hug and a little treat, often a lollipop. But she never usually popped by this late.

"Jacinta, I'm just in the middle of—," she said, pulling open the door.

But it wasn't the babysitter. It was Robert, and he was bearing a huge assortment of flowers, which Lily noticed on closer inspection was predominantly made up of a variety of white lilies—callas, Asiatic and tiger lilies—plus a smattering of white orchids and roses. The foyer filled with their sweet scent as soon as Robert stepped through the front door.

Robert took in Lily's appearance, the formal gown, the disheveled hair, the look of surprise on her face. He wasn't quite sure what to make of it. "Is this a bad time?"

"No, it's okay. I was just trying this on."

"Oh," he said.

Lily noted the relief in his voice. *Did he think I had been out on a date, that I had a man here?* She couldn't help but snicker at the thought. In a twisted way, the thought of Robert assuming she was already seeing someone new cheered her. Not that she was the least bit ready to begin dating again, but she liked the idea of him being jealous. "Allison and Kate convinced me to go to this silly benefit next week. They wouldn't leave me alone until I agreed," she explained.

"There's no reason you shouldn't go. Don't you think it's time you get out and about? Have some fun? You can't stay in hiding forever."

Lily bristled. When Robert had left her, he'd given up his right to advise her on anything besides their child. Her personal life was exactly that: *her* personal life. She didn't want his input, not now. "Who says I'm in hiding. I'm over the social scene, Robert. I have no intention of getting, as you say, out and about again, thank you. Now is there anything I can do for you? Will's asleep."

"I didn't come to see Will."

Lily stared at him. The way he was looking at her, the flowers he was holding, was he here because he wanted her back? No, she couldn't jump to such conclusions. Maybe he felt guilty about the way he'd handled their breakup and just wanted to be nice so they could be friends. Confused, she threw her hands up in the air. "Robert, I give up. In addition to being over the socialite rat race, I'm over playing guessing games. Why are you here?"

"To give you these flowers," he said, holding the bouquet out to her. "Here."

"Thank you," she said, accepting the bouquet. They were nice flowers, from a real florist's, not a corner bodega. But they looked slightly droopy. She imagined that he'd gotten them on his lunch break and left them sitting on his desk for a few hours. "I should put these in water," she said.

Lily headed for the kitchen, where she unpacked the flowers in the sink. Turning on the tap, she filled a large glass vase halfway with water and took a deep breath. She had to get away from

Robert for a second to regain her composure. She'd made a fool of herself the last time he was here; she'd practically begged him to come back to her. And now he was here, smiling at her, being charming, bearing flowers. Did he show up just to torture her? Rub in her face what she'd lost? With a pair of large shears she started cutting each of the stems under the water.

Robert pushed his way through the swinging door. "Can I lend a hand?" he asked, rubbing his hands together as if in preparation for a major task.

Lily backed away from the sink. "Be my guest."

He took over the job, snipping a diagonal tip on a calla lily before dropping it in the vase. She'd have to redo the arrangement later, but she wasn't about to stop him. *Let him work while I relax. For once.*

"I didn't drop by just to bring you flowers. I have news." He turned around from the sink and studied her face.

She gave him her best blank stare.

"I've sold the Porsche."

"Oh?" Lily knew he wanted a big reaction, but she wasn't about to give him that. He continued to stare at her expectantly, waiting for her to say something, praise his level-headedness. "Why are you telling me this?" she finally asked.

"Because I love you and I want us to get back together."

She couldn't believe what she was hearing. After spending so many months wishing to hear those exact words, she'd given up hope. He'd humiliated her the last time he came over for dinner. He had been cold. He had been cruel. Now he expected her to accept him back in her life, just like that? "Too little, too late," she said.

"I've changed, Lily," he said.

"Selling your sports car won't solve the problems we have."

"I know, but it's a start, right? The Porsche is gone, and I'm leaving IIPG for another hedge fund. That's what I've been working on these last few months. Today was my last day there. I knew

I couldn't stay there after everything that happened, but I didn't want us to get back together until we could really put this chapter behind us."

"I'm happy you've left that firm. Any place that would employ a jerk like Christian is bad news to me. But, again, I don't see how that has any bearing on the problems between *us*."

He snipped the last stem and turned off the water. "If we don't get back together, I don't think Colette will ever forgive me. She says you're like the sister she never had." Robert took a step toward Lily and grabbed her by the elbows. "Please, Lily. I *love* you. Let's start over."

She took a step away from him and shook her head. "Why the sudden change of heart? I thought you were enjoying the single life in your very own bachelor pad, hitting the bars with Henry whenever you weren't saddled with the baby."

"Do you honestly think I've been out there sleeping around? I haven't even *looked* at another woman since I moved out. The only times I've been out is to meet with other hedge funds. I've been stuck at the office otherwise."

"I have trouble believing this."

"Lily, you're the only one for me. Ever since we met that day at the office party. I was over and done that day forward. And I got the studio, which just so you know is the farthest thing from a bachelor pad—there's a crib in there for God's sake, not to mention piles of toys and diapers everywhere—because I couldn't deal with Henry anymore. He's a fun guy, but he's in his mid-thirties and he doesn't even have a steady girlfriend. It's sad, you know? His life is so lonely and empty and he doesn't even know it. He thinks happiness is a summer fling with a twenty-year-old model."

"So, that's why you want me back? Because the alternative of being alone is too depressing?" Lily crossed her arms. She liked watching him squirm, making him sort through and explain his emotions. She had spent their marriage trying to divine his inner thoughts, but she wasn't going to do that anymore. From now on he was going to have to tell her in words—not grunts or shrugs or furrowed brows—what he was thinking.

"Well, to be honest, that's partly true. But I don't want to be with just anyone. I want to be with you."

"And when did you figure this out?"

"When I saw you on the street with Will. It was a couple weeks ago, late in the afternoon. You were on your way back from the park, I think."

"I didn't see you. Why didn't you say hello?"

"You were oblivious to anything besides Will and the traffic lights. And I was going to say hello, but then, well, your hair was a mess and you were wearing sweat pants and tennis shoes, and I knew you'd be embarrassed seeing me that way."

"Well, I pretty much live in sweats now. When I'm not trying on old ball gowns, that is. And my hair is always a mess." She gestured at the tangled topknot on her head.

Robert laughed. "You looked great on the street. Better than great. Lovely, adorable. But I knew you'd be embarrassed."

"You're probably right about that," she conceded.

"Anyway, you were waiting at an intersection for the light to change, and you bent down and smoothed Will's hair to the side and kissed him on the forehead. And that's when I realized that I wanted to be there, standing beside you, hearing all about your day and Will's. You're a great mother. And you were an amazing wife. I'm sorry I never told you how much I appreciated you. Maybe I didn't appreciate you enough. But Lily, I miss you. Now I realize what we had."

"What we lost."

"All I can think about is touching you," he said, his voice suddenly deep and serious. His eyes bore into her, aflame with passion and an urgency she hadn't seen for a long time. "At night, I lay awake in bed thinking about making love to you. All day long, I dream of being inside you again."

She felt a bolt of electricity crackle between them. It was not unlike the first time they had met. The feeling caught her off guard, and she fumbled for the right words, finding none. She wanted to kiss him again, to let him fuck her on the floor of the kitchen right then and there, but she couldn't let herself give in to her desire. Having sex with Robert wouldn't change the fact that he'd wronged her or that, perhaps, they were wrong for each other. Either way, she couldn't just take him back in her arms like nothing had happened. They'd been living apart for months and up until tonight, she'd been steeling herself for life as a single mother. "I'm not a switch, Robert. You can't just turn me on and off."

"I know that. And I'm sorry. I was an ass. I was a mess. But I can't lose you. You give meaning to everything I do. I could make all the money in the world, and if I didn't have you and Will, it would mean nothing. Somehow," he paused, reflecting, "I lost sight of that. But my intentions were good. You know that."

"Robert, you turned your back on me. And then instead of sticking around and figuring things out, you bolted. We're going to have more problems in our lives. If this is how you handle them, then—"

"Next time will be different. I won't make the same mistake over again. We've both learned from this experience."

"But next time—"

"Next time we'll talk things through. We'll fight for each other. We'll be prepared next time."

"I just don't know."

"Think of Will. Think of everything good that we have between us. We can't throw it away like it's nothing. It's not too late for us. We're not even divorced yet."

"But in my heart we already are. This was how you wanted it, Robert. *I* gave you a chance and *you* walked out."

"You don't have to give me your answer now. I can wait. I made you wait; now it's my turn. Just promise me you'll think about it."

She looked into his eyes, the same pools of blue she'd stared into almost every day for close to three years. It seemed like ages, not just a few years, since they had first met. "I'll think about it, but I'm not making any promises," she said.

"Good enough." He kissed her on the cheek and let himself out the front door. "I'll take what I can get."

Chapter 44

The night of Allison and Kate's gala Lily washed her hair and blew it dry, and then, after dusting off her collection of eye shadows and pencils, she went to work making up her face. When she was done, she looked in the mirror and saw that her hair didn't look as sleek as it did when Nesto or Lucas blew it out and that her face lacked the porcelain perfection expected of a New York socialite. But by most standards she looked pretty, and that was more than enough for her. She smiled at her reflection, stuck a pair of diamond solitaires in her ears, and kissed Will good-bye for the night.

"I shouldn't be gone more than two, three hours," she told Jacinta on her way out.

"Take your time, mamita," Jacinta said, hugging her in the doorway. "Try to have some fun. Shake your *toto* a little," she teased, moving her considerable bottom back and forth. Will clapped his chubby toddler hands and giggled.

Lily took a taxi to the dinner, which was being held at the Metropolitan Club, a private club that was built by J. P. Morgan in 1894 and had counted among its first members the Whitneys, Roosevelts, and Vanderbilts. Mingling alongside Kate in the venue's grand marble entrance, she noticed that all of the usual faces were there: the social girls and their walkers; the gossip kings; the fashion pack; and the photographers. At one point, she thought she caught Morgan and Di glaring at her, but then again, they could have been glaring at someone else.

After the dinner bell rang, Lily and Kate threaded their way through the dining room, which was decorated in tall golden pillars, red and white floral arrangements, and canopies of airy muslin. Once the women were halfway through the room, Kate turned to Lily and winked, "I think Allison is planning on seating you next to someone special tonight."

"No! She didn't! How could she? She knows I'm still thinking about getting back together with Robert!"

Kate smiled mysteriously and linked her arm in Lily's. "Should we go see who your dinner companion is?"

Together they entered the dining room. Hoping for an advance peek at her blind date, Lily peered across the sea of decorated tables in the direction of theirs. But the centerpieces, giant arrangements of snow-white delphinium, amaryllis, and crimson roses bursting from a tall crystal vase, obscured her view. She walked toward their table slowly, feeling full of dread.

I'm not ready for this, not now and not ever.

There was only one man she wanted to be with, and that was Robert. As much as he had hurt her, she knew she had to forgive him. They both had made horrible miscalculations and faulty assumptions—the baby's arrival had thrown them both off course in different ways—but she believed that they could learn from their mistakes and move forward.

Lily realized that she had to go and find Robert tonight. She could hear herself telling him "Yes, I want you back." She could see herself unpacking his clothes as fast as she could, making love to him as soon as Will had been put to bed. How happy their little baby would be to see his parents together. Just the thought of Will's happy little face made her eyes well with emotion. Suddenly she was crying.

"I can't stay," Lily said, swiping a stream of tears from her cheek. "Will you tell Allison I had to go home?"

"You can't leave." Kate's grip tightened.

She pulled away. "Kate, listen. I have to go find Robert. Now."

"I think, in that case, you really do need to stay."

Lily looked at her puzzlingly.

"Look over there. Your dinner partner is waiting for you."

Lily followed Kate's gaze to find Robert sitting quietly, bent over the dinner menu, a branch of delphinium curved over his head. A moment later, he looked at her.

She walked to their table.

"You look breathtaking," he said, standing up and pulling out her chair.

"I thought I was Allison's guest," she stammered, confused. "I wasn't expecting to see you." Lily hadn't heard from him since he left her apartment a week ago. He was still waiting for her response.

"I know, I wanted it to be a surprise," he smiled. "I made Kate and Allison swear they wouldn't tell you I was coming. Last week, when I saw you in this dress, I knew I *had* to be here tonight. I couldn't stand the thought of you dancing with another man." Lily opened her mouth to tell him that she couldn't stand the thought either, but then Allison and the rest of their tablemates arrived en masse.

At the beginning of dinner, during the first course, she tried to pretend as though she wasn't sitting next to her (up until that night) soon-to-be ex-husband and that everyone at their table didn't notice the frissons of passion passing between them. But then Kate, who had been making a valiant effort to keep the conversation lively and off the topic of divorce (not easy in a social season teeming with them), winked at Lily and she allowed herself to relax and enjoy the evening.

She felt Robert's hand grasp hers under the table. "Are you having a good time?" he asked.

She looked into his blue eyes. "Yes, the best."

"Better than that time we found that diner open at three in the morning and ate Belgian waffles in our black tie?" he asked, chuckling at the memory of Lily seated in a corner booth, plastic bib tucked into the top of her Valentino bustier, inhaling forkfuls of waffle.

"I got whipped cream all over my face," she laughed. "And you leaned over and kissed it all off."

"Yeah, and got maple syrup all over my tux." Robert smiled. "Those were good times." He squeezed her hand under the table. "By the way, I'm never letting go of this."

"Of what, my hand?"

"Your hand. Attached to the rest of you, of course. I want the total package."

"But I might need my hand to change diapers once in a while."

"How about I change them all for you."

"Even when you're at work?"

"*Err* no, but all of them when I'm at home."

"I think I can live with that arrangement."

The dinner hour passed more quickly than Lily had anticipated, and after the dessert plates had been cleared and the band started to play some slower tunes, Robert leaned over and whispered in her ear. "May I have this dance?"

Not making any eye contact with him or anyone else at the table—she was sure they were all watching—Lily nodded and grabbed her clutch. That way she wouldn't have to come back to the table for her purse after she'd danced with him. She wanted to take him away from all this and get him home and in her bed. No, correction: in their bed. Tomorrow she'd call Allison and Kate and tell them all about their reconciliation (minus whatever happened in the bedroom, of course).

Robert led Lily to a spot in the middle of the dance floor. "Here?" She blushed, looking around. There were only a handful of other couples dancing, the rest having abandoned the floor in search of refreshments.

Not waiting for an answer, Robert pulled her in, not too close, and placed his hand on the small of her back. The band was playing a cover of "Don't Dream It's Over" by Crowded House, and she allowed herself to succumb to the nostalgic crooning.

Robert dipped Lily backward, her head almost touching the floor before he lifted her back up again. "Put your hand in my pocket," he instructed.

This time she did as she was told without hesitation and pulled the now-familiar vine of diamonds and platinum from his trouser pocket.

"Can we start over?" he pleaded.

Lily lifted her eyes to meet his. "No," she said, shaking her head. "Let's continue."

Acknowledgments

I will be forever indebted to the many people who have made the publication of this novel possible. I am grateful to my lovely editor, Lucia Macro, for her brilliant direction and good humor, and to the rest of the team at Avon Books and William Morrow, especially Esi Sogah, Liate Stehlik, Pamela Spengler-Jaffee, Debbie Stier, and Sarah Burningham, for their fantastic ideas and enthusiasm. My agents Diane Bartoli and Joe Veltre cheered me on through every step and offered indispensable advice at critical stages in this novel's evolution.

I would also like to thank the many talented editors I've been fortunate to work with during the course of my journalistic career: Jill Abramson, Eva Rodriguez, Richard Barbieri, Amy Virshup, Alanna Stang, Vanessa Friedman, Edwina Ings-Chambers, Trip Gabriel, and Victoria Vila, to name a few. Much gratitude and affection goes to my oldest friend, Sarahbeth Purcell, who inspired me to try writing fiction in the first place, and Karen Quinn, who spent countless hours teaching me how to craft a good story. Bridie Clarke, Faye Bender, and Beth Waltemath all read early versions of this work and provided valuable insight. To Yvette Corporon-Manessis, Laurie Dhue, Paula Froelich, Gigi Howard, Elke Koosman, Laura Lachman, Leslie Schnur, Jamie Wells, and Margaret Wray, thank you for your friendship and encouragement.

I owe so much to my parents, Lawrence and Milena, who taught me that with a hefty amount of determination and hard work anything is possible, and to my sister, Natasha, for making a fist with me when it mattered most. My children, Valentina and Enrico, bring me endless joy, as does my husband, Max, who believed in me even before I had written word one of this novel. You are so good and so loyal; I love you deeply. A big thank you as well to my husband's family, especially to my mother-in-law, Camilla, who, for the record, has flat abs and great taste, but not much else in common with the mother-in-law in this book.

Last, many thanks to all the socialites out there, for being such good sports.

A+
AUTHOR
INSIGHTS,
EXTRAS, &
MORE...

FROM

**TATIANA
BONCOMPAGNI**

AND

AVON A

Top Ten Tips to Becoming a Top Girl (A Tongue-in-Cheek Guide)

1. Lose weight. A top girl is as useful as an ice cube in Antarctica if she can't fit into a sample size. Bulimia will do the trick, but there's no risk of getting vomit on your Valentino with self-starvation.

2. Get a nose job. And cheek implants. And hair extensions. What's that you say, your grandmother says she can't recognize you? You're on your way, girlfriend!

3. Make friends with other top girls—or just pretend to. As long as they are willing to pose with you in party pictures, who's gonna know the difference anyway? Just don't make the mistake of giving out TMI while you're zooming around town in the back of your supposed BFF's town car. That girl spilling the beans about you on ParkAvenue-Peerage? Yep, that's her.

4. Find a walker. A gay male socialite is the top girl's true best friend. Why? He'll do all the dirty work for you, from planting awful rumors on the Internet about your biggest rival to getting her blackballed by the best charity benefit committees. Bonus points awarded when your male-socialite BFF writes about you for *W* magazine (but only if you don't look like a tranny in the accompanying photo spread).

5. Hire a publicist, even if it bankrupts your father. A top girl is only as good as the ink she gets. The pinnacle of respectability? Cover of the *New York Times Sunday Styles* section or *Vogue*'s "Girl of the Moment" page. It's a toss-up.

6. Become a publicist. Check out the party pages in your latest society monthly. Those girls smirking back at you? Mostly publicists. After all, they control the guest list, decide who gets to borrow the best dresses, and—surprise—they're the ones hiring the photographers.

7. If you aren't already rich and Daddy refuses to mortgage the family home to turn his ugly duckling into a social swan, try prostitution. It's not so bad! High-class hooking is glamorous. And giving sweaty paparazzi free blow jobs is fun.

8. Land a modeling or "ambassadorial" campaign. The talent agent you swear you don't have can help hook you up with this. Best part is that you don't even have to be pretty (just thin).

9. Still not getting enough attention? Make up a story about another top girl trying to steal your husband/kick you in the shins/besmirch your good name, and then manipulate your best friend's boyfriend into writing about it for a respectable magazine. *Instafame!*

10. Launch your own clothing/handbag/jewelry line in Tokyo and New York and rake in the green. Forget to pay Daddy back/dump drug-dealing John/get a quickie divorce from earnest husband, and then hightail it out to Los Angeles for the *real* red carpets.

What inspired you to write *Gilding Lily*?

I sat down at the computer on the morning of my twenty-eighth birthday knowing that I wanted to write a novel, but not much else. I wanted to write something entertaining and fun, the kind of book that I would look forward to reading at the end of a long day. Very quickly into the writing process I figured out that my main character would be a woman who had lost her sense of self somewhere between saying I do and pushing a nearly ten-pound baby out of her vagina. And then, after writing a few more chapters, I realized that by setting Lily's story in the ultraglam, ultraexclusive world of the New York socialite, everything awful and humiliating about new motherhood would be magnified tenfold. As humbling and profound as motherhood is, the socialite world is (from a certain point of view) egocentric and shallow. I liked how polar opposite these two main elements of the book were. From there, things started to take shape.

Is the book based on your life?

My life was a starting point for *Gilding Lily*, yes. But the vast majority of what happens in the book is entirely fictional. I was recently at the launch of a socialite's clothing line during New York's fashion week and met the talented actress Bebe Neuwirth, who upon hearing about my book asked, "Is it based on reality or is it a hundred percent verbatim?" I laughed and said that she had asked the right question. Then she asked if I was prepared to lose all my friends. (Gosh I hope not.)

The thing is that I don't know any authors who don't use things from their own life in their fiction. Like Bebe said, it's not a question of *if* but of *how much*. *Gilding Lily* might have more real life inspiration than most novels, so for the record, here's what Lily and I have in common and what we don't:

We're both writers, mothers, and married to men with recognizable last names. We also are both from Nashville (although I was born in South Dakota and also lived in Minneapolis, Puerto Rico, and Brussels while I was growing up), and we both gained a lot of weight during our pregnancies.

Lily's a hell of a lot more fabulous than I am. I never was a *Vogue* Girl of the Moment—although my picture once did appear in the magazine a long time ago—and believe me, no designer is clamoring to loan me clothes. It's a good night if a photographer doesn't bump me over while trying to get pictures of Tinsley Mortimer, the charismatic, bubbly New York socialite famous for wearing girly dresses and her hair in flaxen ringlets.

Oh, and my mother-in-law is not Josephine and my husband is not even nearly like Robert (except he is gorgeous!), in case anyone out there is wondering. That's not to say I've never argued with my husband or had issues with my mother-in-law, but my family members just aren't capable of behaving as badly as their fictional counterparts in my novel.

Speaking of socialites, are they really as bad as you make them seem in your book?

For the record, none of the socialite characters in my book are based on real people, and I don't think anyone on the social scene is as cruel as Diana and Morgan are. The majority of the socialites I know are lovely, friendly, gracious, and polite. They use their status to help people they care about and causes that do an incredible amount of good. However, for every five smart, kind, hard-working social women I've had the pleasure of meeting, there's one hideous, manipulating diva out there calling herself a socialite. I think that a lot of the top girls today say they don't like being called a socialite because of a small handful of women who give the term a bad name.

It used to be that socialites were privileged women who had a deep understanding of what the French call *noblesse oblige*, which translates roughly as "noble birth obligates (one to do good)." In other words, with wealth comes the responsibility to give back to one's community. These women donated their time and effort to raise money for deserving cultural institutions and charities. Now, more and more, the women cochairing benefits are concerned with promoting their own interests rather than the charities for which they supposedly work. This said, I'm pretty sure the economist Adam Smith, who wrote the capitalist tome *An Inquiry into the Nature and Causes of the Wealth of Nations*, wouldn't have a problem with the current quid pro quo between charities and socialites, since these girls ultimately do raise considerable funds because their very names on an invitation will compel smart people to part with hundreds of dollars (sometimes thousands) for a seat at a charity dinner (far away from the socialites, mind you).

Lily Bart is the protagonist of Edith Wharton's *House of Mirth*. Did you reference that novel in *Gilding Lily*?

Edith Wharton is one of my favorite authors and *House of Mirth* is one of my favorite books, so I named my main character Lily Bartholomew as a kind of ode to Wharton and the original Lily. There is one plot similarity between *House of Mirth* and *Gilding Lily* that I intentionally included in the book: Lily Bartholomew, like Lily Bart, careens toward her social death and is ultimately tricked by a wealthy man who wants to bed her.

I also wanted to reference the Gilded Age, the time in which Wharton's characters existed, the time in which Wharton wrote. Many believe we are living in the New Gilded Age, and I also see many commonalities between our contemporary consumerist culture and the conspicuous consumption of the era of the robber barons. So by naming my novel *Gilding Lily*, I hoped to hint to the reader that the book is about, in part, the corruptive influence of too much wealth.

Why did Emily Leiberwaller have to die?

Emily died because she's the book's martyr. Through her death I was able to show the potential for a tragedy of this magnitude to occur when bullies like Morgan and Diana are allowed to rule the roost with no checks or balances. I'm not sure if anyone is going to catch this, but I named my villains Morgan and Diana—Morg and Di, or *morgue* and *die*—to conjure up the image of death. They ultimately were the pallbearers for Emily's literal death and Lily's social one.

Also I didn't want to make Emily overly likable. She had to have a lack of self-awareness and have major psychological problems so that it would be believable that she would kill herself, but as sad a case as she is, I think most people can see a little bit of themselves in Emily. We all have a piece of us that is broken and we all just want to feel like we belong sometimes. It's human nature. Lily, for example, wanted to feel like she belonged; that's what got her into so much trouble.

Is *Townhouse* a real magazine?

No, I based *Townhouse* on another magazine called *Quest*. I read *Quest* every month when it arrives at my gym. It makes thirty minutes on the elliptical trainer disappear like nobody's business. *Quest* often features writing by some of my friends and runs lots of great pictures of social types I know (and like, for the most part). I've met the Meighers, the family who publishes *Quest*, and they are wonderful, genuine people, nothing like Verushka and Jerry Kravis. But for the purposes of this book I thought it would be more interesting to write about what sort of hijinks might occur if unscrupulous people ran the city's best-read society monthly.

Will you write about socialites again?

Yes, probably. But I don't think I'll focus on them so completely. I'm working on my next novel right now, and one of the three main female characters is a socialite, but the other two are just your average, run-of-the-mill, millionaires next door. You can check out my website (www.boncompagni.net) to check on my progress. Feel free to contact me through my site. I'd LOVE to hear from you!

Tatiana Boncompagni

TATIANA BONCOMPAGNI is a freelance journalist based in New York City. Her writing has appeared in the *New York Times, Wall Street Journal, Financial Times* and *Vogue*. She is married with two children. This is her first novel.